CU00722945

John Griffith London (born **John Griffith Chaney**; January 12, 1876 – November 22, 1916) was an American novelist, journalist, and social activist. A pioneer in the world of commercial magazine fiction, he was one of the first writers to become a worldwide celebrity and earn a large fortune from writing. He was also an innovator in the genre that would later become known as science fiction. His most famous works include The Call of the Wild and White Fang, both set in the Klondike Gold Rush, as well as the short stories "To Build a Fire", "An Odyssey of the North", and "Love of Life". He also wrote about the South Pacific in stories such as "The Pearls of Parlay" and "The Heathen". London was part of the radical literary group "The Crowd" in San Francisco and a passionate advocate of unionization, socialism, and the rights of workers. He wrote several powerful works dealing with these topics, such as his dystopian novel The Iron Heel, his non-fiction exposé The People of the Abyss, and The War of the Classes. (Source: Wikipedia)

Literary works:
The Cruise of the Dazzler (1902)
A Daughter of the Snows (1902)
The Call of the Wild (1903)
The Kempton-Wace Letters (1903)
The Sea-Wolf (1904)
The Game (1905)
White Fang (1906)
Before Adam (1907)
The Iron Heel (1908)
Martin Eden (1909)
Burning Daylight (1910)
Adventure (1911)
The Scarlet Plague (1912)
A Son of the Sun (1912)
The Abysmal Brute (1913)
The Valley of the Moon (1913)

THRONE CLASSICS

CHILDREN OF THE FROST
&
THE CRUISE OF THE DAZZLER

JACK LONDON

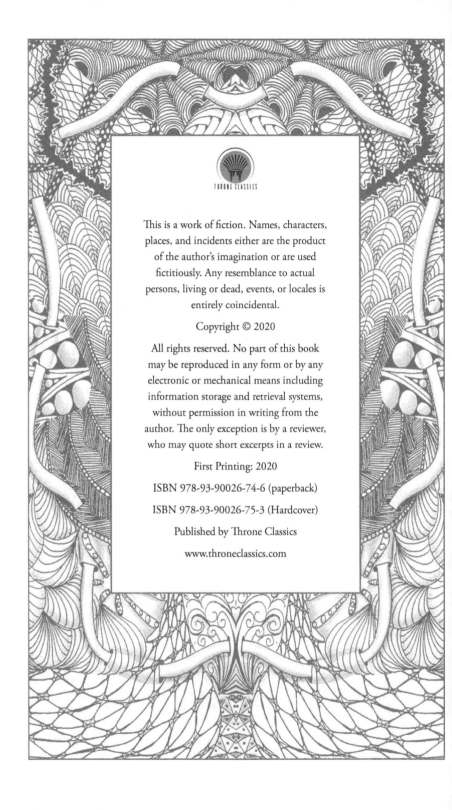

This is a work of fiction. Names, characters, places, and incidents either are the product of the author's imagination or are used fictitiously. Any resemblance to actual persons, living or dead, events, or locales is entirely coincidental.

Copyright © 2020

All rights reserved. No part of this book may be reproduced in any form or by any electronic or mechanical means including information storage and retrieval systems, without permission in writing from the author. The only exception is by a reviewer, who may quote short excerpts in a review.

First Printing: 2020

ISBN 978-93-90026-74-6 (paperback)

ISBN 978-93-90026-75-3 (Hardcover)

Published by Throne Classics

www.throneclassics.com

Contents

CHILDREN OF THE FROST
&
THE CRUISE OF THE DAZZLER

CHILDREN OF THE FROST

IN THE FORESTS OF THE NORTH

A weary journey beyond the last scrub timber and straggling copses, into the heart of the Barrens where the niggard North is supposed to deny the Earth, are to be found great sweeps of forests and stretches of smiling land. But this the world is just beginning to know. The world's explorers have known it, from time to time, but hitherto they have never returned to tell the world.

The Barrens—well, they are the Barrens, the bad lands of the Arctic, the deserts of the Circle, the bleak and bitter home of the musk-ox and the lean plains wolf. So Avery Van Brunt found them, treeless and cheerless, sparsely clothed with moss and lichens, and altogether uninviting. At least so he found them till he penetrated to the white blank spaces on the map, and came upon undreamed-of rich spruce forests and unrecorded Eskimo tribes. It had been his intention, (and his bid for fame), to break up these white blank spaces and diversify them with the black markings of mountain-chains, sinks and basins, and sinuous river courses; and it was with added delight that he came to speculate upon the possibilities of timber belts and native villages.

Avery Van Brunt, or, in full distinction, Professor A. Van Brunt of the Geological Survey, was second in command of the expedition, and first in command of the sub-expedition which he had led on a side tour of some half a thousand miles up one of the branches of the Thelon and which he was now leading into one of his unrecorded villages. At his back plodded eight men, two of them French-Canadian voyageurs, and the remainder strapping Crees from Manitoba-way. He, alone, was full-blooded Saxon, and his blood was pounding fiercely through his veins to the traditions of his race. Clive and Hastings, Drake and Raleigh, Hengest and Horsa, walked with him. First of all men of his breed was he to enter this lone Northland village, and at the thought an exultancy came upon him, an exaltation, and his followers noted that his leg-weariness fell from him and that he insensibly quickened the pace.

The village emptied itself, and a motley crowd trooped out to meet him, men in the forefront, with bows and spears clutched menacingly, and women and children faltering timidly in the rear. Van Brunt lifted his right arm and made the universal peace sign, a sign which all peoples know, and the villagers answered in peace. But to his chagrin, a skin-clad man ran forward and thrust out his hand with a familiar "Hello." He was a bearded man, with cheeks and brow bronzed to copper-brown, and in him Van Brunt knew his kind.

"Who are you?" he asked, gripping the extended hand. "Andrée?"

"Who's Andrée?" the man asked back.

Van Brunt looked at him more sharply. "By George, you've been here some time."

"Five years," the man answered, a dim flicker of pride in his eyes. "But come on, let's talk."

"Let them camp alongside of me," he answered Van Brunt's glance at his party. "Old Tantlatch will take care of them. Come on."

He swung off in a long stride, Van Brunt following at his heels through the village. In irregular fashion, wherever the ground favored, the lodges of moose hide were pitched. Van Brunt ran his practised eye over them and calculated.

"Two hundred, not counting the young ones," he summed up.

The man nodded. "Pretty close to it. But here's where I live, out of the thick of it, you know—more privacy and all that. Sit down. I'll eat with you when your men get something cooked up. I've forgotten what tea tastes like.... Five years and never a taste or smell.... Any tobacco?... Ah, thanks, and a pipe? Good. Now for a fire-stick and we'll see if the weed has lost its cunning."

He scratched the match with the painstaking care of the woodsman, cherished its young flame as though there were never another in all the world, and drew in the first mouthful of smoke. This he retained meditatively for a time, and blew out through his pursed lips slowly and caressingly. Then his face seemed to soften as he leaned back, and a soft blur to film his eyes. He sighed heavily, happily, with immeasurable content, and then said suddenly:

"God! But that tastes good!"

Van Brunt nodded sympathetically. "Five years, you say?"

"Five years." The man sighed again. "And you, I presume, wish to know about it, being naturally curious, and this a sufficiently strange situation, and all that. But it's not much. I came in from Edmonton after musk-ox, and like Pike and the rest of them, had my mischances, only I lost my party and outfit. Starvation, hardship, the regular tale, you know, sole survivor and all that, till I crawled into Tantlatch's, here, on hand and knee."

"Five years," Van Brunt murmured retrospectively, as though turning things over in his mind.

"Five years on February last. I crossed the Great Slave early in May—"

"And you are ... Fairfax?" Van Brunt interjected.

The man nodded.

"Let me see ... John, I think it is, John Fairfax."

"How did you know?" Fairfax queried lazily, half-absorbed in curling smoke-spirals upward in the quiet air.

"The papers were full of it at the time. Prevanche—"

"Prevanche!" Fairfax sat up, suddenly alert. "He was lost in the Smoke Mountains."

"Yes, but he pulled through and came out."

Fairfax settled back again and resumed his smoke-spirals. "I am glad to hear it," he remarked reflectively. "Prevanche was a bully fellow if he did have ideas about head-straps, the beggar. And he pulled through? Well, I'm glad."

Five years ... the phrase drifted recurrently through Van Brunt's thought,

13

and somehow the face of Emily Southwaithe seemed to rise up and take form before him. Five years ... A wedge of wild-fowl honked low overhead and at sight of the encampment veered swiftly to the north into the smouldering sun. Van Brunt could not follow them. He pulled out his watch. It was an hour past midnight. The northward clouds flushed bloodily, and rays of sombre-red shot southward, firing the gloomy woods with a lurid radiance. The air was in breathless calm, not a needle quivered, and the least sounds of the camp were distinct and clear as trumpet calls. The Crees and voyageurs felt the spirit of it and mumbled in dreamy undertones, and the cook unconsciously subdued the clatter of pot and pan. Somewhere a child was crying, and from the depths of the forest, like a silver thread, rose a woman's voice in mournful chant: "O-o-o-o-o-o-a-haa-ha-a-ha-aa-a-a, O-o-o-o-o-o-a-ha-a-ha-a."

Van Brunt shivered and rubbed the backs of his hands briskly.

"And they gave me up for dead?" his companion asked slowly.

"Well, you never came back, so your friends—"

"Promptly forgot." Fairfax laughed harshly, defiantly.

"Why didn't you come out?"

"Partly disinclination, I suppose, and partly because of circumstances over which I had no control. You see, Tantlatch, here, was down with a broken leg when I made his acquaintance,—a nasty fracture,—and I set it for him and got him into shape. I stayed some time, getting my strength back. I was the first white man he had seen, and of course I seemed very wise and showed his people no end of things. Coached them up in military tactics, among other things, so that they conquered the four other tribal villages, (which you have not yet seen), and came to rule the land. And they naturally grew to think a good deal of me, so much so that when I was ready to go they wouldn't hear of it. Were most hospitable, in fact. Put a couple of guards over me and watched me day and night. And then Tantlatch offered me inducements,—in a sense, inducements,—so to say, and as it didn't matter much one way or the other, I reconciled myself to remaining."

"I knew your brother at Freiburg. I am Van Brunt."

Fairfax reached forward impulsively and shook his hand. "You were Billy's friend, eh? Poor Billy! He spoke of you often."

"Rum meeting place, though," he added, casting an embracing glance over the primordial landscape and listening for a moment to the woman's mournful notes. "Her man was clawed by a bear, and she's taking it hard."

"Beastly life!" Van Brunt grimaced his disgust. "I suppose, after five years of it, civilization will be sweet? What do you say?"

Fairfax's face took on a stolid expression. "Oh, I don't know. At least they're honest folk and live according to their lights. And then they are amazingly simple. No complexity about them, no thousand and one subtle ramifications to every single emotion they experience. They love, fear, hate, are angered, or made happy, in common, ordinary, and unmistakable terms. It may be a beastly life, but at least it is easy to live. No philandering, no dallying. If a woman likes you, she'll not be backward in telling you so. If she hates you, she'll tell you so, and then, if you feel inclined, you can beat her, but the thing is, she knows precisely what you mean, and you know precisely what she means. No mistakes, no misunderstandings. It has its charm, after civilization's fitful fever. Comprehend?"

"No, it's a pretty good life," he continued, after a pause; "good enough for me, and I intend to stay with it."

Van Brunt lowered his head in a musing manner, and an imperceptible smile played on his mouth. No philandering, no dallying, no misunderstanding. Fairfax also was taking it hard, he thought, just because Emily Southwaithe had been mistakenly clawed by a bear. And not a bad sort of a bear, either, was Carlton Southwaithe.

"But you are coming along with me," Van Brunt said deliberately.

"No, I'm not."

"Yes, you are."

"Life's too easy here, I tell you." Fairfax spoke with decision. "I understand everything, and I am understood. Summer and winter alternate like the sun flashing through the palings of a fence, the seasons are a blur of

15

light and shade, and time slips by, and life slips by, and then ... a wailing in the forest, and the dark. Listen!"

He held up his hand, and the silver thread of the woman's sorrow rose through the silence and the calm. Fairfax joined in softly.

"O-o-o-o-o-o-a-haa-ha-a-ha-aa-a-a, O-o-o-o-o-a-ha-a-ha-a," he sang. "Can't you hear it? Can't you see it? The women mourning? the funeral chant? my hair white-locked and patriarchal? my skins wrapped in rude splendor about me? my hunting-spear by my side? And who shall say it is not well?"

Van Brunt looked at him coolly. "Fairfax, you are a damned fool. Five years of this is enough to knock any man, and you are in an unhealthy, morbid condition. Further, Carlton Southwaithe is dead."

Van Brunt filled his pipe and lighted it, the while watching slyly and with almost professional interest. Fairfax's eyes flashed on the instant, his fists clenched, he half rose up, then his muscles relaxed and he seemed to brood. Michael, the cook, signalled that the meal was ready, but Van Brunt motioned back to delay. The silence hung heavy, and he fell to analyzing the forest scents, the odors of mould and rotting vegetation, the resiny smells of pine cones and needles, the aromatic savors of many camp-smokes. Twice Fairfax looked up, but said nothing, and then:

"And ... Emily ...?"

"Three years a widow; still a widow."

Another long silence settled down, to be broken by Fairfax finally with a naïve smile. "I guess you're right, Van Brunt. I'll go along."

"I knew you would." Van Brunt laid his hand on Fairfax's shoulder. "Of course, one cannot know, but I imagine—for one in her position—she has had offers—"

"When do you start?" Fairfax interrupted.

"After the men have had some sleep. Which reminds me, Michael is getting angry, so come and eat."

16

After supper, when the Crees and voyageurs had rolled into their blankets, snoring, the two men lingered by the dying fire. There was much to talk about,—wars and politics and explorations, the doings of men and the happening of things, mutual friends, marriages, deaths,—five years of history for which Fairfax clamored.

"So the Spanish fleet was bottled up in Santiago," Van Brunt was saying, when a young woman stepped lightly before him and stood by Fairfax's side. She looked swiftly into his face, then turned a troubled gaze upon Van Brunt.

"Chief Tantlatch's daughter, sort of princess," Fairfax explained, with an honest flush. "One of the inducements, in short, to make me stay. Thom, this is Van Brunt, friend of mine."

Van Brunt held out his hand, but the woman maintained a rigid repose quite in keeping with her general appearance. Not a line of her face softened, not a feature unbent. She looked him straight in the eyes, her own piercing, questioning, searching.

"Precious lot she understands," Fairfax laughed. "Her first introduction, you know. But as you were saying, with the Spanish fleet bottled up in Santiago?"

Thom crouched down by her husband's side, motionless as a bronze statue, only her eyes flashing from face to face in ceaseless search. And Avery Van Brunt, as he talked on and on, felt a nervousness under the dumb gaze. In the midst of his most graphic battle descriptions, he would become suddenly conscious of the black eyes burning into him, and would stumble and flounder till he could catch the gait and go again. Fairfax, hands clasped round knees, pipe out, absorbed, spurred him on when he lagged, and repictured the world he thought he had forgotten.

One hour passed, and two, and Fairfax rose reluctantly to his feet. "And Cronje was cornered, eh? Well, just wait a moment till I run over to Tantlatch. He'll be expecting you, and I'll arrange for you to see him after breakfast. That will be all right, won't it?"

He went off between the pines, and Van Brunt found himself staring into Thom's warm eyes. Five years, he mused, and she can't be more than twenty now. A most remarkable creature. Being Eskimo, she should have a little flat excuse for a nose, and lo, it is neither broad nor flat, but aquiline, with nostrils delicately and sensitively formed as any fine lady's of a whiter breed—the Indian strain somewhere, be assured, Avery Van Brunt. And, Avery Van Brunt, don't be nervous, she won't eat you; she's only a woman, and not a bad-looking one at that. Oriental rather than aborigine. Eyes large and fairly wide apart, with just the faintest hint of Mongol obliquity. Thom, you're an anomaly. You're out of place here among these Eskimos, even if your father is one. Where did your mother come from? or your grandmother? And Thom, my dear, you're a beauty, a frigid, frozen little beauty with Alaskan lava in your blood, and please don't look at me that way.

He laughed and stood up. Her insistent stare disconcerted him. A dog was prowling among the grub-sacks. He would drive it away and place them into safety against Fairfax's return. But Thom stretched out a detaining hand and stood up, facing him.

"You?" she said, in the Arctic tongue which differs little from Greenland to Point Barrow. "You?"

And the swift expression of her face demanded all for which "you" stood, his reason for existence, his presence there, his relation to her husband—everything.

"Brother," he answered in the same tongue, with a sweeping gesture to the south. "Brothers we be, your man and I."

She shook her head. "It is not good that you be here."

"After one sleep I go."

"And my man?" she demanded, with tremulous eagerness.

Van Brunt shrugged his shoulders. He was aware of a certain secret shame, of an impersonal sort of shame, and an anger against Fairfax. And he felt the warm blood in his face as he regarded the young savage. She was just a woman. That was all—a woman. The whole sordid story over again, over and over again, as old as Eve and young as the last new love-light.

"My man! My man! My man!" she was reiterating vehemently, her face passionately dark, and the ruthless tenderness of the Eternal Woman, the Mate-Woman, looking out at him from her eyes.

"Thom," he said gravely, in English, "you were born in the Northland forest, and you have eaten fish and meat, and fought with frost and famine, and lived simply all the days of your life. And there are many things, indeed not simple, which you do not know and cannot come to understand. You do not know what it is to long for the fleshpots afar, you cannot understand what it is to yearn for a fair woman's face. And the woman is fair, Thom, the woman is nobly fair. You have been woman to this man, and you have been your all, but your all is very little, very simple. Too little and too simple, and he is an alien man. Him you have never known, you can never know. It is so ordained. You held him in your arms, but you never held his heart, this man with his blurring seasons and his dreams of a barbaric end. Dreams and dream-dust, that is what he has been to you. You clutched at form and gripped shadow, gave yourself to a man and bedded with the wraith of a man. In such manner, of old, did the daughters of men whom the gods found fair. And, Thom, Thom, I should not like to be John Fairfax in the night-watches of the years to come, in the night-watches, when his eyes shall see, not the sun-gloried hair of the woman by his side, but the dark tresses of a mate forsaken in the forests of the North."

Though she did not understand, she had listened with intense attention, as though life hung on his speech. But she caught at her husband's name and cried out in Eskimo:—

"Yes! Yes! Fairfax! My man!"

"Poor little fool, how could he be your man?"

But she could not understand his English tongue, and deemed that she was being trifled with. The dumb, insensate anger of the Mate-Woman flamed in her face, and it almost seemed to the man as though she crouched panther-like for the spring.

He cursed softly to himself and watched the fire fade from her face and the soft luminous glow of the appealing woman spring up, of the appealing woman who foregoes strength and panoplies herself wisely in her weakness.

"He is my man," she said gently. "Never have I known other. It cannot be that I should ever know other. Nor can it be that he should go from me."

"Who has said he shall go from thee?" he demanded sharply, half in exasperation, half in impotence.

"It is for thee to say he shall not go from me," she answered softly, a half-sob in her throat.

Van Brunt kicked the embers of the fire savagely and sat down.

"It is for thee to say. He is my man. Before all women he is my man. Thou art big, thou art strong, and behold, I am very weak. See, I am at thy feet. It is for thee to deal with me. It is for thee."

"Get up!" He jerked her roughly erect and stood up himself. "Thou art a woman. Wherefore the dirt is no place for thee, nor the feet of any man."

"He is my man."

"Then Jesus forgive all men!" Van Brunt cried out passionately.

"He is my man," she repeated monotonously, beseechingly.

"He is my brother," he answered.

"My father is Chief Tantlatch. He is a power over five villages. I will see that the five villages be searched for thy choice of all maidens, that thou mayest stay here by thy brother, and dwell in comfort."

"After one sleep I go."

"And my man?"

"Thy man comes now. Behold!"

From among the gloomy spruces came the light carolling of Fairfax's voice.

As the day is quenched by a sea of fog, so his song smote the light out of her face. "It is the tongue of his own people," she said; "the tongue of his own people."

She turned, with the free movement of a lithe young animal, and made off into the forest.

"It's all fixed," Fairfax called as he came up. "His regal highness will receive you after breakfast."

"Have you told him?" Van Brunt asked.

"No. Nor shall I tell him till we're ready to pull out."

Van Brunt looked with moody affection over the sleeping forms of his men.

"I shall be glad when we are a hundred leagues upon our way," he said.

Thom raised the skin-flap of her father's lodge. Two men sat with him, and the three looked at her with swift interest. But her face betokened nothing as she entered and took seat quietly, without speech. Tantlatch drummed with his knuckles on a spear-heft across his knees, and gazed idly along the path of a sun-ray which pierced a lacing-hole and flung a glittering track across the murky atmosphere of the lodge. To his right, at his shoulder, crouched Chugungatte, the shaman. Both were old men, and the weariness of many years brooded in their eyes. But opposite them sat Keen, a young man and chief favorite in the tribe. He was quick and alert of movement, and his black eyes flashed from face to face in ceaseless scrutiny and challenge.

Silence reigned in the place. Now and again camp noises penetrated, and from the distance, faint and far, like the shadows of voices, came the wrangling of boys in thin shrill tones. A dog thrust his head into the entrance and blinked wolfishly at them for a space, the slaver dripping from his ivory-white fangs. After a time he growled tentatively, and then, awed by the immobility of the human figures, lowered his head and grovelled away backward. Tantlatch glanced apathetically at his daughter.

"And thy man, how is it with him and thee?"

"He sings strange songs," Thom made answer, "and there is a new look on his face."

"So? He hath spoken?"

"Nay, but there is a new look on his face, a new light in his eyes, and with the New-Comer he sits by the fire, and they talk and talk, and the talk is without end."

Chugungatte whispered in his master's ear, and Keen leaned forward from his hips.

"There be something calling him from afar," she went on, "and he seems to sit and listen, and to answer, singing, in his own people's tongue."

Again Chugungatte whispered and Keen leaned forward, and Thom held her speech till her father nodded his head that she might proceed.

"It be known to thee, O Tantlatch, that the wild goose and the swan and the little ringed duck be born here in the low-lying lands. It be known that they go away before the face of the frost to unknown places. And it be known, likewise, that always do they return when the sun is in the land and the waterways are free. Always do they return to where they were born, that new life may go forth. The land calls to them and they come. And now there is another land that calls, and it is calling to my man,—the land where he was born,—and he hath it in mind to answer the call. Yet is he my man. Before all women is he my man."

"Is it well, Tantlatch? Is it well?" Chugungatte demanded, with the hint of menace in his voice.

"Ay, it is well!" Keen cried boldly. "The land calls to its children, and all lands call their children home again. As the wild goose and the swan and the little ringed duck are called, so is called this Stranger Man who has lingered with us and who now must go. Also there be the call of kind. The goose mates with the goose, nor does the swan mate with the little ringed duck. It is not well that the swan should mate with the little ringed duck. Nor is it well that stranger men should mate with the women of our villages. Wherefore I say the man should go, to his own kind, in his own land."

"He is my own man," Thom answered, "and he is a great man."

"Ay, he is a great man." Chugungatte lifted his head with a faint recrudescence of youthful vigor. "He is a great man, and he put strength in thy arm, O Tantlatch, and gave thee power, and made thy name to be feared in the land, to be feared and to be respected. He is very wise, and there be much profit in his wisdom. To him are we beholden for many things,—for the cunning in war and the secrets of the defence of a village and a rush in the forest, for the discussion in council and the undoing of enemies by word of mouth and the hard-sworn promise, for the gathering of game and the making of traps and the preserving of food, for the curing of sickness and mending of hurts of trail and fight. Thou, Tantlatch, wert a lame old man this day, were it not that the Stranger Man came into our midst and attended on thee. And ever, when in doubt on strange questions, have we gone to him, that out of his wisdom he might make things clear, and ever has he made things clear. And there be questions yet to arise, and needs upon his wisdom yet to come, and we cannot bear to let him go. It is not well that we should let him go."

Tantlatch continued to drum on the spear-haft, and gave no sign that he had heard. Thom studied his face in vain, and Chugungatte seemed to shrink together and droop down as the weight of years descended upon him again.

"No man makes my kill." Keen smote his breast a valorous blow. "I make my own kill. I am glad to live when I make my own kill. When I creep through the snow upon the great moose, I am glad. And when I draw the bow, so, with my full strength, and drive the arrow fierce and swift and to the heart, I am glad. And the meat of no man's kill tastes as sweet as the meat of my kill. I am glad to live, glad in my own cunning and strength, glad that I am a doer of things, a doer of things for myself. Of what other reason to live than that? Why should I live if I delight not in myself and the things I do? And it is because I delight and am glad that I go forth to hunt and fish, and it is because I go forth to hunt and fish that I grow cunning and strong. The man who stays in the lodge by the fire grows not cunning and strong. He is

23

not made happy in the eating of my kill, nor is living to him a delight. He does not live. And so I say it is well this Stranger Man should go. His wisdom does not make us wise. If he be cunning, there is no need that we be cunning. If need arise, we go to him for his cunning. We eat the meat of his kill, and it tastes unsweet. We merit by his strength, and in it there is no delight. We do not live when he does our living for us. We grow fat and like women, and we are afraid to work, and we forget how to do things for ourselves. Let the man go, O Tantlatch, that we may be men! I am Keen, a man, and I make my own kill!"

Tantlatch turned a gaze upon him in which seemed the vacancy of eternity. Keen waited the decision expectantly; but the lips did not move, and the old chief turned toward his daughter.

"That which be given cannot be taken away," she burst forth. "I was but a girl when this Stranger Man, who is my man, came among us. And I knew not men, or the ways of men, and my heart was in the play of girls, when thou, Tantlatch, thou and none other, didst call me to thee and press me into the arms of the Stranger Man. Thou and none other, Tantlatch; and as thou didst give me to the man, so didst thou give the man to me. He is my man. In my arms has he slept, and from my arms he cannot be taken."

"It were well, O Tantlatch," Keen followed quickly, with a significant glance at Thom, "it were well to remember that that which be given cannot be taken away."

Chugungatte straightened up. "Out of thy youth, Keen, come the words of thy mouth. As for ourselves, O Tantlatch, we be old men and we understand. We, too, have looked into the eyes of women and felt our blood go hot with strange desires. But the years have chilled us, and we have learned the wisdom of the council, the shrewdness of the cool head and hand, and we know that the warm heart be over-warm and prone to rashness. We know that Keen found favor in thy eyes. We know that Thom was promised him in the old days when she was yet a child. And we know that the new days came, and the Stranger Man, and that out of our wisdom and desire for welfare was Thom lost to Keen and the promise broken."

The old shaman paused, and looked directly at the young man.

"And be it known that I, Chugungatte, did advise that the promise be broken."

"Nor have I taken other woman to my bed," Keen broke in. "And I have builded my own fire, and cooked my own food, and ground my teeth in my loneliness."

Chugungatte waved his hand that he had not finished. "I am an old man and I speak from understanding. It be good to be strong and grasp for power. It be better to forego power that good come out of it. In the old days I sat at thy shoulder, Tantlatch, and my voice was heard over all in the council, and my advice taken in affairs of moment. And I was strong and held power. Under Tantlatch I was the greatest man. Then came the Stranger Man, and I saw that he was cunning and wise and great. And in that he was wiser and greater than I, it was plain that greater profit should arise from him than from me. And I had thy ear, Tantlatch, and thou didst listen to my words, and the Stranger Man was given power and place and thy daughter, Thom. And the tribe prospered under the new laws in the new days, and so shall it continue to prosper with the Stranger Man in our midst. We be old men, we two, O Tantlatch, thou and I, and this be an affair of head, not heart. Hear my words, Tantlatch! Hear my words! The man remains!"

There was a long silence. The old chief pondered with the massive certitude of God, and Chugungatte seemed to wrap himself in the mists of a great antiquity. Keen looked with yearning upon the woman, and she, unnoting, held her eyes steadfastly upon her father's face. The wolf-dog shoved the flap aside again, and plucking courage at the quiet, wormed forward on his belly. He sniffed curiously at Thom's listless hand, cocked ears challengingly at Chugungatte, and hunched down upon his haunches before Tantlatch. The spear rattled to the ground, and the dog, with a frightened yell, sprang sideways, snapping in mid-air, and on the second leap cleared the entrance.

Tantlatch looked from face to face, pondering each one long and carefully. Then he raised his head, with rude royalty, and gave judgment in cold and even tones: "The man remains. Let the hunters be called together. Send a runner to the next village with word to bring on the fighting men. I shall not see the New-Comer. Do thou, Chugungatte, have talk with him. Tell him he may go at once, if he would go in peace. And if fight there be, kill, kill, kill, to the last man; but let my word go forth that no harm befall our man,—the man whom my daughter hath wedded. It is well."

Chugungatte rose and tottered out; Thom followed; but as Keen stooped to the entrance the voice of Tantlatch stopped him.

"Keen, it were well to hearken to my word. The man remains. Let no harm befall him."

Because of Fairfax's instructions in the art of war, the tribesmen did not hurl themselves forward boldly and with clamor. Instead, there was great restraint and self-control, and they were content to advance silently, creeping and crawling from shelter to shelter. By the river bank, and partly protected by a narrow open space, crouched the Crees and voyageurs. Their eyes could see nothing, and only in vague ways did their ears hear, but they felt the thrill of life which ran through the forest, the indistinct, indefinable movement of an advancing host.

"Damn them," Fairfax muttered. "They've never faced powder, but I taught them the trick."

Avery Van Brunt laughed, knocked the ashes out of his pipe, and put it carefully away with the pouch, and loosened the hunting-knife in its sheath at his hip.

"Wait," he said. "We'll wither the face of the charge and break their hearts."

"They'll rush scattered if they remember my teaching."

"Let them. Magazine rifles were made to pump. We'll—good! First blood! Extra tobacco, Loon!"

Loon, a Cree, had spotted an exposed shoulder and with a stinging bullet apprised its owner of his discovery.

"If we can tease them into breaking forward," Fairfax muttered,—"if we can only tease them into breaking forward."

Van Brunt saw a head peer from behind a distant tree, and with a quick shot sent the man sprawling to the ground in a death struggle. Michael potted a third, and Fairfax and the rest took a hand, firing at every exposure and into each clump of agitated brush. In crossing one little swale out of cover, five of the tribesmen remained on their faces, and to the left, where the covering was sparse, a dozen men were struck. But they took the punishment with sullen steadiness, coming on cautiously, deliberately, without haste and without lagging.

Ten minutes later, when they were quite close, all movement was suspended, the advance ceased abruptly, and the quietness that followed was portentous, threatening. Only could be seen the green and gold of the woods, and undergrowth, shivering and trembling to the first faint puffs of the day-wind. The wan white morning sun mottled the earth with long shadows and streaks of light. A wounded man lifted his head and crawled painfully out of the swale, Michael following him with his rifle but forbearing to shoot. A whistle ran along the invisible line from left to right, and a flight of arrows arched through the air.

"Get ready," Van Brunt commanded, a new metallic note in his voice. "Now!"

They broke cover simultaneously. The forest heaved into sudden life. A great yell went up, and the rifles barked back sharp defiance. Tribesmen knew their deaths in mid-leap, and as they fell, their brothers surged over them in a roaring, irresistible wave. In the forefront of the rush, hair flying and arms swinging free, flashing past the tree-trunks, and leaping the obstructing logs, came Thom. Fairfax sighted on her and almost pulled trigger ere he knew her.

"The woman! Don't shoot!" he cried. "See! She is unarmed!"

The Crees never heard, nor Michael and his brother voyageur, nor Van Brunt, who was keeping one shell continuously in the air. But Thom bore straight on, unharmed, at the heels of a skin-clad hunter who had veered

27

in before her from the side. Fairfax emptied his magazine into the men to right and left of her, and swung his rifle to meet the big hunter. But the man, seeming to recognize him, swerved suddenly aside and plunged his spear into the body of Michael. On the moment Thom had one arm passed around her husband's neck, and twisting half about, with voice and gesture was splitting the mass of charging warriors. A score of men hurled past on either side, and Fairfax, for a brief instant's space, stood looking upon her and her bronze beauty, thrilling, exulting, stirred to unknown deeps, visioning strange things, dreaming, immortally dreaming. Snatches and scraps of old-world philosophies and new-world ethics floated through his mind, and things wonderfully concrete and woefully incongruous—hunting scenes, stretches of sombre forest, vastnesses of silent snow, the glittering of ballroom lights, great galleries and lecture halls, a fleeting shimmer of glistening test-tubes, long rows of book-lined shelves, the throb of machinery and the roar of traffic, a fragment of forgotten song, faces of dear women and old chums, a lonely watercourse amid upstanding peaks, a shattered boat on a pebbly strand, quiet moonlit fields, fat vales, the smell of hay....

A hunter, struck between the eyes with a rifle-ball, pitched forward lifeless, and with the momentum of his charge slid along the ground. Fairfax came back to himself. His comrades, those that lived, had been swept far back among the trees beyond. He could hear the fierce "Hia! Hia!" of the hunters as they closed in and cut and thrust with their weapons of bone and ivory. The cries of the stricken men smote him like blows. He knew the fight was over, the cause was lost, but all his race traditions and race loyalty impelled him into the welter that he might die at least with his kind.

"My man! My man!" Thom cried. "Thou art safe!"

He tried to struggle on, but her dead weight clogged his steps.

"There is no need! They are dead, and life be good!"

She held him close around the neck and twined her limbs about his till he tripped and stumbled, reeled violently to recover footing, tripped again, and fell backward to the ground. His head struck a jutting root, and he was half-stunned and could struggle but feebly. In the fall she had heard the feathered swish of an arrow darting past, and she covered his body with hers, as with a shield, her arms holding him tightly, her face and lips pressed upon his neck.

Then it was that Keen rose up from a tangled thicket a score of feet away. He looked about him with care. The fight had swept on and the cry of the last man was dying away. There was no one to see. He fitted an arrow to the string and glanced at the man and woman. Between her breast and arm the flesh of the man's side showed white. Keen bent the bow and drew back the arrow to its head. Twice he did so, calmly and for certainty, and then drove the bone-barbed missile straight home to the white flesh, gleaming yet more white in the dark-armed, dark-breasted embrace.

THE LAW OF LIFE

Old Koskoosh listened greedily. Though his sight had long since faded, his hearing was still acute, and the slightest sound penetrated to the glimmering intelligence which yet abode behind the withered forehead, but which no longer gazed forth upon the things of the world. Ah! that was Sit-cum-to-ha, shrilly anathematizing the dogs as she cuffed and beat them into the harnesses. Sit-cum-to-ha was his daughter's daughter, but she was too busy to waste a thought upon her broken grandfather, sitting alone there in the snow, forlorn and helpless. Camp must be broken. The long trail waited while the short day refused to linger. Life called her, and the duties of life, not death. And he was very close to death now.

The thought made the old man panicky for the moment, and he stretched forth a palsied hand which wandered tremblingly over the small heap of dry wood beside him. Reassured that it was indeed there, his hand returned to the shelter of his mangy furs, and he again fell to listening. The sulky crackling of half-frozen hides told him that the chief's moose-skin lodge had been struck, and even then was being rammed and jammed into portable compass. The chief was his son, stalwart and strong, head man of the tribesmen, and a mighty hunter. As the women toiled with the camp luggage, his voice rose, chiding them for their slowness. Old Koskoosh strained his ears. It was the last time he would hear that voice. There went Geehow's lodge! And Tusken's! Seven, eight, nine; only the shaman's could be still standing. There! They were at work upon it now. He could hear the shaman grunt as he piled it on the sled. A child whimpered, and a woman soothed it with soft, crooning gutturals. Little Koo-tee, the old man thought, a fretful child, and not overstrong. It would die soon, perhaps, and they would burn a hole through the frozen tundra and pile rocks above to keep the wolverines away. Well, what did it matter? A few years at best, and as many an empty belly as a full one. And in the end, Death waited, ever-hungry and hungriest of them all.

What was that? Oh, the men lashing the sleds and drawing tight the thongs. He listened, who would listen no more. The whip-lashes snarled and bit among the dogs. Hear them whine! How they hated the work and the trail! They were off! Sled after sled churned slowly away into the silence. They were gone. They had passed out of his life, and he faced the last bitter hour alone. No. The snow crunched beneath a moccasin; a man stood beside him; upon his head a hand rested gently. His son was good to do this thing. He remembered other old men whose sons had not waited after the tribe. But his son had. He wandered away into the past, till the young man's voice brought him back.

"Is it well with you?" he asked.

And the old man answered, "It is well."

"There be wood beside you," the younger man continued, "and the fire burns bright. The morning is gray, and the cold has broken. It will snow presently. Even now is it snowing."

"Ay, even now is it snowing."

"The tribesmen hurry. Their bales are heavy, and their bellies flat with lack of feasting. The trail is long and they travel fast. I go now. It is well?"

"It is well. I am as a last year's leaf, clinging lightly to the stem. The first breath that blows, and I fall. My voice is become like an old woman's. My eyes no longer show me the way of my feet, and my feet are heavy, and I am tired. It is well."

He bowed his head in content till the last noise of the complaining snow had died away, and he knew his son was beyond recall. Then his hand crept out in haste to the wood. It alone stood between him and the eternity that yawned in upon him. At last the measure of his life was a handful of fagots. One by one they would go to feed the fire, and just so, step by step, death would creep upon him. When the last stick had surrendered up its heat, the frost would begin to gather strength. First his feet would yield, then his hands; and the numbness would travel, slowly, from the extremities to the body. His head would fall forward upon his knees, and he would rest. It was easy. All men must die.

He did not complain. It was the way of life, and it was just. He had been born close to the earth, close to the earth had he lived, and the law thereof was not new to him. It was the law of all flesh. Nature was not kindly to the flesh. She had no concern for that concrete thing called the individual. Her interest lay in the species, the race. This was the deepest abstraction old Koskoosh's barbaric mind was capable of, but he grasped it firmly. He saw it exemplified in all life. The rise of the sap, the bursting greenness of the willow bud, the fall of the yellow leaf—in this alone was told the whole history. But one task did Nature set the individual. Did he not perform it, he died. Did he perform it, it was all the same, he died. Nature did not care; there were plenty who were obedient, and it was only the obedience in this matter, not the obedient, which lived and lived always. The tribe of Koskoosh was very old. The old men he had known when a boy, had known old men before them. Therefore it was true that the tribe lived, that it stood for the obedience of all its members, way down into the forgotten past, whose very resting-places were unremembered. They did not count; they were episodes. They had passed away like clouds from a summer sky. He also was an episode, and would pass away. Nature did not care. To life she set one task, gave one law. To perpetuate was the task of life, its law was death. A maiden was a good creature to look upon, full-breasted and strong, with spring to her step and light in her eyes. But her task was yet before her. The light in her eyes brightened, her step quickened, she was now bold with the young men, now timid, and she gave them of her own unrest. And ever she grew fairer and yet fairer to look upon, till some hunter, able no longer to withhold himself, took her to his lodge to cook and toil for him and to become the mother of his children. And with the coming of her offspring her looks left her. Her limbs dragged and shuffled, her eyes dimmed and bleared, and only the little children found joy against the withered cheek of the old squaw by the fire. Her task was done. But a little while, on the first pinch of famine or the first long trail, and she would be left, even as he had been left, in the snow, with a little pile of wood. Such was the law.

He placed a stick carefully upon the fire and resumed his meditations. It was the same everywhere, with all things. The mosquitoes vanished with the first frost. The little tree-squirrel crawled away to die. When age settled upon the rabbit it became slow and heavy, and could no longer outfoot its enemies.

Even the big bald-face grew clumsy and blind and quarrelsome, in the end to be dragged down by a handful of yelping huskies. He remembered how he had abandoned his own father on an upper reach of the Klondike one winter, the winter before the missionary came with his talk-books and his box of medicines. Many a time had Koskoosh smacked his lips over the recollection of that box, though now his mouth refused to moisten. The "painkiller" had been especially good. But the missionary was a bother after all, for he brought no meat into the camp, and he ate heartily, and the hunters grumbled. But he chilled his lungs on the divide by the Mayo, and the dogs afterwards nosed the stones away and fought over his bones.

Koskoosh placed another stick on the fire and harked back deeper into the past. There was the time of the Great Famine, when the old men crouched empty-bellied to the fire, and let fall from their lips dim traditions of the ancient day when the Yukon ran wide open for three winters, and then lay frozen for three summers. He had lost his mother in that famine. In the summer the salmon run had failed, and the tribe looked forward to the winter and the coming of the caribou. Then the winter came, but with it there were no caribou. Never had the like been known, not even in the lives of the old men. But the caribou did not come, and it was the seventh year, and the rabbits had not replenished, and the dogs were naught but bundles of bones. And through the long darkness the children wailed and died, and the women, and the old men; and not one in ten of the tribe lived to meet the sun when it came back in the spring. That was a famine!

But he had seen times of plenty, too, when the meat spoiled on their hands, and the dogs were fat and worthless with overeating—times when they let the game go unkilled, and the women were fertile, and the lodges were cluttered with sprawling men-children and women-children. Then it was the men became high-stomached, and revived ancient quarrels, and crossed the divides to the south to kill the Pellys, and to the west that they might sit by the dead fires of the Tananas. He remembered, when a boy, during a time of plenty, when he saw a moose pulled down by the wolves. Zing-ha lay with him in the snow and watched—Zing-ha, who later became the craftiest of hunters, and who, in the end, fell through an air-hole on the Yukon. They found him, a month afterward, just as he had crawled halfway out and frozen stiff to the ice.

But the moose. Zing-ha and he had gone out that day to play at hunting after the manner of their fathers. On the bed of the creek they struck the fresh track of a moose, and with it the tracks of many wolves. "An old one," Zing-ha, who was quicker at reading the sign, said—"an old one who cannot keep up with the herd. The wolves have cut him out from his brothers, and they will never leave him." And it was so. It was their way. By day and by night, never resting, snarling on his heels, snapping at his nose, they would stay by him to the end. How Zing-ha and he felt the blood-lust quicken! The finish would be a sight to see!

Eager-footed, they took the trail, and even he, Koskoosh, slow of sight and an unversed tracker, could have followed it blind, it was so wide. Hot were they on the heels of the chase, reading the grim tragedy, fresh-written, at every step. Now they came to where the moose had made a stand. Thrice the length of a grown man's body, in every direction, had the snow been stamped about and uptossed. In the midst were the deep impressions of the splay-hoofed game, and all about, everywhere, were the lighter footmarks of the wolves. Some, while their brothers harried the kill, had lain to one side and rested. The full-stretched impress of their bodies in the snow was as perfect as though made the moment before. One wolf had been caught in a wild lunge of the maddened victim and trampled to death. A few bones, well picked, bore witness.

Again, they ceased the uplift of their snowshoes at a second stand. Here the great animal had fought desperately. Twice had he been dragged down, as the snow attested, and twice had he shaken his assailants clear and gained footing once more. He had done his task long since, but none the less was life dear to him. Zing-ha said it was a strange thing, a moose once down to get free again; but this one certainly had. The shaman would see signs and wonders in this when they told him.

And yet again, they come to where the moose had made to mount the bank and gain the timber. But his foes had laid on from behind, till he reared and fell back upon them, crushing two deep into the snow. It was plain the kill was at hand, for their brothers had left them untouched. Two more stands were hurried past, brief in time-length and very close together. The trail was red now, and the clean stride of the great beast had grown short and slovenly. Then they heard the first sounds of the battle—not the full-throated chorus of the chase, but the short, snappy bark which spoke of close quarters and teeth to flesh. Crawling up the wind, Zing-ha bellied it through the snow, and with him crept he, Koskoosh, who was to be chief of the tribesmen in the years to come. Together they shoved aside the under branches of a young spruce and peered forth. It was the end they saw.

The picture, like all of youth's impressions, was still strong with him, and his dim eyes watched the end played out as vividly as in that far-off time. Koskoosh marvelled at this, for in the days which followed, when he was a leader of men and a head of councillors, he had done great deeds and made his name a curse in the mouths of the Pellys, to say naught of the strange white man he had killed, knife to knife, in open fight.

For long he pondered on the days of his youth, till the fire died down and the frost bit deeper. He replenished it with two sticks this time, and gauged his grip on life by what remained. If Sit-cum-to-ha had only remembered her grandfather, and gathered a larger armful, his hours would have been longer. It would have been easy. But she was ever a careless child, and honored not her ancestors from the time the Beaver, son of the son of Zing-ha, first cast eyes upon her. Well, what mattered it? Had he not done likewise in his own quick youth? For a while he listened to the silence. Perhaps the heart of his son might soften, and he would come back with the dogs to take his old father on with the tribe to where the caribou ran thick and the fat hung heavy upon them.

He strained his ears, his restless brain for the moment stilled. Not a stir, nothing. He alone took breath in the midst of the great silence. It was very lonely. Hark! What was that? A chill passed over his body. The familiar, long-drawn howl broke the void, and it was close at hand. Then on his darkened eyes was projected the vision of the moose—the old bull moose—the torn flanks and bloody sides, the riddled mane, and the great branching horns, down low

35

and tossing to the last. He saw the flashing forms of gray, the gleaming eyes, the lolling tongues, the slavered fangs. And he saw the inexorable circle close in till it became a dark point in the midst of the stamped snow.

A cold muzzle thrust against his cheek, and at its touch his soul leaped back to the present. His hand shot into the fire and dragged out a burning faggot. Overcome for the nonce by his hereditary fear of man, the brute retreated, raising a prolonged call to his brothers; and greedily they answered, till a ring of crouching, jaw-slobbered gray was stretched round about. The old man listened to the drawing in of this circle. He waved his brand wildly, and sniffs turned to snarls; but the panting brutes refused to scatter. Now one wormed his chest forward, dragging his haunches after, now a second, now a third; but never a one drew back. Why should he cling to life? he asked, and dropped the blazing stick into the snow. It sizzled and went out. The circle grunted uneasily, but held its own. Again he saw the last stand of the old bull moose, and Koskoosh dropped his head wearily upon his knees. What did it matter after all? Was it not the law of life?

NAM-BOK THE UNVERACIOUS

"A bidarka, is it not so? Look! a bidarka, and one man who drives clumsily with a paddle!"

Old Bask-Wah-Wan rose to her knees, trembling with weakness and eagerness, and gazed out over the sea.

"Nam-Bok was ever clumsy at the paddle," she maundered reminiscently, shading the sun from her eyes and staring across the silver-spilled water. "Nam-Bok was ever clumsy. I remember...."

But the women and children laughed loudly, and there was a gentle mockery in their laughter, and her voice dwindled till her lips moved without sound.

Koogah lifted his grizzled head from his bone-carving and followed the path of her eyes. Except when wide yaws took it off its course, a bidarka was heading in for the beach. Its occupant was paddling with more strength than dexterity, and made his approach along the zigzag line of most resistance. Koogah's head dropped to his work again, and on the ivory tusk between his knees he scratched the dorsal fin of a fish the like of which never swam in the sea.

"It is doubtless the man from the next village," he said finally, "come to consult with me about the marking of things on bone. And the man is a clumsy man. He will never know how."

"It is Nam-Bok," old Bask-Wah-Wan repeated. "Should I not know my son?" she demanded shrilly. "I say, and I say again, it is Nam-Bok."

"And so thou hast said these many summers," one of the women chided softly. "Ever when the ice passed out of the sea hast thou sat and watched through the long day, saying at each chance canoe, 'This is Nam-Bok.' Nam-Bok is dead, O Bask-Wah-Wan, and the dead do not come back. It cannot be that the dead come back."

"Nam-Bok!" the old woman cried, so loud and clear that the whole village was startled and looked at her.

She struggled to her feet and tottered down the sand. She stumbled over a baby lying in the sun, and the mother hushed its crying and hurled harsh words after the old woman, who took no notice. The children ran down the beach in advance of her, and as the man in the bidarka drew closer, nearly capsizing with one of his ill-directed strokes, the women followed. Koogah dropped his walrus tusk and went also, leaning heavily upon his staff, and after him loitered the men in twos and threes.

The bidarka turned broadside and the ripple of surf threatened to swamp it, only a naked boy ran into the water and pulled the bow high up on the sand. The man stood up and sent a questing glance along the line of villagers. A rainbow sweater, dirty and the worse for wear, clung loosely to his broad shoulders, and a red cotton handkerchief was knotted in sailor fashion about his throat. A fisherman's tam-o'-shanter on his close-clipped head, and dungaree trousers and heavy brogans, completed his outfit.

But he was none the less a striking personage to these simple fisherfolk of the great Yukon Delta, who, all their lives, had stared out on Bering Sea and in that time seen but two white men,—the census enumerator and a lost Jesuit priest. They were a poor people, with neither gold in the ground nor valuable furs in hand, so the whites had passed them afar. Also, the Yukon, through the thousands of years, had shoaled that portion of the sea with the detritus of Alaska till vessels grounded out of sight of land. So the sodden coast, with its long inside reaches and huge mud-land archipelagoes, was avoided by the ships of men, and the fisherfolk knew not that such things were.

Koogah, the Bone-Scratcher, retreated backward in sudden haste, tripping over his staff and falling to the ground. "Nam-Bok!" he cried, as he scrambled wildly for footing. "Nam-Bok, who was blown off to sea, come back!"

The men and women shrank away, and the children scuttled off between their legs. Only Opee-Kwan was brave, as befitted the head man of the village.

He strode forward and gazed long and earnestly at the new-comer.

"It is Nam-Bok," he said at last, and at the conviction in his voice the women wailed apprehensively and drew farther away.

The lips of the stranger moved indecisively, and his brown throat writhed and wrestled with unspoken words.

"La la, it is Nam-Bok," Bask-Wah-Wan croaked, peering up into his face. "Ever did I say Nam-Bok would come back."

"Ay, it is Nam-Bok come back." This time it was Nam-Bok himself who spoke, putting a leg over the side of the bidarka and standing with one foot afloat and one ashore. Again his throat writhed and wrestled as he grappled after forgotten words. And when the words came forth they were strange of sound and a spluttering of the lips accompanied the gutturals. "Greeting, O brothers," he said, "brothers of old time before I went away with the off-shore wind."

He stepped out with both feet on the sand, and Opee-Kwan waved him back.

"Thou art dead, Nam-Bok," he said.

Nam-Bok laughed. "I am fat."

"Dead men are not fat," Opee-Kwan confessed. "Thou hast fared well, but it is strange. No man may mate with the off-shore wind and come back on the heels of the years."

"I have come back," Nam-Bok answered simply.

"Mayhap thou art a shadow, then, a passing shadow of the Nam-Bok that was. Shadows come back."

"I am hungry. Shadows do not eat."

But Opee-Kwan doubted, and brushed his hand across his brow in sore puzzlement. Nam-Bok was likewise puzzled, and as he looked up and down the line found no welcome in the eyes of the fisherfolk. The men and women whispered together. The children stole timidly back among their elders, and bristling dogs fawned up to him and sniffed suspiciously.

"I bore thee, Nam-Bok, and I gave thee suck when thou wast little," Bask-Wah-Wan whimpered, drawing closer; "and shadow though thou be, or no shadow, I will give thee to eat now."

Nam-Bok made to come to her, but a growl of fear and menace warned him back. He said something in a strange tongue which sounded like "Goddam," and added, "No shadow am I, but a man."

"Who may know concerning the things of mystery?" Opee-Kwan demanded, half of himself and half of his tribespeople. "We are, and in a breath we are not. If the man may become shadow, may not the shadow become man? Nam-Bok was, but is not. This we know, but we do not know if this be Nam-Bok or the shadow of Nam-Bok."

Nam-Bok cleared his throat and made answer. "In the old time long ago, thy father's father, Opee-Kwan, went away and came back on the heels of the years. Nor was a place by the fire denied him. It is said ..." He paused significantly, and they hung on his utterance. "It is said," he repeated, driving his point home with deliberation, "that Sipsip, his klooch, bore him two sons after he came back."

"But he had no doings with the off-shore wind," Opee-Kwan retorted. "He went away into the heart of the land, and it is in the nature of things that a man may go on and on into the land."

"And likewise the sea. But that is neither here nor there. It is said ... that thy father's father told strange tales of the things he saw."

"Ay, strange tales he told."

"I, too, have strange tales to tell," Nam-Bok stated insidiously. And, as they wavered, "And presents likewise."

He pulled from the bidarka a shawl, marvellous of texture and color, and flung it about his mother's shoulders. The women voiced a collective sigh of admiration, and old Bask-Wah-Wan ruffled the gay material and patted it and crooned in childish joy.

"He has tales to tell," Koogah muttered. "And presents," a woman seconded.

And Opee-Kwan knew that his people were eager, and further, he was aware himself of an itching curiosity concerning those untold tales. "The fishing has been good," he said judiciously, "and we have oil in plenty. So come, Nam-Bok, let us feast."

Two of the men hoisted the bidarka on their shoulders and carried it up to the fire. Nam-Bok walked by the side of Opee-Kwan, and the villagers followed after, save those of the women who lingered a moment to lay caressing fingers on the shawl.

There was little talk while the feast went on, though many and curious were the glances stolen at the son of Bask-Wah-Wan. This embarrassed him— not because he was modest of spirit, however, but for the fact that the stench of the seal-oil had robbed him of his appetite, and that he keenly desired to conceal his feelings on the subject.

"Eat; thou art hungry," Opee-Kwan commanded, and Nam-Bok shut both his eyes and shoved his fist into the big pot of putrid fish.

"La la, be not ashamed. The seal were many this year, and strong men are ever hungry." And Bask-Wah-Wan sopped a particularly offensive chunk of salmon into the oil and passed it fondly and dripping to her son.

In despair, when premonitory symptoms warned him that his stomach was not so strong as of old, he filled his pipe and struck up a smoke. The people fed on noisily and watched. Few of them could boast of intimate acquaintance with the precious weed, though now and again small quantities and abominable qualities were obtained in trade from the Eskimos to the northward. Koogah, sitting next to him, indicated that he was not averse to taking a draw, and between two mouthfuls, with the oil thick on his lips, sucked away at the amber stem. And thereupon Nam-Bok held his stomach with a shaky hand and declined the proffered return. Koogah could keep the pipe, he said, for he had intended so to honor him from the first. And the people licked their fingers and approved of his liberality.

Opee-Kwan rose to his feet "And now, O Nam-Bok, the feast is ended, and we would listen concerning the strange things you have seen."

The fisherfolk applauded with their hands, and gathering about them their work, prepared to listen. The men were busy fashioning spears and carving on ivory, while the women scraped the fat from the hides of the hair seal and made them pliable or sewed muclucs with threads of sinew. Nam-Bok's eyes roved over the scene, but there was not the charm about it that his recollection had warranted him to expect. During the years of his wandering he had looked forward to just this scene, and now that it had come he was disappointed. It was a bare and meagre life, he deemed, and not to be compared to the one to which he had become used. Still, he would open their eyes a bit, and his own eyes sparkled at the thought.

"Brothers," he began, with the smug complacency of a man about to relate the big things he has done, "it was late summer of many summers back, with much such weather as this promises to be, when I went away. You all remember the day, when the gulls flew low, and the wind blew strong from the land, and I could not hold my bidarka against it. I tied the covering of the bidarka about me so that no water could get in, and all of the night I fought with the storm. And in the morning there was no land,—only the sea,—and the off-shore wind held me close in its arms and bore me along. Three such nights whitened into dawn and showed me no land, and the off-shore wind would not let me go.

"And when the fourth day came, I was as a madman. I could not dip my paddle for want of food; and my head went round and round, what of the thirst that was upon me. But the sea was no longer angry, and the soft south wind was blowing, and as I looked about me I saw a sight that made me think I was indeed mad."

Nam-Bok paused to pick away a sliver of salmon lodged between his teeth, and the men and women, with idle hands and heads craned forward, waited.

"It was a canoe, a big canoe. If all the canoes I have ever seen were made into one canoe, it would not be so large."

There were exclamations of doubt, and Koogah, whose years were many, shook his head.

"If each bidarka were as a grain of sand," Nam-Bok defiantly continued, "and if there were as many bidarkas as there be grains of sand in this beach, still would they not make so big a canoe as this I saw on the morning of the fourth day. It was a very big canoe, and it was called a schooner. I saw this thing of wonder, this great schooner, coming after me, and on it I saw men—"

"Hold, O Nam-Bok!" Opee-Kwan broke in. "What manner of men were they?—big men?"

"Nay, mere men like you and me."

"Did the big canoe come fast?"

"Ay."

"The sides were tall, the men short." Opee-Kwan stated the premises with conviction. "And did these men dip with long paddles?"

Nam-Bok grinned. "There were no paddles," he said.

Mouths remained open, and a long silence dropped down. Opee-Kwan borrowed Koogah's pipe for a couple of contemplative sucks. One of the younger women giggled nervously and drew upon herself angry eyes.

"There were no paddles?" Opee-Kwan asked softly, returning the pipe.

"The south wind was behind," Nam-Bok explained.

"But the wind-drift is slow."

"The schooner had wings—thus." He sketched a diagram of masts and sails in the sand, and the men crowded around and studied it. The wind was blowing briskly, and for more graphic elucidation he seized the corners of his mother's shawl and spread them out till it bellied like a sail. Bask-Wah-Wan scolded and struggled, but was blown down the beach for a score of feet and left breathless and stranded in a heap of driftwood. The men uttered sage grunts of comprehension, but Koogah suddenly tossed back his hoary head.

"Ho! Ho!" he laughed. "A foolish thing, this big canoe! A most foolish thing! The plaything of the wind! Wheresoever the wind goes, it goes too. No man who journeys therein may name the landing beach, for always he goes with the wind, and the wind goes everywhere, but no man knows where."

"It is so," Opee-Kwan supplemented gravely. "With the wind the going is easy, but against the wind a man striveth hard; and for that they had no paddles these men on the big canoe did not strive at all."

"Small need to strive," Nam-Bok cried angrily. "The schooner went likewise against the wind."

"And what said you made the sch—sch—schooner go?" Koogah asked, tripping craftily over the strange word.

"The wind," was the impatient response.

"Then the wind made the sch—sch—schooner go against the wind." Old Koogah dropped an open leer to Opee-Kwan, and, the laughter growing around him, continued: "The wind blows from the south and blows the schooner south. The wind blows against the wind. The wind blows one way and the other at the same time. It is very simple. We understand, Nam-Bok. We clearly understand."

"Thou art a fool!"

"Truth falls from thy lips," Koogah answered meekly. "I was over-long in understanding, and the thing was simple."

But Nam-Bok's face was dark, and he said rapid words which they had never heard before. Bone-scratching and skin-scraping were resumed, but he shut his lips tightly on the tongue that could not be believed.

"This sch—sch—schooner," Koogah imperturbably asked; "it was made of a big tree?"

"It was made of many trees," Nam-Bok snapped shortly. "It was very big."

He lapsed into sullen silence again, and Opee-Kwan nudged Koogah, who shook his head with slow amazement and murmured, "It is very strange."

Nam-bok took the bait. "That is nothing," he said airily; "you should see the steamer. As the grain of sand is to the bidarka, as the bidarka is to the schooner, so the schooner is to the steamer. Further, the steamer is made of iron. It is all iron."

"Nay, nay, Nam-Bok," cried the head man; "how can that be? Always iron goes to the bottom. For behold, I received an iron knife in trade from the head man of the next village, and yesterday the iron knife slipped from my fingers and went down, down, into the sea. To all things there be law. Never was there one thing outside the law. This we know. And, moreover, we know that things of a kind have the one law, and that all iron has the one law. So unsay thy words, Nam-Bok, that we may yet honor thee."

"It is so," Nam-Bok persisted. "The steamer is all iron and does not sink."

"Nay, nay; this cannot be."

"With my own eyes I saw it."

"It is not in the nature of things."

"But tell me, Nam-Bok," Koogah interrupted, for fear the tale would go no farther, "tell me the manner of these men in finding their way across the sea when there is no land by which to steer."

"The sun points out the path."

"But how?"

"At midday the head man of the schooner takes a thing through which his eye looks at the sun, and then he makes the sun climb down out of the sky to the edge of the earth."

"Now this be evil medicine!" cried Opee-Kwan, aghast at the sacrilege.

The men held up their hands in horror, and the women moaned. "This be evil medicine. It is not good to misdirect the great sun which drives away the night and gives us the seal, the salmon, and warm weather."

"What if it be evil medicine?" Nam-Bok demanded truculently. "I, too, have looked through the thing at the sun and made the sun climb down out of the sky."

Those who were nearest drew away from him hurriedly, and a woman covered the face of a child at her breast so that his eye might not fall upon it.

"But on the morning of the fourth day, O Nam-Bok," Koogah suggested; "on the morning of the fourth day when the sch—sch—schooner came after thee?"

"I had little strength left in me and could not run away. So I was taken on board and water was poured down my throat and good food given me. Twice, my brothers, you have seen a white man. These men were all white and as many as have I fingers and toes. And when I saw they were full of kindness, I took heart, and I resolved to bring away with me report of all that I saw. And they taught me the work they did, and gave me good food and a place to sleep.

"And day after day we went over the sea, and each day the head man drew the sun down out of the sky and made it tell where we were. And when the waves were kind, we hunted the fur seal and I marvelled much, for always did they fling the meat and the fat away and save only the skin."

Opee-Kwan's mouth was twitching violently, and he was about to make denunciation of such waste when Koogah kicked him to be still.

"After a weary time, when the sun was gone and the bite of the frost come into the air, the head man pointed the nose of the schooner south. South and east we travelled for days upon days, with never the land in sight, and we were near to the village from which hailed the men—"

"How did they know they were near?" Opee-Kwan, unable to contain himself longer, demanded. "There was no land to see."

Nam-Bok glowered on him wrathfully. "Did I not say the head man brought the sun down out of the sky?"

Koogah interposed, and Nam-Bok went on.

"As I say, when we were near to that village a great storm blew up, and in the night we were helpless and knew not where we were—"

"Thou hast just said the head man knew—"

"Oh, peace, Opee-Kwan! Thou art a fool and cannot understand. As I say, we were helpless in the night, when I heard, above the roar of the storm, the sound of the sea on the beach. And next we struck with a mighty crash and I was in the water, swimming. It was a rock-bound coast, with one patch of beach in many miles, and the law was that I should dig my hands into the sand and draw myself clear of the surf. The other men must have pounded against the rocks, for none of them came ashore but the head man, and him I knew only by the ring on his finger.

"When day came, there being nothing of the schooner, I turned my face to the land and journeyed into it that I might get food and look upon the faces of the people. And when I came to a house I was taken in and given to eat, for I had learned their speech, and the white men are ever kindly. And it was a house bigger than all the houses built by us and our fathers before us."

"It was a mighty house," Koogah said, masking his unbelief with wonder.

"And many trees went into the making of such a house," Opee-Kwan added, taking the cue.

"That is nothing." Nam-Bok shrugged his shoulders in belittling fashion. "As our houses are to that house, so that house was to the houses I was yet to see."

"And they are not big men?"

"Nay; mere men like you and me," Nam-Bok answered. "I had cut a stick that I might walk in comfort, and remembering that I was to bring report to you, my brothers, I cut a notch in the stick for each person who lived in that house. And I stayed there many days, and worked, for which they gave me money—a thing of which you know nothing, but which is very good.

"And one day I departed from that place to go farther into the land. And as I walked I met many people, and I cut smaller notches in the stick, that there might be room for all. Then I came upon a strange thing. On the ground before me was a bar of iron, as big in thickness as my arm, and a long step away was another bar of iron—"

"Then wert thou a rich man," Opee-Kwan asserted; "for iron be worth more than anything else in the world. It would have made many knives."

"Nay, it was not mine."

"It was a find, and a find be lawful."

"Not so; the white men had placed it there And further, these bars were so long that no man could carry them away—so long that as far as I could see there was no end to them."

"Nam-Bok, that is very much iron," Opee-Kwan cautioned.

"Ay, it was hard to believe with my own eyes upon it; but I could not gainsay my eyes. And as I looked I heard...." He turned abruptly upon the head man. "Opee-Kwan, thou hast heard the sea-lion bellow in his anger. Make it plain in thy mind of as many sea-lions as there be waves to the sea, and make it plain that all these sea-lions be made into one sea-lion, and as that one sea-lion would bellow so bellowed the thing I heard."

The fisherfolk cried aloud in astonishment, and Opee-Kwan's jaw lowered and remained lowered.

"And in the distance I saw a monster like unto a thousand whales. It was one-eyed, and vomited smoke, and it snorted with exceeding loudness. I was afraid and ran with shaking legs along the path between the bars. But it came with the speed of the wind, this monster, and I leaped the iron bars with its breath hot on my face...."

Opee-Kwan gained control of his jaw again. "And—and then, O Nam-

Bok?"

"Then it came by on the bars, and harmed me not; and when my legs could hold me up again it was gone from sight. And it is a very common thing in that country. Even the women and children are not afraid. Men make them to do work, these monsters."

"As we make our dogs do work?" Koogah asked, with sceptic twinkle in his eye.

"Ay, as we make our dogs do work."

"And how do they breed these—these things?" Opee-Kwan questioned.

"They breed not at all. Men fashion them cunningly of iron, and feed them with stone, and give them water to drink. The stone becomes fire, and the water becomes steam, and the steam of the water is the breath of their nostrils, and—"

"There, there, O Nam-Bok," Opee-Kwan interrupted. "Tell us of other wonders. We grow tired of this which we may not understand."

"You do not understand?" Nam-Bok asked despairingly.

"Nay, we do not understand," the men and women wailed back. "We cannot understand."

Nam-Bok thought of a combined harvester, and of the machines wherein visions of living men were to be seen, and of the machines from which came the voices of men, and he knew his people could never understand.

"Dare I say I rode this iron monster through the land?" he asked bitterly.

Opee-Kwan threw up his hands, palms outward, in open incredulity. "Say on; say anything. We listen."

"Then did I ride the iron monster, for which I gave money—"

"Thou saidst it was fed with stone."

"And likewise, thou fool, I said money was a thing of which you know nothing. As I say, I rode the monster through the land, and through many

49

villages, until I came to a big village on a salt arm of the sea. And the houses shoved their roofs among the stars in the sky, and the clouds drifted by them, and everywhere was much smoke. And the roar of that village was like the roar of the sea in storm, and the people were so many that I flung away my stick and no longer remembered the notches upon it."

"Hadst thou made small notches," Koogah reproved, "thou mightst have brought report."

Nam-Bok whirled upon him in anger. "Had I made small notches! Listen, Koogah, thou scratcher of bone! If I had made small notches, neither the stick, nor twenty sticks, could have borne them—nay, not all the driftwood of all the beaches between this village and the next. And if all of you, the women and children as well, were twenty times as many, and if you had twenty hands each, and in each hand a stick and a knife, still the notches could not be cut for the people I saw, so many were they and so fast did they come and go."

"There cannot be so many people in all the world," Opee-Kwan objected, for he was stunned and his mind could not grasp such magnitude of numbers.

"What dost thou know of all the world and how large it is?" Nam-Bok demanded.

"But there cannot be so many people in one place."

"Who art thou to say what can be and what cannot be?"

"It stands to reason there cannot be so many people in one place. Their canoes would clutter the sea till there was no room. And they could empty the sea each day of its fish, and they would not all be fed."

"So it would seem," Nam-Bok made final answer; "yet it was so. With my own eyes I saw, and flung my stick away." He yawned heavily and rose to his feet. "I have paddled far. The day has been long, and I am tired. Now I will sleep, and to-morrow we will have further talk upon the things I have seen."

Bask-Wah-Wan, hobbling fearfully in advance, proud indeed, yet awed by her wonderful son, led him to her igloo and stowed him away among the

50

greasy, ill-smelling furs. But the men lingered by the fire, and a council was held wherein was there much whispering and low-voiced discussion.

An hour passed, and a second, and Nam-Bok slept, and the talk went on. The evening sun dipped toward the northwest, and at eleven at night was nearly due north. Then it was that the head man and the bone-scratcher separated themselves from the council and aroused Nam-Bok. He blinked up into their faces and turned on his side to sleep again. Opee-Kwan gripped him by the arm and kindly but firmly shook his senses back into him.

"Come, Nam-Bok, arise!" he commanded. "It be time."

"Another feast?" Nam-Bok cried. "Nay, I am not hungry. Go on with the eating and let me sleep."

"Time to be gone!" Koogah thundered.

But Opee-Kwan spoke more softly. "Thou wast bidarka-mate with me when we were boys," he said. "Together we first chased the seal and drew the salmon from the traps. And thou didst drag me back to life, Nam-Bok, when the sea closed over me and I was sucked down to the black rocks. Together we hungered and bore the chill of the frost, and together we crawled beneath the one fur and lay close to each other. And because of these things, and the kindness in which I stood to thee, it grieves me sore that thou shouldst return such a remarkable liar. We cannot understand, and our heads be dizzy with the things thou hast spoken. It is not good, and there has been much talk in the council. Wherefore we send thee away, that our heads may remain clear and strong and be not troubled by the unaccountable things."

"These things thou speakest of be shadows," Koogah took up the strain. "From the shadow-world thou hast brought them, and to the shadow-world thou must return them. Thy bidarka be ready, and the tribespeople wait. They may not sleep until thou art gone."

Nam-Bok was perplexed, but hearkened to the voice of the head man.

"If thou art Nam-Bok," Opee-Kwan was saying, "thou art a fearful and most wonderful liar; if thou art the shadow of Nam-Bok, then thou speakest of shadows, concerning which it is not good that living men have knowledge. This great village thou hast spoken of we deem the village of shadows. Therein flutter the souls of the dead; for the dead be many and the living few. The dead do not come back. Never have the dead come back—save thou with thy wonder-tales. It is not meet that the dead come back, and should we permit it, great trouble may be our portion."

Nam-Bok knew his people well and was aware that the voice of the council was supreme. So he allowed himself to be led down to the water's edge, where he was put aboard his bidarka and a paddle thrust into his hand. A stray wild-fowl honked somewhere to seaward, and the surf broke limply and hollowly on the sand. A dim twilight brooded over land and water, and in the north the sun smouldered, vague and troubled, and draped about with blood-red mists. The gulls were flying low. The off-shore wind blew keen and chill, and the black-massed clouds behind it gave promise of bitter weather.

"Out of the sea thou earnest," Opee-Kwan chanted oracularly, "and back into the sea thou goest. Thus is balance achieved and all things brought to law."

Bask-Wah-Wan limped to the froth-mark and cried, "I bless thee, Nam-Bok, for that thou remembered me."

But Koogah, shoving Nam-Bok clear of the beach, tore the shawl from her shoulders and flung it into the bidarka.

"It is cold in the long nights," she wailed; "and the frost is prone to nip old bones."

"The thing is a shadow," the bone-scratcher answered, "and shadows cannot keep thee warm."

Nam-Bok stood up that his voice might carry. "O Bask-Wah-Wan, mother that bore me!" he called. "Listen to the words of Nam-Bok, thy son. There be room in his bidarka for two, and he would that thou camest with him. For his journey is to where there are fish and oil in plenty. There the frost comes not, and life is easy, and the things of iron do the work of men. Wilt thou come, O Bask-Wah-Wan?"

She debated a moment, while the bidarka drifted swiftly from her, then raised her voice to a quavering treble. "I am old, Nam-Bok, and soon I shall pass down among the shadows. But I have no wish to go before my time. I am old, Nam-Bok, and I am afraid."

A shaft of light shot across the dim-lit sea and wrapped boat and man in a splendor of red and gold. Then a hush fell upon the fisherfolk, and only was heard the moan of the off-shore wind and the cries of the gulls flying low in the air.

THE MASTER OF MYSTERY

There was complaint in the village. The women chattered together with shrill, high-pitched voices. The men were glum and doubtful of aspect, and the very dogs wandered dubiously about, alarmed in vague ways by the unrest of the camp, and ready to take to the woods on the first outbreak of trouble. The air was filled with suspicion. No man was sure of his neighbor, and each was conscious that he stood in like unsureness with his fellows. Even the children were oppressed and solemn, and little Di Ya, the cause of it all, had been soundly thrashed, first by Hooniah, his mother, and then by his father, Bawn, and was now whimpering and looking pessimistically out upon the world from the shelter of the big overturned canoe on the beach.

And to make the matter worse, Scundoo, the shaman, was in disgrace, and his known magic could not be called upon to seek out the evil-doer. Forsooth, a month gone, he had promised a fair south wind so that the tribe might journey to the potlatch at Tonkin, where Taku Jim was giving away the savings of twenty years; and when the day came, lo, a grievous north wind blew, and of the first three canoes to venture forth, one was swamped in the big seas, and two were pounded to pieces on the rocks, and a child was drowned. He had pulled the string of the wrong bag, he explained,—a mistake. But the people refused to listen; the offerings of meat and fish and fur ceased to come to his door; and he sulked within—so they thought, fasting in bitter penance; in reality, eating generously from his well-stored cache and meditating upon the fickleness of the mob.

The blankets of Hooniah were missing. They were good blankets, of most marvellous thickness and warmth, and her pride in them was greatened in that they had been come by so cheaply. Ty-Kwan, of the next village but one, was a fool to have so easily parted with them. But then, she did not know they were the blankets of the murdered Englishman, because of whose take-off the United States cutter nosed along the coast for a time, while its launches puffed and snorted among the secret inlets. And not knowing that Ty-Kwan had disposed of them in haste so that his own people might not have to render account to the Government, Hooniah's pride was unshaken. And because the women envied her, her pride was without end and boundless, till it filled the village and spilled over along the Alaskan shore from Dutch Harbor to St. Mary's. Her totem had become justly celebrated, and her name known on the lips of men wherever men fished and feasted, what of the blankets and their marvellous thickness and warmth. It was a most mysterious happening, the manner of their going.

"I but stretched them up in the sun by the side-wall of the house," Hooniah disclaimed for the thousandth time to her Thlinget sisters. "I but stretched them up and turned my back; for Di Ya, dough-thief and eater of raw flour that he is, with head into the big iron pot, overturned and stuck there, his legs waving like the branches of a forest tree in the wind. And I did but drag him out and twice knock his head against the door for riper understanding, and behold, the blankets were not!"

"The blankets were not!" the women repeated in awed whispers.

"A great loss," one added. A second, "Never were there such blankets." And a third, "We be sorry, Hooniah, for thy loss." Yet each woman of them was glad in her heart that the odious, dissension-breeding blankets were gone. "I but stretched them up in the sun," Hooniah began for the thousand and first time.

"Yea, yea," Bawn spoke up, wearied. "But there were no gossips in the village from other places. Wherefore it be plain that some of our own tribespeople have laid unlawful hand upon the blankets."

"How can that be, O Bawn?" the women chorussed indignantly. "Who should there be?"

"Then has there been witchcraft," Bawn continued stolidly enough, though he stole a sly glance at their faces.

"Witchcraft!" And at the dread word their voices hushed and each looked fearfully at each.

"Ay," Hooniah affirmed, the latent malignancy of her nature flashing into a moment's exultation. "And word has been sent to Klok-No-Ton, and strong paddles. Truly shall he be here with the afternoon tide."

The little groups broke up, and fear descended upon the village. Of all misfortune, witchcraft was the most appalling. With the intangible and unseen things only the shamans could cope, and neither man, woman, nor child could know, until the moment of ordeal, whether devils possessed their souls or not. And of all shamans, Klok-No-Ton, who dwelt in the next village, was the most terrible. None found more evil spirits than he, none visited his victims with more frightful tortures. Even had he found, once, a devil residing within the body of a three-months babe—a most obstinate devil which could only be driven out when the babe had lain for a week on thorns and briers. The body was thrown into the sea after that, but the waves tossed it back again and again as a curse upon the village, nor did it finally go away till two strong men were staked out at low tide and drowned.

And Hooniah had sent for this Klok-No-Ton. Better had it been if Scundoo, their own shaman, were undisgraced. For he had ever a gentler way, and he had been known to drive forth two devils from a man who afterward begat seven healthy children. But Klok-No-Ton! They shuddered with dire foreboding at thought of him, and each one felt himself the centre of accusing eyes, and looked accusingly upon his fellows—each one and all, save Sime, and Sime was a scoffer whose evil end was destined with a certitude his successes could not shake.

"Hoh! Hoh!" he laughed. "Devils and Klok-No-Ton!—than whom no greater devil can be found in Thlinket Land."

"Thou fool! Even now he cometh with witcheries and sorceries; so beware thy tongue, lest evil befall thee and thy days be short in the land!"

So spoke La-lah, otherwise the Cheater, and Sime laughed scornfully.

"I am Sime, unused to fear, unafraid of the dark. I am a strong man, as my father before me, and my head is clear. Nor you nor I have seen with our eyes the unseen evil things—"

"But Scundoo hath," La-lah made answer. "And likewise Klok-No-Ton.

This we know."

"How dost thou know, son of a fool?" Sime thundered, the choleric blood darkening his thick bull neck.

"By the word of their mouths—even so."

Sime snorted. "A shaman is only a man. May not his words be crooked, even as thine and mine? Bah! Bah! And once more, bah! And this for thy shamans and thy shamans' devils! and this! and this!"

And snapping his fingers to right and left, Sime strode through the on-lookers, who made over-zealous and fearsome way for him.

"A good fisher and strong hunter, but an evil man," said one.

"Yet does he flourish," speculated another.

"Wherefore be thou evil and flourish," Sime retorted over his shoulder. "And were all evil, there would be no need for shamans. Bah! You children-afraid-of-the-dark!"

And when Klok-No-Ton arrived on the afternoon tide, Sime's defiant laugh was unabated; nor did he forbear to make a joke when the shaman tripped on the sand in the landing. Klok-No-Ton looked at him sourly, and without greeting stalked straight through their midst to the house of Scundoo.

Of the meeting with Scundoo none of the tribespeople might know, for they clustered reverently in the distance and spoke in whispers while the masters of mystery were together.

"Greeting, O Scundoo!" Klok-No-Ton rumbled, wavering perceptibly from doubt of his reception.

He was a giant in stature, and towered massively above little Scundoo, whose thin voice floated upward like the faint far rasping of a cricket.

"Greeting, Klok-No-Ton," he returned. "The day is fair with thy coming."

"Yet it would seem ..." Klok-No-Ton hesitated.

"Yea, yea," the little shaman put in impatiently, "that I have fallen on ill days, else would I not stand in gratitude to you in that you do my work."

"It grieves me, friend Scundoo ..."

"Nay, I am made glad, Klok-No-Ton."

"But will I give thee half of that which be given me."

"Not so, good Klok-No-Ton," murmured Scundoo, with a deprecatory wave of the hand. "It is I who am thy slave, and my days shall be filled with desire to befriend thee."

"As I—"

"As thou now befriendest me."

"That being so, it is then a bad business, these blankets of the woman Hooniah?"

The big shaman blundered tentatively in his quest, and Scundoo smiled a wan, gray smile, for he was used to reading men, and all men seemed very small to him.

"Ever hast thou dealt in strong medicine," he said. "Doubtless the evil-doer will be briefly known to thee."

"Ay, briefly known when I set eyes upon him." Again Klok-No-Ton hesitated. "Have there been gossips from other places?" he asked.

Scundoo shook his head. "Behold! Is this not a most excellent mucluc?"

He held up the foot-covering of sealskin and walrus hide, and his visitor examined it with secret interest.

"It did come to me by a close-driven bargain."

Klok-No-Ton nodded attentively.

"I got it from the man La-lah. He is a remarkable man, and often have I thought ..."

"So?" Klok-No-Ton ventured impatiently.

"Often have I thought," Scundoo concluded, his voice falling as he came to a full pause. "It is a fair day, and thy medicine be strong, Klok-No-Ton."

Klok-No-Ton's face brightened. "Thou art a great man, Scundoo, a shaman of shamans. I go now. I shall remember thee always. And the man La-lah, as you say, is a remarkable man."

Scundoo smiled yet more wan and gray, closed the door on the heels of his departing visitor, and barred and double-barred it.

Sime was mending his canoe when Klok-No-Ton came down the beach, and he broke off from his work only long enough to ostentatiously load his rifle and place it near him.

The shaman noted the action and called out: "Let all the people come together on this spot! It is the word of Klok-No-Ton, devil-seeker and driver of devils!"

He had been minded to assemble them at Hooniah's house, but it was necessary that all should be present, and he was doubtful of Sime's obedience and did not wish trouble. Sime was a good man to let alone, his judgment ran, and withal, a bad one for the health of any shaman.

"Let the woman Hooniah be brought," Klok-No-Ton commanded, glaring ferociously about the circle and sending chills up and down the spines of those he looked upon.

Hooniah waddled forward, head bent and gaze averted.

"Where be thy blankets?"

"I but stretched them up in the sun, and behold, they were not!" she whined.

"So?"

"It was because of Di Ya."

"So?"

"Him have I beaten sore, and he shall yet be beaten, for that he brought

59

trouble upon us who be poor people."

"The blankets!" Klok-No-Ton bellowed hoarsely, foreseeing her desire to lower the price to be paid. "The blankets, woman! Thy wealth is known."

"I but stretched them up in the sun," she sniffled, "and we be poor people and have nothing."

He stiffened suddenly, with a hideous distortion of the face, and Hooniah shrank back. But so swiftly did he spring forward, with in-turned eyeballs and loosened jaw, that she stumbled and fell down grovelling at his feet. He waved his arms about, wildly flagellating the air, his body writhing and twisting in torment. An epilepsy seemed to come upon him. A white froth flecked his lips, and his body was convulsed with shiverings and tremblings.

The women broke into a wailing chant, swaying backward and forward in abandonment, while one by one the men succumbed to the excitement till only Sime remained. He, perched upon his canoe, looked on in mockery; yet the ancestors whose seed he bore pressed heavily upon him, and he swore his strongest oaths that his courage might be cheered. Klok-No-Ton was horrible to behold. He had cast off his blanket and torn his clothes from him, so that he was quite naked, save for a girdle of eagle-claws about his thighs. Shrieking and yelling, his long black hair flying like a blot of night, he leaped frantically about the circle. A certain rude rhythm characterized his frenzy, and when all were under its sway, swinging their bodies in accord with his and venting their cries in unison, he sat bolt upright, with arm outstretched and long, talon-like finger extended. A low moaning, as of the dead, greeted this, and the people cowered with shaking knees as the dread finger passed them slowly by. For death went with it, and life remained with those who watched it go; and being rejected, they watched with eager intentness.

Finally, with a tremendous cry, the fateful finger rested upon La-lah. He shook like an aspen, seeing himself already dead, his household goods divided, and his widow married to his brother. He strove to speak, to deny, but his tongue clove to his mouth and his throat was sanded with an intolerable thirst. Klok-No-Ton seemed to half swoon away, now that his work was done; but he waited, with closed eyes, listening for the great blood-cry to go up—

the great blood-cry, familiar to his ear from a thousand conjurations, when the tribespeople flung themselves like wolves upon the trembling victim. But only was there silence, then a low tittering, from nowhere in particular, which spread and spread until a vast laughter welled up to the sky.

"Wherefore?" he cried.

"Na! Na!" the people laughed. "Thy medicine be ill, O Klok-No-Ton!"

"It be known to all," La-lah stuttered. "For eight weary months have I been gone afar with the Siwash sealers, and but this day am I come back to find the blankets of Hooniah gone ere I came!"

"It be true!" they cried with one accord. "The blankets of Hooniah were gone ere he came!"

"And thou shalt be paid nothing for thy medicine which is of no avail," announced Hooniah, on her feet once more and smarting from a sense of ridiculousness.

But Klok-No-Ton saw only the face of Scundoo and its wan, gray smile, heard only the faint far cricket's rasping. "I got it from the man La-lah, and often have I thought," and, "It is a fair day and thy medicine be strong."

He brushed by Hooniah, and the circle instinctively gave way for him to pass. Sime flung a jeer from the top of the canoe, the women snickered in his face, cries of derision rose in his wake, but he took no notice, pressing onward to the house of Scundoo. He hammered on the door, beat it with his fists, and howled vile imprecations. Yet there was no response, save that in the lulls Scundoo's voice rose eerily in incantation. Klok-No-Ton raged about like a madman, but when he attempted to break in the door with a huge stone, murmurs arose from the men and women. And he, Klok-No-Ton, knew that he stood shorn of his strength and authority before an alien people. He saw a man stoop for a stone, and a second, and a bodily fear ran through him.

"Harm not Scundoo, who is a master!" a woman cried out.

"Better you return to your own village," a man advised menacingly.

Klok-No-Ton turned on his heel and went down among them to the beach, a bitter rage at his heart, and in his head a just apprehension for his defenceless back. But no stones were cast. The children swarmed mockingly about his feet, and the air was wild with laughter and derision, but that was all. Yet he did not breathe freely until the canoe was well out upon the water, when he rose up and laid a futile curse upon the village and its people, not forgetting to particularly specify Scundoo who had made a mock of him.

Ashore there was a clamor for Scundoo, and the whole population crowded his door, entreating and imploring in confused babel till he came forth and raised his hand.

"In that ye are my children I pardon freely," he said. "But never again. For the last time thy foolishness goes unpunished. That which ye wish shall be granted, and it be already known to me. This night, when the moon has gone behind the world to look upon the mighty dead, let all the people gather in the blackness before the house of Hooniah. Then shall the evil-doer stand forth and take his merited reward. I have spoken."

"It shall be death!" Bawn vociferated, "for that it hath brought worry upon us, and shame."

"So be it," Scundoo replied, and shut his door.

"Now shall all be made clear and plain, and content rest upon us once again," La-lah declaimed oracularly.

"Because of Scundoo, the little man," Sime sneered.

"Because of the medicine of Scundoo, the little man," La-lah corrected.

"Children of foolishness, these Thlinket people!" Sime smote his thigh a resounding blow. "It passeth understanding that grown women and strong men should get down in the dirt to dream-things and wonder tales."

"I am a travelled man," La-lah answered. "I have journeyed on the deep seas and seen signs and wonders, and I know that these things be so. I am La-lah—"

"The Cheater—"

"So called, but the Far-Journeyer right-named."

"I am not so great a traveller—" Sime began.

"Then hold thy tongue," Bawn cut in, and they separated in anger.

When the last silver moonlight had vanished beyond the world, Scundoo came among the people huddled about the house of Hooniah. He walked with a quick, alert step, and those who saw him in the light of Hooniah's slush-lamp noticed that he came empty-handed, without rattles, masks, or shaman's paraphernalia, save for a great sleepy raven carried under one arm.

"Is there wood gathered for a fire, so that all may see when the work be done?" he demanded.

"Yea," Bawn answered. "There be wood in plenty."

"Then let all listen, for my words be few. With me have I brought Jelchs, the Raven, diviner of mystery and seer of things. Him, in his blackness, shall I place under the big black pot of Hooniah, in the blackest corner of her house. The slush-lamp shall cease to burn, and all remain in outer darkness. It is very simple. One by one shall ye go into the house, lay hand upon the pot for the space of one long intake of the breath, and withdraw again. Doubtless Jelchs will make outcry when the hand of the evil-doer is nigh him. Or who knows but otherwise he may manifest his wisdom. Are ye ready?"

"We be ready," came the multi-voiced response.

"Then will I call the name aloud, each in his turn and hers, till all are called."

Thereat La-lah was first chosen, and he passed in at once. Every ear strained, and through the silence they could hear his footsteps creaking across the rickety floor. But that was all. Jelchs made no outcry, gave no sign. Bawn was next chosen, for it well might be that a man should steal his own blankets with intent to cast shame upon his neighbors. Hooniah followed, and other women and children, but without result.

"Sime!" Scundoo called out.

"Sime!" he repeated.

But Sime did not stir.

"Art thou afraid of the dark?" La-lah, his own integrity being proved, demanded fiercely.

Sime chuckled. "I laugh at it all, for it is a great foolishness. Yet will I go in, not in belief in wonders, but in token that I am unafraid."

And he passed in boldly, and came out still mocking.

"Some day shalt thou die with great suddenness," La-lah whispered, righteously indignant.

"I doubt not," the scoffer answered airily. "Few men of us die in our beds, what of the shamans and the deep sea."

When half the villagers had safely undergone the ordeal, the excitement, because of its repression, was painfully intense. When two-thirds had gone through, a young woman, close on her first child-bed, broke down and in nervous shrieks and laughter gave form to her terror.

Finally the turn came for the last of all to go in, and nothing had happened. And Di Ya was the last of all. It must surely be he. Hooniah let out a lament to the stars, while the rest drew back from the luckless lad. He was half-dead from fright, and his legs gave under him so that he staggered on the threshold and nearly fell. Scundoo shoved him inside and closed the door. A long time went by, during which could be heard only the boy's weeping. Then, very slowly, came the creak of his steps to the far corner, a pause, and the creaking of his return. The door opened and he came forth. Nothing had happened, and he was the last.

"Let the fire be lighted," Scundoo commanded.

The bright flames rushed upward, revealing faces yet marked with vanishing fear, but also clouded with doubt.

"Surely the thing has failed," Hooniah whispered hoarsely.

"Yea," Bawn answered complacently. "Scundoo groweth old, and we stand in need of a new shaman."

"Where now is the wisdom of Jelchs?" Sime snickered in La-lah's ear.

La-lah brushed his brow in a puzzled manner and said nothing.

Sime threw his chest out arrogantly and strutted up to the little shaman. "Hoh! Hoh! As I said, nothing has come of it!"

"So it would seem, so it would seem," Scundoo answered meekly. "And it would seem strange to those unskilled in the affairs of mystery."

"As thou?" Sime queried audaciously.

"Mayhap even as I," Scundoo spoke quite softly, his eyelids drooping, slowly drooping, down, down, till his eyes were all but hidden. "So I am minded of another test. Let every man, woman, and child, now and at once, hold their hands well up above their heads!"

So unexpected was the order, and so imperatively was it given, that it was obeyed without question. Every hand was in the air.

"Let each look on the other's hands, and let all look," Scundoo commanded, "so that—"

But a noise of laughter, which was more of wrath, drowned his voice. All eyes had come to rest upon Sime. Every hand but his was black with soot, and his was guiltless of the smirch of Hooniah's pot.

A stone hurtled through the air and struck him on the cheek.

"It is a lie!" he yelled. "A lie! I know naught of Hooniah's blankets!"

A second stone gashed his brow, a third whistled past his head, the great blood-cry went up, and everywhere were people groping on the ground for missiles. He staggered and half sank down.

"It was a joke! Only a joke!" he shrieked. "I but took them for a joke!"

"Where hast thou hidden them?" Scundoo's shrill, sharp voice cut through the tumult like a knife.

"In the large skin-bale in my house, the one slung by the ridge-pole," came the answer. "But it was a joke, I say, only—"

Scundoo nodded his head, and the air went thick with flying stones. Sime's wife was crying silently, her head upon her knees; but his little boy, with shrieks and laughter, was flinging stones with the rest.

Hooniah came waddling back with the precious blankets. Scundoo stopped her.

"We be poor people and have little," she whimpered. "So be not hard upon us, O Scundoo."

The people ceased from the quivering stone-pile they had builded, and looked on.

"Nay, it was never my way, good Hooniah," Scundoo made answer, reaching for the blankets. "In token that I am not hard, these only shall I take."

"Am I not wise, my children?" he demanded.

"Thou art indeed wise, O Scundoo!" they cried in one voice.

And he went away into the darkness, the blankets around him, and Jelchs nodding sleepily under his arm.

THE SUNLANDERS

Mandell is an obscure village on the rim of the polar sea. It is not large, and the people are peaceable, more peaceable even than those of the adjacent tribes. There are few men in Mandell, and many women; wherefore a wholesome and necessary polygamy is in practice; the women bear children with ardor, and the birth of a man-child is hailed with acclamation. Then there is Aab-Waak, whose head rests always on one shoulder, as though at some time the neck had become very tired and refused forevermore its wonted duty.

The cause of all these things,—the peaceableness, and the polygamy, and the tired neck of Aab-Waak,—goes back among the years to the time when the schooner Search dropped anchor in Mandell Bay, and when Tyee, chief man of the tribe, conceived a scheme of sudden wealth. To this day the story of things that happened is remembered and spoken of with bated breath by the people of Mandell, who are cousins to the Hungry Folk who live in the west. Children draw closer when the tale is told, and marvel sagely to themselves at the madness of those who might have been their forebears had they not provoked the Sunlanders and come to bitter ends.

It began to happen when six men came ashore from the Search, with heavy outfits, as though they had come to stay, and quartered themselves in Neegah's igloo. Not but that they paid well in flour and sugar for the lodging, but Neegah was aggrieved because Mesahchie, his daughter, elected to cast her fortunes and seek food and blanket with Bill-Man, who was leader of the party of white men.

"She is worth a price," Neegah complained to the gathering by the council-fire, when the six white men were asleep. "She is worth a price, for we have more men than women, and the men be bidding high. The hunter Ounenk offered me a kayak, new-made, and a gun which he got in trade from the Hungry Folk. This was I offered, and behold, now she is gone and I have nothing!"

"I, too, did bid for Mesahchie," grumbled a voice, in tones not altogether joyless, and Peelo shoved his broad-cheeked, jovial face for a moment into the light.

"Thou, too," Neegah affirmed. "And there were others. Why is there such a restlessness upon the Sunlanders?" he demanded petulantly. "Why do they not stay at home? The Snow People do not wander to the lands of the Sunlanders."

"Better were it to ask why they come," cried a voice from the darkness, and Aab-Waak pushed his way to the front.

"Ay! Why they come!" clamored many voices, and Aab-Waak waved his hand for silence.

"Men do not dig in the ground for nothing," he began. "And I have it in mind of the Whale People, who are likewise Sunlanders, and who lost their ship in the ice. You all remember the Whale People, who came to us in their broken boats, and who went away into the south with dogs and sleds when the frost arrived and snow covered the land. And you remember, while they waited for the frost, that one man of them dug in the ground, and then two men and three, and then all men of them, with great excitement and much disturbance. What they dug out of the ground we do not know, for they drove us away so we could not see. But afterward, when they were gone, we looked and found nothing. Yet there be much ground and they did not dig it all."

"Ay, Aab-Waak! Ay!" cried the people in admiration.

"Wherefore I have it in mind," he concluded, "that one Sunlander tells another, and that these Sunlanders have been so told and are come to dig in the ground."

"But how can it be that Bill-Man speaks our tongue?" demanded a little weazened old hunter,—"Bill-Man, upon whom never before our eyes have rested?"

"Bill-Man has been other times in the Snow Lands," Aab-Waak

68

answered, "else would he not speak the speech of the Bear People, which is like the speech of the Hungry Folk, which is very like the speech of the Mandells. For there have been many Sunlanders among the Bear People, few among the Hungry Folk, and none at all among the Mandells, save the Whale People and those who sleep now in the igloo of Neegah."

"Their sugar is very good," Neegah commented, "and their flour."

"They have great wealth," Ounenk added. "Yesterday I was to their ship, and beheld most cunning tools of iron, and knives, and guns, and flour, and sugar, and strange foods without end."

"It is so, brothers!" Tyee stood up and exulted inwardly at the respect and silence his people accorded him. "They be very rich, these Sunlanders. Also, they be fools. For behold! They come among us boldly, blindly, and without thought for all of their great wealth. Even now they snore, and we are many and unafraid."

"Mayhap they, too, are unafraid, being great fighters," the weazened little old hunter objected.

But Tyee scowled upon him. "Nay, it would not seem so. They live to the south, under the path of the sun, and are soft as their dogs are soft. You remember the dog of the Whale People? Our dogs ate him the second day, for he was soft and could not fight. The sun is warm and life easy in the Sun Lands, and the men are as women, and the women as children."

Heads nodded in approval, and the women craned their necks to listen.

"It is said they are good to their women, who do little work," tittered Likeeta, a broad-hipped, healthy young woman, daughter to Tyee himself.

"Thou wouldst follow the feet of Mesahchie, eh?" he cried angrily. Then he turned swiftly to the tribesmen. "Look you, brothers, this is the way of the Sunlanders! They have eyes for our women, and take them one by one. As Mesahchie has gone, cheating Neegah of her price, so will Likeeta go, so will they all go, and we be cheated. I have talked with a hunter from the Bear People, and I know. There be Hungry Folk among us; let them speak if my

69

words be true."

The six hunters of the Hungry Folk attested the truth and fell each to telling his neighbor of the Sunlanders and their ways. There were mutterings from the younger men, who had wives to seek, and from the older men, who had daughters to fetch prices, and a low hum of rage rose higher and clearer.

"They are very rich, and have cunning tools of iron, and knives, and guns without end," Tyee suggested craftily, his dream of sudden wealth beginning to take shape.

"I shall take the gun of Bill-Man for myself," Aab-Waak suddenly proclaimed.

"Nay, it shall be mine!" shouted Neegah; "for there is the price of Mesahchie to be reckoned."

"Peace! O brothers!" Tyee swept the assembly with his hands. "Let the women and children go to their igloos. This is the talk of men; let it be for the ears of men."

"There be guns in plenty for all," he said when the women had unwillingly withdrawn. "I doubt not there will be two guns for each man, without thought of the flour and sugar and other things. And it is easy. The six Sunlanders in Neegah's igloo will we kill to-night while they sleep. To-morrow will we go in peace to the ship to trade, and there, when the time favors, kill all their brothers. And to-morrow night there shall be feasting and merriment and division of wealth. And the least man shall possess more than did ever the greatest before. Is it wise, that which I have spoken, brothers?"

A low growl of approval answered him, and preparation for the attack was begun. The six Hungry Folk, as became members of a wealthier tribe, were armed with rifles and plenteously supplied with ammunition. But it was only here and there that a Mandell possessed a gun, many of which were broken, and there was a general slackness of powder and shells. This poverty of war weapons, however, was relieved by myriads of bone-headed arrows and casting-spears for work at a distance, and for close quarters steel knives of Russian and Yankee make.

"Let there be no noise," Tyee finally instructed; "but be there many on every side of the igloo, and close, so that the Sunlanders may not break through. Then do you, Neegah, with six of the young men behind, crawl in to where they sleep. Take no guns, which be prone to go off at unexpected times, but put the strength of your arms into the knives."

"And be it understood that no harm befall Mesahchie, who is worth a price," Neegah whispered hoarsely.

Flat upon the ground, the small army concentred on the igloo, and behind, deliciously expectant, crouched many women and children, come out to witness the murder. The brief August night was passing, and in the gray of dawn could be dimly discerned the creeping forms of Neegah and the young men. Without pause, on hands and knees, they entered the long passageway and disappeared. Tyee rose up and rubbed his hands. All was going well. Head after head in the big circle lifted and waited. Each man pictured the scene according to his nature—the sleeping men, the plunge of the knives, and the sudden death in the dark.

A loud hail, in the voice of a Sunlander, rent the silence, and a shot rang out. Then an uproar broke loose inside the igloo. Without premeditation, the circle swept forward into the passageway. On the inside, half a dozen repeating rifles began to chatter, and the Mandells, jammed in the confined space, were powerless. Those at the front strove madly to retreat from the fire-spitting guns in their very faces, and those in the rear pressed as madly forward to the attack. The bullets from the big 45:90's drove through half a dozen men at a shot, and the passageway, gorged with surging, helpless men, became a shambles. The rifles, pumped without aim into the mass, withered it away like a machine gun, and against that steady stream of death no man could advance.

"Never was there the like!" panted one of the Hungry Folk. "I did but look in, and the dead were piled like seals on the ice after a killing!"

"Did I not say, mayhap, they were fighters?" cackled the weazened old hunter.

"It was to be expected," Aab-Waak answered stoutly. "We fought in a trap of our making."

"O ye fools!" Tyee chided. "Ye sons of fools! It was not planned, this thing ye have done. To Neegah and the six young men only was it given to go inside. My cunning is superior to the cunning of the Sunlanders, but ye take away its edge, and rob me of its strength, and make it worse than no cunning at all!"

No one made reply, and all eyes centred on the igloo, which loomed vague and monstrous against the clear northeast sky. Through a hole in the roof the smoke from the rifles curled slowly upward in the pulseless air, and now and again a wounded man crawled painfully through the gray.

"Let each ask of his neighbor for Neegah and the six young men," Tyee commanded.

And after a time the answer came back, "Neegah and the six young men are not."

"And many more are not!" wailed a woman to the rear.

"The more wealth for those who are left," Tyee grimly consoled. Then, turning to Aab-Waak, he said: "Go thou, and gather together many sealskins filled with oil. Let the hunters empty them on the outside wood of the igloo and of the passage. And let them put fire to it ere the Sunlanders make holes in the igloo for their guns."

Even as he spoke a hole appeared in the dirt plastered between the logs, a rifle muzzle protruded, and one of the Hungry Folk clapped hand to his side and leaped in the air. A second shot, through the lungs, brought him to the ground. Tyee and the rest scattered to either side, out of direct range, and Aab-Waak hastened the men forward with the skins of oil. Avoiding the loopholes, which were making on every side of the igloo, they emptied the skins on the dry drift-logs brought down by the Mandell River from the tree-lands to the south. Ounenk ran forward with a blazing brand, and the flames leaped upward. Many minutes passed, without sign, and they held their weapons ready as the fire gained headway.

Tyee rubbed his hands gleefully as the dry structure burned and crackled.

"Now we have them, brothers! In the trap!"

"And no one may gainsay me the gun of Bill-Man," Aab-Waak announced.

"Save Bill-Man," squeaked the old hunter. "For behold, he cometh now!"

Covered with a singed and blackened blanket, the big white man leaped out of the blazing entrance, and on his heels, likewise shielded, came Mesahchie, and the five other Sunlanders. The Hungry Folk tried to check the rush with an ill-directed volley, while the Mandells hurled in a cloud of spears and arrows. But the Sunlanders cast their flaming blankets from them as they ran, and it was seen that each bore on his shoulders a small pack of ammunition. Of all their possessions, they had chosen to save that. Running swiftly and with purpose, they broke the circle and headed directly for the great cliff, which towered blackly in the brightening day a half-mile to the rear of the village.

But Tyee knelt on one knee and lined the sights of his rifle on the rearmost Sunlander. A great shout went up when he pulled the trigger and the man fell forward, struggled partly up, and fell again. Without regard for the rain of arrows, another Sunlander ran back, bent over him, and lifted him across his shoulders. But the Mandell spearmen were crowding up into closer range, and a strong cast transfixed the wounded man. He cried out and became swiftly limp as his comrade lowered him to the ground. In the meanwhile, Bill-Man and the three others had made a stand and were driving a leaden hail into the advancing spearmen. The fifth Sunlander bent over his stricken fellow, felt the heart, and then coolly cut the straps of the pack and stood up with the ammunition and extra gun.

"Now is he a fool!" cried Tyee, leaping high, as he ran forward, to clear the squirming body of one of the Hungry Folk.

His own rifle was clogged so that he could not use it, and he called out for some one to spear the Sunlander, who had turned and was running for safety under the protecting fire. The little old hunter poised his spear on the throwing-stick, swept his arm back as he ran, and delivered the cast.

"By the body of the Wolf, say I, it was a good throw!" Tyee praised, as the fleeing man pitched forward, the spear standing upright between his shoulders and swaying slowly forward and back.

The little weazened old man coughed and sat down. A streak of red showed on his lips and welled into a thick stream. He coughed again, and a strange whistling came and went with his breath.

"They, too, are unafraid, being great fighters," he wheezed, pawing aimlessly with his hands. "And behold! Bill-Man comes now!"

Tyee glanced up. Four Mandells and one of the Hungry Folk had rushed upon the fallen man and were spearing him from his knees back to the earth. In the twinkling of an eye, Tyee saw four of them cut down by the bullets of the Sunlanders. The fifth, as yet unhurt, seized the two rifles, but as he stood up to make off he was whirled almost completely around by the impact of a bullet in the arm, steadied by a second, and overthrown by the shock of a third. A moment later and Bill-Man was on the spot, cutting the pack-straps and picking up the guns.

This Tyee saw, and his own people falling as they straggled forward, and he was aware of a quick doubt, and resolved to lie where he was and see more. For some unaccountable reason, Mesahchie was running back to Bill-Man; but before she could reach him, Tyee saw Peelo run out and throw arms about her. He essayed to sling her across his shoulder, but she grappled with him, tearing and scratching at his face. Then she tripped him, and the pair fell heavily. When they regained their feet, Peelo had shifted his grip so that one arm was passed under her chin, the wrist pressing into her throat and strangling her. He buried his face in her breast, taking the blows of her hands on his thick mat of hair, and began slowly to force her off the field. Then it was, retreating with the weapons of his fallen comrades, that Bill-Man came upon them. As Mesahchie saw him, she twirled the victim around and held him steady. Bill-Man swung the rifle in his right hand, and hardly easing his stride, delivered the blow. Tyee saw Peelo drive to the earth as smote by a falling star, and the Sunlander and Neegah's daughter fleeing side by side.

A bunch of Mandells, led by one of the Hungry Folk, made a futile rush which melted away into the earth before the scorching fire.

Tyee caught his breath and murmured, "Like the young frost in the morning sun."

"As I say, they are great fighters," the old hunter whispered weakly, far gone in hemorrhage. "I know. I have heard. They be sea-robbers and hunters of seals; and they shoot quick and true, for it is their way of life and the work of their hands."

"Like the young frost in the morning sun," Tyee repeated, crouching for shelter behind the dying man and peering at intervals about him.

It was no longer a fight, for no Mandell man dared venture forward, and as it was, they were too close to the Sunlanders to go back. Three tried it, scattering and scurrying like rabbits; but one came down with a broken leg, another was shot through the body, and the third, twisting and dodging, fell on the edge of the village. So the tribesmen crouched in the hollow places and burrowed into the dirt in the open, while the Sunlanders' bullets searched the plain.

"Move not," Tyee pleaded, as Aab-Waak came worming over the ground to him. "Move not, good Aab-Waak, else you bring death upon us."

"Death sits upon many," Aab-Waak laughed; "wherefore, as you say, there will be much wealth in division. My father breathes fast and short behind the big rock yon, and beyond, twisted like in a knot, lieth my brother. But their share shall be my share, and it is well."

"As you say, good Aab-Waak, and as I have said; but before division must come that which we may divide, and the Sunlanders be not yet dead."

A bullet glanced from a rock before them, and singing shrilly, rose low over their heads on its second flight. Tyee ducked and shivered, but Aab-Waak grinned and sought vainly to follow it with his eyes.

"So swiftly they go, one may not see them," he observed.

"But many be dead of us," Tyee went on.

"And many be left," was the reply. "And they hug close to the earth, for they have become wise in the fashion of righting. Further, they are angered. Moreover, when we have killed the Sunlanders on the ship, there will remain but four on the land. These may take long to kill, but in the end it will happen."

"How may we go down to the ship when we cannot go this way or that?" Tyee questioned.

"It is a bad place where lie Bill-Man and his brothers," Aab-Waak explained. "We may come upon them from every side, which is not good. So they aim to get their backs against the cliff and wait until their brothers of the ship come to give them aid."

"Never shall they come from the ship, their brothers! I have said it."

Tyee was gathering courage again, and when the Sunlanders verified the prediction by retreating to the cliff, he was light-hearted as ever.

"There be only three of us!" complained one of the Hungry Folk as they came together for council.

"Therefore, instead of two, shall you have four guns each," was Tyee's rejoinder.

"We did good fighting."

"Ay; and if it should happen that two of you be left, then will you have six guns each. Therefore, fight well."

"And if there be none of them left?" Aab-Waak whispered slyly.

"Then will we have the guns, you and I," Tyee whispered back.

However, to propitiate the Hungry Folk, he made one of them leader of the ship expedition. This party comprised fully two-thirds of the tribesmen, and departed for the coast, a dozen miles away, laden with skins and things to trade. The remaining men were disposed in a large half-circle about the breastwork which Bill-Man and his Sunlanders had begun to throw up. Tyee was quick to note the virtues of things, and at once set his men to digging shallow trenches.

"The time will go before they are aware," he explained to Aab-Waak; "and their minds being busy, they will not think overmuch of the dead that are, nor gather trouble to themselves. And in the dark of night they may creep closer, so that when the Sunlanders look forth in the morning light they will find us very near."

In the midday heat the men ceased from their work and made a meal of dried fish and seal oil which the women brought up. There was some clamor for the food of the Sunlanders in the igloo of Neegah, but Tyee refused to divide it until the return of the ship party. Speculations upon the outcome became rife, but in the midst of it a dull boom drifted up over the land from the sea. The keen-eyed ones made out a dense cloud of smoke, which quickly disappeared, and which they averred was directly over the ship of the Sunlanders. Tyee was of the opinion that it was a big gun. Aab-Waak did not know, but thought it might be a signal of some sort. Anyway, he said, it was time something happened.

Five or six hours afterward a solitary man was descried coming across the wide flat from the sea, and the women and children poured out upon him in a body. It was Ounenk, naked, winded, and wounded. The blood still trickled down his face from a gash on the forehead. His left arm, frightfully mangled, hung helpless at his side. But most significant of all, there was a wild gleam in his eyes which betokened the women knew not what.

"Where be Peshack?" an old squaw queried sharply.

"And Olitlie?" "And Polak?" "And Mah-Kook?" the voices took up the cry.

But he said nothing, brushing his way through the clamorous mass and directing his staggering steps toward Tyee. The old squaw raised the wail, and one by one the women joined her as they swung in behind. The men crawled out of their trenches and ran back to gather about Tyee, and it was noticed that the Sunlanders climbed upon their barricade to see.

Ounenk halted, swept the blood from his eyes, and looked about. He strove to speak, but his dry lips were glued together. Likeeta fetched him water, and he grunted and drank again.

"Was it a fight?" Tyee demanded finally,—"a good fight?"

"Ho! ho! ho!" So suddenly and so fiercely did Ounenk laugh that every voice hushed. "Never was there such a fight! So I say, I, Ounenk, fighter beforetime of beasts and men. And ere I forget, let me speak fat words and wise. By fighting will the Sunlanders teach us Mandell Folk how to fight. And if we fight long enough, we shall be great fighters, even as the Sunlanders, or else we shall be—dead. Ho! ho! ho! It was a fight!"

"Where be thy brothers?" Tyee shook him till he shrieked from the pain of his hurts.

Ounenk sobered. "My brothers? They are not."

"And Pome-Lee?" cried one of the two Hungry Folk; "Pome-Lee, the son of my mother?"

"Pome-Lee is not," Ounenk answered in a monotonous voice.

"And the Sunlanders?" from Aab-Waak.

"The Sunlanders are not."

"Then the ship of the Sunlanders, and the wealth and guns and things?" Tyee demanded.

"Neither the ship of the Sunlanders, nor the wealth and guns and things," was the unvarying response. "All are not. Nothing is. I only am."

"And thou art a fool."

"It may be so," Ounenk answered, unruffled.

"I have seen that which would well make me a fool."

Tyee held his tongue, and all waited till it should please Ounenk to tell the story in his own way.

"We took no guns, O Tyee," he at last began; "no guns, my brothers—

only knives and hunting bows and spears. And in twos and threes, in our kayaks, we came to the ship. They were glad to see us, the Sunlanders, and we spread our skins and they brought out their articles of trade, and everything was well. And Pome-Lee waited—waited till the sun was well overhead and they sat at meat, when he gave the cry and we fell upon them. Never was there such a fight, and never such fighters. Half did we kill in the quickness of surprise, but the half that was left became as devils, and they multiplied themselves, and everywhere they fought like devils. Three put their backs against the mast of the ship, and we ringed them with our dead before they died. And some got guns and shot with both eyes wide open, and very quick and sure. And one got a big gun, from which at one time he shot many small bullets. And so, behold!"

Ounenk pointed to his ear, neatly pierced by a buckshot.

"But I, Ounenk, drove my spear through his back from behind. And in such fashion, one way and another, did we kill them all—all save the head man. And him we were about, many of us, and he was alone, when he made a great cry and broke through us, five or six dragging upon him, and ran down inside the ship. And then, when the wealth of the ship was ours, and only the head man down below whom we would kill presently, why then there was a sound as of all the guns in the world—a mighty sound! And like a bird I rose up in the air, and the living Mandell Folk, and the dead Sunlanders, the little kayaks, the big ship, the guns, the wealth—everything rose up in the air. So I say, I, Ounenk, who tell the tale, am the only one left."

A great silence fell upon the assemblage. Tyee looked at Aab-Waak with awe-struck eyes, but forbore to speak. Even the women were too stunned to wail the dead.

Ounenk looked about him with pride. "I, only, am left," he repeated.

But at that instant a rifle cracked from Bill-Man's barricade, and there was a sharp spat and thud on the chest of Ounenk. He swayed backward and came forward again, a look of startled surprise on his face. He gasped, and his lips writhed in a grim smile. There was a shrinking together of the shoulders and a bending of the knees. He shook himself, as might a drowsing man, and straightened up. But the shrinking and bending began again, and he sank down slowly, quite slowly, to the ground.

It was a clean mile from the pit of the Sunlanders, and death had spanned it. A great cry of rage went up, and in it there was much of blood-vengeance, much of the unreasoned ferocity of the brute. Tyee and Aab-Waak tried to hold the Mandell Folk back, were thrust aside, and could only turn and watch the mad charge. But no shots came from the Sunlanders, and ere half the distance was covered, many, affrighted by the mysterious silence of the pit, halted and waited. The wilder spirits bore on, and when they had cut the remaining distance in half, the pit still showed no sign of life. At two hundred yards they slowed down and bunched; at one hundred, they stopped, a score of them, suspicious, and conferred together.

Then a wreath of smoke crowned the barricade, and they scattered like a handful of pebbles thrown at random. Four went down, and four more, and they continued swiftly to fall, one and two at a time, till but one remained, and he in full flight with death singing about his ears. It was Nok, a young hunter, long-legged and tall, and he ran as never before. He skimmed across the naked open like a bird, and soared and sailed and curved from side to side. The rifles in the pit rang out in solid volley; they flut-flut-flut-flutted in ragged sequence; and still Nok rose and dipped and rose again unharmed. There was a lull in the firing, as though the Sunlanders had given over, and Nok curved less and less in his flight till he darted straight forward at every leap. And then, as he leaped cleanly and well, one lone rifle barked from the pit, and he doubled up in mid-air, struck the ground in a ball, and like a ball bounced from the impact, and came down in a broken heap.

"Who so swift as the swift-winged lead?" Aab-Waak pondered.

Tyee grunted and turned away. The incident was closed and there was more pressing matter at hand. One Hungry Man and forty fighters, some of them hurt, remained; and there were four Sunlanders yet to reckon with.

"We will keep them in their hole by the cliff," he said, "and when famine has gripped them hard we will slay them like children."

"But of what matter to fight?" queried Oloof, one of the younger men.

"The wealth of the Sunlanders is not; only remains that in the igloo of Neegah, a paltry quantity—"

He broke off hastily as the air by his ear split sharply to the passage of a bullet.

Tyee laughed scornfully. "Let that be thy answer. What else may we do with this mad breed of Sunlanders which will not die?"

"What a thing is foolishness!" Oloof protested, his ears furtively alert for the coming of other bullets. "It is not right that they should fight so, these Sunlanders. Why will they not die easily? They are fools not to know that they are dead men, and they give us much trouble."

"We fought before for great wealth; we fight now that we may live," Aab-Waak summed up succinctly.

That night there was a clash in the trenches, and shots exchanged. And in the morning the igloo of Neegah was found empty of the Sunlanders' possessions. These they themselves had taken, for the signs of their trail were visible to the sun. Oloof climbed to the brow of the cliff to hurl great stones down into the pit, but the cliff overhung, and he hurled down abuse and insult instead, and promised bitter torture to them in the end. Bill-Man mocked him back in the tongue of the Bear Folk, and Tyee, lifting his head from a trench to see, had his shoulder scratched deeply by a bullet.

And in the dreary days that followed, and in the wild nights when they pushed the trenches closer, there was much discussion as to the wisdom of letting the Sunlanders go. But of this they were afraid, and the women raised a cry always at the thought This much they had seen of the Sunlanders; they cared to see no more. All the time the whistle and blub-blub of bullets filled the air, and all the time the death-list grew. In the golden sunrise came the faint, far crack of a rifle, and a stricken woman would throw up her hands on the distant edge of the village; in the noonday heat, men in the trenches heard the shrill sing-song and knew their deaths; or in the gray afterglow of evening, the dirt kicked up in puffs by the winking fires. And through the nights the long "Wah-hoo-ha-a wah-hoo-ha-a!" of mourning women held dolorous sway.

As Tyee had promised, in the end famine gripped the Sunlanders. And once, when an early fall gale blew, one of them crawled through the darkness past the trenches and stole many dried fish.

But he could not get back with them, and the sun found him vainly hiding in the village. So he fought the great fight by himself, and in a narrow ring of Mandell Folk shot four with his revolver, and ere they could lay hands on him for the torture, turned it on himself and died.

This threw a gloom upon the people. Oloof put the question, "If one man die so hard, how hard will die the three who yet are left?"

Then Mesahchie stood up on the barricade and called in by name three dogs which had wandered close,—meat and life,—which set back the day of reckoning and put despair in the hearts of the Mandell Folk. And on the head of Mesahchie were showered the curses of a generation.

The days dragged by. The sun hurried south, the nights grew long and longer, and there was a touch of frost in the air. And still the Sunlanders held the pit. Hearts were breaking under the unending strain, and Tyee thought hard and deep. Then he sent forth word that all the skins and hides of all the tribe be collected. These he had made into huge cylindrical bales, and behind each bale he placed a man.

When the word was given the brief day was almost spent, and it was slow work and tedious, rolling the big bales forward foot by foot The bullets of the Sunlanders blub-blubbed and thudded against them, but could not go through, and the men howled their delight But the dark was at hand, and Tyee, secure of success, called the bales back to the trenches.

In the morning, in the face of an unearthly silence from the pit, the real advance began. At first with large intervals between, the bales slowly converged as the circle drew in. At a hundred yards they were quite close together, so that Tyee's order to halt was passed along in whispers. The pit showed no sign of life. They watched long and sharply, but nothing stirred. The advance was taken up and the manoeuvre repeated at fifty yards. Still no sign nor sound. Tyee shook his head, and even Aab-Waak was dubious. But the order was given to go on, and go on they did, till bale touched bale and a solid rampart of skin and hide bowed out from the cliff about the pit and back to the cliff again.

Tyee looked back and saw the women and children clustering blackly in the deserted trenches. He looked ahead at the silent pit. The men were wriggling nervously, and he ordered every second bale forward. This double line advanced till bale touched bale as before. Then Aab-Waak, of his own will, pushed one bale forward alone. When it touched the barricade, he waited a long while. After that he tossed unresponsive rocks over into the pit, and finally, with great care, stood up and peered in. A carpet of empty cartridges, a few white-picked dog bones, and a soggy place where water dripped from a crevice, met his eyes. That was all. The Sunlanders were gone.

There were murmurings of witchcraft, vague complaints, dark looks which foreshadowed to Tyee dread things which yet might come to pass, and he breathed easier when Aab-Waak took up the trail along the base of the cliff.

"The cave!" Tyee cried. "They foresaw my wisdom of the skin-bales and fled away into the cave!"

The cliff was honey-combed with a labyrinth of subterranean passages which found vent in an opening midway between the pit and where the trench tapped the wall. Thither, and with many exclamations, the tribesmen followed Aab-Waak, and, arrived, they saw plainly where the Sunlanders had climbed to the mouth, twenty and odd feet above.

"Now the thing is done," Tyee said, rubbing his hands. "Let word go forth that rejoicing be made, for they are in the trap now, these Sunlanders, in the trap. The young men shall climb up, and the mouth of the cave be filled with stones, so that Bill-Man and his brothers and Mesahchie shall by famine be pinched to shadows and die cursing in the silence and dark."

Cries of delight and relief greeted this, and Howgah, the last of the Hungry Folk, swarmed up the steep slant and drew himself, crouching, upon the lip of the opening. But as he crouched, a muffled report rushed forth, and as he clung desperately to the slippery edge, a second. His grip loosed with reluctant weakness, and he pitched down at the feet of Tyee, quivered for a moment like some monstrous jelly, and was still.

"How should I know they were great fighters and unafraid?" Tyee demanded, spurred to defence by recollection of the dark looks and vague complaints.

"We were many and happy," one of the men stated baldly. Another fingered his spear with a prurient hand.

But Oloof cried them cease. "Give ear, my brothers! There be another way! As a boy I chanced upon it playing along the steep. It is hidden by the rocks, and there is no reason that a man should go there; wherefore it is secret, and no man knows. It is very small, and you crawl on your belly a long way, and then you are in the cave. To-night we will so crawl, without noise, on our bellies, and come upon the Sunlanders from behind. And to-morrow we will be at peace, and never again will we quarrel with the Sunlanders in the years to come."

"Never again!" chorussed the weary men. "Never again!" And Tyee joined with them.

That night, with the memory of their dead in their hearts, and in their hands stones and spears and knives, the horde of women and children collected about the known mouth of the cave. Down the twenty and odd precarious feet to the ground no Sunlander could hope to pass and live. In the village remained only the wounded men, while every able man—and there were thirty of them—followed Oloof to the secret opening. A hundred feet of broken ledges and insecurely heaped rocks were between it and the earth, and because of the rocks, which might be displaced by the touch of hand or foot, but one man climbed at a time. Oloof went up first, called softly for the next to come on, and disappeared inside. A man followed, a second, and a third, and so on, till only Tyee remained. He received the call of the last man, but a quick doubt assailed him and he stayed to ponder. Half an hour later he swung up to the opening and peered in. He could feel the narrowness of the passage, and the darkness before him took on solidity. The fear of the walled-in earth chilled him and he could not venture. All the men who had died, from Neegah the first of the Mandells, to Howgah the last of the Hungry Folk, came and sat with him, but he chose the terror of their company rather than face the horror which he felt to lurk in the thick blackness. He had been sitting long when something soft and cold fluttered lightly on his cheek, and he knew the first winter's snow was falling. The dim dawn came, and after that the bright day, when he heard a low guttural sobbing, which came and went at intervals along the passage and which drew closer each time and more distinct He slipped over the edge, dropped his feet to the first ledge, and waited.

That which sobbed made slow progress, but at last, after many halts, it reached him, and he was sure no Sunlander made the noise. So he reached a hand inside, and where there should have been a head felt the shoulders of a man uplifted on bent arms. The head he found later, not erect, but hanging straight down so that the crown rested on the floor of the passage.

"Is it you, Tyee?" the head said. "For it is I, Aab-Waak, who am helpless and broken as a rough-flung spear. My head is in the dirt, and I may not climb down unaided."

Tyee clambered in, dragged him up with his back against the wall, but the head hung down on the chest and sobbed and wailed.

"Ai-oo-o, ai-oo-o!" it went "Oloof forgot, for Mesahchie likewise knew the secret and showed the Sunlanders, else they would not have waited at the end of the narrow way. Wherefore, I am a broken man, and helpless—ai-oo-o, ai-oo-o!"

"And did they die, the cursed Sunlanders, at the end of the narrow way?" Tyee demanded.

"How should I know they waited?" Aab-Waak gurgled. "For my brothers had gone before, many of them, and there was no sound of struggle. How should I know why there should be no sound of struggle? And ere I knew, two hands were about my neck so that I could not cry out and warn my brothers yet to come. And then there were two hands more on my head, and two more on my feet. In this fashion the three Sunlanders had me. And while the hands held my head in the one place, the hands on my feet swung my body around, and as we wring the neck of a duck in the marsh, so my week was wrung.

"But it was not given that I should die," he went on, a remnant of pride yet glimmering. "I, only, am left. Oloof and the rest lie on their backs in a row, and their faces turn this way and that, and the faces of some be underneath where the backs of their heads should be. It is not good to look upon; for when life returned to me I saw them all by the light of a torch which the Sunlanders left, and I had been laid with them in the row."

"So? So?" Tyee mused, too stunned for speech.

He started suddenly, and shivered, for the voice of Bill-Man shot out at him from the passage.

"It is well," it said. "I look for the man who crawls with the broken neck, and lo, do I find Tyee. Throw down thy gun, Tyee, so that I may hear it strike among the rocks."

Tyee obeyed passively, and Bill-Man crawled forward into the light. Tyee looked at him curiously. He was gaunt and worn and dirty, and his eyes burned like twin coals in their cavernous sockets.

"I am hungry, Tyee," he said. "Very hungry."

"And I am dirt at thy feet," Tyee responded.

"Thy word is my law. Further, I commanded my people not to withstand thee. I counselled—"

But Bill-Man had turned and was calling back into the passage. "Hey! Charley! Jim! Fetch the woman along and come on!"

"We go now to eat," he said, when his comrades and Mesahchie had joined him.

Tyee rubbed his hands deprecatingly. "We have little, but it is thine."

"After that we go south on the snow," Bill-Man continued.

"May you go without hardship and the trail be easy."

"It is a long way. We will need dogs and food—much!"

"Thine the pick of our dogs and the food they may carry."

Bill-Man slipped over the edge of the opening and prepared to descend. "But we come again, Tyee. We come again, and our days shall be long in the land."

And so they departed into the trackless south, Bill-Man, his brothers, and Mesahchie. And when the next year came, the Search Number Two rode at anchor in Mandell Bay. The few Mandell men, who survived because their wounds had prevented their crawling into the cave, went to work at the best of the Sunlanders and dug in the ground. They hunt and fish no more, but receive a daily wage, with which they buy flour, sugar, calico, and such things which the Search Number Two brings on her yearly trip from the Sunlands.

And this mine is worked in secret, as many Northland mines have been worked; and no white man outside the Company, which is Bill-Man, Jim, and Charley, knows the whereabouts of Mandell on the rim of the polar sea. Aab-Waak still carries his head on one shoulder, is become an oracle, and preaches peace to the younger generation, for which he receives a pension from the Company. Tyee is foreman of the mine. But he has achieved a new theory concerning the Sunlanders.

"They that live under the path of the sun are not soft," he says, smoking his pipe and watching the day-shift take itself off and the night-shift go on. "For the sun enters into their blood and burns them with a great fire till they are filled with lusts and passions. They burn always, so that they may not know when they are beaten. Further, there is an unrest in them, which is a devil, and they are flung out over the earth to toil and suffer and fight without end. I know. I am Tyee."

THE SICKNESS OF LONE CHIEF

This is a tale that was told to me by two old men. We sat in the smoke of a mosquito-smudge, in the cool of the day, which was midnight; and ever and anon, throughout the telling, we smote lustily and with purpose at such of the winged pests as braved the smoke for a snack at our hides. To the right, beneath us, twenty feet down the crumbling bank, the Yukon gurgled lazily. To the left, on the rose-leaf rim of the low-lying hills, smouldered the sleepy sun, which saw no sleep that night nor was destined to see sleep for many nights to come.

The old men who sat with me and valorously slew mosquitoes were Lone Chief and Mutsak, erstwhile comrades in arms, and now withered repositories of tradition and ancient happening. They were the last of their generation and without honor among the younger set which had grown up on the farthest fringe of a mining civilization. Who cared for tradition in these days, when spirits could be evoked from black bottles, and black bottles could be evoked from the complaisant white men for a few hours' sweat or a mangy fur? Of what potency the fearful rites and masked mysteries of shamanism, when daily that living wonder, the steamboat, coughed and spluttered up and down the Yukon in defiance of all law, a veritable fire-breathing monster? And of what value was hereditary prestige, when he who now chopped the most wood, or best conned a stern-wheeler through the island mazes, attained the chiefest consideration of his fellows?

Of a truth, having lived too long, they had fallen on evil days, these two old men, Lone Chief and Mutsak, and in the new order they were without honor or place. So they waited drearily for death, and the while their hearts warmed to the strange white man who shared with them the torments of the mosquito-smudge and lent ready ear to their tales of old time before the steamboat came.

"So a girl was chosen for me," Lone Chief was saying. His voice, shrill and piping, ever and again dropped plummet-like into a hoarse and rattling bass, and, just as one became accustomed to it, soaring upward into the thin treble—alternate cricket chirpings and bullfrog croakings, as it were.

"So a girl was chosen for me," he was saying. "For my father, who was Kask-ta-ka, the Otter, was angered because I looked not with a needful eye upon women. He was an old man, and chief of his tribe. I was the last of his sons to be alive, and through me, only, could he look to see his blood go down among those to come after and as yet unborn. But know, O White Man, that I was very sick; and when neither the hunting nor the fishing delighted me, and by meat my belly was not made warm, how should I look with favor upon women? or prepare for the feast of marriage? or look forward to the prattle and troubles of little children?"

"Ay," Mutsak interrupted. "For had not Lone Chief fought in the arms of a great bear till his head was cracked and blood ran from out his ears?"

Lone Chief nodded vigorously. "Mutsak speaks true. In the time that followed, my head was well, and it was not well. For though the flesh healed and the sore went away, yet was I sick inside. When I walked, my legs shook under me, and when I looked at the light, my eyes became filled with tears. And when I opened my eyes, the world outside went around and around, and when I closed my eyes, my head inside went around and around, and all the things I had ever seen went around and around inside my head. And above my eyes there was a great pain, as though something heavy rested always upon me, or like a band that is drawn tight and gives much hurt. And speech was slow to me, and I waited long for each right word to come to my tongue. And when I waited not long, all manner of words crowded in, and my tongue spoke foolishness. I was very sick, and when my father, the Otter, brought the girl Kasaan before me—"

"Who was a young girl, and strong, my sister's child," Mutsak broke in. "Strong-hipped for children was Kasaan, and straight-legged and quick of foot. She made better moccasins than any of all the young girls, and the bark-rope she braided was the stoutest. And she had a smile in her eyes, and a laugh on her lips; and her temper was not hasty, nor was she unmindful that men give the law and women ever obey."

"As I say, I was very sick," Lone Chief went on. "And when my father, the Otter, brought the girl Kasaan before me, I said rather should they make me ready for burial than for marriage. Whereat the face of my father went black with anger, and he said that I should be served according to my wish, and that I who was yet alive should be made ready for death as one already dead—"

"Which be not the way of our people, O White Man," spoke up Mutsak. "For know that these things that were done to Lone Chief it was our custom to do only to dead men. But the Otter was very angry."

"Ay," said Lone Chief. "My father, the Otter, was a man short of speech and swift of deed. And he commanded the people to gather before the lodge wherein I lay. And when they were gathered, he commanded them to mourn for his son who was dead—"

"And before the lodge they sang the death-song—O-o-o-o-o-a-haa-ha-a-ich-klu-kuk-ich-klu-kuk," wailed Mutsak, in so excellent an imitation that all the tendrils of my spine crawled and curved in sympathy.

"And inside the lodge," continued Lone Chief, "my mother blackened her face with soot, and flung ashes upon her head, and mourned for me as one already dead; for so had my father commanded. So Okiakuta, my mother, mourned with much noise, and beat her breasts and tore her hair; and likewise Hooniak, my sister, and Seenatah, my mother's sister; and the noise they made caused a great ache in my head, and I felt that I would surely and immediately die.

"And the elders of the tribe gathered about me where I lay and discussed the journey my soul must take. One spoke of the thick and endless forests where lost souls wandered crying, and where I, too, might chance to wander and never see the end. And another spoke of the big rivers, rapid with bad water, where evil spirits shrieked and lifted up their formless arms to drag one down by the hair. For these rivers, all said together, a canoe must be provided me. And yet another spoke of the storms, such as no live man ever saw, when the stars rained down out of the sky, and the earth gaped wide in many cracks, and all the rivers in the heart of the earth rushed out and in.

Whereupon they that sat by me flung up their arms and wailed loudly; and those outside heard, and wailed more loudly. And as to them I was as dead, so was I to my own mind dead. I did not know when, or how, yet did I know that I had surely died.

"And Okiakuta, my mother, laid beside me my squirrel-skin parka. Also she laid beside me my parka of caribou hide, and my rain coat of seal gut, and my wet-weather muclucs, that my soul should be warm and dry on its long journey. Further, there was mention made of a steep hill, thick with briers and devil's-club, and she fetched heavy moccasins to make the way easy for my feet.

"And when the elders spoke of the great beasts I should have to slay, the young men laid beside me my strongest bow and straightest arrows, my throwing-stick, my spear and knife. And when the elders spoke of the darkness and silence of the great spaces my soul must wander through, my mother wailed yet more loudly and flung yet more ashes upon her head.

"And the girl, Kasaan, crept in, very timid and quiet, and dropped a little bag upon the things for my journey. And in the little bag, I knew, were the flint and steel and the well-dried tinder for the fires my soul must build. And the blankets were chosen which were to be wrapped around me. Also were the slaves selected that were to be killed that my soul might have company. There were seven of these slaves, for my father was rich and powerful, and it was fit that I, his son, should have proper burial. These slaves we had got in war from the Mukumuks, who live down the Yukon. On the morrow, Skolka, the shaman, would kill them, one by one, so that their souls should go questing with mine through the Unknown. Among other things, they would carry my canoe till we came to the big river, rapid with bad water. And there being no room, and their work being done, they would come no farther, but remain and howl forever in the dark and endless forest.

"And as I looked on my fine warm clothes, and my blankets and weapons of war, and as I thought of the seven slaves to be slain, I felt proud of my burial and knew that I must be the envy of many men. And all the while my father, the Otter, sat silent and black. And all that day and night the people sang my death-song and beat the drums, till it seemed that I had surely died a thousand times.

"But in the morning my father arose and made talk. He had been a fighting man all his days, he said, as the people knew. Also the people knew that it were a greater honor to die fighting in battle than on the soft skins by the fire. And since I was to die anyway, it were well that I should go against the Mukumuks and be slain. Thus would I attain honor and chieftainship in the final abode of the dead, and thus would honor remain to my father, who was the Otter. Wherefore he gave command that a war party be made ready to go down the river. And that when we came upon the Mukumuks I was to go forth alone from my party, giving semblance of battle, and so be slain."

"Nay, but hear, O White Man!" cried Mutsak, unable longer to contain himself. "Skolka, the shaman, whispered long that night in the ear of the Otter, and it was his doing that Lone Chief should be sent forth to die. For the Otter being old, and Lone Chief the last of his sons, Skolka had it in mind to become chief himself over the people. And when the people had made great noise for a day and a night and Lone Chief was yet alive, Skolka was become afraid that he would not die. So it was the counsel of Skolka, with fine words of honor and deeds, that spoke through the mouth of the Otter.

"Ay," replied Lone Chief. "Well did I know it was the doing of Skolka, but I was unmindful, being very sick. I had no heart for anger, nor belly for stout words, and I cared little, one way or the other, only I cared to die and have done with it all. So, O White Man, the war party was made ready. No tried fighters were there, nor elders, crafty and wise—naught but five score of young men who had seen little fighting. And all the village gathered together above the bank of the river to see us depart. And we departed amid great rejoicing and the singing of my praises. Even thou, O White Man, wouldst rejoice at sight of a young man going forth to battle, even though doomed to die.

"So we went forth, the five score young men, and Mutsak came also, for he was likewise young and untried. And by command of my father, the Otter, my canoe was lashed on either side to the canoe of Mutsak and the canoe of

Kannakut. Thus was my strength saved me from the work of the paddles, so that, for all of my sickness, I might make a brave show at the end. And thus we went down the river.

"Nor will I weary thee with the tale of the journey, which was not long. And not far above the village of the Mukumuks we came upon two of their fighting men in canoes, that fled at the sight of us. And then, according to the command of my father, my canoe was cast loose and I was left to drift down all alone. Also, according to his command, were the young men to see me die, so that they might return and tell the manner of my death. Upon this, my father, the Otter, and Skolka, the shaman, had been very clear, with stern promises of punishment in case they were not obeyed.

"I dipped my paddle and shouted words of scorn after the fleeing warriors. And the vile things I shouted made them turn their heads in anger, when they beheld that the young men held back, and that I came on alone. Whereupon, when they had made a safe distance, the two warriors drew their canoes somewhat apart and waited side by side for me to come between. And I came between, spear in hand, and singing the war-song of my people. Each flung a spear, but I bent my body, and the spears whistled over me, and I was unhurt. Then, and we were all together, we three, I cast my spear at the one to the right, and it drove into his throat and he pitched backward into the water.

"Great was my surprise thereat, for I had killed a man. I turned to the one on the left and drove strong with my paddle, to meet Death face to face; but the man's second spear, which was his last, but bit into the flesh of my shoulder. Then was I upon him, making no cast, but pressing the point into his breast and working it through him with both my hands. And while I worked, pressing with all my strength, he smote me upon my head, once and twice, with the broad of his paddle.

"Even as the point of the spear sprang out beyond his back, he smote me upon the head. There was a flash, as of bright light, and inside my head I felt something give, with a snap—just like that, with a snap. And the weight that pressed above my eyes so long was lifted, and the band that bound my brows so tight was broken. And a great gladness came upon me, and my heart sang with joy.

"This be death, I thought; wherefore I thought that death was very good. And then I saw the two empty canoes, and I knew that I was not dead, but well again. The blows of the man upon my head had made me well. I knew that I had killed, and the taste of the blood made me fierce, and I drove my paddle into the breast of the Yukon and urged my canoe toward the village of the Mukumuks. The young men behind me gave a great cry. I looked over my shoulder and saw the water foaming white from their paddles—"

"Ay, it foamed white from our paddles," said Mutsak. "For we remembered the command of the Otter, and of Skolka, that we behold with our own eyes the manner of Lone Chief's death. A young man of the Mukumuks, on his way to a salmon trap, beheld the coming of Lone Chief, and of the five score men behind him. And the young man fled in his canoe, straight for the village, that alarm might be given and preparation made. But Lone Chief hurried after him, and we hurried after Lone Chief to behold the manner of his death. Only, in the face of the village, as the young man leaped to the shore, Lone Chief rose up in his canoe and made a mighty cast. And the spear entered the body of the young man above the hips, and the young man fell upon his face.

"Whereupon Lone Chief leaped up the bank war-club in hand and a great war-cry on his lips, and dashed into the village. The first man he met was Itwilie, chief over the Mukumuks, and him Lone Chief smote upon the head with his war-club, so that he fell dead upon the ground. And for fear we might not behold the manner of his death, we too, the five score young men, leaped to the shore and followed Lone Chief into the village. Only the Mukumuks did not understand, and thought we had come to fight; so their bow-thongs sang and their arrows whistled among us. Whereat we forgot our errand, and fell upon them with our spears and clubs; and they being unprepared, there was great slaughter—"

"With my own hands I slew their shaman," proclaimed Lone Chief, his withered face a-work with memory of that old-time day. "With my own hands I slew him, who was a greater shaman than Skolka, our own shaman.

And each time I faced a man, I thought, 'Now cometh Death; and each time I slew the man, and Death came not. It seemed the breath of life was strong in my nostrils and I could not die—"

"And we followed Lone Chief the length of the village and back again," continued Mutsak. "Like a pack of wolves we followed him, back and forth, and here and there, till there were no more Mukumuks left to fight. Then we gathered together five score men-slaves, and double as many women, and countless children, and we set fire and burned all the houses and lodges, and departed. And that was the last of the Mukumuks."

"And that was the last of the Mukumuks," Lone Chief repeated exultantly. "And when we came to our own village, the people were amazed at our burden of wealth and slaves, and in that I was still alive they were more amazed. And my father, the Otter, came trembling with gladness at the things I had done. For he was an old man, and I the last of his sons. And all the tried fighting men came, and the crafty and wise, till all the people were gathered together. And then I arose, and with a voice like thunder, commanded Skolka, the shaman, to stand forth—"

"Ay, O White Man," exclaimed Mutsak. "With a voice like thunder, that made the people shake at the knees and become afraid."

"And when Skolka had stood forth," Lone Chief went on, "I said that I was not minded to die. Also, I said it were not well that disappointment come to the evil spirits that wait beyond the grave. Wherefore I deemed it fit that the soul of Skolka fare forth into the Unknown, where doubtless it would howl forever in the dark and endless forest. And then I slew him, as he stood there, in the face of all the people. Even I, Lone Chief, with my own hands, slew Skolka, the shaman, in the face of all the people. And when a murmuring arose, I cried aloud—"

"With a voice like thunder," prompted Mutsak.

"Ay, with a voice like thunder I cried aloud: 'Behold, O ye people! I am Lone Chief, slayer of Skolka, the false shaman! Alone among men, have I passed down through the gateway of Death and returned again. Mine eyes have looked upon the unseen things. Mine ears have heard the unspoken words. Greater am I than Skolka, the shaman. Greater than all shamans am I. Likewise am I a greater chief than my father, the Otter. All his days did he fight with the Mukumuks, and lo, in one day have I destroyed them all. As with the breathing of a breath have I destroyed them. Wherefore, my father, the Otter, being old, and Skolka, the shaman, being dead, I shall be both chief and shaman. Henceforth shall I be both chief and shaman to you, O my people. And if any man dispute my word, let that man stand forth!'

"I waited, but no man stood forth. Then I cried: 'Hoh! I have tasted blood! Now bring meat, for I am hungry. Break open the caches, tear down the fish-racks, and let the feast be big. Let there be merriment, and songs, not of burial, but marriage. And last of all, let the girl Kasaan be brought. The girl Kasaan, who is to be the mother of the children of Lone Chief!'

"And at my words, and because that he was very old, my father, the Otter, wept like a woman, and put his arms about my knees. And from that day I was both chief and shaman. And great honor was mine, and all men yielded me obedience."

"Until the steamboat came," Mutsak prompted.

"Ay," said Lone Chief. "Until the steamboat came."

KEESH, THE SON OF KEESH

"Thus will I give six blankets, warm and double; six files, large and hard; six Hudson Bay knives, keen-edged and long; two canoes, the work of Mogum, The Maker of Things; ten dogs, heavy-shouldered and strong in the harness; and three guns—the trigger of one be broken, but it is a good gun and can doubtless be mended."

Keesh paused and swept his eyes over the circle of intent faces. It was the time of the Great Fishing, and he was bidding to Gnob for Su-Su his daughter. The place was the St. George Mission by the Yukon, and the tribes had gathered for many a hundred miles. From north, south, east, and west they had come, even from Tozikakat and far Tana-naw.

"And further, O Gnob, thou art chief of the Tana-naw; and I, Keesh, the son of Keesh, am chief of the Thlunget. Wherefore, when my seed springs from the loins of thy daughter, there shall be a friendship between the tribes, a great friendship, and Tana-naw and Thlunget shall be brothers of the blood in the time to come. What I have said I will do, that will I do. And how is it with you, O Gnob, in this matter?"

Gnob nodded his head gravely, his gnarled and age-twisted face inscrutably masking the soul that dwelt behind. His narrow eyes burned like twin coals through their narrow slits, as he piped in a high-cracked voice, "But that is not all."

"What more?" Keesh demanded. "Have I not offered full measure? Was there ever yet a Tana-naw maiden who fetched so great a price? Then name her!"

An open snicker passed round the circle, and Keesh knew that he stood in shame before these people.

"Nay, nay, good Keesh, thou dost not understand." Gnob made a soft, stroking gesture. "The price is fair. It is a good price. Nor do I question the broken trigger. But that is not all. What of the man?"

"Ay, what of the man?" the circle snarled.

"It is said," Gnob's shrill voice piped, "it is said that Keesh does not walk in the way of his fathers. It is said that he has wandered into the dark, after strange gods, and that he is become afraid."

The face of Keesh went dark. "It is a lie!" he thundered. "Keesh is afraid of no man!"

"It is said," old Gnob piped on, "that he has harkened to the speech of the white man up at the Big House, and that he bends head to the white man's god, and, moreover, that blood is displeasing to the white man's god."

Keesh dropped his eyes, and his hands clenched passionately. The savage circle laughed derisively, and in the ear of Gnob whispered Madwan, the shaman, high-priest of the tribe and maker of medicine.

The shaman poked among the shadows on the rim of the firelight and roused up a slender young boy, whom he brought face to face with Keesh; and in the hand of Keesh he thrust a knife.

Gnob leaned forward. "Keesh! O Keesh! Darest thou to kill a man? Behold! This be Kitz-noo, a slave. Strike, O Keesh, strike with the strength of thy arm!"

The boy trembled and waited the stroke. Keesh looked at him, and thoughts of Mr. Brown's higher morality floated through his mind, and strong upon him was a vision of the leaping flames of Mr. Brown's particular brand of hell-fire. The knife fell to the ground, and the boy sighed and went out beyond the firelight with shaking knees. At the feet of Gnob sprawled a wolf-dog, which bared its gleaming teeth and prepared to spring after the boy. But the shaman ground his foot into the brute's body, and so doing, gave Gnob an idea.

"And then, O Keesh, what wouldst thou do, should a man do this thing to you?"—as he spoke, Gnob held a ribbon of salmon to White Fang, and when the animal attempted to take it, smote him sharply on the nose with a stick. "And afterward, O Keesh, wouldst thou do thus?"—White Fang was cringing back on his belly and fawning to the hand of Gnob.

"Listen!"—leaning on the arm of Madwan, Gnob had risen to his feet. "I am very old, and because I am very old I will tell thee things. Thy father, Keesh, was a mighty man. And he did love the song of the bowstring in battle, and these eyes have beheld him cast a spear till the head stood out beyond a man's body. But thou art unlike. Since thou left the Raven to worship the Wolf, thou art become afraid of blood, and thou makest thy people afraid. This is not good. For behold, when I was a boy, even as Kitz-noo there, there was no white man in all the land. But they came, one by one, these white men, till now they are many. And they are a restless breed, never content to rest by the fire with a full belly and let the morrow bring its own meat. A curse was laid upon them, it would seem, and they must work it out in toil and hardship."

Keesh was startled. A recollection of a hazy story told by Mr. Brown of one Adam, of old time, came to him, and it seemed that Mr. Brown had spoken true.

"So they lay hands upon all they behold, these white men, and they go everywhere and behold all things. And ever do more follow in their steps, so that if nothing be done they will come to possess all the land and there will be no room for the tribes of the Raven. Wherefore it is meet that we fight with them till none are left. Then will we hold the passes and the land, and perhaps our children and our children's children shall flourish and grow fat. There is a great struggle to come, when Wolf and Raven shall grapple; but Keesh will not fight, nor will he let his people fight. So it is not well that he should take to him my daughter. Thus have I spoken, I, Gnob, chief of the Tana-naw."

"But the white men are good and great," Keesh made answer. "The white men have taught us many things. The white men have given us blankets and knives and guns, such as we have never made and never could make. I remember in what manner we lived before they came. I was unborn then, but I have it from my father. When we went on the hunt we must creep so close to the moose that a spear-cast would cover the distance. To-day we use the white man's rifle, and farther away than can a child's cry be heard. We ate fish and meat and berries—there was nothing else to eat—and we ate without salt. How many be there among you who care to go back to the fish and meat without salt?"

It would have sunk home, had not Madwan leaped to his feet ere silence could come. "And first a question to thee, Keesh. The white man up at the Big House tells you that it is wrong to kill. Yet do we not know that the white men kill? Have we forgotten the great fight on the Koyokuk? or the great fight at Nuklukyeto, where three white men killed twenty of the Tozikakats? Do you think we no longer remember the three men of the Tana-naw that the white man Macklewrath killed? Tell me, O Keesh, why does the Shaman Brown teach you that it is wrong to fight, when all his brothers fight?"

"Nay, nay, there is no need to answer," Gnob piped, while Keesh struggled with the paradox. "It is very simple. The Good Man Brown would hold the Raven tight whilst his brothers pluck the feathers." He raised his voice. "But so long as there is one Tana-naw to strike a blow, or one maiden to bear a man-child, the Raven shall not be plucked!"

Gnob turned to a husky young man across the fire. "And what sayest thou, Makamuk, who art brother to Su-Su?"

Makamuk came to his feet. A long face-scar lifted his upper lip into a perpetual grin which belied the glowing ferocity of his eyes. "This day," he began with cunning irrelevance, "I came by the Trader Macklewrath's cabin. And in the door I saw a child laughing at the sun. And the child looked at me with the Trader Macklewrath's eyes, and it was frightened. The mother ran to it and quieted it. The mother was Ziska, the Thlunget woman."

A snarl of rage rose up and drowned his voice, which he stilled by turning dramatically upon Keesh with outstretched arm and accusing finger.

"So? You give your women away, you Thlunget, and come to the Tana-naw for more? But we have need of our women, Keesh; for we must breed men, many men, against the day when the Raven grapples with the Wolf."

Through the storm of applause, Gnob's voice shrilled clear. "And thou, Nossabok, who art her favorite brother?"

100

The young fellow was slender and graceful, with the strong aquiline nose and high brows of his type; but from some nervous affliction the lid of one eye drooped at odd times in a suggestive wink. Even as he arose it so drooped and rested a moment against his cheek. But it was not greeted with the accustomed laughter. Every face was grave. "I, too, passed by the Trader Macklewrath's cabin," he rippled in soft, girlish tones, wherein there was much of youth and much of his sister. "And I saw Indians with the sweat running into their eyes and their knees shaking with weariness—I say, I saw Indians groaning under the logs for the store which the Trader Macklewrath is to build. And with my eyes I saw them chopping wood to keep the Shaman Brown's Big House warm through the frost of the long nights. This be squaw work. Never shall the Tana-naw do the like. We shall be blood brothers to men, not squaws; and the Thlunget be squaws."

A deep silence fell, and all eyes centred on Keesh. He looked about him carefully, deliberately, full into the face of each grown man. "So," he said passionlessly. And "So," he repeated. Then turned on his heel without further word and passed out into the darkness.

Wading among sprawling babies and bristling wolf-dogs, he threaded the great camp, and on its outskirts came upon a woman at work by the light of a fire. With strings of bark stripped from the long roots of creeping vines, she was braiding rope for the Fishing. For some time, without speech, he watched her deft hands bringing law and order out of the unruly mass of curling fibres. She was good to look upon, swaying there to her task, strong-limbed, deep-chested, and with hips made for motherhood. And the bronze of her face was golden in the flickering light, her hair blue-black, her eyes jet.

"O Su-Su," he spoke finally, "thou hast looked upon me kindly in the days that have gone and in the days yet young—"

"I looked kindly upon thee for that thou wert chief of the Thlunget," she answered quickly, "and because thou wert big and strong."

"Ay—"

"But that was in the old days of the Fishing," she hastened to add, "before the Shaman Brown came and taught thee ill things and led thy feet on strange trails."

"But I would tell thee the—"

She held up one hand in a gesture which reminded him of her father. "Nay, I know already the speech that stirs in thy throat, O Keesh, and I make answer now. It so happeneth that the fish of the water and the beasts of the forest bring forth after their kind. And this is good. Likewise it happeneth to women. It is for them to bring forth their kind, and even the maiden, while she is yet a maiden, feels the pang of the birth, and the pain of the breast, and the small hands at the neck. And when such feeling is strong, then does each maiden look about her with secret eyes for the man—for the man who shall be fit to father her kind. So have I felt. So did I feel when I looked upon thee and found thee big and strong, a hunter and fighter of beasts and men, well able to win meat when I should eat for two, well able to keep danger afar off when my helplessness drew nigh. But that was before the day the Shaman Brown came into the land and taught thee—"

"But it is not right, Su-Su. I have it on good word—"

"It is not right to kill. I know what thou wouldst say. Then breed thou after thy kind, the kind that does not kill; but come not on such quest among the Tana-naw. For it is said in the time to come, that the Raven shall grapple with the Wolf. I do not know, for this be the affair of men; but I do know that it is for me to bring forth men against that time."

"Su-Su," Keesh broke in, "thou must hear me—"

"A man would beat me with a stick and make me hear," she sneered. "But thou ... here!" She thrust a bunch of bark into his hand. "I cannot give thee myself, but this, yes. It looks fittest in thy hands. It is squaw work, so braid away."

He flung it from him, the angry blood pounding a muddy path under his bronze.

"One thing more," she went on. "There be an old custom which thy father and mine were not strangers to. When a man falls in battle, his scalp is carried away in token. Very good. But thou, who have forsworn the Raven, must do more. Thou must bring me, not scalps, but heads, two heads, and then will I give thee, not bark, but a brave-beaded belt, and sheath, and long Russian knife. Then will I look kindly upon thee once again, and all will be well."

"So," the man pondered. "So." Then he turned and passed out through the light.

"Nay, O Keesh!" she called after him. "Not two heads, but three at least!"

But Keesh remained true to his conversion, lived uprightly, and made his tribespeople obey the gospel as propounded by the Rev. Jackson Brown. Through all the time of the Fishing he gave no heed to the Tana-naw, nor took notice of the sly things which were said, nor of the laughter of the women of the many tribes. After the Fishing, Gnob and his people, with great store of salmon, sun-dried and smoke-cured, departed for the Hunting on the head reaches of the Tana-naw. Keesh watched them go, but did not fail in his attendance at Mission service, where he prayed regularly and led the singing with his deep bass voice.

The Rev. Jackson Brown delighted in that deep bass voice, and because of his sterling qualities deemed him the most promising convert. Macklewrath doubted this. He did not believe in the efficacy of the conversion of the heathen, and he was not slow in speaking his mind. But Mr. Brown was a large man, in his way, and he argued it out with such convincingness, all of one long fall night, that the trader, driven from position after position, finally announced in desperation, "Knock out my brains with apples, Brown, if I don't become a convert myself, if Keesh holds fast, true blue, for two years!" Mr. Brown never lost an opportunity, so he clinched the matter on the spot with a virile hand-grip, and thenceforth the conduct of Keesh was to determine the ultimate abiding-place of Macklewrath's soul.

But there came news one day, after the winter's rime had settled down over the land sufficiently for travel. A Tana-naw man arrived at the St. George

Mission in quest of ammunition and bringing information that Su-Su had set eyes on Nee-Koo, a nervy young hunter who had bid brilliantly for her by old Gnob's fire. It was at about this time that the Rev. Jackson Brown came upon Keesh by the wood-trail which leads down to the river. Keesh had his best dogs in the harness, and shoved under the sled-lashings was his largest and finest pair of snow-shoes.

"Where goest thou, O Keesh? Hunting?" Mr. Brown asked, falling into the Indian manner.

Keesh looked him steadily in the eyes for a full minute, then started up his dogs. Then again, turning his deliberate gaze upon the missionary, he answered, "No; I go to hell."

In an open space, striving to burrow into the snow as though for shelter from the appalling desolateness, huddled three dreary lodges. Ringed all about, a dozen paces away, was the sombre forest. Overhead there was no keen, blue sky of naked space, but a vague, misty curtain, pregnant with snow, which had drawn between. There was no wind, no sound, nothing but the snow and silence. Nor was there even the general stir of life about the camp; for the hunting party had run upon the flank of the caribou herd and the kill had been large. Thus, after the period of fasting had come the plenitude of feasting, and thus, in broad daylight, they slept heavily under their roofs of moosehide.

By a fire, before one of the lodges, five pairs of snow-shoes stood on end in their element, and by the fire sat Su-Su. The hood of her squirrel-skin parka was about her hair, and well drawn up around her throat; but her hands were unmittened and nimbly at work with needle and sinew, completing the last fantastic design on a belt of leather faced with bright scarlet cloth. A dog, somewhere at the rear of one of the lodges, raised a short, sharp bark, then ceased as abruptly as it had begun. Once, her father, in the lodge at her back, gurgled and grunted in his sleep. "Bad dreams," she smiled to herself. "He grows old, and that last joint was too much."

She placed the last bead, knotted the sinew, and replenished the fire. Then, after gazing long into the flames, she lifted her head to the harsh crunch-crunch of a moccasined foot against the flinty snow granules. Keesh was at her side, bending slightly forward to a load which he bore upon his back. This was wrapped loosely in a soft-tanned moosehide, and he dropped it carelessly into the snow and sat down. They looked at each other long and without speech.

"It is a far fetch, O Keesh," she said at last, "a far fetch from St. George Mission by the Yukon."

"Ay," he made answer, absently, his eyes fixed keenly upon the belt and taking note of its girth. "But where is the knife?" he demanded.

"Here." She drew it from inside her parka and flashed its naked length in the firelight. "It is a good knife."

"Give it me!" he commanded.

"Nay, O Keesh," she laughed. "It may be that thou wast not born to wear it."

"Give it me!" he reiterated, without change of tone. "I was so born."

But her eyes, glancing coquettishly past him to the moosehide, saw the snow about it slowly reddening. "It is blood, Keesh?" she asked.

"Ay, it is blood. But give me the belt and the long Russian knife."

She felt suddenly afraid, but thrilled when he took the belt roughly from her, thrilled to the roughness. She looked at him softly, and was aware of a pain at the breast and of small hands clutching her throat.

"It was made for a smaller man," he remarked grimly, drawing in his abdomen and clasping the buckle at the first hole.

Su-Su smiled, and her eyes were yet softer. Again she felt the soft hands at her throat. He was good to look upon, and the belt was indeed small, made for a smaller man; but what did it matter? She could make many belts.

"But the blood?" she asked, urged on by a hope new-born and growing. "The blood, Keesh? Is it ... are they ... heads?"

"Ay."

"They must be very fresh, else would the blood be frozen."

"Ay, it is not cold, and they be fresh, quite fresh."

"Oh, Keesh!" Her face was warm and bright. "And for me?"

"Ay; for thee."

He took hold of a corner of the hide, flirted it open, and rolled the heads out before her.

"Three," he whispered savagely; "nay, four at least."

But she sat transfixed. There they lay—the soft-featured Nee-Koo; the gnarled old face of Gnob; Makamuk, grinning at her with his lifted upper lip; and lastly, Nossabok, his eyelid, up to its old trick, drooped on his girlish cheek in a suggestive wink. There they lay, the firelight flashing upon and playing over them, and from each of them a widening circle dyed the snow to scarlet.

Thawed by the fire, the white crust gave way beneath the head of Gnob, which rolled over like a thing alive, spun around, and came to rest at her feet. But she did not move. Keesh, too, sat motionless, his eyes unblinking, centred steadfastly upon her.

Once, in the forest, an overburdened pine dropped its load of snow, and the echoes reverberated hollowly down the gorge; but neither stirred. The short day had been waning fast, and darkness was wrapping round the camp when White Fang trotted up toward the fire. He paused to reconnoitre, but not being driven back, came closer. His nose shot swiftly to the side, nostrils a-tremble and bristles rising along the spine; and straight and true, he followed the sudden scent to his master's head. He sniffed it gingerly at first and licked the forehead with his red lolling tongue. Then he sat abruptly down, pointed his nose up at the first faint star, and raised the long wolf-howl.

This brought Su-Su to herself. She glanced across at Keesh, who had unsheathed the Russian knife and was watching her intently. His face was firm and set, and in it she read the law. Slipping back the hood of her parka, she bared her neck and rose to her feet There she paused and took a long look about her, at the rimming forest, at the faint stars in the sky, at the camp, at the snow-shoes in the snow—a last long comprehensive look at life. A light breeze stirred her hair from the side, and for the space of one deep breath she turned her head and followed it around until she met it full-faced.

Then she thought of her children, ever to be unborn, and she walked over to Keesh and said, "I am ready."

THE DEATH OF LIGOUN

Blood for blood, rank for rank.

—Thlinket Code.

"Hear now the death of Ligoun—"

The speaker ceased, or rather suspended utterance, and gazed upon me with an eye of understanding. I held the bottle between our eyes and the fire, indicated with my thumb the depth of the draught, and shoved it over to him; for was he not Palitlum, the Drinker? Many tales had he told me, and long had I waited for this scriptless scribe to speak of the things concerning Ligoun; for he, of all men living, knew these things best.

He tilted back his head with a grunt that slid swiftly into a gurgle, and the shadow of a man's torso, monstrous beneath a huge inverted bottle, wavered and danced on the frown of the cliff at our backs. Palitlum released his lips from the glass with a caressing suck and glanced regretfully up into the ghostly vault of the sky where played the wan white light of the summer borealis.

"It be strange," he said; "cold like water and hot like fire. To the drinker it giveth strength, and from the drinker it taketh away strength. It maketh old men young, and young men old. To the man who is weary it leadeth him to get up and go onward, and to the man unweary it burdeneth him into sleep. My brother was possessed of the heart of a rabbit, yet did he drink of it, and forthwith slay four of his enemies. My father was like a great wolf, showing his teeth to all men, yet did he drink of it and was shot through the back, running swiftly away. It be most strange."

"It is 'Three Star,' and a better than what they poison their bellies with down there," I answered, sweeping my hand, as it were, over the yawning chasm of blackness and down to where the beach fires glinted far below—tiny jets of flame which gave proportion and reality to the night.

Palitlum sighed and shook his head. "Wherefore I am here with thee."

And here he embraced the bottle and me in a look which told more eloquently than speech of his shameless thirst.

"Nay," I said, snuggling the bottle in between my knees. "Speak now of Ligoun. Of the 'Three Star' we will hold speech hereafter."

"There be plenty, and I am not wearied," he pleaded brazenly. "But the feel of it on my lips, and I will speak great words of Ligoun and his last days."

"From the drinker it taketh away strength," I mocked, "and to the man unweary it burdeneth him into sleep."

"Thou art wise," he rejoined, without anger and pridelessly. "Like all of thy brothers, thou art wise. Waking or sleeping, the 'Three Star' be with thee, yet never have I known thee to drink overlong or overmuch. And the while you gather to you the gold that hides in our mountains and the fish that swim in our seas; and Palitlum, and the brothers of Palitlum, dig the gold for thee and net the fish, and are glad to be made glad when out of thy wisdom thou deemest it fit that the 'Three Star' should wet our lips."

"I was minded to hear of Ligoun," I said impatiently. "The night grows short, and we have a sore journey to-morrow."

I yawned and made as though to rise, but Palitlum betrayed a quick anxiety, and with abruptness began:—

"It was Ligoun's desire, in his old age, that peace should be among the tribes. As a young man he had been first of the fighting men and chief over the war-chiefs of the Islands and the Passes. All his days had been full of fighting. More marks he boasted of bone and lead and iron than any other man. Three wives he had, and for each wife two sons; and the sons, eldest born and last and all died by his side in battle. Restless as the bald-face, he ranged wide and far—north to Unalaska and the Shallow Sea; south to the Queen Charlottes, ay, even did he go with the Kakes, it is told, to far Puget Sound, and slay thy brothers in their sheltered houses.

"But, as I say, in his old age he looked for peace among the tribes. Not that he was become afraid, or overfond of the corner by the fire and the well-filled pot. For he slew with the shrewdness and blood-hunger of the fiercest, drew in his belly to famine with the youngest, and with the stoutest faced the bitter seas and stinging trail. But because of his many deeds, and in punishment, a warship carried him away, even to thy country, O Hair-Face and Boston Man; and the years were many ere he came back, and I was grown to something more than a boy and something less than a young man. And Ligoun, being childless in his old age, made much of me, and grown wise, gave me of his wisdom.

"'It be good to fight, O Palitlum,' said he. Nay, O Hair-Face, for I was unknown as Palitlum in those days, being called Olo, the Ever-Hungry. The drink was to come after. 'It be good to fight,' spoke Ligoun, 'but it be foolish. In the Boston Man Country, as I saw with mine eyes, they are not given to fighting one with another, and they be strong. Wherefore, of their strength, they come against us of the Islands and Passes, and we are as camp smoke and sea mist before them. Wherefore I say it be good to fight, most good, but it be likewise foolish.'

"And because of this, though first always of the fighting men, Ligoun's voice was loudest, ever, for peace. And when he was very old, being greatest of chiefs and richest of men, he gave a potlatch. Never was there such a potlatch. Five hundred canoes were lined against the river bank, and in each canoe there came not less than ten of men and women. Eight tribes were there; from the first and oldest man to the last and youngest babe were they there. And then there were men from far-distant tribes, great travellers and seekers who had heard of the potlatch of Ligoun. And for the length of seven days they filled their bellies with his meat and drink. Eight thousand blankets did he give to them, as I well know, for who but I kept the tally and apportioned according to degree and rank? And in the end Ligoun was a poor man; but his name was on all men's lips, and other chiefs gritted their teeth in envy that he should be so great.

"And so, because there was weight to his words, he counselled peace; and he journeyed to every potlatch and feast and tribal gathering that he might counsel peace. And so it came that we journeyed together, Ligoun and

I, to the great feast given by Niblack, who was chief over the river Indians of the Skoot, which is not far from the Stickeen. This was in the last days, and Ligoun was very old and very close to death. He coughed of cold weather and camp smoke, and often the red blood ran from out his mouth till we looked for him to die.

"'Nay,' he said once at such time; 'it were better that I should die when the blood leaps to the knife, and there is a clash of steel and smell of powder, and men crying aloud what of the cold iron and quick lead.' So, it be plain, O Hair-Face, that his heart was yet strong for battle.

"It is very far from the Chilcat to the Skoot, and we were many days in the canoes. And the while the men bent to the paddles, I sat at the feet of Ligoun and received the Law. Of small need for me to say the Law, O Hair-Face, for it be known to me that in this thou art well skilled. Yet do I speak of the Law of blood for blood, and rank for rank. Also did Ligoun go deeper into the matter, saying:—

"'But know this, O Olo, that there be little honor in the killing of a man less than thee. Kill always the man who is greater, and thy honor shall be according to his greatness. But if, of two men, thou killest the lesser, then is shame thine, for which the very squaws will lift their lips at thee. As I say, peace be good; but remember, O Olo, if kill thou must, that thou killest by the Law.'

"It is a way of the Thlinket-folk," Palitlum vouchsafed half apologetically.

And I remembered the gun-fighters and bad men of my own Western land, and was not perplexed at the way of the Thlinket-folk.

"In time," Palitlum continued, "we came to Chief Niblack and the Skoots. It was a feast great almost as the potlatch of Ligoun. There were we of the Chilcat, and the Sitkas, and the Stickeens who are neighbors to the Skoots, and the Wrangels and the Hoonahs. There were Sundowns and Tahkos from Port Houghton, and their neighbors the Awks from Douglass Channel; the Naass River people, and the Tongas from north of Dixon, and the Kakes who come from the island called Kupreanoff. Then there were

111

Siwashes from Vancouver, Cassiars from the Gold Mountains, Teslin men, and even Sticks from the Yukon Country.

"It was a mighty gathering. But first of all, there was to be a meeting of the chiefs with Niblack, and a drowning of all enmities in quass. The Russians it was who showed us the way of making quass, for so my father told me,—my father, who got it from his father before him. But to this quass had Niblack added many things, such as sugar, flour, dried apples, and hops, so that it was a man's drink, strong and good. Not so good as 'Three Star,' O Hair-Face, yet good.

"This quass-feast was for the chiefs, and the chiefs only, and there was a score of them. But Ligoun being very old and very great, it was given that I walk with him that he might lean upon my shoulder and that I might ease him down when he took his seat and raise him up when he arose. At the door of Niblack's house, which was of logs and very big, each chief, as was the custom, laid down his spear or rifle and his knife. For as thou knowest, O Hair-Face, strong drink quickens, and old hates flame up, and head and hand are swift to act. But I noted that Ligoun had brought two knives, the one he left outside the door, the other slipped under his blanket, snug to the grip. The other chiefs did likewise, and I was troubled for what was to come.

"The chiefs were ranged, sitting, in a big circle about the room. I stood at Ligoun's elbow. In the middle was the barrel of quass, and by it a slave to serve the drink. First, Niblack made oration, with much show of friendship and many fine words. Then he gave a sign, and the slave dipped a gourd full of quass and passed it to Ligoun, as was fit, for his was the highest rank.

"Ligoun drank it, to the last drop, and I gave him my strength to get on his feet so that he, too, might make oration. He had kind speech for the many tribes, noted the greatness of Niblack to give such a feast, counselled for peace as was his custom, and at the end said that the quass was very good.

"Then Niblack drank, being next of rank to Ligoun, and after him one chief and another in degree and order. And each spoke friendly words and said that the quass was good, till all had drunk. Did I say all? Nay, not all, O Hair-Face. For last of them was one, a lean and catlike man, young of face,

112

with a quick and daring eye, who drank darkly, and spat forth upon the ground, and spoke no word.

"To not say that the quass was good were insult; to spit forth upon the ground were worse than insult. And this very thing did he do. He was known for a chief over the Sticks of the Yukon, and further naught was known of him.

"As I say, it was an insult. But mark this, O Hair-Face: it was an insult, not to Niblack the feast-giver, but to the man chiefest of rank who sat among those of the circle. And that man was Ligoun. There was no sound. All eyes were upon him to see what he might do. He made no movement. His withered lips trembled not into speech; nor did a nostril quiver, nor an eyelid droop. But I saw that he looked wan and gray, as I have seen old men look of bitter mornings when famine pressed, and the women wailed and the children whimpered, and there was no meat nor sign of meat. And as the old men looked, so looked Ligoun.

"There was no sound. It were as a circle of the dead, but that each chief felt beneath his blanket to make sure, and that each chief glanced to his neighbor, right and left, with a measuring eye. I was a stripling; the things I had seen were few; yet I knew it to be the moment one meets but once in all a lifetime.

"The Stick rose up, with every eye upon him, and crossed the room till he stood before Ligoun.

"'I am Opitsah, the Knife,' he said.

"But Ligoun said naught, nor looked at him, but gazed unblinking at the ground.

"'You are Ligoun,' Opitsah said. 'You have killed many men. I am still alive.'

"And still Ligoun said naught, though he made the sign to me and with my strength arose and stood upright on his two feet. He was as an old pine, naked and gray, but still a-shoulder to the frost and storm. His eyes were unblinking, and as he had not heard Opitsah, so it seemed he did not see him.

"And Opitsah was mad with anger, and danced stiff-legged before him, as men do when they wish to give another shame. And Opitsah sang a song of his own greatness and the greatness of his people, filled with bad words for the Chilcats and for Ligoun. And as he danced and sang, Opitsah threw off his blanket and with his knife drew bright circles before the face of Ligoun. And the song he sang was the Song of the Knife.

"And there was no other sound, only the singing of Opitsah, and the circle of chiefs that were as dead, save that the flash of the knife seemed to draw smouldering fire from their eyes. And Ligoun, also, was very still. Yet did he know his death, and was unafraid. And the knife sang closer and yet closer to his face, but his eyes were unblinking and he swayed not to right or left, or this way or that.

"And Opitsah drove in the knife, so, twice on the forehead of Ligoun, and the red blood leaped after it. And then it was that Ligoun gave me the sign to bear up under him with my youth that he might walk. And he laughed with a great scorn, full in the face of Opitsah, the Knife. And he brushed Opitsah to the side, as one brushes to the side a low-hanging branch on the trail and passes on.

"And I knew and understood, for there was but shame in the killing of Opitsah before the faces of a score of greater chiefs. I remembered the Law, and knew Ligoun had it in mind to kill by the Law. And who, chiefest of rank but himself, was there but Niblack? And toward Niblack, leaning on my arm, he walked. And to his other arm, clinging and striking, was Opitsah, too small to soil with his blood the hands of so great a man. And though the knife of Opitsah bit in again and again, Ligoun noted it not, nor winced. And in this fashion we three went our way across the room, Niblack sitting in his blanket and fearful of our coming.

"And now old hates flamed up and forgotten grudges were remembered. Lamuk, a Kake, had had a brother drowned in the bad water of the Stickeen, and the Stickeens had not paid in blankets for their bad water, as was the custom to pay. So Lamuk drove straight with his long knife to the heart of

Klok-Kutz the Stickeen. And Katchahook remembered a quarrel of the Naass River people with the Tongas of north of Dixon, and the chief of the Tongas he slew with a pistol which made much noise. And the blood-hunger gripped all the men who sat in the circle, and chief slew chief, or was slain, as chance might be. Also did they stab and shoot at Ligoun, for whoso killed him won great honor and would be unforgotten for the deed. And they were about him like wolves about a moose, only they were so many they were in their own way, and they slew one another to make room. And there was great confusion.

"But Ligoun went slowly, without haste, as though many years were yet before him. It seemed that he was certain he would make his kill, in his own way, ere they could slay him. And as I say, he went slowly, and knives bit into him, and he was red with blood. And though none sought after me, who was a mere stripling, yet did the knives find me, and the hot bullets burn me. And still Ligoun leaned his weight on my youth, and Opitsah struck at him, and we three went forward. And when we stood by Niblack, he was afraid, and covered his head with his blanket. The Skoots were ever cowards.

"And Goolzug and Kadishan, the one a fish-eater and the other a meat-killer, closed together for the honor of their tribes. And they raged madly about, and in their battling swung against the knees of Opitsah, who was overthrown and trampled upon. And a knife, singing through the air, smote Skulpin, of the Sitkas, in the throat, and he flung his arms out blindly, reeling, and dragged me down in his fall.

"And from the ground I beheld Ligoun bend over Niblack, and uncover the blanket from his head, and turn up his face to the light. And Ligoun was in no haste. Being blinded with his own blood, he swept it out of his eyes with the back of his hand, so he might see and be sure. And when he was sure that the upturned face was the face of Niblack, he drew the knife across his throat as one draws a knife across the throat of a trembling deer. And then Ligoun stood erect, singing his death-song and swaying gently to and fro. And Skulpin, who had dragged me down, shot with a pistol from where he lay, and Ligoun toppled and fell, as an old pine topples and falls in the teeth of the wind."

Palitlum ceased. His eyes, smouldering moodily, were bent upon the fire, and his cheek was dark with blood.

"And thou, Palitlum?" I demanded. "And thou?"

"I? I did remember the Law, and I slew Opitsah the Knife, which was well. And I drew Ligoun's own knife from the throat of Niblack, and slew Skulpin, who had dragged me down. For I was a stripling, and I could slay any man and it were honor. And further, Ligoun being dead, there was no need for my youth, and I laid about me with his knife, choosing the chiefest of rank that yet remained."

Palitlum fumbled under his shirt and drew forth a beaded sheath, and from the sheath, a knife. It was a knife home-wrought and crudely fashioned from a whip-saw file; a knife such as one may find possessed by old men in a hundred Alaskan villages.

"The knife of Ligoun?" I said, and Palitlum nodded.

"And for the knife of Ligoun," I said, "will I give thee ten bottles of 'Three Star.'"

But Palitlum looked at me slowly. "Hair-Face, I am weak as water, and easy as a woman. I have soiled my belly with quass, and hooch, and 'Three Star.' My eyes are blunted, my ears have lost their keenness, and my strength has gone into fat. And I am without honor in these days, and am called Palitlum, the Drinker. Yet honor was mine at the potlatch of Niblack, on the Skoot, and the memory of it, and the memory of Ligoun, be dear to me. Nay, didst thou turn the sea itself into 'Three Star' and say that it were all mine for the knife, yet would I keep the knife. I am Palitlum, the Drinker, but I was once Olo, the Ever-Hungry, who bore up Ligoun with his youth!"

"Thou art a great man, Palitlum," I said, "and I honor thee."

Palitlum reached out his hand.

"The 'Three Star' between thy knees be mine for the tale I have told," he said.

And as I looked on the frown of the cliff at our backs, I saw the shadow of a man's torso, monstrous beneath a huge inverted bottle.

LI WAN, THE FAIR

"The sun sinks, Canim, and the heat of the day is gone!"

So called Li Wan to the man whose head was hidden beneath the squirrel-skin robe, but she called softly, as though divided between the duty of waking him and the fear of him awake. For she was afraid of this big husband of hers, who was like unto none of the men she had known. The moose-meat sizzled uneasily, and she moved the frying-pan to one side of the red embers. As she did so she glanced warily at the two Hudson Bay dogs dripping eager slaver from their scarlet tongues and following her every movement. They were huge, hairy fellows, crouched to leeward in the thin smoke-wake of the fire to escape the swarming myriads of mosquitoes. As Li Wan gazed down the steep to where the Klondike flung its swollen flood between the hills, one of the dogs bellied its way forward like a worm, and with a deft, catlike stroke of the paw dipped a chunk of hot meat out of the pan to the ground. But Li Wan caught him from out the tail of her eye, and he sprang back with a snap and a snarl as she rapped him over the nose with a stick of firewood.

"Nay, Olo," she laughed, recovering the meat without removing her eye from him. "Thou art ever hungry, and for that thy nose leads thee into endless troubles."

But the mate of Olo joined him, and together they defied the woman. The hair on their backs and shoulders bristled in recurrent waves of anger, and the thin lips writhed and lifted into ugly wrinkles, exposing the flesh-tearing fangs, cruel and menacing. Their very noses serrulated and shook in brute passion, and they snarled as the wolves snarl, with all the hatred and malignity of the breed impelling them to spring upon the woman and drag her down.

"And thou, too, Bash, fierce as thy master and never at peace with the hand that feeds thee! This is not thy quarrel, so that be thine! and that!"

As she cried, she drove at them with the firewood, but they avoided the blows and refused to retreat. They separated and approached her from either side, crouching low and snarling. Li Wan had struggled with the wolf-dog for mastery from the time she toddled among the skin-bales of the teepee, and she knew a crisis was at hand. Bash had halted, his muscles stiff and tense for the spring; Olo was yet creeping into striking distance.

Grasping two blazing sticks by the charred ends, she faced the brutes. The one held back, but Bash sprang, and she met him in mid-air with the flaming weapon. There were sharp yelps of pain and swift odors of burning hair and flesh as he rolled in the dirt and the woman ground the fiery embers into his mouth. Snapping wildly, he flung himself sidewise out of her reach and in a frenzy of fear scrambled for safety. Olo, on the other side, had begun his retreat, when Li Wan reminded him of her primacy by hurling a heavy stick of wood into his ribs. Then the pair retreated under a rain of firewood, and on the edge of the camp fell to licking their wounds and whimpering by turns and snarling.

Li Wan blew the ashes off the meat and sat down again. Her heart had not gone up a beat, and the incident was already old, for this was the routine of life. Canim had not stirred during the disorder, but instead had set up a lusty snoring.

"Come, Canim!" she called. "The heat of the day is gone, and the trail waits for our feet."

The squirrel-skin robe was agitated and cast aside by a brown arm. Then the man's eyelids fluttered and drooped again.

"His pack is heavy," she thought, "and he is tired with the work of the morning."

A mosquito stung her on the neck, and she daubed the unprotected spot with wet clay from a ball she had convenient to hand. All morning, toiling up the divide and enveloped in a cloud of the pests, the man and woman had plastered themselves with the sticky mud, which, drying in the sun, covered their faces with masks of clay. These masks, broken in divers places by the movement of the facial muscles, had constantly to be renewed, so that the deposit was irregular of depth and peculiar of aspect.

Li Wan shook Canim gently but with persistence till he roused and sat up. His first glance was to the sun, and after consulting the celestial timepiece he hunched over to the fire and fell-to ravenously on the meat. He was a large Indian fully six feet in height, deep-chested and heavy-muscled, and his eyes were keener and vested with greater mental vigor than the average of his kind. The lines of will had marked his face deeply, and this, coupled with a sternness and primitiveness, advertised a native indomitability, unswerving of purpose, and prone, when thwarted, to sullen cruelty.

"To-morrow, Li Wan, we shall feast." He sucked a marrow-bone clean and threw it to the dogs. "We shall have flapjacks fried in bacon grease, and sugar, which is more toothsome—"

"Flapjacks?" she questioned, mouthing the word curiously.

"Ay," Canim answered with superiority; "and I shall teach you new ways of cookery. Of these things I speak you are ignorant, and of many more things besides. You have lived your days in a little corner of the earth and know nothing. But I,"—he straightened himself and looked at her pridefully,—"I am a great traveller, and have been all places, even among the white people, and I am versed in their ways, and in the ways of many peoples. I am not a tree, born to stand in one place always and know not what there be over the next hill; for I am Canim, the Canoe, made to go here and there and to journey and quest up and down the length and breadth of the world."

She bowed her head humbly. "It is true. I have eaten fish and meat and berries all my days and lived in a little corner of the earth. Nor did I dream the world was so large until you stole me from my people and I cooked and carried for you on the endless trails." She looked up at him suddenly. "Tell me, Canim, does this trail ever end?"

"Nay," he answered. "My trail is like the world; it never ends. My trail is the world, and I have travelled it since the time my legs could carry me, and I shall travel it until I die. My father and my mother may be dead, but it is long since I looked upon them, and I do not care. My tribe is like your tribe.

119

It stays in the one place—which is far from here,—but I care naught for my tribe, for I am Canim, the Canoe!"

"And must I, Li Wan, who am weary, travel always your trail until I die?"

"You, Li Wan, are my wife, and the wife travels the husband's trail wheresoever it goes. It is the law. And were it not the law, yet would it be the law of Canim, who is lawgiver unto himself and his."

She bowed her head again, for she knew no other law than that man was the master of woman.

"Be not in haste," Canim cautioned her, as she began to strap the meagre camp outfit to her pack. "The sun is yet hot, and the trail leads down and the footing is good."

She dropped her work obediently and resumed her seat.

Canim regarded her with speculative interest. "You do not squat on your hams like other women," he remarked.

"No," she answered. "It never came easy. It tires me, and I cannot take my rest that way."

"And why is it your feet point not straight before you?"

"I do not know, save that they are unlike the feet of other women."

A satisfied light crept into his eyes, but otherwise he gave no sign.

"Like other women, your hair is black; but have you ever noticed that it is soft and fine, softer and finer than the hair of other women?"

"I have noticed," she answered shortly, for she was not pleased at such cold analysis of her sex-deficiencies.

"It is a year, now, since I took you from your people," he went on, "and you are nigh as shy and afraid of me as when first I looked upon you. How does this thing be?"

Li Wan shook her head. "I am afraid of you, Canim, you are so big and strange. And further, before you looked upon me even, I was afraid of all the young men. I do not know ... I cannot say ... only it seemed, somehow, as though I should not be for them, as though ..."

"Ay," he encouraged, impatient at her faltering.

"As though they were not my kind."

"Not your kind?" he demanded slowly. "Then what is your kind?"

"I do not know, I ..." She shook her head in a bewildered manner. "I cannot put into words the way I felt. It was strangeness in me. I was unlike other maidens, who sought the young men slyly. I could not care for the young men that way. It would have been a great wrong, it seemed, and an ill deed."

"What is the first thing you remember?" Canim asked with abrupt irrelevance.

"Pow-Wah-Kaan, my mother."

"And naught else before Pow-Wah-Kaan?"

"Naught else."

But Canim, holding her eyes with his, searched her secret soul and saw it waver.

"Think, and think hard, Li Wan!" he threatened.

She stammered, and her eyes were piteous and pleading, but his will dominated her and wrung from her lips the reluctant speech.

"But it was only dreams, Canim, ill dreams of childhood, shadows of things not real, visions such as the dogs, sleeping in the sun-warmth, behold and whine out against."

"Tell me," he commanded, "of the things before Pow-Wah-Kaan, your mother."

"They are forgotten memories," she protested. "As a child I dreamed

121

awake, with my eyes open to the day, and when I spoke of the strange things I saw I was laughed at, and the other children were afraid and drew away from me. And when I spoke of the things I saw to Pow-Wah-Kaan, she chided me and said they were evil; also she beat me. It was a sickness, I believe, like the falling-sickness that comes to old men; and in time I grew better and dreamed no more. And now ... I cannot remember"—she brought her hand in a confused manner to her forehead—"they are there, somewhere, but I cannot find them, only ..."

"Only," Canim repeated, holding her.

"Only one thing. But you will laugh at its foolishness, it is so unreal."

"Nay, Li Wan. Dreams are dreams. They may be memories of other lives we have lived. I was once a moose. I firmly believe I was once a moose, what of the things I have seen in dreams, and heard."

Strive as he would to hide it, a growing anxiety was manifest, but Li Wan, groping after the words with which to paint the picture, took no heed.

"I see a snow-tramped space among the trees," she began, "and across the snow the sign of a man where he has dragged himself heavily on hand and knee. And I see, too, the man in the snow, and it seems I am very close to him when I look. He is unlike real men, for he has hair on his face, much hair, and the hair of his face and head is yellow like the summer coat of the weasel. His eyes are closed, but they open and search about. They are blue like the sky, and look into mine and search no more. And his hand moves, slow, as from weakness, and I feel ..."

"Ay," Canim whispered hoarsely. "You feel—?"

"No! no!" she cried in haste. "I feel nothing. Did I say 'feel'? I did not mean it. It could not be that I should mean it. I see, and I see only, and that is all I see—a man in the snow, with eyes like the sky, and hair like the weasel. I have seen it many times, and always it is the same—a man in the snow—"

"And do you see yourself?" he asked, leaning forward and regarding her intently. "Do you ever see yourself and the man in the snow?"

"Why should I see myself? Am I not real?"

His muscles relaxed and he sank back, an exultant satisfaction in his eyes which he turned from her so that she might not see.

"I will tell you, Li Wan," he spoke decisively; "you were a little bird in some life before, a little moose-bird, when you saw this thing, and the memory of it is with you yet. It is not strange. I was once a moose, and my father's father afterward became a bear—so said the shaman, and the shaman cannot lie. Thus, on the Trail of the Gods we pass from life to life, and the gods know only and understand. Dreams and the shadows of dreams be memories, nothing more, and the dog, whining asleep in the sun-warmth, doubtless sees and remembers things gone before. Bash, there, was a warrior once. I do firmly believe he was once a warrior."

Canim tossed a bone to the brute and got upon his feet. "Come, let us begone. The sun is yet hot, but it will get no cooler."

"And these white people, what are they like?" Li Wan made bold to ask.

"Like you and me," he answered, "only they are less dark of skin. You will be among them ere the day is dead."

Canim lashed the sleeping-robe to his one-hundred-and-fifty-pound pack, smeared his face with wet clay, and sat down to rest till Li Wan had finished loading the dogs. Olo cringed at sight of the club in her hand, and gave no trouble when the bundle of forty pounds and odd was strapped upon him. But Bash was aggrieved and truculent, and could not forbear to whimper and snarl as he was forced to receive the burden. He bristled his back and bared his teeth as she drew the straps tight, the while throwing all the malignancy of his nature into the glances shot at her sideways and backward. And Canim chuckled and said, "Did I not say he was once a very great warrior?"

"These furs will bring a price," he remarked as he adjusted his head-strap and lifted his pack clear of the ground. "A big price. The white men pay well for such goods, for they have no time to hunt and are soft to the cold. Soon shall we feast, Li Wan, as you have feasted never in all the lives you have lived before."

She grunted acknowledgment and gratitude for her lord's condescension, slipped into the harness, and bent forward to the load.

"The next time I am born, I would be born a white man," he added, and swung off down the trail which dived into the gorge at his feet.

The dogs followed close at his heels, and Li Wan brought up the rear. But her thoughts were far away, across the Ice Mountains to the east, to the little corner of the earth where her childhood had been lived. Ever as a child, she remembered, she had been looked upon as strange, as one with an affliction. Truly she had dreamed awake and been scolded and beaten for the remarkable visions she saw, till, after a time, she had outgrown them. But not utterly. Though they troubled her no more waking, they came to her in her sleep, grown woman that she was, and many a night of nightmare was hers, filled with fluttering shapes, vague and meaningless. The talk with Canim had excited her, and down all the twisted slant of the divide she harked back to the mocking fantasies of her dreams.

"Let us take breath," Canim said, when they had tapped midway the bed of the main creek.

He rested his pack on a jutting rock, slipped the head-strap, and sat down. Li Wan joined him, and the dogs sprawled panting on the ground beside them. At their feet rippled the glacial drip of the hills, but it was muddy and discolored, as if soiled by some commotion of the earth.

"Why is this?" Li Wan asked.

"Because of the white men who work in the ground. Listen!" He held up his hand, and they heard the ring of pick and shovel, and the sound of men's voices. "They are made mad by gold, and work without ceasing that they may find it. Gold? It is yellow and comes from the ground, and is considered of great value. It is also a measure of price."

But Li Wan's roving eyes had called her attention from him. A few yards below and partly screened by a clump of young spruce, the tiered logs of a

124

cabin rose to meet its overhanging roof of dirt. A thrill ran through her, and all her dream-phantoms roused up and stirred about uneasily.

"Canim," she whispered in an agony of apprehension. "Canim, what is that?"

"The white man's teepee, in which he eats and sleeps."

She eyed it wistfully, grasping its virtues at a glance and thrilling again at the unaccountable sensations it aroused. "It must be very warm in time of frost," she said aloud, though she felt that she must make strange sounds with her lips.

She felt impelled to utter them, but did not, and the next instant Canim said, "It is called a cabin."

Her heart gave a great leap. The sounds! the very sounds! She looked about her in sudden awe. How should she know that strange word before ever she heard it? What could be the matter? And then with a shock, half of fear and half of delight, she realized that for the first time in her life there had been sanity and significance in the promptings of her dreams.

"Cabin" she repeated to herself. "Cabin." An incoherent flood of dream-stuff welled up and up till her head was dizzy and her heart seemed bursting. Shadows, and looming bulks of things, and unintelligible associations fluttered and whirled about, and she strove vainly with her consciousness to grasp and hold them. For she felt that there, in that welter of memories, was the key of the mystery; could she but grasp and hold it, all would be clear and plain—

O Canim! O Pow-Wah-Kaan! O shades and shadows, what was that?

She turned to Canim, speechless and trembling, the dream-stuff in mad, overwhelming riot. She was sick and fainting, and could only listen to the ravishing sounds which proceeded from the cabin in a wonderful rhythm.

"Hum, fiddle," Canim vouchsafed.

But she did not hear him, for in the ecstasy she was experiencing, it seemed at last that all things were coming clear. Now! now! she thought. A sudden moisture swept into her eyes, and the tears trickled down her cheeks. The mystery was unlocking, but the faintness was overpowering her. If only she could hold herself long enough! If only—but the landscape bent and crumpled up, and the hills swayed back and forth across the sky as she sprang upright and screamed, "Daddy! Daddy!" Then the sun reeled, and darkness smote her, and she pitched forward limp and headlong among the rocks.

Canim looked to see if her neck had been broken by the heavy pack, grunted his satisfaction, and threw water upon her from the creek. She came to slowly, with choking sobs, and sat up.

"It is not good, the hot sun on the head," he ventured.

And she answered, "No, it is not good, and the pack bore upon me hard."

"We shall camp early, so that you may sleep long and win strength," he said gently. "And if we go now, we shall be the quicker to bed."

Li Wan said nothing, but tottered to her feet in obedience and stirred up the dogs. She took the swing of his pace mechanically, and followed him past the cabin, scarce daring to breathe. But no sounds issued forth, though the door was open and smoke curling upward from the sheet-iron stovepipe.

They came upon a man in the bend of the creek, white of skin and blue of eye, and for a moment Li Wan saw the other man in the snow. But she saw dimly, for she was weak and tired from what she had undergone. Still, she looked at him curiously, and stopped with Canim to watch him at his work. He was washing gravel in a large pan, with a circular, tilting movement; and as they looked, giving a deft flirt, he flashed up the yellow gold in a broad streak across the bottom of the pan.

"Very rich, this creek," Canim told her, as they went on. "Sometime I will find such a creek, and then I shall be a big man."

Cabins and men grew more plentiful, till they came to where the main portion of the creek was spread out before them. It was the scene of a vast devastation. Everywhere the earth was torn and rent as though by a Titan's struggles. Where there were no upthrown mounds of gravel, great holes and trenches yawned, and chasms where the thick rime of the earth had been peeled to bed-rock. There was no worn channel for the creek, and its waters, dammed up, diverted, flying through the air on giddy flumes, trickling into sinks and low places, and raised by huge water-wheels, were used and used again a thousand times. The hills had been stripped of their trees, and their raw sides gored and perforated by great timber-slides and prospect holes. And over all, like a monstrous race of ants, was flung an army of men—mud-covered, dirty, dishevelled men, who crawled in and out of the holes of their digging, crept like big bugs along the flumes, and toiled and sweated at the gravel-heaps which they kept in constant unrest—men, as far as the eye could see, even to the rims of the hilltops, digging, tearing, and scouring the face of nature.

Li Wan was appalled at the tremendous upheaval. "Truly, these men are mad," she said to Canim.

"Small wonder. The gold they dig after is a great thing," he replied. "It is the greatest thing in the world."

For hours they threaded the chaos of greed, Canim eagerly intent, Li Wan weak and listless. She knew she had been on the verge of disclosure, and she felt that she was still on the verge of disclosure, but the nervous strain she had undergone had tired her, and she passively waited for the thing, she knew not what, to happen. From every hand her senses snatched up and conveyed to her innumerable impressions, each of which became a dull excitation to her jaded imagination. Somewhere within her, responsive notes were answering to the things without, forgotten and undreamed-of correspondences were being renewed; and she was aware of it in an incurious way, and her soul was troubled, but she was not equal to the mental exultation necessary to transmute and understand. So she plodded wearily on at the heels of her lord, content to wait for that which she knew, somewhere, somehow, must happen.

After undergoing the mad bondage of man, the creek finally returned to its ancient ways, all soiled and smirched from its toil, and coiled lazily among the broad flats and timbered spaces where the valley widened to its mouth. Here the "pay" ran out, and men were loth to loiter with the lure yet beyond. And here, as Li Wan paused to prod Olo with her staff, she heard the mellow silver of a woman's laughter.

Before a cabin sat a woman, fair of skin and rosy as a child, dimpling with glee at the words of another woman in the doorway. But the woman who sat shook about her great masses of dark, wet hair which yielded up its dampness to the warm caresses of the sun.

For an instant Li Wan stood transfixed. Then she was aware of a blinding flash, and a snap, as though something gave way; and the woman before the cabin vanished, and the cabin and the tall spruce timber, and the jagged skyline, and Li Wan saw another woman, in the shine of another sun, brushing great masses of black hair, and singing as she brushed. And Li Wan heard the words of the song, and understood, and was a child again. She was smitten with a vision, wherein all the troublesome dreams merged and became one, and shapes and shadows took up their accustomed round, and all was clear and plain and real. Many pictures jostled past, strange scenes, and trees, and flowers, and people; and she saw them and knew them all.

"When you were a little bird, a little moose-bird," Canim said, his eyes upon her and burning into her.

"When I was a little moose-bird," she whispered, so faint and low he scarcely heard. And she knew she lied, as she bent her head to the strap and took the swing of the trail.

And such was the strangeness of it, the real now became unreal. The mile tramp and the pitching of camp by the edge of the stream seemed like a passage in a nightmare. She cooked the meat, fed the dogs, and unlashed the packs as in a dream, and it was not until Canim began to sketch his next wandering that she became herself again.

"The Klondike runs into the Yukon," he was saying; "a mighty river, mightier than the Mackenzie, of which you know. So we go, you and I, down to Fort o' Yukon. With dogs, in time of winter, it is twenty sleeps. Then we follow the Yukon away into the west—one hundred sleeps, two hundred—I have never heard. It is very far. And then we come to the sea. You know nothing of the sea, so let me tell you. As the lake is to the island, so the sea is to the land; all the rivers run to it, and it is without end. I have seen it at Hudson Bay; I have yet to see it in Alaska. And then we may take a great canoe upon the sea, you and I, Li Wan, or we may follow the land into the south many a hundred sleeps. And after that I do not know, save that I am Canim, the Canoe, wanderer and far-journeyer over the earth!"

She sat and listened, and fear ate into her heart as she pondered over this plunge into the illimitable wilderness. "It is a weary way," was all she said, head bowed on knee in resignation.

Then it was a splendid thought came to her, and at the wonder of it she was all aglow. She went down to the stream and washed the dried clay from her face. When the ripples died away, she stared long at her mirrored features; but sun and weather-beat had done their work, and, what of roughness and bronze, her skin was not soft and dimpled as a child's. But the thought was still splendid and the glow unabated as she crept in beside her husband under the sleeping-robe.

She lay awake, staring up at the blue of the sky and waiting for Canim to sink into the first deep sleep. When this came about, she wormed slowly and carefully away, tucked the robe around him, and stood up. At her second step, Bash growled savagely. She whispered persuasively to him and glanced at the man. Canim was snoring profoundly. Then she turned, and with swift, noiseless feet sped up the back trail.

Mrs. Evelyn Van Wyck was just preparing for bed. Bored by the duties put upon her by society, her wealth, and widowed blessedness, she had journeyed into the Northland and gone to housekeeping in a cosey cabin on the edge of the diggings. Here, aided and abetted by her friend and companion, Myrtle Giddings, she played at living close to the soil, and cultivated the primitive with refined abandon.

She strove to get away from the generations of culture and parlor selection, and sought the earth-grip her ancestors had forfeited. Likewise she induced mental states which she fondly believed to approximate those of the stone-folk, and just now, as she put up her hair for the pillow, she was indulging her fancy with a palaeolithic wooing. The details consisted principally of cave-dwellings and cracked marrow-bones, intersprinkled with fierce carnivora, hairy mammoths, and combats with rude flaked knives of flint; but the sensations were delicious. And as Evelyn Van Wyck fled through the sombre forest aisles before the too arduous advances of her slant-browed, skin-clad wooer, the door of the cabin opened, without the courtesy of a knock, and a skin-clad woman, savage and primitive, came in.

"Mercy!"

With a leap that would have done credit to a cave-woman, Miss Giddings landed in safety behind the table. But Mrs. Van Wyck held her ground. She noticed that the intruder was laboring under a strong excitement, and cast a swift glance backward to assure herself that the way was clear to the bunk, where the big Colt's revolver lay beneath a pillow.

"Greeting, O Woman of the Wondrous Hair," said Li Wan.

But she said it in her own tongue, the tongue spoken in but a little corner of the earth, and the women did not understand.

"Shall I go for help?" Miss Giddings quavered.

"The poor creature is harmless, I think," Mrs. Van Wyck replied. "And just look at her skin-clothes, ragged and trail-worn and all that. They are certainly unique. I shall buy them for my collection. Get my sack, Myrtle, please, and set up the scales."

Li Wan followed the shaping of the lips, but the words were unintelligible, and then, and for the first time, she realized, in a moment of suspense and indecision, that there was no medium of communication between them.

And at the passion of her dumbness she cried out, with arms stretched wide apart, "O Woman, thou art sister of mine!"

The tears coursed down her cheeks as she yearned toward them, and the break in her voice carried the sorrow she could not utter. But Miss Giddings was trembling, and even Mrs. Van Wyck was disturbed.

"I would live as you live. Thy ways are my ways, and our ways be one. My husband is Canim, the Canoe, and he is big and strange, and I am afraid. His trail is all the world and never ends, and I am weary. My mother was like you, and her hair was as thine, and her eyes. And life was soft to me then, and the sun warm."

She knelt humbly, and bent her head at Mrs. Van Wyck's feet. But Mrs. Van Wyck drew away, frightened at her vehemence.

Li Wan stood up, panting for speech. Her dumb lips could not articulate her overmastering consciousness of kind.

"Trade? you trade?" Mrs. Van Wyck questioned, slipping, after the fashion of the superior peoples, into pigeon tongue.

She touched Li Wan's ragged skins to indicate her choice, and poured several hundreds of gold into the blower. She stirred the dust about and trickled its yellow lustre temptingly through her fingers. But Li Wan saw only the fingers, milk-white and shapely, tapering daintily to the rosy, jewel-like nails. She placed her own hand alongside, all work-worn and calloused, and wept.

Mrs. Van Wyck misunderstood. "Gold," she encouraged. "Good gold! You trade? You changee for changee?" And she laid her hand again on Li Wan's skin garments.

"How much? You sell? How much?" she persisted, running her hand against the way of the hair so that she might make sure of the sinew-thread seam.

But Li Wan was deaf as well, and the woman's speech was without significance. Dismay at her failure sat upon her. How could she identify herself with these women? For she knew they were of the one breed, blood-sisters among men and the women of men. Her eyes roved wildly about the interior, taking in the soft draperies hanging around, the feminine garments, the oval mirror, and the dainty toilet accessories beneath. And the things haunted her, for she had seen like things before; and as she looked at them her lips involuntarily formed sounds which her throat trembled to utter. Then a thought flashed upon her, and she steadied herself. She must be calm. She must control herself, for there must be no misunderstanding this time, or else,—and she shook with a storm of suppressed tears and steadied herself again.

She put her hand on the table. "Table," she clearly and distinctly enunciated. "Table," she repeated.

She looked at Mrs. Van Wyck, who nodded approbation. Li Wan exulted, but brought her will to bear and held herself steady. "Stove" she went on. "Stove."

And at every nod of Mrs. Van Wyck, Li Wan's excitement mounted. Now stumbling and halting, and again in feverish haste, as the recrudescence of forgotten words was fast or slow, she moved about the cabin, naming article after article. And when she paused finally, it was in triumph, with body erect and head thrown back, expectant, waiting.

"Cat," Mrs. Van Wyck, laughing, spelled out in kindergarten fashion. "I—see—the—cat—catch—the—rat."

Li Wan nodded her head seriously. They were beginning to understand her at last, these women. The blood flushed darkly under her bronze at the thought, and she smiled and nodded her head still more vigorously.

Mrs. Van Wyck turned to her companion. "Received a smattering of mission education somewhere, I fancy, and has come to show it off."

"Of course," Miss Giddings tittered. "Little fool! We shall lose our sleep with her vanity."

"All the same I want that jacket. If it is old, the workmanship is good—a most excellent specimen." She returned to her visitor. "Changee for changee? You! Changee for changee? How much? Eh? How much, you?"

"Perhaps she'd prefer a dress or something," Miss Giddings suggested.

Mrs. Van Wyck went up to Li Wan and made signs that she would exchange her wrapper for the jacket. And to further the transaction, she took Li Wan's hand and placed it amid the lace and ribbons of the flowing bosom, and rubbed the fingers back and forth so they might feel the texture. But the jewelled butterfly which loosely held the fold in place was insecurely fastened, and the front of the gown slipped to the side, exposing a firm white breast, which had never known the lip-clasp of a child.

Mrs. Van Wyck coolly repaired the mischief; but Li Wan uttered a loud cry, and ripped and tore at her skin-shirt till her own breast showed firm and white as Evelyn Van Wyck's. Murmuring inarticulately and making swift signs, she strove to establish the kinship.

"A half-breed," Mrs. Van Wyck commented. "I thought so from her hair."

Miss Giddings made a fastidious gesture. "Proud of her father's white skin. It's beastly! Do give her something, Evelyn, and make her go."

But the other woman sighed. "Poor creature, I wish I could do something for her."

A heavy foot crunched the gravel without. Then the cabin door swung wide, and Canim stalked in. Miss Giddings saw a vision of sudden death, and screamed; but Mrs. Van Wyck faced him composedly.

"What do you want?" she demanded.

"How do?" Canim answered suavely and directly, pointing at the same time to Li Wan. "Um my wife."

He reached out for her, but she waved him back.

"Speak, Canim! Tell them that I am—"

"Daughter of Pow-Wah-Kaan? Nay, of what is it to them that they should care? Better should I tell them thou art an ill wife, given to creeping from thy husband's bed when sleep is heavy in his eyes."

Again he reached out for her, but she fled away from him to Mrs. Van Wyck, at whose feet she made frenzied appeal, and whose knees she tried to clasp. But the lady stepped back and gave permission with her eyes to Canim. He gripped Li Wan under the shoulders and raised her to her feet. She fought with him, in a madness of despair, till his chest was heaving with the exertion, and they had reeled about over half the room.

"Let me go, Canim," she sobbed.

But he twisted her wrist till she ceased to struggle. "The memories of the little moose-bird are overstrong and make trouble," he began.

"I know! I know!" she broke in. "I see the man in the snow, and as never before I see him crawl on hand and knee. And I, who am a little child, am carried on his back. And this is before Pow-Wah-Kaan and the time I came to live in a little corner of the earth."

"You know," he answered, forcing her toward the door; "but you will go with me down the Yukon and forget."

"Never shall I forget! So long as my skin is white shall I remember!" She clutched frantically at the door-post and looked a last appeal to Mrs. Evelyn Van Wyck.

"Then will I teach thee to forget, I, Canim, the Canoe!"

As he spoke he pulled her fingers clear and passed out with her upon the trail.

THE LEAGUE OF THE OLD MEN

At the Barracks a man was being tried for his life. He was an old man, a native from the Whitefish River, which empties into the Yukon below Lake Le Barge. All Dawson was wrought up over the affair, and likewise the Yukon-dwellers for a thousand miles up and down. It has been the custom of the land-robbing and sea-robbing Anglo-Saxon to give the law to conquered peoples, and ofttimes this law is harsh. But in the case of Imber the law for once seemed inadequate and weak. In the mathematical nature of things, equity did not reside in the punishment to be accorded him. The punishment was a foregone conclusion, there could be no doubt of that; and though it was capital, Imber had but one life, while the tale against him was one of scores.

In fact, the blood of so many was upon his hands that the killings attributed to him did not permit of precise enumeration. Smoking a pipe by the trail-side or lounging around the stove, men made rough estimates of the numbers that had perished at his hand. They had been whites, all of them, these poor murdered people, and they had been slain singly, in pairs, and in parties. And so purposeless and wanton had been these killings, that they had long been a mystery to the mounted police, even in the time of the captains, and later, when the creeks realized, and a governor came from the Dominion to make the land pay for its prosperity.

But more mysterious still was the coming of Imber to Dawson to give himself up. It was in the late spring, when the Yukon was growling and writhing under its ice, that the old Indian climbed painfully up the bank from the river trail and stood blinking on the main street. Men who had witnessed his advent, noted that he was weak and tottery, and that he staggered over to a heap of cabin-logs and sat down. He sat there a full day, staring straight before him at the unceasing tide of white men that flooded past. Many a head jerked curiously to the side to meet his stare, and more than one remark was dropped anent the old Siwash with so strange a look upon his face. No end of men remembered afterward that they had been struck by his extraordinary figure, and forever afterward prided themselves upon their swift discernment of the unusual.

But it remained for Dickensen, Little Dickensen, to be the hero of the occasion. Little Dickensen had come into the land with great dreams and a pocketful of cash; but with the cash the dreams vanished, and to earn his passage back to the States he had accepted a clerical position with the brokerage firm of Holbrook and Mason. Across the street from the office of Holbrook and Mason was the heap of cabin-logs upon which Imber sat. Dickensen looked out of the window at him before he went to lunch; and when he came back from lunch he looked out of the window, and the old Siwash was still there.

Dickensen continued to look out of the window, and he, too, forever afterward prided himself upon his swiftness of discernment. He was a romantic little chap, and he likened the immobile old heathen to the genius of the Siwash race, gazing calm-eyed upon the hosts of the invading Saxon. The hours swept along, but Imber did not vary his posture, did not by a hair's-breadth move a muscle; and Dickensen remembered the man who once sat upright on a sled in the main street where men passed to and fro. They thought the man was resting, but later, when they touched him, they found him stiff and cold, frozen to death in the midst of the busy street. To undouble him, that he might fit into a coffin, they had been forced to lug him to a fire and thaw him out a bit. Dickensen shivered at the recollection.

Later on, Dickensen went out on the sidewalk to smoke a cigar and cool off; and a little later Emily Travis happened along. Emily Travis was dainty and delicate and rare, and whether in London or Klondike she gowned herself as befitted the daughter of a millionnaire mining engineer. Little Dickensen deposited his cigar on an outside window ledge where he could find it again, and lifted his hat.

They chatted for ten minutes or so, when Emily Travis, glancing past Dickensen's shoulder, gave a startled little scream. Dickensen turned about to see, and was startled, too. Imber had crossed the street and was standing there, a gaunt and hungry-looking shadow, his gaze riveted upon the girl.

"What do you want?" Little Dickensen demanded, tremulously plucky.

Imber grunted and stalked up to Emily Travis. He looked her over, keenly and carefully, every square inch of her. Especially did he appear interested in her silky brown hair, and in the color of her cheek, faintly sprayed and soft, like the downy bloom of a butterfly wing. He walked around her, surveying her with the calculating eye of a man who studies the lines upon which a horse or a boat is builded. In the course of his circuit the pink shell of her ear came between his eye and the westering sun, and he stopped to contemplate its rosy transparency. Then he returned to her face and looked long and intently into her blue eyes. He grunted and laid a hand on her arm midway between the shoulder and elbow. With his other hand he lifted her forearm and doubled it back. Disgust and wonder showed in his face, and he dropped her arm with a contemptuous grunt. Then he muttered a few guttural syllables, turned his back upon her, and addressed himself to Dickensen.

Dickensen could not understand his speech, and Emily Travis laughed. Imber turned from one to the other, frowning, but both shook their heads. He was about to go away, when she called out:

"Oh, Jimmy! Come here!"

Jimmy came from the other side of the street. He was a big, hulking Indian clad in approved white-man style, with an Eldorado king's sombrero on his head. He talked with Imber, haltingly, with throaty spasms. Jimmy was a Sitkan, possessed of no more than a passing knowledge of the interior dialects.

"Him Whitefish man," he said to Emily Travis. "Me savve um talk no very much. Him want to look see chief white man."

"The Governor," suggested Dickensen.

Jimmy talked some more with the Whitefish man, and his face went grave and puzzled.

"I t'ink um want Cap'n Alexander," he explained. "Him say um kill white man, white woman, white boy, plenty kill um white people. Him want to die."

"Insane, I guess," said Dickensen.

"What you call dat?" queried Jimmy.

Dickensen thrust a finger figuratively inside his head and imparted a rotary motion thereto.

"Mebbe so, mebbe so," said Jimmy, returning to Imber, who still demanded the chief man of the white men.

A mounted policeman (unmounted for Klondike service) joined the group and heard Imber's wish repeated. He was a stalwart young fellow, broad-shouldered, deep-chested, legs cleanly built and stretched wide apart, and tall though Imber was, he towered above him by half a head. His eyes were cool, and gray, and steady, and he carried himself with the peculiar confidence of power that is bred of blood and tradition. His splendid masculinity was emphasized by his excessive boyishness,—he was a mere lad,—and his smooth cheek promised a blush as willingly as the cheek of a maid.

Imber was drawn to him at once. The fire leaped into his eyes at sight of a sabre slash that scarred his cheek. He ran a withered hand down the young fellow's leg and caressed the swelling thew. He smote the broad chest with his knuckles, and pressed and prodded the thick muscle-pads that covered the shoulders like a cuirass. The group had been added to by curious passers-by—husky miners, mountaineers, and frontiersmen, sons of the long-legged and broad-shouldered generations. Imber glanced from one to another, then he spoke aloud in the Whitefish tongue.

"What did he say?" asked Dickensen.

"Him say um all the same one man, dat p'liceman," Jimmy interpreted.

Little Dickensen was little, and what of Miss Travis, he felt sorry for having asked the question.

The policeman was sorry for him and stepped into the breach. "I fancy there may be something in his story. I'll take him up to the captain for examination. Tell him to come along with me, Jimmy."

Jimmy indulged in more throaty spasms, and Imber grunted and looked satisfied.

"But ask him what he said, Jimmy, and what he meant when he took hold of my arm."

So spoke Emily Travis, and Jimmy put the question and received the answer.

"Him say you no afraid," said Jimmy.

Emily Travis looked pleased.

"Him say you no skookum, no strong, all the same very soft like little baby. Him break you, in um two hands, to little pieces. Him t'ink much funny, very strange, how you can be mother of men so big, so strong, like dat p'liceman."

Emily Travers kept her eyes up and unfaltering, but her cheeks were sprayed with scarlet. Little Dickensen blushed and was quite embarrassed. The policeman's face blazed with his boy's blood.

"Come along, you," he said gruffly, setting his shoulder to the crowd and forcing a way.

Thus it was that Imber found his way to the Barracks, where he made full and voluntary confession, and from the precincts of which he never emerged.

Imber looked very tired. The fatigue of hopelessness and age was in his face. His shoulders drooped depressingly, and his eyes were lack-lustre. His mop of hair should have been white, but sun and weatherbeat had burned and bitten it so that it hung limp and lifeless and colorless. He took no interest in what went on around him. The courtroom was jammed with the men of the creeks and trails, and there was an ominous note in the rumble and grumble of their low-pitched voices, which came to his ears like the growl of the sea from deep caverns.

He sat close by a window, and his apathetic eyes rested now and again on the dreary scene without. The sky was overcast, and a gray drizzle was falling. It was flood-time on the Yukon. The ice was gone, and the river was up in the town. Back and forth on the main street, in canoes and poling-boats, passed the people that never rested. Often he saw these boats turn aside from the street and enter the flooded square that marked the Barracks' parade-ground. Sometimes they disappeared beneath him, and he heard them jar against the house-logs and their occupants scramble in through the window. After that came the slush of water against men's legs as they waded across the lower room and mounted the stairs. Then they appeared in the doorway, with doffed hats and dripping sea-boots, and added themselves to the waiting crowd.

And while they centred their looks on him, and in grim anticipation enjoyed the penalty he was to pay, Imber looked at them, and mused on their ways, and on their Law that never slept, but went on unceasing, in good times and bad, in flood and famine, through trouble and terror and death, and which would go on unceasing, it seemed to him, to the end of time.

A man rapped sharply on a table, and the conversation droned away into silence. Imber looked at the man. He seemed one in authority, yet Imber divined the square-browed man who sat by a desk farther back to be the one chief over them all and over the man who had rapped. Another man by the same table uprose and began to read aloud from many fine sheets of paper. At the top of each sheet he cleared his throat, at the bottom moistened his fingers. Imber did not understand his speech, but the others did, and he knew that it made them angry. Sometimes it made them very angry, and once a man cursed him, in single syllables, stinging and tense, till a man at the table rapped him to silence.

For an interminable period the man read. His monotonous, sing-song utterance lured Imber to dreaming, and he was dreaming deeply when the man ceased. A voice spoke to him in his own Whitefish tongue, and he roused up, without surprise, to look upon the face of his sister's son, a young man who had wandered away years agone to make his dwelling with the whites.

"Thou dost not remember me," he said by way of greeting.

"Nay," Imber answered. "Thou art Howkan who went away. Thy mother

140

be dead."

"She was an old woman," said Howkan.

But Imber did not hear, and Howkan, with hand upon his shoulder, roused him again.

"I shall speak to thee what the man has spoken, which is the tale of the troubles thou hast done and which thou hast told, O fool, to the Captain Alexander. And thou shalt understand and say if it be true talk or talk not true. It is so commanded."

Howkan had fallen among the mission folk and been taught by them to read and write. In his hands he held the many fine sheets from which the man had read aloud, and which had been taken down by a clerk when Imber first made confession, through the mouth of Jimmy, to Captain Alexander. Howkan began to read. Imber listened for a space, when a wonderment rose up in his face and he broke in abruptly.

"That be my talk, Howkan. Yet from thy lips it comes when thy ears have not heard."

Howkan smirked with self-appreciation. His hair was parted in the middle. "Nay, from the paper it comes, O Imber. Never have my ears heard. From the paper it comes, through my eyes, into my head, and out of my mouth to thee. Thus it comes."

"Thus it comes? It be there in the paper?" Imber's voice sank in whisperful awe as he crackled the sheets 'twixt thumb and finger and stared at the charactery scrawled thereon. "It be a great medicine, Howkan, and thou art a worker of wonders."

"It be nothing, it be nothing," the young man responded carelessly and pridefully. He read at hazard from the document: "In that year, before the break of the ice, came an old man, and a boy who was lame of one foot. These also did I kill, and the old man made much noise—"

"It be true," Imber interrupted breathlessly. "He made much noise and would not die for a long time. But how dost thou know, Howkan? The chief man of the white men told thee, mayhap? No one beheld me, and him alone have I told."

Howkan shook his head with impatience. "Have I not told thee it be there in the paper, O fool?"

Imber stared hard at the ink-scrawled surface. "As the hunter looks upon the snow and says, Here but yesterday there passed a rabbit; and here by the willow scrub it stood and listened, and heard, and was afraid; and here it turned upon its trail; and here it went with great swiftness, leaping wide; and here, with greater swiftness and wider leapings, came a lynx; and here, where the claws cut deep into the snow, the lynx made a very great leap; and here it struck, with the rabbit under and rolling belly up; and here leads off the trail of the lynx alone, and there is no more rabbit,—as the hunter looks upon the markings of the snow and says thus and so and here, dost thou, too, look upon the paper and say thus and so and here be the things old Imber hath done?"

"Even so," said Howkan. "And now do thou listen, and keep thy woman's tongue between thy teeth till thou art called upon for speech."

Thereafter, and for a long time, Howkan read to him the confession, and Imber remained musing and silent At the end, he said:

"It be my talk, and true talk, but I am grown old, Howkan, and forgotten things come back to me which were well for the head man there to know. First, there was the man who came over the Ice Mountains, with cunning traps made of iron, who sought the beaver of the Whitefish. Him I slew. And there were three men seeking gold on the Whitefish long ago. Them also I slew, and left them to the wolverines. And at the Five Fingers there was a man with a raft and much meat."

At the moments when Imber paused to remember, Howkan translated and a clerk reduced to writing. The courtroom listened stolidly to each unadorned little tragedy, till Imber told of a red-haired man whose eyes were crossed and whom he had killed with a remarkably long shot.

"Hell," said a man in the forefront of the onlookers. He said it soulfully and sorrowfully. He was red-haired. "Hell," he repeated. "That was my brother Bill." And at regular intervals throughout the session, his solemn "Hell" was heard in the courtroom; nor did his comrades check him, nor did the man at the table rap him to order.

Imber's head drooped once more, and his eyes went dull, as though a film rose up and covered them from the world. And he dreamed as only age can dream upon the colossal futility of youth.

Later, Howkan roused him again, saying: "Stand up, O Imber. It be commanded that thou tellest why you did these troubles, and slew these people, and at the end journeyed here seeking the Law."

Imber rose feebly to his feet and swayed back and forth. He began to speak in a low and faintly rumbling voice, but Howkan interrupted him.

"This old man, he is damn crazy," he said in English to the square-browed man. "His talk is foolish and like that of a child."

"We will hear his talk which is like that of a child," said the square-browed man. "And we will hear it, word for word, as he speaks it. Do you understand?"

Howkan understood, and Imber's eyes flashed, for he had witnessed the play between his sister's son and the man in authority. And then began the story, the epic of a bronze patriot which might well itself be wrought into bronze for the generations unborn. The crowd fell strangely silent, and the square-browed judge leaned head on hand and pondered his soul and the soul of his race. Only was heard the deep tones of Imber, rhythmically alternating with the shrill voice of the interpreter, and now and again, like the bell of the Lord, the wondering and meditative "Hell" of the red-haired man.

"I am Imber of the Whitefish people." So ran the interpretation of Howkan, whose inherent barbarism gripped hold of him, and who lost his mission culture and veneered civilization as he caught the savage ring and rhythm of old Imber's tale. "My father was Otsbaok, a strong man. The land was warm with sunshine and gladness when I was a boy. The people did not hunger after strange things, nor hearken to new voices, and the ways of their fathers were their ways. The women found favor in the eyes of the young men, and the young men looked upon them with content. Babes hung at the breasts of the women, and they were heavy-hipped with increase of the tribe. Men were men in those days. In peace and plenty, and in war and famine, they were men.

"At that time there was more fish in the water than now, and more meat in the forest. Our dogs were wolves, warm with thick hides and hard to the frost and storm. And as with our dogs so with us, for we were likewise hard to the frost and storm. And when the Pellys came into our land we slew them and were slain. For we were men, we Whitefish, and our fathers and our fathers' fathers had fought against the Pellys and determined the bounds of the land.

"As I say, with our dogs, so with us. And one day came the first white man. He dragged himself, so, on hand and knee, in the snow. And his skin was stretched tight, and his bones were sharp beneath. Never was such a man, we thought, and we wondered of what strange tribe he was, and of its land. And he was weak, most weak, like a little child, so that we gave him a place by the fire, and warm furs to lie upon, and we gave him food as little children are given food.

"And with him was a dog, large as three of our dogs, and very weak. The hair of this dog was short, and not warm, and the tail was frozen so that the end fell off. And this strange dog we fed, and bedded by the fire, and fought from it our dogs, which else would have killed him. And what of the moose meat and the sun-dried salmon, the man and dog took strength to themselves; and what of the strength they became big and unafraid. And the man spoke loud words and laughed at the old men and young men, and looked boldly upon the maidens. And the dog fought with our dogs, and for all of his short hair and softness slew three of them in one day.

"When we asked the man concerning his people, he said, 'I have many brothers,' and laughed in a way that was not good. And when he was in his full strength he went away, and with him went Noda, daughter to the chief. First, after that, was one of our bitches brought to pup. And never was there such a breed of dogs,—big-headed, thick-jawed, and short-haired, and helpless. Well do I remember my father, Otsbaok, a strong man. His face was black with anger at such helplessness, and he took a stone, so, and so, and there was no more helplessness. And two summers after that came Noda back to us with a man-child in the hollow of her arm.

"And that was the beginning. Came a second white man, with short-haired dogs, which he left behind him when he went. And with him went six of our strongest dogs, for which, in trade, he had given Koo-So-Tee, my mother's brother, a wonderful pistol that fired with great swiftness six times. And Koo-So-Tee was very big, what of the pistol, and laughed at our bows and arrows. 'Woman's things,' he called them, and went forth against the bald-face grizzly, with the pistol in his hand. Now it be known that it is not good to hunt the bald-face with a pistol, but how were we to know? and how was Koo-So-Tee to know? So he went against the bald-face, very brave, and fired the pistol with great swiftness six times; and the bald-face but grunted and broke in his breast like it were an egg, and like honey from a bee's nest dripped the brains of Koo-So-Tee upon the ground. He was a good hunter, and there was no one to bring meat to his squaw and children. And we were bitter, and we said, 'That which for the white men is well, is for us not well.' And this be true. There be many white men and fat, but their ways have made us few and lean.

"Came the third white man, with great wealth of all manner of wonderful foods and things. And twenty of our strongest dogs he took from us in trade. Also, what of presents and great promises, ten of our young hunters did he take with him on a journey which fared no man knew where. It is said they died in the snow of the Ice Mountains where man has never been, or in the Hills of Silence which are beyond the edge of the earth. Be that as it may, dogs and young hunters were seen never again by the Whitefish people.

"And more white men came with the years, and ever, with pay and presents, they led the young men away with them. And sometimes the young men came back with strange tales of dangers and toils in the lands beyond the Pellys, and sometimes they did not come back. And we said: 'If they be unafraid of life, these white men, it is because they have many lives; but we be few by the Whitefish, and the young men shall go away no more.' But the young men did go away; and the young women went also; and we were very wroth.

"It be true, we ate flour, and salt pork, and drank tea which was a great delight; only, when we could not get tea, it was very bad and we became short of speech and quick of anger. So we grew to hunger for the things the white men brought in trade. Trade! trade! all the time was it trade! One winter we sold our meat for clocks that would not go, and watches with broken guts, and files worn smooth, and pistols without cartridges and worthless. And then came famine, and we were without meat, and two score died ere the break of spring.

"'Now are we grown weak,' we said; 'and the Pellys will fall upon us, and our bounds be overthrown.' But as it fared with us, so had it fared with the Pellys, and they were too weak to come against us.

"My father, Otsbaok, a strong man, was now old and very wise. And he spoke to the chief, saying: 'Behold, our dogs be worthless. No longer are they thick-furred and strong, and they die in the frost and harness. Let us go into the village and kill them, saving only the wolf ones, and these let us tie out in the night that they may mate with the wild wolves of the forest. Thus shall we have dogs warm and strong again.'

"And his word was harkened to, and we Whitefish became known for our dogs, which were the best in the land. But known we were not for ourselves. The best of our young men and women had gone away with the white men to wander on trail and river to far places. And the young women came back old and broken, as Noda had come, or they came not at all. And the young men came back to sit by our fires for a time, full of ill speech and rough ways, drinking evil drinks and gambling through long nights and days, with a great unrest always in their hearts, till the call of the white men came to them and they went away again to the unknown places. And they were without honor and respect, jeering the old-time customs and laughing in the faces of chief and shamans.

"As I say, we were become a weak breed, we Whitefish. We sold our warm skins and furs for tobacco and whiskey and thin cotton things that left us shivering in the cold. And the coughing sickness came upon us, and men and women coughed and sweated through the long nights, and the hunters on trail spat blood upon the snow. And now one, and now another, bled swiftly from the mouth and died. And the women bore few children, and those they bore were weak and given to sickness. And other sicknesses came to us from the white men, the like of which we had never known and could not understand. Smallpox, likewise measles, have I heard these sicknesses named, and we died of them as die the salmon in the still eddies when in the fall their eggs are spawned and there is no longer need for them to live.

"And yet, and here be the strangeness of it, the white men come as the breath of death; all their ways lead to death, their nostrils are filled with it; and yet they do not die. Theirs the whiskey, and tobacco, and short-haired dogs; theirs the many sicknesses, the smallpox and measles, the coughing and mouth-bleeding; theirs the white skin, and softness to the frost and storm; and theirs the pistols that shoot six times very swift and are worthless. And yet they grow fat on their many ills, and prosper, and lay a heavy hand over all the world and tread mightily upon its peoples. And their women, too, are soft as little babes, most breakable and never broken, the mothers of men. And out of all this softness, and sickness, and weakness, come strength, and power, and authority. They be gods, or devils, as the case may be. I do not know. What do I know, I, old Imber of the Whitefish? Only do I know that they are past understanding, these white men, far-wanderers and fighters over the earth that they be.

"As I say, the meat in the forest became less and less. It be true, the white man's gun is most excellent and kills a long way off; but of what worth the gun, when there is no meat to kill? When I was a boy on the Whitefish there was moose on every hill, and each year came the caribou uncountable. But now the hunter may take the trail ten days and not one moose gladden his eyes, while the caribou uncountable come no more at all. Small worth the gun, I say, killing a long way off, when there be nothing to kill.

"And I, Imber, pondered upon these things, watching the while the Whitefish, and the Pellys, and all the tribes of the land, perishing as perished the meat of the forest. Long I pondered. I talked with the shamans and the old men who were wise. I went apart that the sounds of the village might not disturb me, and I ate no meat so that my belly should not press upon me and make me slow of eye and ear. I sat long and sleepless in the forest, wide-eyed for the sign, my ears patient and keen for the word that was to come. And I wandered alone in the blackness of night to the river bank, where was wind-moaning and sobbing of water, and where I sought wisdom from the ghosts of old shamans in the trees and dead and gone.

"And in the end, as in a vision, came to me the short-haired and detestable dogs, and the way seemed plain. By the wisdom of Otsbaok, my father and a strong man, had the blood of our own wolf-dogs been kept clean, wherefore had they remained warm of hide and strong in the harness. So I returned to my village and made oration to the men. 'This be a tribe, these white men,' I said. 'A very large tribe, and doubtless there is no longer meat in their land, and they are come among us to make a new land for themselves. But they weaken us, and we die. They are a very hungry folk. Already has our meat gone from us, and it were well, if we would live, that we deal by them as we have dealt by their dogs.'

"And further oration I made, counselling fight. And the men of the Whitefish listened, and some said one thing, and some another, and some spoke of other and worthless things, and no man made brave talk of deeds and war. But while the young men were weak as water and afraid, I watched that the old men sat silent, and that in their eyes fires came and went. And later, when the village slept and no one knew, I drew the old men away into the forest and made more talk. And now we were agreed, and we remembered the good young days, and the free land, and the times of plenty, and the gladness and sunshine; and we called ourselves brothers, and swore great secrecy, and a mighty oath to cleanse the land of the evil breed that had come upon it. It be plain we were fools, but how were we to know, we old men of the Whitefish?

"And to hearten the others, I did the first deed. I kept guard upon the Yukon till the first canoe came down. In it were two white men, and when I stood upright upon the bank and raised my hand they changed their course and drove in to me. And as the man in the bow lifted his head, so, that he

148

might know wherefore I wanted him, my arrow sang through the air straight to his throat, and he knew. The second man, who held paddle in the stern, had his rifle half to his shoulder when the first of my three spear-casts smote him.

"'These be the first,' I said, when the old men had gathered to me. 'Later we will bind together all the old men of all the tribes, and after that the young men who remain strong, and the work will become easy.'

"And then the two dead white men we cast into the river. And of the canoe, which was a very good canoe, we made a fire, and a fire, also, of the things within the canoe. But first we looked at the things, and they were pouches of leather which we cut open with our knives. And inside these pouches were many papers, like that from which thou hast read, O Howkan, with markings on them which we marvelled at and could not understand. Now, I am become wise, and I know them for the speech of men as thou hast told me."

A whisper and buzz went around the courtroom when Howkan finished interpreting the affair of the canoe, and one man's voice spoke up: "That was the lost '91 mail, Peter James and Delaney bringing it in and last spoken at Le Barge by Matthews going out." The clerk scratched steadily away, and another paragraph was added to the history of the North.

"There be little more," Imber went on slowly. "It be there on the paper, the things we did. We were old men, and we did not understand. Even I, Imber, do not now understand. Secretly we slew, and continued to slay, for with our years we were crafty and we had learned the swiftness of going without haste. When white men came among us with black looks and rough words, and took away six of the young men with irons binding them helpless, we knew we must slay wider and farther. And one by one we old men departed up river and down to the unknown lands. It was a brave thing. Old we were, and unafraid, but the fear of far places is a terrible fear to men who are old.

"So we slew, without haste and craftily. On the Chilcoot and in the Delta we slew, from the passes to the sea, wherever the white men camped or broke their trails. It be true, they died, but it was without worth. Ever did they come over the mountains, ever did they grow and grow, while we, being old, became less and less. I remember, by the Caribou Crossing, the camp of a white man. He was a very little white man, and three of the old men came upon him in his sleep. And the next day I came upon the four of them. The white man alone still breathed, and there was breath in him to curse me once and well before he died.

"And so it went, now one old man, and now another. Sometimes the word reached us long after of how they died, and sometimes it did not reach us. And the old men of the other tribes were weak and afraid, and would not join with us. As I say, one by one, till I alone was left. I am Imber, of the Whitefish people. My father was Otsbaok, a strong man. There are no Whitefish now. Of the old men I am the last. The young men and young women are gone away, some to live with the Pellys, some with the Salmons, and more with the white men. I am very old, and very tired, and it being vain fighting the Law, as thou sayest, Howkan, I am come seeking the Law."

"O Imber, thou art indeed a fool," said Howkan.

But Imber was dreaming. The square-browed judge likewise dreamed, and all his race rose up before him in a mighty phantasmagoria—his steel-shod, mail-clad race, the lawgiver and world-maker among the families of men. He saw it dawn red-flickering across the dark forests and sullen seas; he saw it blaze, bloody and red, to full and triumphant noon; and down the shaded slope he saw the blood-red sands dropping into night. And through it all he observed the Law, pitiless and potent, ever unswerving and ever ordaining, greater than the motes of men who fulfilled it or were crushed by it, even as it was greater than he, his heart speaking for softness.

THE CRUISE OF THE DAZZLER

PART I

CHAPTER I. BROTHER AND SISTER

They ran across the shining sand, the Pacific thundering its long surge at their backs, and when they gained the roadway leaped upon bicycles and dived at faster pace into the green avenues of the park. There were three of them, three boys, in as many bright-colored sweaters, and they "scorched" along the cycle-path as dangerously near the speed-limit as is the custom of boys in bright-colored sweaters to go. They may have exceeded the speed-limit. A mounted park policeman thought so, but was not sure, and contented himself with cautioning them as they flashed by. They acknowledged the warning promptly, and on the next turn of the path as promptly forgot it, which is also a custom of boys in bright-colored sweaters.

Shooting out through the entrance to Golden Gate Park, they turned into San Francisco, and took the long sweep of the descending hills at a rate that caused pedestrians to turn and watch them anxiously. Through the city streets the bright sweaters flew, turning and twisting to escape climbing the steeper hills, and, when the steep hills were unavoidable, doing stunts to see which would first gain the top.

The boy who more often hit up the pace, led the scorching, and instituted the stunts was called Joe by his companions. It was "follow the leader," and he led, the merriest and boldest in the bunch. But as they pedaled into the Western Addition, among the large and comfortable residences, his laughter became less loud and frequent, and he unconsciously lagged in the rear. At Laguna and Vallejo streets his companions turned off to the right.

"So long, Fred," he called as he turned his wheel to the left. "So long, Charley."

"See you to-night!" they called back.

"No—I can't come," he answered.

"Aw, come on," they begged.

"No, I've got to dig.—So long!"

As he went on alone, his face grew grave and a vague worry came into his eyes. He began resolutely to whistle, but this dwindled away till it was a thin and very subdued little sound, which ceased altogether as he rode up the driveway to a large two-storied house.

"Oh, Joe!"

He hesitated before the door to the library. Bessie was there, he knew, studiously working up her lessons. She must be nearly through with them, too, for she was always done before dinner, and dinner could not be many minutes away. As for his lessons, they were as yet untouched. The thought made him angry. It was bad enough to have one's sister—and two years younger at that—in the same grade, but to have her continually head and shoulders above him in scholarship was a most intolerable thing. Not that he was dull. No one knew better than himself that he was not dull. But somehow—he did not quite know how—his mind was on other things and he was usually unprepared.

"Joe—please come here." There was the slightest possible plaintive note in her voice this time.

"Well?" he said, thrusting aside the portière with an impetuous movement.

He said it gruffly, but he was half sorry for it the next instant when he saw a slender little girl regarding him with wistful eyes across the big reading-table heaped with books. She was curled up, with pencil and pad, in an easy-chair of such generous dimensions that it made her seem more delicate and fragile than she really was.

"What is it, Sis?" he asked more gently, crossing over to her side.

She took his hand in hers and pressed it against her cheek, and as he stood beside her came closer to him with a nestling movement.

"What is the matter, Joe dear?" she asked softly. "Won't you tell me?"

He remained silent. It struck him as ridiculous to confess his troubles to a little sister, even if her reports were higher than his. And the little sister struck him as ridiculous to demand his troubles of him. "What a soft cheek she has!" he thought as she pressed her face gently against his hand. If he could but tear himself away—it was all so foolish! Only he might hurt her feelings, and, in his experience, girls' feelings were very easily hurt.

She opened his fingers and kissed the palm of his hand. It was like a rose-leaf falling; it was also her way of asking her question over again.

"Nothing 's the matter," he said decisively. And then, quite inconsistently, he blurted out, "Father!"

His worry was now in her eyes. "But father is so good and kind, Joe," she began. "Why don't you try to please him? He does n't ask much of you, and it 's all for your own good. It 's not as though you were a fool, like some boys. If you would only study a little bit—"

"That 's it! Lecturing!" he exploded, tearing his hand roughly away. "Even you are beginning to lecture me now. I suppose the cook and the stable-boy will be at it next."

He shoved his hands into his pockets and looked forward into a melancholy and desolate future filled with interminable lectures and lecturers innumerable.

"Was that what you wanted me for?" he demanded, turning to go.

She caught at his hand again. "No, it wasn't; only you looked so worried that I thought—I—" Her voice broke, and she began again freshly. "What I wanted to tell you was that we're planning a trip across the bay to Oakland, next Saturday, for a tramp in the hills."

"Who 's going?"

"Myrtle Hayes—"

"What! That little softy?" he interrupted.

"I don't think she is a softy," Bessie answered with spirit. "She 's one of the sweetest girls I know."

"Which is n't saying much, considering the girls you know. But go on. Who are the others?"

"Pearl Sayther, and her sister Alice, and Jessie Hilborn, and Sadie French, and Edna Crothers. That 's all the girls."

Joe sniffed disdainfully. "Who are the fellows, then?"

"Maurice and Felix Clement, Dick Schofield, Burt Layton, and—"

"That 's enough. Milk-and-water chaps, all of them."

"I—I wanted to ask you and Fred and Charley," she said in a quavering voice. "That 's what I called you in for—to ask you to come."

"And what are you going to do?" he asked.

"Walk, gather wild flowers,—the poppies are all out now,—eat luncheon at some nice place, and—and—"

"Come home," he finished for her.

Bessie nodded her head. Joe put his hands in his pockets again, and walked up and down.

"A sissy outfit, that 's what it is," he said abruptly; "and a sissy program. None of it in mine, please."

She tightened her trembling lips and struggled on bravely. "What would you rather do?" she asked.

"I 'd sooner take Fred and Charley and go off somewhere and do something—well, anything."

He paused and looked at her. She was waiting patiently for him to proceed. He was aware of his inability to express in words what he felt and wanted, and all his trouble and general dissatisfaction rose up and gripped hold of him.

"Oh, you can't understand!" he burst out. "You can't understand. You 're a girl. You like to be prim and neat, and to be good in deportment and ahead in your studies. You don't care for danger and adventure and such things, and you don't care for boys who are rough, and have life and go in them, and all that. You like good little boys in white collars, with clothes always clean and hair always combed, who like to stay in at recess and be petted by the teacher and told how they're always up in their studies; nice little boys who never get into scrapes—who are too busy walking around and picking flowers and eating lunches with girls, to get into scrapes. Oh, I know the kind—afraid of their own shadows, and no more spunk in them than in so many sheep. That 's what they are—sheep. Well, I 'm not a sheep, and there 's no more to be said. And I don't want to go on your picnic, and, what 's more, I 'm not going."

The tears welled up in Bessie's brown eyes, and her lips were trembling. This angered him unreasonably. What were girls good for, anyway?—always blubbering, and interfering, and carrying on. There was no sense in them.

"A fellow can't say anything without making you cry," he began, trying to appease her. "Why, I did n't mean anything, Sis. I did n't, sure. I—"

He paused helplessly and looked down at her. She was sobbing, and at the same time shaking with the effort to control her sobs, while big tears were rolling down her cheeks.

"Oh, you—you girls!" he cried, and strode wrathfully out of the room.

CHAPTER II. "THE DRACONIAN REFORMS"

A few minutes later, and still wrathful, Joe went in to dinner. He ate silently, though his father and mother and Bessie kept up a genial flow of conversation. There she was, he communed savagely with his plate, crying one minute, and the next all smiles and laughter. Now that was n't his way. If he had anything sufficiently important to cry about, rest assured he would n't get over it for days. Girls were hypocrites, that was all there was to it. They did n't feel one hundredth part of all that they said when they cried. It stood to reason that they did n't. It must be that they just carried on because they enjoyed it. It made them feel good to make other people miserable, especially boys. That was why they were always interfering.

Thus reflecting sagely, he kept his eyes on his plate and did justice to the fare; for one cannot scorch from the Cliff House to the Western Addition via the park without being guilty of a healthy appetite.

Now and then his father directed a glance at him in a certain mildly anxious way. Joe did not see these glances, but Bessie saw them, every one. Mr. Bronson was a middle-aged man, well developed and of heavy build, though not fat. His was a rugged face, square-jawed and stern-featured, though his eyes were kindly and there were lines about the mouth that betokened laughter rather than severity. A close examination was not required to discover the resemblance between him and Joe. The same broad forehead and strong jaw characterized them both, and the eyes, taking into consideration the difference of age, were as like as peas from one pod.

"How are you getting on, Joe?" Mr. Bronson asked finally. Dinner was over and they were about to leave the table.

"Oh, I don't know," Joe answered carelessly, and then added: "We have examinations to-morrow. I'll know then."

"Whither bound?" his mother questioned, as he turned to leave the room. She was a slender, willowy woman, whose brown eyes Bessie's were, and likewise her tender ways.

"To my room," Joe answered. "To work," he supplemented.

She rumpled his hair affectionately, and bent and kissed him. Mr. Bronson smiled approval at him as he went out, and he hurried up the stairs, resolved to dig hard and pass the examinations of the coming day.

Entering his room, he locked the door and sat down at a desk most comfortably arranged for a boy's study. He ran his eye over his text-books. The history examination came the first thing in the morning, so he would begin on that. He opened the book where a page was turned down, and began to read:

Shortly after the Draconian reforms, a war broke out between Athens and Megara respecting the island of Salamis, to which both cities laid claim.

That was easy; but what were the Draconian reforms? He must look them up. He felt quite studious as he ran over the back pages, till he chanced to raise his eyes above the top of the book and saw on a chair a baseball mask and a catcher's glove. They should n't have lost that game last Saturday, he thought, and they would n't have, either, if it had n't been for Fred. He wished Fred would n't fumble so. He could hold a hundred difficult balls in succession, but when a critical point came, he 'd let go of even a dewdrop. He 'd have to send him out in the field and bring in Jones to first base. Only Jones was so excitable. He could hold any kind of a ball, no matter how critical the play was, but there was no telling what he would do with the ball after he got it.

Joe came to himself with a start. A pretty way of studying history! He buried his head in his book and began:

Shortly after the Draconian reforms—

He read the sentence through three times, and then recollected that he had not looked up the Draconian reforms.

A knock came at the door. He turned the pages over with a noisy flutter, but made no answer.

The knock was repeated, and Bessie's "Joe, dear" came to his ears.

"What do you want?" he demanded. But before she could answer he hurried on: "No admittance. I 'm busy."

"I came to see if I could help you," she pleaded. "I 'm all done, and I thought—"

"Of course you 're all done!" he shouted. "You always are!"

He held his head in both his hands to keep his eyes on the book. But the baseball mask bothered him. The more he attempted to keep his mind on the history the more in his mind's eye he saw the mask resting on the chair and all the games in which it had played its part.

This would never do. He deliberately placed the book face downward on the desk and walked over to the chair. With a swift sweep he sent both mask and glove hurtling under the bed, and so violently that he heard the mask rebound from the wall.

Shortly after the Draconian reforms, a war broke out between Athens and Megara—

The mask had rolled back from the wall. He wondered if it had rolled back far enough for him to see it. No, he would n't look. What did it matter if it had rolled out? That was n't history. He wondered—

He peered over the top of the book, and there was the mask peeping out at him from under the edge of the bed. This was not to be borne. There was no use attempting to study while that mask was around. He went over and fished it out, crossed the room to the closet, and tossed it inside, then locked the door. That was settled, thank goodness! Now he could do some work.

He sat down again.

Shortly after the Draconian reforms, a war broke out between Athens and Megara respecting the island of Salamis, to which, both cities laid claim.

Which was all very well, if he had only found out what the Draconian reforms were. A soft glow pervaded the room, and he suddenly became aware of it. What could cause it? He looked out of the window. The setting sun was slanting its long rays against low-hanging masses of summer clouds, turning them to warm scarlet and rosy red; and it was from them that the red light, mellow and glowing, was flung earthward.

His gaze dropped from the clouds to the bay beneath. The sea-breeze was dying down with the day, and off Fort Point a fishing-boat was creeping into port before the last light breeze. A little beyond, a tug was sending up a twisted pillar of smoke as it towed a three-masted schooner to sea. His eyes wandered over toward the Marin County shore. The line where land and water met was already in darkness, and long shadows were creeping up the hills toward Mount Tamalpais, which was sharply silhouetted against the western sky.

Oh, if he, Joe Bronson, were only on that fishing-boat and sailing in with a deep-sea catch! Or if he were on that schooner, heading out into the sunset, into the world! That was life, that was living, doing something and being something in the world. And, instead, here he was, pent up in a close room, racking his brains about people dead and gone thousands of years before he was born.

He jerked himself away from the window as though held there by some physical force, and resolutely carried his chair and history into the farthest corner of the room, where he sat down with his back to the window.

An instant later, so it seemed to him, he found himself again staring out of the window and dreaming. How he had got there he did not know. His last recollection was the finding of a subheading on a page on the right-hand side of the book which read: "The Laws and Constitution of Draco." And then, evidently like walking in one's sleep, he had come to the window. How long had he been there? he wondered. The fishing-boat which he had seen off Fort Point was now crawling into Meiggs's Wharf. This denoted nearly an hour's lapse of time. The sun had long since set; a solemn grayness was brooding over the water, and the first faint stars were beginning to twinkle over the crest of Mount Tamalpais.

He turned, with a sigh, to go back into his corner, when a long whistle, shrill and piercing, came to his ears. That was Fred. He sighed again. The whistle repeated itself. Then another whistle joined it. That was Charley. They were waiting on the corner—lucky fellows!

Well, they would n't see him this night. Both whistles arose in duet. He writhed in his chair and groaned. No, they would n't see him this night, he reiterated, at the same time rising to his feet. It was certainly impossible for him to join them when he had not yet learned about the Draconian reforms. The same force which had held him to the window now seemed drawing him across the room to the desk. It made him put the history on top of his school-books, and he had the door unlocked and was half-way into the hall before he realized it. He started to return, but the thought came to him that he could go out for a little while and then come back and do his work.

A very little while, he promised himself, as he went down-stairs. He went down faster and faster, till at the bottom he was going three steps at a time. He popped his cap on his head and went out of the side entrance in a rush; and ere he reached the corner the reforms of Draco were as far away in the past as Draco himself, while the examinations on the morrow were equally far away in the future.

CHAPTER III. "BRICK," "SORREL-TOP," AND "REDDY"

"What 's up?" Joe asked, as he joined Fred and Charley.

"Kites," Charley answered. "Come on. We 're tired out waiting for you."

The three set off down the street to the brow of the hill, where they looked down upon Union Street, far below and almost under their feet. This they called the Pit, and it was well named. Themselves they called the Hill-dwellers, and a descent into the Pit by the Hill-dwellers was looked upon by them as a great adventure.

Scientific kite-flying was one of the keenest pleasures of these three particular Hill-dwellers, and six or eight kites strung out on a mile of twine and soaring into the clouds was an ordinary achievement for them. They were compelled to replenish their kite-supply often; for whenever an accident occurred, and the string broke, or a ducking kite dragged down the rest, or the wind suddenly died out, their kites fell into the Pit, from which place they were unrecoverable. The reason for this was the young people of the Pit were a piratical and robber race with peculiar ideas of ownership and property rights.

On a day following an accident to a kite of one of the Hill-dwellers, the self-same kite could be seen riding the air attached to a string which led down into the Pit to the lairs of the Pit People. So it came about that the Pit People, who were a poor folk and unable to afford scientific kite-flying, developed great proficiency in the art when their neighbors the Hill-dwellers took it up.

There was also an old sailorman who profited by this recreation of the Hill-dwellers; for he was learned in sails and air-currents, and being deft of hand and cunning, he fashioned the best-flying kites that could be obtained. He lived in a rattletrap shanty close to the water, where he could still watch with dim eyes the ebb and flow of the tide, and the ships pass out and in, and where he could revive old memories of the days when he, too, went down to the sea in ships.

To reach his shanty from the Hill one had to pass through the Pit, and thither the three boys were bound. They had often gone for kites in the daytime, but this was their first trip after dark, and they felt it to be, as it indeed was, a hazardous adventure.

In simple words, the Pit was merely the cramped and narrow quarters of the poor, where many nationalities crowded together in cosmopolitan confusion, and lived as best they could, amid much dirt and squalor. It was still early evening when the boys passed through on their way to the sailorman's shanty, and no mishap befell them, though some of the Pit boys stared at them savagely and hurled a taunting remark after them, now and then.

The sailorman made kites which were not only splendid fliers but which folded up and were very convenient to carry. Each of the boys bought a few, and, with them wrapped in compact bundles and under their arms, started back on the return journey.

"Keep a sharp lookout for the b'ys," the kite-maker cautioned them. "They 're like to be cruisin' round after dark."

"We 're not afraid," Charley assured him; "and we know how to take care of ourselves."

Used to the broad and quiet streets of the Hill, the boys were shocked and stunned by the life that teemed in the close-packed quarter. It seemed some thick and monstrous growth of vegetation, and that they were wading through it. They shrank closely together in the tangle of narrow streets as though for protection, conscious of the strangeness of it all, and how unrelated they were to it.

Children and babies sprawled on the sidewalk and under their feet. Bareheaded and unkempt women gossiped in the doorways or passed back and forth with scant marketings in their arms. There was a general odor of decaying fruit and fish, a smell of staleness and putridity. Big hulking men slouched by, and ragged little girls walked gingerly through the confusion with foaming buckets of beer in their hands. There was a clatter and garble of foreign tongues and brogues, shrill cries, quarrels and wrangles, and the

Pit pulsed with a great and steady murmur, like the hum of the human hive that it was.

"Phew! I 'll be glad when we 're out of it," Fred said.

He spoke in a whisper, and Joe and Charley nodded grimly that they agreed with him. They were not inclined to speech, and they walked as rapidly as the crowd permitted, with much the same feelings as those of travelers in a dangerous and hostile jungle.

And danger and hostility stalked in the Pit. The inhabitants seemed to resent the presence of these strangers from the Hill. Dirty little urchins abused them as they passed, snarling with assumed bravery, and prepared to run away at the first sign of attack. And still other little urchins formed a noisy parade at the heels of the boys, and grew bolder with increasing numbers.

"Don't mind them," Joe cautioned. "Take no notice, but keep right on. We 'll soon be out of it."

"No; we 're in for it," said Fred, in an undertone. "Look there!"

On the corner they were approaching, four or five boys of about their own age were standing. The light from a street-lamp fell upon them and disclosed one with vivid red hair. It could be no other than "Brick" Simpson, the redoubtable leader of a redoubtable gang. Twice within their memory he had led his gang up the Hill and spread panic and terror among the Hill-dwelling young folk, who fled wildly to their homes, while their fathers and mothers hurriedly telephoned for the police.

At sight of the group on the corner, the rabble at the heels of the three boys melted away on the instant with like manifestations of fear. This but increased the anxiety of the boys, though they held boldly on their way.

The red-haired boy detached himself from the group, and stepped before them, blocking their path. They essayed to go around him, but he stretched out his arm.

"Wot yer doin' here?" he snarled. "Why don't yer stay where yer b'long?"

"We 're just going home," Fred said mildly.

165

Brick looked at Joe. "Wot yer got under yer arm?" he demanded.

Joe contained himself and took no heed of him. "Come on," he said to Fred and Charley, at the same time starting to brush past the gang-leader.

But with a quick blow Brick Simpson struck him in the face, and with equal quickness snatched the bundle of kites from under his arm.

Joe uttered an inarticulate cry of rage, and, all caution flung to the winds, sprang at his assailant.

This was evidently a surprise to the gang-leader, who expected least of all to be attacked in his own territory. He retreated backward, still clutching the kites, and divided between desire to fight and desire to retain his capture.

The latter desire dominated him, and he turned and fled swiftly down the narrow side-street into a labyrinth of streets and alleys. Joe knew that he was plunging into the wilderness of the enemy's country, but his sense of both property and pride had been offended, and he took up the pursuit hot-footed.

Fred and Charley followed after, though he outdistanced them, and behind came the three other members of the gang, emitting a whistling call while they ran which was evidently intended for the assembling of the rest of the band. As the chase proceeded, these whistles were answered from many different directions, and soon a score of dark figures were tagging at the heels of Fred and Charley, who, in turn, were straining every muscle to keep the swifter-footed Joe in sight.

Brick Simpson darted into a vacant lot, aiming for a "slip," as such things are called which are prearranged passages through fences and over sheds and houses and around dark holes and corners, where the unfamiliar pursuer must go more carefully and where the chances are many that he will soon lose the track.

But Joe caught Brick before he could attain his end, and together they rolled over and over in the dirt, locked in each other's arms. By the time Fred and Charley and the gang had come up, they were on their feet, facing each other.

166

"Wot d' ye want, eh?" the red-headed gang-leader was saying in a bullying tone. "Wot d' ye want? That 's wot I wanter know."

"I want my kites," Joe answered.

Brick Simpson's eyes sparkled at the intelligence. Kites were something he stood in need of himself.

"Then you 've got to fight fer 'em," he announced.

"Why should I fight for them?" Joe demanded indignantly. "They 're mine." Which went to show how ignorant he was of the ideas of ownership and property rights which obtained among the People of the Pit.

A chorus of jeers and catcalls went up from the gang, which clustered behind its leader like a pack of wolves.

"Why should I fight for them?" Joe reiterated.

"'Cos I say so," Simpson replied. "An' wot I say goes. Understand?"

But Joe did not understand. He refused to understand that Brick Simpson's word was law in San Francisco, or any part of San Francisco. His love of honesty and right dealing was offended, and all his fighting blood was up.

"You give those kites to me, right here and now," he threatened, reaching out his hand for them.

But Simpson jerked them away. "D' ye know who I am?" he demanded. "I 'm Brick Simpson, an' I don't 'low no one to talk to me in that tone of voice."

"Better leave him alone," Charley whispered in Joe's ear. "What are a few kites? Leave him alone and let 's get out of this."

"They 're my kites," Joe said slowly in a dogged manner. "They 're my kites, and I 'm going to have them."

"You can't fight the crowd," Fred interfered; "and if you do get the best of him they 'll all pile on you."

The gang, observing this whispered colloquy, and mistaking it for hesitancy on the part of Joe, set up its wolf-like howling again.

"Afraid! afraid!" the young roughs jeered and taunted. "He 's too high-toned, he is! Mebbe he 'll spoil his nice clean shirt, and then what 'll mama say?"

"Shut up!" their leader snapped authoritatively, and the noise obediently died away.

"Will you give me those kites?" Joe demanded, advancing determinedly.

"Will you fight for 'em?" was Simpson's counter-demand.

"Yes," Joe answered.

"Fight! fight!" the gang began to howl again.

"And it 's me that 'll see fair play," said a man's heavy voice.

All eyes were instantly turned upon the man who had approached unseen and made this announcement. By the electric light, shining brightly on them from the corner, they made him out to be a big, muscular fellow, clad in a working-man's garments. His feet were incased in heavy brogans, a narrow strap of black leather held his overalls about his waist, and a black and greasy cap was on his head. His face was grimed with coal-dust, and a coarse blue shirt, open at the neck, revealed a wide throat and massive chest.

"An' who 're you?" Simpson snarled, angry at the interruption.

"None of yer business," the newcomer retorted tartly. "But, if it 'll do you any good, I 'm a fireman on the China steamers, and, as I said, I 'm goin' to see fair play. That 's my business. Your business is to give fair play. So pitch in, and don't be all night about it."

The three boys were as pleased by the appearance of the fireman as Simpson and his followers were displeased. They conferred together for several minutes, when Simpson deposited the bundle of kites in the arms of one of his gang and stepped forward.

"Come on, then," he said, at the same time pulling off his coat.

Joe handed his to Fred, and sprang toward Brick. They put up their fists and faced each other. Almost instantly Simpson drove in a fierce blow and ducked cleverly away and out of reach of the blow which Joe returned. Joe felt a sudden respect for the abilities of his antagonist, but the only effect upon him was to arouse all the doggedness of his nature and make him utterly determined to win.

Awed by the presence of the fireman, Simpson's followers confined themselves to cheering Brick and jeering Joe. The two boys circled round and round, attacking, feinting, and guarding, and now one and then the other getting in a telling blow. Their positions were in marked contrast. Joe stood erect, planted solidly on his feet, with legs wide apart and head up. On the other hand, Simpson crouched till his head was nearly lost between his shoulders, and all the while he was in constant motion, leaping and springing and manoeuvering in the execution of a score or more of tricks quite new and strange to Joe.

At the end of a quarter of an hour, both were very tired, though Joe was much fresher. Tobacco, ill food, and unhealthy living were telling on the gang-leader, who was panting and sobbing for breath. Though at first (and because of superior skill) he had severely punished Joe, he was now weak and his blows were without force. Growing desperate, he adopted what might be called not an unfair but a mean method of attack: he would manoeuver, leap in and strike swiftly, and then, ducking forward, fall to the ground at Joe's feet. Joe could not strike him while he was down, and so would step back until he could get on his feet again, when the thing would be repeated.

But Joe grew tired of this, and prepared for him. Timing his blow with Simpson's attack, he delivered it just as Simpson was ducking forward to fall. Simpson fell, but he fell over on one side, whither he had been driven by the impact of Joe's fist upon his head. He rolled over and got half-way to his feet, where he remained, crying and gasping. His followers called upon him to get up, and he tried once or twice, but was too exhausted and stunned.

"I give in," he said. "I 'm licked."

The gang had become silent and depressed at its leader's defeat.

Joe stepped forward.

"I 'll trouble you for those kites," he said to the boy who was holding them.

"Oh, I dunno," said another member of the gang, shoving in between Joe and his property. His hair was also a vivid red. "You 've got to lick me before you kin have 'em."

"I don't see that," Joe said bluntly. "I 've fought and I 've won, and there 's nothing more to it."

"Oh, yes, there is," said the other. "I 'm 'Sorrel-top' Simpson. Brick 's my brother. See?"

And so, in this fashion, Joe learned another custom of the Pit People of which he had been ignorant.

"All right," he said, his fighting blood more fully aroused than ever by the unjustness of the proceeding. "Come on."

Sorrel-top Simpson, a year younger than his brother, proved to be a most unfair fighter, and the good-natured fireman was compelled to interfere several times before the second of the Simpson clan lay on the ground and acknowledged defeat.

This time Joe reached for his kites without the slightest doubt that he was to get them. But still another lad stepped in between him and his property. The telltale hair, vividly red, sprouted likewise on this lad's head, and Joe knew him at once for what he was, another member of the Simpson clan. He was a younger edition of his brothers, somewhat less heavily built, with a face covered with a vast quantity of freckles, which showed plainly under the electric light.

"You don't git them there kites till you git me," he challenged in a piping little voice. "I 'm 'Reddy' Simpson, an' you ain't licked the fambly till you 've licked me."

The gang cheered admiringly, and Reddy stripped a tattered jacket preparatory for the fray.

"Git ready," he said to Joe.

Joe's knuckles were torn, his nose was bleeding, his lip was cut and swollen, while his shirt had been ripped down from throat to waist. Further, he was tired, and breathing hard.

"How many more are there of you Simpsons?" he asked. "I 've got to get home, and if your family 's much larger this thing is liable to keep on all night."

"I 'm the last an' the best," Reddy replied. "You gits me an' you gits the kites. Sure."

"All right," Joe sighed. "Come on."

While the youngest of the clan lacked the strength and skill of his elders, he made up for it by a wildcat manner of fighting that taxed Joe severely. Time and again it seemed to him that he must give in to the little whirlwind; but each time he pulled himself together and went doggedly on. For he felt that he was fighting for principle, as his forefathers had fought for principle; also, it seemed to him that the honor of the Hill was at stake, and that he, as its representative, could do nothing less than his very best.

So he held on and managed to endure his opponent's swift and continuous rushes till that young and less experienced person at last wore himself out with his own exertions, and from the ground confessed that, for the first time in its history, the "Simpson fambly was beat."

CHAPTER IV. THE BITER BITTEN

But life in the Pit at best was a precarious affair, as the three Hill-dwellers were quickly to learn. Before Joe could even possess himself of his kites, his astonished eyes were greeted with the spectacle of all his enemies, the fireman included, taking to their heels in wild flight. As the little girls and urchins had melted away before the Simpson gang, so was melting away the Simpson gang before some new and correspondingly awe-inspiring group of predatory creatures.

Joe heard terrified cries of "Fish gang!" "Fish gang!" from those who fled, and he would have fled himself from this new danger, only he was breathless from his last encounter, and knew the impossibility of escaping whatever threatened. Fred and Charley felt mighty longings to run away from a danger great enough to frighten the redoubtable Simpson gang and the valorous fireman, but they could not desert their comrade.

Dark forms broke into the vacant lot, some surrounding the boys and others dashing after the fugitives. That the laggards were overtaken was evidenced by the cries of distress that went up, and when later the pursuers returned, they brought with them the luckless and snarling Brick, still clinging fast to the bundle of kites.

Joe looked curiously at this latest band of marauders. They were young men of from seventeen and eighteen to twenty-three and -four years of age, and bore the unmistakable stamp of the hoodlum class. There were vicious faces among them—faces so vicious as to make Joe's flesh creep as he looked at them. A couple grasped him tightly by the arms, and Fred and Charley were similarly held captive.

"Look here, you," said one who spoke with the authority of leader, "we 've got to inquire into this. Wot 's be'n goin' on here? Wot 're you up to, Red-head? Wot you be'n doin'?"

"Ain't be'n doin' nothin'," Simpson whined.

"Looks like it." The leader turned up Brick's face to the electric light. "Who 's been paintin' you up like that?" he demanded.

Brick pointed at Joe, who was forthwith dragged to the front.

"Wot was you scrappin' about?"

"Kites—my kites," Joe spoke up boldly. "That fellow tried to take them away from me. He 's got them under his arm now."

"Oh, he has, has he? Look here, you Brick, we don't put up with stealin' in this territory. See? You never rightly owned nothin'. Come, fork over the kites. Last call."

The leader tightened his grasp threateningly, and Simpson, weeping tears of rage, surrendered the plunder.

"Wot yer got under yer arm?" the leader demanded abruptly of Fred, at the same time jerking out the bundle. "More kites, eh? Reg'lar kite-factory gone and got itself lost," he remarked finally, when he had appropriated Charley's bundle. "Now, wot I wants to know is wot we 're goin' to do to you t'ree chaps?" he continued in a judicial tone.

"What for?" Joe demanded hotly. "For being robbed of our kites?"

"Not at all, not at all," the leader responded politely; "but for luggin' kites round these quarters an' causin' all this unseemly disturbance. It 's disgraceful; that 's wot it is—disgraceful."

At this juncture, when the Hill-dwellers were the center of attraction, Brick suddenly wormed out of his jacket, squirmed away from his captors, and dashed across the lot to the slip for which he had been originally headed when overtaken by Joe. Two or three of the gang shot over the fence after him in noisy pursuit. There was much barking and howling of back-yard dogs and clattering of shoes over sheds and boxes. Then there came a splashing of water, as though a barrel of it had been precipitated to the ground. Several minutes later the pursuers returned, very sheepish and very wet from the deluge presented them by the wily Brick, whose voice, high up in the air from some friendly housetop, could be heard defiantly jeering them.

This event apparently disconcerted the leader of the gang, and just as he turned to Joe and Fred and Charley, a long and peculiar whistle came to their ears from the street—the warning signal, evidently, of a scout posted to keep a lookout. The next moment the scout himself came flying back to the main body, which was already beginning to retreat.

"Cops!" he panted.

Joe looked, and he saw two helmeted policemen approaching, with bright stars shining on their breasts.

"Let 's get out of this," he whispered to Fred and Charley.

The gang had already taken to flight, and they blocked the boys' retreat in one quarter, and in another they saw the policemen advancing. So they took to their heels in the direction of Brick Simpson's slip, the policemen hot after them and yelling bravely for them to halt.

But young feet are nimble, and young feet when frightened become something more than nimble, and the boys were first over the fence and plunging wildly through a maze of back yards. They soon found that the policemen were discreet. Evidently they had had experiences in slips, and they were satisfied to give over the chase at the first fence.

No street-lamps shed their light here, and the boys blundered along through the blackness with their hearts in their mouths. In one yard, filled with mountains of crates and fruit-boxes, they were lost for a quarter of an hour. Feel and quest about as they would, they encountered nothing but endless heaps of boxes. From this wilderness they finally emerged by way of a shed roof, only to fall into another yard, cumbered with countless empty chicken-coops.

Farther on they came upon the contrivance which had soaked Brick Simpson's pursuers with water. It was a cunning arrangement. Where the slip led through a fence with a board missing, a long slat was so arranged that the ignorant wayfarer could not fail to strike against it. This slat was the spring of the trap. A light touch upon it was sufficient to disconnect a heavy stone from a barrel perched overhead and nicely balanced. The disconnecting of the stone permitted the barrel to turn over and spill its contents on the one beneath who touched the slat.

The boys examined the arrangement with keen appreciation. Luckily for them, the barrel was overturned, or they too would have received a ducking, for Joe, who was in advance, had blundered against the slat.

"I wonder if this is Simpson's back yard?" he queried softly.

"It must be," Fred concluded, "or else the back yard of some member of his gang."

Charley put his hands warningly on both their arms.

"Hist! What 's that?" he whispered.

They crouched down on the ground. Not far away was the sound of some one moving about. Then they heard a noise of falling water, as from a faucet into a bucket. This was followed by steps boldly approaching. They crouched lower, breathless with apprehension.

A dark form passed by within arm's reach and mounted on a box to the fence. It was Brick himself, resetting the trap. They heard him arrange the slat and stone, then right the barrel and empty into it a couple of buckets of water. As he came down from the box to go after more water, Joe sprang upon him, tripped him up, and held him to the ground.

"Don't make any noise," he said. "I want you to listen to me."

"Oh, it 's you, is it?" Simpson replied, with such obvious relief in his voice as to make them feel relieved also. "Wot d' ye want here?"

"We want to get out of here," Joe said, "and the shortest way 's the best. There 's three of us, and you 're only one—"

"That 's all right, that 's all right," the gang-leader interrupted. "I 'd just as soon show you the way out as not. I ain't got nothin' 'gainst you. Come on an' follow me, an' don't step to the side, an' I 'll have you out in no time."

Several minutes later they dropped from the top of a high fence into a dark alley.

"Follow this to the street," Simpson directed; "turn to the right two blocks, turn to the right again for three, an' yer on Union. Tra-la-loo."

They said good-by, and as they started down the alley received the following advice:

"Nex' time you bring kites along, you 'd best leave 'em to home."

CHAPTER V. HOME AGAIN

Following Brick Simpson's directions, they came into Union Street, and without further mishap gained the Hill. From the brow they looked down into the Pit, whence arose that steady, indefinable hum which comes from crowded human places.

"I 'll never go down there again, not as long as I live," Fred said with a great deal of savagery in his voice. "I wonder what became of the fireman."

"We 're lucky to get back with whole skins," Joe cheered them philosophically.

"I guess we left our share, and you more than yours," laughed Charley.

"Yes," Joe answered. "And I 've got more trouble to face when I get home. Good night, fellows."

As he expected, the door on the side porch was locked, and he went around to the dining-room and entered like a burglar through a window. As he crossed the wide hall, walking softly toward the stairs, his father came out of the library. The surprise was mutual, and each halted aghast.

Joe felt a hysterical desire to laugh, for he thought that he knew precisely how he looked. In reality he looked far worse than he imagined. What Mr. Bronson saw was a boy with hat and coat covered with dirt, his whole face smeared with the stains of conflict, and, in particular, a badly swollen nose, a bruised eyebrow, a cut and swollen lip, a scratched cheek, knuckles still bleeding, and a shirt torn open from throat to waist.

"What does this mean, sir?" Mr. Bronson finally managed to articulate.

Joe stood speechless. How could he tell, in one brief sentence, all the whole night's happenings?—for all that must be included in the explanation of what his luckless disarray meant.

"Have you lost your tongue?" Mr. Bronson demanded with an

appearance of impatience.

"I 've—I 've—"

"Yes, yes," his father encouraged.

"I 've—well, I 've been down in the Pit," Joe succeeded in blurting out.

"I must confess that you look like it—very much like it indeed." Mr. Bronson spoke severely, but if ever by great effort he conquered a smile, that was the time. "I presume," he went on, "that you do not refer to the abiding-place of sinners, but rather to some definite locality in San Francisco. Am I right?"

Joe swept his arm in a descending gesture toward Union Street, and said: "Down there, sir."

"And who gave it that name?"

"I did," Joe answered, as though confessing to a specified crime.

"It 's most appropriate, I 'm sure, and denotes imagination. It could n't really be bettered. You must do well at school, sir, with your English."

This did not increase Joe's happiness, for English was the only study of which he did not have to feel ashamed.

And, while he stood thus a silent picture of misery and disgrace, Mr. Bronson looked upon him through the eyes of his own boyhood with an understanding which Joe could not have believed possible.

"However, what you need just now is not a discourse, but a bath and court-plaster and witch-hazel and cold-water bandages," Mr. Bronson said; "so to bed with you. You 'll need all the sleep you can get, and you 'll feel stiff and sore to-morrow morning, I promise you."

The clock struck one as Joe pulled the bedclothes around him; and the next he knew he was being worried by a soft, insistent rapping, which seemed to continue through several centuries, until at last, unable to endure it longer, he opened his eyes and sat up.

The day was streaming in through the window—bright and sunshiny day. He stretched his arms to yawn; but a shooting pain darted through all the muscles, and his arms came down more rapidly than they had gone up. He looked at them with a bewildered stare, till suddenly the events of the night rushed in upon him, and he groaned.

The rapping still persisted, and he cried: "Yes, I hear. What time is it?"

"Eight o'clock," Bessie's voice came to him through the door. "Eight o'clock, and you 'll have to hurry if you don't want to be late for school."

"Goodness!" He sprang out of bed precipitately, groaned with the pain from all his stiff muscles, and collapsed slowly and carefully on a chair. "Why did n't you call me sooner?" he growled.

"Father said to let you sleep."

Joe groaned again, in another fashion Then his history-book caught his eye, and he groaned yet again and in still another fashion.

"All right," he called. "Go on. I 'll be down in a jiffy."

He did come down in fairly brief order; but if Bessie had watched him descend the stairs she would have been astounded at the remarkable caution he observed and at the twinges of pain that every now and then contorted his face. As it was, when she came upon him in the dining-room she uttered a frightened cry and ran over to him.

"What 's the matter, Joe?" she asked tremulously. "What has happened?"

"Nothing," he grunted, putting sugar on his porridge.

"But surely—" she began.

"Please don't bother me," he interrupted. "I 'm late, and I want to eat my breakfast."

And just then Mrs. Bronson caught Bessie's eye, and that young lady, still mystified, made haste to withdraw herself.

Joe was thankful to his mother for that, and thankful that she refrained from remarking upon his appearance. Father had told her; that was one thing sure. He could trust her not to worry him; it was never her way.

And, meditating in this way, he hurried through with his solitary breakfast, vaguely conscious in an uncomfortable way that his mother was fluttering anxiously about him. Tender as she always was, he noticed that she kissed him with unusual tenderness as he started out with his books swinging at the end of a strap; and he also noticed, as he turned the corner, that she was still looking after him through the window.

But of more vital importance than that, to him, was his stiffness and soreness. As he walked along, each step was an effort and a torment. Severely as the reflected sunlight from the cement sidewalk hurt his bruised eye, and severely as his various wounds pained him, still more severely did he suffer from his muscles and joints. He had never imagined such stiffness. Each individual muscle in his whole body protested when called upon to move. His fingers were badly swollen, and it was agony to clasp and unclasp them; while his arms were sore from wrist to elbow. This, he said to himself, was caused by the many blows which he had warded off from his face and body. He wondered if Brick Simpson was in similar plight, and the thought of their mutual misery made him feel a certain kinship for that redoubtable young ruffian.

When he entered the school-yard he quickly became aware that he was the center of attraction for all eyes. The boys crowded around in an awe-stricken way, and even his classmates and those with whom he was well acquainted looked at him with a certain respect he had never seen before.

CHAPTER VI. EXAMINATION DAY

It was plain that Fred and Charley had spread the news of their descent into the Pit, and of their battle with the Simpson clan and the Fishes. He heard the nine-o'clock bell with feelings of relief, and passed into the school, a mark for admiring glances from all the boys. The girls, too, looked at him in a timid and fearful way—as they might have looked at Daniel when he came out of the lions' den, Joe thought, or at David after his battle with Goliath. It made him uncomfortable and painfully self-conscious, this hero-worshiping, and he wished heartily that they would look in some other direction for a change.

Soon they did look in another direction. While big sheets of foolscap were being distributed to every desk, Miss Wilson, the teacher (an austere-looking young woman who went through the world as though it were a refrigerator, and who, even on the warmest days in the classroom, was to be found with a shawl or cape about her shoulders), arose, and on the blackboard where all could see wrote the Roman numeral "I." Every eye, and there were fifty pairs of them, hung with expectancy upon her hand, and in the pause that followed the room was quiet as the grave.

Underneath the Roman numeral "I" she wrote: **"(a) What were the laws of Draco? (b) Why did an Athenian orator say that they were written 'not in ink, but in blood'?"**

Forty-nine heads bent down and forty-nine pens scratched lustily across as many sheets of foolscap. Joe's head alone remained up, and he regarded the blackboard with so blank a stare that Miss Wilson, glancing over her shoulder after having written "II," stopped to look at him. Then she wrote:

"(a) How did the war between Athens and Megara, respecting the island of Salamis, bring about the reforms of Solon? (b) In what way did they differ from the laws of Draco?"

She turned to look at Joe again. He was staring as blankly as ever.

"What is the matter, Joe?" she asked. "Have you no paper?"

"Yes, I have, thank you," he answered, and began moodily to sharpen a lead-pencil.

He made a fine point to it. Then he made a very fine point. Then, and with infinite patience, he proceeded to make it very much finer. Several of his classmates raised their heads inquiringly at the noise. But he did not notice. He was too absorbed in his pencil-sharpening and in thinking thoughts far away from both pencil-sharpening and Greek history.

"Of course you all understand that the examination papers are to be written with ink."

Miss Wilson addressed the class in general, but her eyes rested on Joe.

Just as it was about as fine as it could possibly be the point broke, and Joe began over again.

"I am afraid, Joe, that you annoy the class," Miss Wilson said in final desperation.

He put the pencil down, closed the knife with a snap, and returned to his blank staring at the blackboard. What did he know about Draco? or Solon? or the rest of the Greeks? It was a flunk, and that was all there was to it. No need for him to look at the rest of the questions, and even if he did know the answers to two or three, there was no use in writing them down. It would not prevent the flunk. Besides, his arm hurt him too much to write. It hurt his eyes to look at the blackboard, and his eyes hurt even when they were closed; and it seemed positively to hurt him to think.

So the forty-nine pens scratched on in a race after Miss Wilson, who was covering the blackboard with question after question; and he listened to the scratching, and watched the questions growing under her chalk, and was very miserable indeed. His head seemed whirling around. It ached inside and was sore outside, and he did not seem to have any control of it at all.

He was beset with memories of the Pit, like scenes from some monstrous nightmare, and, try as he would, he could not dispel them. He would fix his mind and eyes on Miss Wilson's face, who was now sitting at her desk, and even as he looked at her the face of Brick Simpson, impudent and pugnacious, would arise before him. It was of no use. He felt sick and sore and tired and worthless. There was nothing to be done but flunk. And when, after an age of waiting, the papers were collected, his went in a blank, save for his name, the name of the examination, and the date, which were written across the top.

After a brief interval, more papers were given out, and the examination in arithmetic began. He did not trouble himself to look at the questions. Ordinarily he might have pulled through such an examination, but in his present state of mind and body he knew it was impossible. He contented himself with burying his face in his hands and hoping for the noon hour. Once, lifting his eyes to the clock, he caught Bessie looking anxiously at him across the room from the girls' side. This but added to his discomfort. Why was she bothering him? No need for her to trouble. She was bound to pass. Then why could n't she leave him alone? So he gave her a particularly glowering look and buried his face in his hands again. Nor did he lift it till the twelve-o'clock gong rang, when he handed in a second blank paper and passed out with the boys.

Fred and Charley and he usually ate lunch in a corner of the yard which they had arrogated to themselves; but this day, by some remarkable coincidence, a score of other boys had elected to eat their lunches on the same spot. Joe surveyed them with disgust. In his present condition he did not feel inclined to receive hero-worship. His head ached too much, and he was troubled over his failure in the examinations; and there were more to come in the afternoon.

He was angry with Fred and Charley. They were chattering like magpies over the adventures of the night (in which, however, they did not fail to give him chief credit), and they conducted themselves in quite a patronizing fashion toward their awed and admiring schoolmates. But every attempt to make Joe talk was a failure. He grunted and gave short answers, and said "yes" and "no" to questions asked with the intention of drawing him out.

He was longing to get away somewhere by himself, to throw himself down some place on the green grass and forget his aches and pains and troubles. He got up to go and find such a place, and found half a dozen of his following tagging after him. He wanted to turn around and scream at them to leave him alone, but his pride restrained him. A great wave of disgust and despair swept over him, and then an idea flashed through his mind. Since he was sure to flunk in his examinations, why endure the afternoon's torture, which could not but be worse than the morning's? And on the impulse of the moment he made up his mind.

He walked straight on to the schoolyard gate and passed out. Here his worshipers halted in wonderment, but he kept on to the corner and out of sight. For some time he wandered along aimlessly, till he came to the tracks of a cable road. A down-town car happening to stop to let off passengers, he stepped aboard and ensconced himself in an outside corner seat. The next thing he was aware of, the car was swinging around on its turn-table and he was hastily scrambling off. The big ferry building stood before him. Seeing and hearing nothing, he had been carried through the heart of the business section of San Francisco.

He glanced up at the tower clock on top of the ferry building. It was ten minutes after one—time enough to catch the quarter-past-one boat. That decided him, and without the least idea in the world as to where he was going, he paid ten cents for a ticket, passed through the gate, and was soon speeding across the bay to the pretty city of Oakland.

In the same aimless and unwitting fashion, he found himself, an hour later, sitting on the string-piece of the Oakland city wharf and leaning his aching head against a friendly timber. From where he sat he could look down upon the decks of a number of small sailing-craft. Quite a crowd of curious idlers had collected to look at them, and Joe found himself growing interested.

There were four boats, and from where he sat he could make out their names. The one directly beneath him had the name Ghost painted in large green letters on its stern. The other three, which lay beyond, were called respectively **La Caprice**, the **Oyster Queen**, and the **Flying Dutchman.**

Each of these boats had cabins built amidships, with short stovepipes projecting through the roofs, and from the pipe of the Ghost smoke was ascending. The cabin doors were open and the roof-slide pulled back, so that Joe could look inside and observe the inmate, a young fellow of nineteen or twenty who was engaged just then in cooking. He was clad in long sea-boots which reached the hips, blue overalls, and dark woolen shirt. The sleeves, rolled back to the elbows, disclosed sturdy, sun-bronzed arms, and when the young fellow looked up his face proved to be equally bronzed and tanned.

The aroma of coffee arose to Joe's nose, and from a light iron pot came the unmistakable smell of beans nearly done. The cook placed a frying-pan on the stove, wiped it around with a piece of suet when it had heated, and tossed in a thick chunk of beefsteak. While he worked he talked with a companion on deck, who was busily engaged in filling a bucket overside and flinging the salt water over heaps of oysters that lay on the deck. This completed, he covered the oysters with wet sacks, and went into the cabin, where a place was set for him on a tiny table, and where the cook served the dinner and joined him in eating it.

All the romance of Joe's nature stirred at the sight. That was life. They were living, and gaining their living, out in the free open, under the sun and sky, with the sea rocking beneath them, and the wind blowing on them, or the rain falling on them, as the chance might be. Each day and every day he sat in a room, pent up with fifty more of his kind, racking his brains and cramming dry husks of knowledge, while they were doing all this, living glad and careless and happy, rowing boats and sailing, and cooking their own food, and certainly meeting with adventures such as one only dreams of in the crowded school-room.

Joe sighed. He felt that he was made for this sort of life and not for the life of a scholar. As a scholar he was undeniably a failure. He had flunked in his examinations, while at that very moment, he knew, Bessie was going triumphantly home, her last examination over and done, and with credit. Oh, it was not to be borne! His father was wrong in sending him to school. That might be well enough for boys who were inclined to study, but it was manifest that he was not so inclined. There were more careers in life than that of the schools. Men had gone down to the sea in the lowest capacity, and risen in greatness, and owned great fleets, and done great deeds, and left their names on the pages of time. And why not he, Joe Bronson?

He closed his eyes and felt immensely sorry for himself; and when he opened his eyes again he found that he had been asleep, and that the sun was sinking fast.

It was after dark when he arrived home, and he went straight to his room and to bed without meeting any one. He sank down between the cool sheets with a sigh of satisfaction at the thought that, come what would, he need no longer worry about his history. Then another and unwelcome thought obtruded itself, and he knew that the next school term would come, and that six months thereafter, another examination in the same history awaited him.

CHAPTER VII. FATHER AND SON

On the following morning, after breakfast, Joe was summoned to the library by his father, and he went in almost with a feeling of gladness that the suspense of waiting was over. Mr. Bronson was standing by the window. A great chattering of sparrows outside seemed to have attracted his attention. Joe joined him in looking out, and saw a fledgeling sparrow on the grass, tumbling ridiculously about in its efforts to stand on its feeble baby legs. It had fallen from the nest in the rose-bush that climbed over the window, and the two parent sparrows were wild with anxiety over its plight.

"It 's a way young birds have," Mr. Bronson remarked, turning to Joe with a serious smile; "and I dare say you are on the verge of a somewhat similar predicament, my boy," he went on. "I am afraid things have reached a crisis, Joe. I have watched it coming on for a year now—your poor scholarship, your carelessness and inattention, your constant desire to be out of the house and away in search of adventures of one sort or another."

He paused, as though expecting a reply; but Joe remained silent.

"I have given you plenty of liberty. I believe in liberty. The finest souls grow in such soil. So I have not hedged you in with endless rules and irksome restrictions. I have asked little of you, and you have come and gone pretty much as you pleased. In a way, I have put you on your honor, made you largely your own master, trusting to your sense of right to restrain you from going wrong and at least to keep you up in your studies. And you have failed me. What do you want me to do? Set you certain bounds and time-limits? Keep a watch over you? Compel you by main strength to go through your books?

"I have here a note," Mr. Bronson said after another pause, in which he picked up an envelop from the table and drew forth a written sheet.

Joe recognized the stiff and uncompromising scrawl of Miss Wilson, and his heart sank.

His father began to read:

"Listlessness and carelessness have characterized his term's work, so that when the examinations came he was wholly unprepared. In neither history nor arithmetic did he attempt to answer a question, passing in his papers perfectly blank. These examinations took place in the morning. In the afternoon he did not take the trouble even to appear for the remainder."

Mr. Bronson ceased reading and looked up.

"Where were you in the afternoon?" he asked.

"I went across on the ferry to Oakland," Joe answered, not caring to offer his aching head and body in extenuation.

"That is what is called 'playing hooky,' is it not?"

"Yes, sir," Joe answered.

"The night before the examinations, instead of studying, you saw fit to wander away and involve yourself in a disgraceful fight with hoodlums. I did not say anything at the time. In my heart I think I might almost have forgiven you that, if you had done well in your school-work."

Joe had nothing to say. He knew that there was his side to the story, but he felt that his father did not understand, and that there was little use of telling him.

"The trouble with you, Joe, is carelessness and lack of concentration. What you need is what I have not given you, and that is rigid discipline. I have been debating for some time upon the advisability of sending you to some military school, where your tasks will be set for you, and what you do every moment in the twenty-four hours will be determined for you—"

"Oh, father, you don't understand, you can't understand!" Joe broke forth at last. "I try to study—I honestly try to study; but somehow—I don't know how—I can't study. Perhaps I am a failure. Perhaps I am not made for study. I want to go out into the world. I want to see life—to live. I don't want any military academy; I 'd sooner go to sea—anywhere where I can do

188

something and be something."

Mr. Bronson looked at him kindly. "It is only through study that you can hope to do something and be something in the world," he said.

Joe threw up his hand with a gesture of despair.

"I know how you feel about it," Mr. Bronson went on; "but you are only a boy, very much like that young sparrow we were watching. If at home you have not sufficient control over yourself to study, then away from home, out in the world which you think is calling to you, you will likewise not have sufficient control over yourself to do the work of that world.

"But I am willing, Joe, I am willing, after you have finished high school and before you go into the university, to let you out into the world for a time."

"Let me go now?" Joe asked impulsively.

"No; it is too early. You have n't your wings yet. You are too unformed, and your ideals and standards are not yet thoroughly fixed."

"But I shall not be able to study," Joe threatened. "I know I shall not be able to study."

Mr. Bronson consulted his watch and arose to go. "I have not made up my mind yet," he said. "I do not know what I shall do—whether I shall give you another trial at the public school or send you to a military academy."

He stopped a moment at the door and looked back. "But remember this, Joe," he said. "I am not angry with you; I am more grieved and hurt. Think it over, and tell me this evening what you intend to do."

His father passed out, and Joe heard the front door close after him. He leaned back in the big easy-chair and closed his eyes. A military school! He feared such an institution as the animal fears a trap. No, he would certainly never go to such a place. And as for public school—He sighed deeply at the thought of it. He was given till evening to make up his mind as to what he intended to do. Well, he knew what he would do, and he did not have to wait till evening to find it out.

He got up with a determined look on his face, put on his hat, and went out the front door. He would show his father that he could do his share of the world's work, he thought as he walked along—he would show him.

By the time he reached the school he had his whole plan worked out definitely. Nothing remained but to put it through. It was the noon hour, and he passed in to his room and packed up his books unnoticed. Coming out through the yard, he encountered Fred and Charley.

"What 's up?" Charley asked.

"Nothing," Joe grunted.

"What are you doing there?"

"Taking my books home, of course. What did you suppose I was doing?"

"Come, come," Fred interposed. "Don't be so mysterious. I don't see why you can't tell us what has happened."

"You 'll find out soon enough," Joe said significantly—more significantly than he had intended.

And, for fear that he might say more, he turned his back on his astonished chums and hurried away. He went straight home and to his room, where he busied himself at once with putting everything in order. His clothes he hung carefully away, changing the suit he had on for an older one. From his bureau he selected a couple of changes of underclothing, a couple of cotton shirts, and half a dozen pairs of socks. To these he added as many handkerchiefs, a comb, and a tooth-brush.

When he had bound the bundle in stout wrapping-paper he contemplated it with satisfaction. Then he went over to his desk and took from a small inner compartment his savings for some months, which amounted to several dollars. This sum he had been keeping for the Fourth of July, but he thrust it into his pocket with hardly a regret. Then he pulled a writing-pad over to him, sat down and wrote:

Don't look for me. I am a failure and I am going away to sea. Don't worry about me. I am all right and able to take care of myself. I shall come back some day, and then you will all be proud of me. Good-by, papa, and mama, and Bessie.

JOE.

This he left lying on his desk where it could easily be seen. He tucked the bundle under his arm, and, with a last farewell look at the room, stole out.

PART II

CHAPTER VIII. 'FRISCO KID AND THE NEW BOY

'Frisco Kid was discontented—discontented and disgusted. This would have seemed impossible to the boys who fished from the dock above and envied him greatly. True, they wore cleaner and better clothes, and were blessed with fathers and mothers; but his was the free floating life of the bay, the domain of moving adventure, and the companionship of men—theirs the rigid discipline and dreary sameness of home life. They did not dream that 'Frisco Kid ever looked up at them from the cockpit of the Dazzler and in turn envied him just those things which sometimes were the most distasteful to them and from which they suffered to repletion. Just as the romance of adventure sang its siren song in their ears and whispered vague messages of strange lands and lusty deeds, so the delicious mysteries of home enticed 'Frisco Kid's roving fancies, and his brightest day-dreams were of the thing's he knew not—brothers, sisters, a father's counsel, a mother's kiss.

He frowned, got up from where he had been sunning himself on top of the Dazzler's cabin, and kicked off his heavy rubber boots. Then he stretched himself on the narrow side-deck and dangled his feet in the cool salt water.

"Now that 's freedom," thought the boys who watched him. Besides, those long sea-boots, reaching to the hips and buckled to the leather strap about the waist, held a strange and wonderful fascination for them. They did not know that 'Frisco Kid did not possess such things as shoes—that the boots were an old pair of Pete Le Maire's and were three sizes too large for him. Nor could they guess how uncomfortable they were to wear on a hot summer day.

The cause of 'Frisco Kid's discontent was those very boys who sat on the string-piece and admired him; but his disgust was the result of quite another event. The Dazzler was short one in its crew, and he had to do more work than was justly his share. He did not mind the cooking, nor the washing down of the decks and the pumping; but when it came to the paint-scrubbing and dishwashing he rebelled. He felt that he had earned the right to be exempt from such scullion work. That was all the green boys were fit for, while he could make or take in sail, lift anchor, steer, and make landings.

"Stan' from un'er!" Pete Le Maire or "French Pete," captain of the Dazzler and lord and master of 'Frisco Kid, threw a bundle into the cockpit and came aboard by the starboard rigging.

"Come! Queeck!" he shouted to the boy who owned the bundle and who now hesitated on the dock. It was a good fifteen feet to the deck of the sloop, and he could not reach the steel stay by which he must descend.

"Now! One, two, three!" the Frenchman counted good-naturedly, after the manner of captains when their crews are short-handed.

The boy swung his body into space and gripped the rigging. A moment later he struck the deck, his hands tingling warmly from the friction.

"Kid, dis is ze new sailor. I make your acquaintance." French Pete smirked and bowed, and stood aside. "Mistaire Sho Bronson," he added as an afterthought.

The two boys regarded each other silently for a moment. They were evidently about the same age, though the stranger looked the heartier and stronger of the two. 'Frisco Kid put out his hand, and they shook.

"So you 're thinking of tackling the water, eh?" he said.

Joe Bronson nodded and glanced curiously about him before answering: "Yes; I think the bay life will suit me for a while, and then, when I 've got used to it, I 'm going to sea in the forecastle."

"In the what?"

"In the forecastle—the place where the sailors live," he explained, flushing and feeling doubtful of his pronunciation.

"Oh, the fo'c'sle. Know anything about going to sea?"

"Yes—no; that is, except what I 've read."

'Frisco Kid whistled, turned on his heel in a lordly manner, and went into the cabin.

"Going to sea," he chuckled to himself as he built the fire and set about cooking supper; "in the 'forecastle,' too; and thinks he 'll like it."

In the meanwhile French Pete was showing the newcomer about the sloop as though he were a guest. Such affability and charm did he display that 'Frisco Kid, popping his head up through the scuttle to call them to supper, nearly choked in his effort to suppress a grin.

Joe Bronson enjoyed that supper. The food was rough but good, and the smack of the salt air and the sea-fittings around him gave zest to his appetite. The cabin was clean and snug, and, though not large, the accommodations surprised him. Every bit of space was utilized. The table swung to the centerboard-case on hinges, so that when not in use it actually occupied no room at all. On either side and partly under the deck were two bunks. The blankets were rolled back, and the boys sat on the well-scrubbed bunk boards while they ate. A swinging sea-lamp of brightly polished brass gave them light, which in the daytime could be obtained through the four deadeyes, or small round panes of heavy glass which were fitted into the walls of the cabin. On one side of the door was the stove and wood-box, on the other the cupboard. The front end of the cabin was ornamented with a couple of rifles and a shot-gun, while exposed by the rolled-back blankets of French Pete's bunk was a cartridge-lined belt carrying a brace of revolvers.

It all seemed like a dream to Joe. Countless times he had imagined scenes somewhat similar to this; but here he was right in the midst of it, and already it seemed as though he had known his two companions for years. French Pete was smiling genially at him across the board. It really was a villainous countenance, but to Joe it seemed only weather-beaten. 'Frisco Kid was describing to him, between mouthfuls, the last sou'easter the Dazzler had weathered, and Joe experienced an increasing awe for this boy who had lived so long upon the water and knew so much about it.

The captain, however, drank a glass of wine, and topped it off with a second and a third, and then, a vicious flush lighting his swarthy face, stretched out on top of his blankets, where he soon was snoring loudly.

"Better turn in and get a couple of hours' sleep," 'Frisco Kid said kindly, pointing Joe's bunk out to him. "We 'll most likely be up the rest of the night."

Joe obeyed, but he could not fall asleep so readily as the others. He lay with his eyes wide open, watching the hands of the alarm-clock that hung in the cabin, and thinking how quickly event had followed event in the last twelve hours. Only that very morning he had been a school-boy, and now he was a sailor, shipped on the Dazzler and bound he knew not whither. His fifteen years increased to twenty at the thought of it, and he felt every inch a man—a sailorman at that. He wished Charley and Fred could see him now. Well, they would hear of it soon enough. He could see them talking it over, and the other boys crowding around. "Who?" "Oh, Joe Bronson; he 's gone to sea. Used to chum with us."

Joe pictured the scene proudly. Then he softened at the thought of his mother worrying, but hardened again at the recollection of his father. Not that his father was not good and kind; but he did not understand boys, Joe thought. That was where the trouble lay. Only that morning he had said that the world was n't a play-ground, and that the boys who thought it was were liable to make sore mistakes and be glad to get home again. Well, he knew that there was plenty of hard work and rough experience in the world; but he also thought boys had some rights. He 'd show him he could take care of himself; and, anyway, he could write home after he got settled down to his new life.

CHAPTER IX. ABOARD THE DAZZLER

A skiff grazed the side of the Dazzler softly and interrupted Joe's reveries. He wondered why he had not heard the sound of the oars in the rowlocks. Then two men jumped over the cockpit-rail and came into the cabin.

"Bli' me, if 'ere they ain't snoozin'," said the first of the newcomers, deftly rolling 'Frisco Kid out of his blankets with one hand and reaching for the wine-bottle with the other.

French Pete put his head up on the other side of the centerboard, his eyes heavy with sleep, and made them welcome.

"'Oo 's this?" asked the Cockney, as he was called, smacking his lips over the wine and rolling Joe out upon the floor. "Passenger?"

"No, no," French Pete made haste to answer. "Ze new sailorman. Vaire good boy."

"Good boy or not, he 's got to keep his tongue atween his teeth," growled the second newcomer, who had not yet spoken, glaring fiercely at Joe.

"I say," queried the other man, "'ow does 'e whack up on the loot? I 'ope as me and Bill 'ave a square deal."

"Ze Dazzler she take one share—what you call—one third; den we split ze rest in five shares. Five men, five shares. Vaire good."

French Pete insisted in excited gibberish that the Dazzler had the right to have three men in its crew, and appealed to 'Frisco Kid to bear him out. But the latter left them to fight it over by themselves, and proceeded to make hot coffee.

It was all Greek to Joe, except he knew that he was in some way the cause of the quarrel. In the end French Pete had his way, and the newcomers gave in after much grumbling. After they had drunk their coffee, all hands went on deck.

"Just stay in the cockpit and keep out of their way," 'Frisco Kid whispered to Joe. "I 'll teach you about the ropes and everything when we ain't in a hurry."

Joe's heart went out to him in sudden gratitude, for the strange feeling came to him that of those on board, to 'Frisco Kid, and to 'Frisco Kid only, could he look for help in time of need. Already a dislike for French Pete was growing up within him. Why, he could not say; he just simply felt it.

A creaking of blocks for'ard, and the huge mainsail loomed above him in the night. Bill cast off the bowline, the Cockney followed suit with the stern, 'Frisco Kid gave her the jib as French Pete jammed up the tiller, and the Dazzler caught the breeze, heeling over for mid-channel. Joe heard talk of not putting up the side-lights, and of keeping a sharp lookout, though all he could comprehend was that some law of navigation was being violated.

The water-front lights of Oakland began to slip past. Soon the stretches of docks and the shadowy ships began to be broken by dim sweeps of marshland, and Joe knew that they were heading out for San Francisco Bay. The wind was blowing from the north in mild squalls, and the Dazzler cut noiselessly through the landlocked water.

"Where are we going?" Joe asked the Cockney, in an endeavor to be friendly and at the same time satisfy his curiosity.

"Oh, my pardner 'ere, Bill, we 're goin' to take a cargo from 'is factory," that worthy airily replied.

Joe thought he was rather a funny-looking individual to own a factory; but, conscious that even stranger things might be found in this new world he was entering, he said nothing. He had already exposed himself to 'Frisco Kid in the matter of his pronunciation of "fo'c'sle," and he had no desire further to advertise his ignorance.

A little after that he was sent in to blow out the cabin lamp. The Dazzler tacked about and began to work in toward the north shore. Everybody kept silent, save for occasional whispered questions and answers which passed between Bill and the captain. Finally the sloop was run into the wind, and the jib and mainsail lowered cautiously.

"Short hawse," French Pete whispered to 'Frisco Kid, who went for'ard and dropped the anchor, paying out the slightest quantity of slack.

The Dazzler's skiff was brought alongside, as was also the small boat in which the two strangers had come aboard.

"See that that cub don't make a fuss," Bill commanded in an undertone, as he joined his partner in his own boat.

"Can you row?" 'Frisco Kid asked as they got into the other boat.

Joe nodded his head.

"Then take these oars, and don't make a racket."

'Frisco Kid took the second pair, while French Pete steered. Joe noticed that the oars were muffled with sennit, and that even the rowlock sockets were protected with leather. It was impossible to make a noise except by a mis-stroke, and Joe had learned to row on Lake Merrit well enough to avoid that. They followed in the wake of the first boat, and, glancing aside, he saw they were running along the length of a pier which jutted out from the land. A couple of ships, with riding-lanterns burning brightly, were moored to it, but they kept just beyond the edge of the light. He stopped rowing at the whispered command of 'Frisco Kid. Then the boats grounded like ghosts on a tiny beach, and they clambered out.

Joe followed the men, who picked their way carefully up a twenty-foot bank. At the top he found himself on a narrow railway track which ran between huge piles of rusty scrap-iron. These piles, separated by tracks, extended in every direction he could not tell how far, though in the distance he could see the vague outlines of some great factory-like building. The men began to carry loads of the iron down to the beach, and French Pete, gripping him by the arm and again warning him not to make any noise, told him to do likewise. At the beach they turned their burdens over to 'Frisco Kid, who loaded them, first in the one skiff and then in the other. As the boats settled under the weight, he kept pushing them farther and farther out, in order that they should keep clear of the bottom.

Joe worked away steadily, though he could not help marveling at the queerness of the whole business. Why should there be such a mystery about it? and why such care taken to maintain silence? He had just begun to ask himself these questions, and a horrible suspicion was forming itself in his mind, when he heard the hoot of an owl from the direction of the beach. Wondering at an owl being in so unlikely a place, he stooped to gather a fresh load of iron. But suddenly a man sprang out of the gloom, flashing a dark lantern full upon him. Blinded by the light, he staggered back. Then a revolver in the man's hand went off like the roar of a cannon. All Joe realized was that he was being shot at, while his legs manifested an overwhelming desire to get away. Even if he had so wished, he could not very well have stayed to explain to the excited man with the smoking revolver. So he took to his heels for the beach, colliding with another man with a dark lantern who came running around the end of one of the piles of iron. This second man quickly regained his feet, and peppered away at Joe as he flew down the bank.

He dashed out into the water for the boat. French Pete at the bow-oars and 'Frisco Kid at the stroke had the skiff's nose pointed seaward and were calmly awaiting his arrival. They had their oars ready for the start, but they held them quietly at rest, for all that both men on the bank had begun to fire at them. The other skiff lay closer inshore, partially aground. Bill was trying to shove it off, and was calling on the Cockney to lend a hand; but that gentleman had lost his head completely, and came floundering through the water hard after Joe. No sooner had Joe climbed in over the stern than he followed him. This extra weight on the stern of the heavily loaded craft nearly swamped them. As it was, a dangerous quantity of water was shipped. In the meantime the men on the bank had reloaded their pistols and opened fire again, this time with better aim. The alarm had spread. Voices and cries could be heard from the ships on the pier, along which men were running. In the distance a police whistle was being frantically blown.

"Get out!" 'Frisco Kid shouted. "You ain't a-going to sink us if I know it. Go and help your pardner."

But the Cockney's teeth were chattering with fright, and he was too unnerved to move or speak.

"T'row ze crazy man out!" French Pete ordered from the bow. At this moment a bullet shattered an oar in his hand, and he coolly proceeded to ship a spare one.

"Give us a hand, Joe," 'Frisco Kid commanded.

Joe understood, and together they seized the terror-stricken creature and flung him overboard. Two or three bullets splashed about him as he came to the surface, just in time to be picked up by Bill, who had at last succeeded in getting clear.

"Now!" French Pete called, and a few strokes into the darkness quickly took them out of the zone of fire.

So much water had been shipped that the light skiff was in danger of sinking at any moment. While the other two rowed, and by the Frenchman's orders, Joe began to throw out the iron. This saved them for the time being. But just as they swept alongside the Dazzler the skiff lurched, shoved a side under, and turned turtle, sending the remainder of the iron to bottom. Joe and 'Frisco Kid came up side by side, and together they clambered aboard with the skiff's painter in tow. French Pete had already arrived, and now helped them out.

By the time they had canted the water out of the swamped boat, Bill and his partner appeared on the scene. All hands worked rapidly, and, almost before Joe could realize, the mainsail and jib had been hoisted, the anchor broken out, and the Dazzler was leaping down the channel. Off a bleak piece of marshland Bill and the Cockney said good-by and cast loose in their skiff. French Pete, in the cabin, bewailed their bad luck in various languages, and sought consolation in the wine-bottle.

CHAPTER X. WITH THE BAY PIRATES

The wind freshened as they got clear of the land, and soon the Dazzler was heeling it with her lee deck buried and the water churning by, half-way up the cockpit-rail. Side-lights had been hung out. 'Frisco Kid was steering, and by his side sat Joe, pondering over the events of the night.

He could no longer blind himself to the facts. His mind was in a whirl of apprehension. If he had done wrong, he reasoned, he had done it through ignorance; and he did not feel shame for the past so much as he did fear for the future. His companions were thieves and robbers—the bay pirates, of whose wild deeds he had heard vague tales. And here he was, right in the midst of them, already possessing information which could send them to State's prison. This very fact, he knew, would force them to keep a sharp watch upon him and so lessen his chances of escape. But escape he would, at the very first opportunity.

At this point his thoughts were interrupted by a sharp squall, which hurled the Dazzler over till the sea rushed inboard. 'Frisco Kid luffed quickly, at the same time slacking off the main-sheet. Then, single-handed,—for French Pete remained below,—and with Joe looking idly on, he proceeded to reef down.

The squall which had so nearly capsized the Dazzler was of short duration, but it marked the rising of the wind, and soon puff after puff was shrieking down upon them out of the north. The mainsail was spilling the wind, and slapping and thrashing about till it seemed it would tear itself to pieces. The sloop was rolling wildly in the quick sea which had come up. Everything was in confusion; but even Joe's untrained eye showed him that it was an orderly confusion. He could see that 'Frisco Kid knew just what to do and just how to do it. As he watched him he learned a lesson, the lack of which has made failures of the lives of many men—the value of knowledge of one's own capacities. 'Frisco Kid knew what he was able to do, and because of this he had confidence in himself. He was cool and self-possessed, working hurriedly but not carelessly. There was no bungling. Every reef-point was drawn down to stay. Other accidents might occur, but the next squall, or the next forty squalls, would not carry one of those reef-knots away.

He called Joe for'ard to help stretch the mainsail by means of swinging on the peak and throat-halyards. To lay out on the long bowsprit and put a single reef in the jib was a slight task compared with what had been already accomplished; so a few moments later they were again in the cockpit. Under the other lad's directions, Joe flattened down the jib-sheet, and, going into the cabin, let down a foot or so of centerboard. The excitement of the struggle had chased all unpleasant thoughts from his mind. Patterning after the other boy, he had retained his coolness. He had executed his orders without fumbling, and at the same time without undue slowness. Together they had exerted their puny strength in the face of violent nature, and together they had outwitted her.

He came back to where his companion stood at the tiller steering, and he felt proud of him and of himself; and when he read the unspoken praise in 'Frisco Kid's eyes he blushed like a girl at her first compliment. But the next instant the thought flashed across him that this boy was a thief, a common thief; and he instinctively recoiled. His whole life had been sheltered from the harsher things of the world. His reading, which had been of the best, had laid a premium upon honesty and uprightness, and he had learned to look with abhorrence upon the criminal classes. So he drew a little away from 'Frisco Kid and remained silent. But 'Frisco Kid, devoting all his energies to the handling of the sloop, had no time in which to remark this sudden change of feeling on the part of his companion.

But there was one thing Joe found in himself that surprised him. While the thought of 'Frisco Kid being a thief was repulsive to him, 'Frisco Kid himself was not. Instead of feeling an honest desire to shun him, he felt drawn toward him. He could not help liking him, though he knew not why. Had he been a little older he would have understood that it was the lad's good qualities which appealed to him—his coolness and self-reliance, his manliness and bravery, and a certain kindliness and sympathy in his nature. As it was, he thought it his own natural badness which prevented him from disliking 'Frisco

Kid; but, while he felt shame at his own weakness, he could not smother the warm regard which he felt growing up for this particular bay pirate.

"Take in two or three feet on the skiff's painter," commanded 'Frisco Kid, who had an eye for everything.

The skiff was towing with too long a painter, and was behaving very badly. Every once in a while it would hold back till the tow-rope tautened, then come leaping ahead and sheering and dropping slack till it threatened to shove its nose under the huge whitecaps which roared so hungrily on every hand. Joe climbed over the cockpit-rail to the slippery after-deck, and made his way to the bitt to which the skiff was fastened.

"Be careful," 'Frisco Kid warned, as a heavy puff struck the Dazzler and careened her dangerously over on her side. "Keep one turn round the bitt, and heave in on it when the painter slacks."

It was ticklish work for a greenhorn. Joe threw off all the turns save the last, which he held with one hand, while with the other he attempted to bring in on the painter. But at that instant it tightened with a tremendous jerk, the boat sheering sharply into the crest of a heavy sea. The rope slipped from his hands and began to fly out over the stern. He clutched it frantically, and was dragged after it over the sloping deck.

"Let her go! Let her go!" 'Frisco Kid shouted.

Joe let go just as he was on the verge of going overboard, and the skiff dropped rapidly astern. He glanced in a shamefaced way at his companion, expecting to be sharply reprimanded for his awkwardness. But 'Frisco Kid smiled good-naturedly.

"That 's all right," he said. "No bones broke and nobody overboard. Better to lose a boat than a man any day; that 's what I say. Besides, I should n't have sent you out there. And there 's no harm done. We can pick it up all right. Go in and drop some more centerboard,—a couple of feet,—and then come out and do what I tell you. But don't be in a hurry. Take it easy and sure."

Joe dropped the centerboard and returned, to be stationed at the jib-sheet.

"Hard a-lee!" 'Frisco Kid cried, throwing the tiller down, and following it with his body. "Cast off! That 's right. Now lend a hand on the main-sheet!"

Together, hand over hand, they came in on the reefed mainsail. Joe began to warm up with the work. The Dazzler turned on her heel like a race-horse, and swept into the wind, her canvas snarling and her sheets slatting like hail.

"Draw down the jib-sheet!"

Joe obeyed, and, the head-sail filling, forced her off on the other tack. This manoeuver had turned French Pete's bunk from the lee to the weather side, and rolled him out on the cabin floor, where he lay in a drunken stupor.

'Frisco Kid, with his back against the tiller and holding the sloop off that it might cover their previous course, looked at him with an expression of disgust, and muttered: "The dog! We could well go to the bottom, for all he 'd care or do!"

Twice they tacked, trying to go over the same ground; and then Joe discovered the skiff bobbing to windward in the star-lit darkness.

"Plenty of time," 'Frisco Kid cautioned, shooting the Dazzler into the wind toward it and gradually losing headway. "Now!"

Joe leaned over the side, grasped the trailing painter, and made it fast to the bitt. Then they tacked ship again and started on their way. Joe still felt ashamed for the trouble he had caused; but 'Frisco Kid quickly put him at ease.

"Oh, that 's nothing," he said. "Everybody does that when they 're beginning. Now some men forget all about the trouble they had in learning, and get mad when a greeny makes a mistake. I never do. Why, I remember—"

And then he told Joe of many of the mishaps which fell to him when, as a little lad, he first went on the water, and of some of the severe punishments for the same which were measured out to him. He had passed the running end of a lanyard over the tiller-neck, and as they talked they sat side by side and close against each other in the shelter of the cockpit.

"What place is that?" Joe asked, as they flew by a lighthouse blinking from a rocky headland.

"Goat Island. They 've got a naval training station for boys over on the other side, and a torpedo-magazine. There 's jolly good fishing, too—rock-cod. We 'll pass to the lee of it, and make across, and anchor in the shelter of Angel Island. There 's a quarantine station there. Then when French Pete gets sober we 'll know where he wants to go. You can turn in now and get some sleep. I can manage all right."

Joe shook his head. There had been too much excitement for him to feel in the least like sleeping. He could not bear to think of it with the Dazzler leaping and surging along and shattering the seas into clouds of spray on her weather bow. His clothes had half dried already, and he preferred to stay on deck and enjoy it.

The lights of Oakland had dwindled till they made only a hazy flare against the sky; but to the south the San Francisco lights, topping hills and sinking into valleys, stretched miles upon miles. Starting from the great ferry building, and passing on to Telegraph Hill, Joe was soon able to locate the principal places of the city. Somewhere over in that maze of light and shadow was the home of his father, and perhaps even now they were thinking and worrying about him; and over there Bessie was sleeping cozily, to wake up in the morning and wonder why her brother Joe did not come down to breakfast. Joe shivered. It was almost morning. Then slowly his head dropped over on 'Frisco Kid's shoulder and he was fast asleep.

CHAPTER XI. CAPTAIN AND CREW

"Come! Wake up! We 're going into anchor."

Joe roused with a start, bewildered at the unusual scene; for sleep had banished his troubles for the time being, and he knew not where he was. Then he remembered. The wind had dropped with the night. Beyond, the heavy after-sea was still rolling; but the Dazzler was creeping up in the shelter of a rocky island. The sky was clear, and the air had the snap and vigor of early morning about it. The rippling water was laughing in the rays of the sun just shouldering above the eastern sky-line. To the south lay Alcatraz Island, and from its gun-crowned heights a flourish of trumpets saluted the day. In the west the Golden Gate yawned between the Pacific Ocean and San Francisco Bay. A full-rigged ship, with her lightest canvas, even to the sky-sails, set, was coming slowly in on the flood-tide.

It was a pretty sight. Joe rubbed the sleep from his eyes and drank in the glory of it till 'Frisco Kid told him to go for'ard and make ready for dropping the anchor.

"Overhaul about fifty fathoms of chain," he ordered, "and then stand by." He eased the sloop gently into the wind, at the same time casting off the jib-sheet. "Let go the jib-halyards and come in on the downhaul!"

Joe had seen the manoeuver performed the previous night, and so was able to carry it out with fair success.

"Now! Over with the mud-hook! Watch out for turns! Lively, now!"

The chain flew out with startling rapidity and brought the Dazzler to rest. 'Frisco Kid went for'ard to help, and together they lowered the mainsail, furled it in shipshape manner and made all fast with the gaskets, and put the crutches under the main-boom.

"Here 's a bucket," said 'Frisco Kid, as he passed him the article in question. "Wash down the decks, and don't be afraid of the water, nor of the dirt either. Here 's a broom. Give it what for, and have everything shining. When you get that done bail out the skiff. She opened her seams a little last night. I 'm going below to cook breakfast."

The water was soon slushing merrily over the deck, while the smoke pouring from the cabin stove carried a promise of good things to come. Time and again Joe lifted his head from his task to take in the scene. It was one to appeal to any healthy boy, and he was no exception. The romance of it stirred him strangely, and his happiness would have been complete could he have escaped remembering who and what his companions were. The thought of this, and of French Pete in his bleary sleep below, marred the beauty of the day. He had been unused to such things and was shocked at the harsh reality of life. But instead of hurting him, as it might a lad of weaker nature, it had the opposite effect. It strengthened his desire to be clean and strong, and to not be ashamed of himself in his own eyes. He glanced about him and sighed. Why could not men be honest and true? It seemed too bad that he must go away and leave all this; but the events of the night were strong upon him, and he knew that in order to be true to himself he must escape.

At this juncture he was called to breakfast. He discovered that 'Frisco Kid was as good a cook as he was a sailor, and made haste to do justice to the fare. There were mush and condensed milk, beefsteak and fried potatoes, and all topped off with good French bread, butter, and coffee. French Pete did not join them, though 'Frisco Kid attempted a couple of times to rouse him. He mumbled and grunted, half opened his bleared eyes, then fell to snoring again.

"Can't tell when he 's going to get those spells," 'Frisco Kid explained, when Joe, having finished washing dishes, came on deck. "Sometimes he won't get that way for a month, and others he won't be decent for a week at a stretch. Sometimes he 's good-natured, and sometimes he 's dangerous; so the best thing to do is to let him alone and keep out of his way; and don't cross him, for if you do there 's liable to be trouble.

"Come on; let 's take a swim," he added, abruptly changing the subject to one more agreeable. "Can you swim?"

207

Joe nodded.

"What 's that place?" he asked, as he poised before diving, pointing toward a sheltered beach on the island where there were several buildings and a large number of tents.

"Quarantine station. Lots of smallpox coming in now on the China steamers, and they make them go there till the doctors say they 're safe to land. I tell you, they 're strict about it, too. Why—"

Splash! Had 'Frisco Kid finished his sentence just then, instead of diving overboard, much trouble might have been saved to Joe. But he did not finish it, and Joe dived after him.

"I 'll tell you what," 'Frisco Kid suggested half an hour later, while they clung to the bobstay preparatory to climbing out. "Let 's catch a mess of fish for dinner, and then turn in and make up for the sleep we lost last night. What d' you say?"

They made a race to clamber aboard, but Joe was shoved over the side again. When he finally did arrive, the other lad had brought to light a pair of heavily leaded, large-hooked lines and a mackerel-keg of salt sardines.

"Bait," he said. "Just shove a whole one on. They 're not a bit partic'lar. Swallow the bait, hook and all, and go—that 's their caper. The fellow that does n't catch the first fish has to clean 'em."

Both sinkers started on their long descent together, and seventy feet of line whizzed out before they came to rest. But at the instant his sinker touched the bottom Joe felt the struggling jerks of a hooked fish. As he began to haul in he glanced at 'Frisco Kid and saw that he too had evidently captured a finny prize. The race between them was exciting. Hand over hand the wet lines flashed inboard. But 'Frisco Kid was more expert, and his fish tumbled into the cockpit first. Joe's followed an instant later—a three-pound rock-cod. He was wild with joy. It was magnificent—the largest fish he had ever landed or ever seen landed. Over went the lines again, and up they came with two mates of the ones already captured. It was sport royal. Joe would certainly have continued till he had fished the bay empty, had not 'Frisco Kid persuaded him to stop.

"We 've got enough for three meals now," he said, "so there 's no use in having them spoil. Besides, the more you catch the more you clean, and you 'd better start in right away. I 'm going to bed."

CHAPTER XII. JOE TRIES TO TAKE FRENCH LEAVE

Joe did not mind. In fact, he was glad he had not caught the first fish, for it helped out a little plan which had come to him while swimming. He threw the last cleaned fish into a bucket of water and glanced about him. The quarantine station was a bare half-mile away, and he could make out a soldier pacing up and down at sentry duty on the beach. Going into the cabin, he listened to the heavy breathing of the sleepers. He had to pass so close to 'Frisco Kid to get his bundle of clothes that he decided not to take it. Returning outside, he carefully pulled the skiff alongside, got aboard with a pair of oars, and cast off.

At first he rowed very gently in the direction of the station, fearing the chance of noise if he made undue haste. But gradually he increased the strength of his strokes till he had settled down to the regular stride. When he had covered half the distance he glanced about. Escape was sure now, for he knew, even if he were discovered, that it would be impossible for the Dazzler to get under way and head him off before he made the land and the protection of that man who wore the uniform of Uncle Sam's soldiers.

The report of a gun came to him from the shore, but his back was in that direction and he did not bother to turn around. A second report followed, and a bullet cut the water within a couple of feet of his oar-blade. This time he did turn around. The soldier on the beach was leveling his rifle at him for a third shot.

Joe was in a predicament, and a very tantalizing one at that. A few minutes of hard rowing would bring him to the beach and to safety; but on that beach, for some unaccountable reason, stood a United States soldier who persisted in firing at him. When Joe saw the gun aimed at him for the third time, he backed water hastily. As a result, the skiff came to a standstill, and the soldier, lowering his rifle, regarded him intently.

"I want to come ashore! Important!" Joe shouted out to him.

The man in uniform shook his head.

"But it 's important, I tell you! Won't you let me come ashore?"

He took a hurried look in the direction of the Dazzler. The shots had evidently awakened French Pete, for the mainsail had been hoisted, and as he looked he saw the anchor broken out and the jib flung to the breeze.

"Can't land here!" the soldier shouted back. "Smallpox!"

"But I must!" he cried, choking down a half-sob and preparing to row.

"Then I 'll shoot you," was the cheering response, and the rifle came to shoulder again.

Joe thought rapidly. The island was large. Perhaps there were no soldiers farther on, and if he only once got ashore he did not care how quickly they captured him. He might catch the smallpox, but even that was better than going back to the bay pirates. He whirled the skiff half about to the right, and threw all his strength against the oars. The cove was quite wide, and the nearest point which he must go around a good distance away. Had he been more of a sailor, he would have gone in the other direction for the opposite point, and thus had the wind on his pursuers. As it was, the Dazzler had a beam wind in which to overtake him.

It was nip and tuck for a while. The breeze was light and not very steady, so sometimes he gained and sometimes they. Once it freshened till the sloop was within a hundred yards of him, and then it dropped suddenly flat, the Dazzler's big mainsail flapping idly from side to side.

"Ah! you steal ze skiff, eh?" French Pete howled at him, running into the cabin for his rifle. "I fix you! You come back queeck, or I kill you!" But he knew the soldier was watching them from the shore, and did not dare to fire, even over the lad's head.

Joe did not think of this, for he, who had never been shot at in all his previous life, had been under fire twice in the last twenty-four hours. Once more or less could n't amount to much. So he pulled steadily away, while French Pete raved like a wild man, threatening him with all manner of punishments once he laid hands upon him again. To complicate matters, 'Frisco Kid waxed mutinous.

"Just you shoot him, and I 'll see you hung for it—see if I don't," he threatened. "You 'd better let him go. He 's a good boy and all right, and not raised for the dirty life you and I are leading."

"You too, eh!" the Frenchman shrieked, beside himself with rage. "Den I fix you, you rat!"

He made a rush for the boy, but 'Frisco Kid led him a lively chase from cockpit to bowsprit and back again. A sharp capful of wind arriving just then, French Pete abandoned the one chase for the other. Springing to the tiller and slacking away on the main-sheet,—for the wind favored,—he headed the sloop down upon Joe. The latter made one tremendous spurt, then gave up in despair and hauled in his oars. French Pete let go the main-sheet, lost steerageway as he rounded up alongside the motionless skiff, and dragged Joe out.

"Keep mum," 'Frisco Kid whispered to him while the irate Frenchman was busy fastening the painter. "Don't talk back. Let him say all he wants to, and keep quiet. It 'll be better for you."

But Joe's Anglo-Saxon blood was up, and he did not heed.

"Look here, Mr. French Pete, or whatever your name is," he commenced; "I give you to understand that I want to quit, and that I 'm going to quit. So you 'd better put me ashore at once. If you don't I 'll put you in prison, or my name 's not Joe Bronson."

'Frisco Kid waited the outcome fearfully. French Pete was aghast. He was being defied aboard his own vessel—and by a boy! Never had such a thing been heard of. He knew he was committing an unlawful act in detaining him, but at the same time he was afraid to let him go with the information he had gathered concerning the sloop and its occupation. The boy had spoken the unpleasant truth when he said he could send him to prison. The only thing for him to do was to bully him.

"You will, eh?" His shrill voice rose wrathfully. "Den you come too. You row ze boat last-a night—answer me dat! You steal ze iron—answer me dat! You run away—answer me dat! And den you say you put me in jail? Bah!"

"But I did n't know," Joe protested.

"Ha, ha! Dat is funny. You tell dat to ze judge; mebbe him laugh, eh?"

"I say I did n't," he reiterated manfully. "I did n't know I 'd shipped along with a lot of thieves."

'Frisco Kid winced at this epithet, and had Joe been looking at him he would have seen a red flush mount to his face.

"And now that I do know," he continued, "I wish to be put ashore. I don't know anything about the law, but I do know something of right and wrong; and I 'm willing to take my chance with any judge for whatever wrong I have done—with all the judges in the United States, for that matter. And that 's more than you can say, Mr. Pete."

"You say dat, eh? Vaire good. But you are one big t'ief—"

"I 'm not—don't you dare call me that again!" Joe's face was pale, and he was trembling—but not with fear.

"T'ief!" the Frenchman taunted back.

"You lie!"

Joe had not been a boy among boys for nothing. He knew the penalty which attached itself to the words he had just spoken, and he expected to receive it. So he was not overmuch surprised when he picked himself up from the floor of the cockpit an instant later, his head still ringing from a stiff blow between the eyes.

"Say dat one time more," French Pete bullied, his fist raised and prepared to strike.

Tears of anger stood in Joe's eyes, but he was calm and in deadly earnest. "When you say I am a thief, Pete, you lie. You can kill me, but still I will say you lie."

"No, you don't!" 'Frisco Kid had darted in like a cat, preventing a second blow, and shoving the Frenchman back across the cockpit.

"You leave the boy alone!" he continued, suddenly unshipping and arming himself with the heavy iron tiller, and standing between them. "This thing 's gone just about as far as it 's going to go. You big fool, can't you see the stuff the boy 's made of? He speaks true. He 's right, and he knows it, and you could kill him and he would n't give in. There 's my hand on it, Joe." He turned and extended his hand to Joe, who returned the grip. "You 've got spunk and you 're not afraid to show it."

French Pete's mouth twisted itself in a sickly smile, but the evil gleam in his eyes gave it the lie. He shrugged his shoulders and said, "Ah! So? He does not dee-sire dat I call him pet names. Ha, ha! It is only ze sailorman play. Let us—what you call—forgive and forget, eh? Vaire good; forgive and forget."

He reached out his hand, but Joe refused to take it. 'Frisco Kid nodded approval, while French Pete, still shrugging his shoulders and smiling, passed into the cabin.

"Slack off ze main-sheet," he called out, "and run down for Hunter's Point. For one time I will cook ze dinner, and den you will say dat it is ze vaire good dinner. Ah! French Pete is ze great cook!"

"That 's the way he always does—gets real good and cooks when he wants to make up," 'Frisco Kid hazarded, slipping the tiller into the rudder-head and obeying the order. "But even then you can't trust him."

Joe nodded his head, but did not speak. He was in no mood for conversation. He was still trembling from the excitement of the last few moments, while deep down he questioned himself on how he had behaved, and found nothing to be ashamed of.

CHAPTER XIII. BEFRIENDING EACH OTHER

The afternoon sea-breeze had sprung up and was now rioting in from the Pacific. Angel Island was fast dropping astern, and the water-front of San Francisco showing up, as the Dazzler plowed along before it. Soon they were in the midst of the shipping, passing in and out among the vessels which had come from the ends of the earth. Later they crossed the fairway, where the ferry steamers, crowded with passengers, passed to and fro between San Francisco and Oakland. One came so close that the passengers crowded to the side to see the gallant little sloop and the two boys in the cockpit. Joe gazed enviously at the row of down-turned faces. They were all going to their homes, while he—he was going he knew not whither, at the will of French Pete. He was half tempted to cry out for help; but the foolishness of such an act struck him, and he held his tongue. Turning his head, his eyes wandered along the smoky heights of the city, and he fell to musing on the strange way of men and ships on the sea.

'Frisco Kid watched him from the corner of his eye, following his thoughts as accurately as though he spoke them aloud.

"Got a home over there somewheres?" he queried suddenly, waving his hand in the direction of the city.

Joe started, so correctly had his thought been guessed. "Yes," he said simply.

"Tell us about it."

Joe rapidly described his home, though forced to go into greater detail because of the curious questions of his companion. 'Frisco Kid was interested in everything, especially in Mrs. Bronson and Bessie. Of the latter he could not seem to tire, and poured forth question after question concerning her. So peculiar and artless were some of them that Joe could hardly forbear to smile.

"Now tell me about yours," he said when he at last had finished.

'Frisco Kid seemed suddenly to harden, and his face took on a stern look which the other had never seen there before. He swung his foot idly to and fro, and lifted a dull eye aloft to the main-peak blocks, with which, by the way, there was nothing the matter.

"Go ahead," the other encouraged.

"I have n't no home."

The four words left his mouth as though they had been forcibly ejected, and his lips came together after them almost with a snap.

Joe saw he had touched a tender spot, and strove to ease the way out of it again. "Then the home you did have." He did not dream that there were lads in the world who never had known homes, or that he had only succeeded in probing deeper.

"Never had none."

"Oh!" His interest was aroused, and he now threw solicitude to the winds. "Any sisters?"

"Nope."

"Mother?"

"I was so young when she died that I don't remember her."

"Father?"

"I never saw much of him. He went to sea—anyhow, he disappeared."

"Oh!" Joe did not know what to say, and an oppressive silence, broken only by the churn of the Dazzler's forefoot, fell upon them.

Just then Pete came out to relieve at the tiller while they went in to eat. Both lads hailed his advent with feelings of relief, and the awkwardness vanished over the dinner, which was all their skipper had claimed it to be. Afterward 'Frisco Kid relieved Pete, and while he was eating Joe washed up the dishes and put the cabin shipshape. Then they all gathered in the stern, where the captain strove to increase the general cordiality by entertaining them with descriptions of life among the pearl-divers of the South Seas.

In this fashion the afternoon wore away. They had long since left San Francisco behind, rounded Hunter's Point, and were now skirting the San Mateo shore. Joe caught a glimpse, once, of a party of cyclists rounding a cliff on the San Bruno Road, and remembered the time when he had gone over the same ground on his own wheel. It was only a month or two before, but it seemed an age to him now, so much had there been to come between.

By the time supper had been eaten and the things cleared away, they were well down the bay, off the marshes behind which Redwood City clustered. The wind had gone down with the sun, and the Dazzler was making but little headway, when they sighted a sloop bearing down upon them on the dying wind. 'Frisco Kid instantly named it as the Reindeer, to which French Pete, after a deep scrutiny, agreed. He seemed very much pleased at the meeting.

"Red Nelson runs her," 'Frisco Kid informed Joe. "And he 's a terror and no mistake. I 'm always afraid of him when he comes near. They 've got something big down here, and they 're always after French Pete to tackle it with them. He knows more about it, whatever it is."

Joe nodded, and looked at the approaching craft curiously. Though somewhat larger, it was built on about the same lines as the Dazzler which meant, above everything else, that it was built for speed. The mainsail was so large that it was more like that of a racing-yacht, and it carried the points for no less than three reefs in case of rough weather. Aloft and on deck everything was in place—nothing was untidy or useless. From running-gear to standing rigging, everything bore evidence of thorough order and smart seamanship.

The Reindeer came up slowly in the gathering twilight and went to anchor a biscuit-toss away. French Pete followed suit with the Dazzler, and then went in the skiff to pay them a visit. The two lads stretched themselves out on top the cabin and awaited his return.

"Do you like the life?" Joe broke silence.

The other turned on his elbow. "Well—I do, and then again I don't. The fresh air, and the salt water, and all that, and the freedom—that 's all right;

but I don't like the—the—" He paused a moment, as though his tongue had failed in its duty, and then blurted out: "the stealing."

"Then why don't you quit it?" Joe liked the lad more than he dared confess to himself, and he felt a sudden missionary zeal come upon him.

"I will just as soon as I can turn my hand to something else."

"But why not now?"

Now is the accepted time was ringing in Joe's ears, and if the other wished to leave, it seemed a pity that he did not, and at once.

"Where can I go? What can I do? There 's nobody in all the world to lend me a hand, just as there never has been. I tried it once, and learned my lesson too well to do it again in a hurry."

"Well, when I get out of this I 'm going home. Guess my father was right, after all. And I don't see, maybe—what 's the matter with you going with me?" He said this last without thinking, impulsively, and 'Frisco Kid knew it.

"You don't know what you 're talking about," he answered. "Fancy me going off with you! What 'd your father say? and—and the rest? How would he think of me? And what 'd he do?"

Joe felt sick at heart. He realized that in the spirit of the moment he had given an invitation which, on sober thought, he knew would be impossible to carry out. He tried to imagine his father receiving in his own house a stranger like 'Frisco Kid—no, that was not to be thought of. Then, forgetting his own plight, he fell to racking his brains for some other method by which 'Frisco Kid could get away from his present surroundings.

"He might turn me over to the police," the other went on, "and send me to a refuge. I 'd die first, before I 'd let that happen to me. And besides, Joe, I 'm not of your kind, and you know it. Why, I 'd be like a fish out of water, what with all the things I did n't know. Nope; I guess I 'll have to wait a little before I strike out. But there 's only one thing for you to do, and that 's to go straight home. First chance I get I 'll land you, and then I 'll deal with

218

French Pete—"

"No, you don't," Joe interrupted hotly. "When I leave I 'm not going to leave you in trouble on my account. So don't you try anything like that. I 'll get away, never fear, and if I can figure it out I want you to come along too; come along anyway, and figure it out afterward. What d' you say?"

'Frisco Kid shook his head, and, gazing up at the starlit heavens, wandered off into dreams of the life he would like to lead but from which he seemed inexorably shut out. The seriousness of life was striking deeper than ever into Joe's heart, and he lay silent, thinking hard. A mumble of heavy voices came to them from the Reindeer; and from the land the solemn notes of a church bell floated across the water, while the summer night wrapped them slowly in its warm darkness.

CHAPTER XIV. AMONG THE OYSTER-BEDS

Time and the world slipped away, and both boys were aroused by the harsh voice of French Pete from the sleep into which they had fallen.

"Get under way!" he was bawling. "Here, you Sho! Cast off ze gaskets! Queeck! Lively! You Kid, ze jib!"

Joe was clumsy in the darkness, not knowing the names of things and the places where they were to be found; but he made fair progress, and when he had tossed the gaskets into the cockpit was ordered forward to help hoist the mainsail. After that the anchor was hove in and the jib set. Then they coiled down the halyards and put everything in order before they returned aft.

"Vaire good, vaire good," the Frenchman praised, as Joe dropped in over the rail. "Splendeed! You make ze good sailorman, I know for sure."

'Frisco Kid lifted the cover of one of the cockpit lockers and glanced questioningly at French Pete.

"For sure," that mariner replied. "Put up ze side-lights."

'Frisco Kid took the red and green lanterns into the cabin to light them, and then went forward with Joe to hang them in the rigging.

"They 're not goin' to tackle it," 'Frisco Kid said in an undertone.

"What?" Joe asked.

"That big thing I was tellin' you was down here somewhere. It 's so big, I guess, that French Pete 's 'most afraid to go in for it. Red Nelson 'd go in quicker 'n a wink, but he don't know enough about it. Can't go in, you see, till Pete gives the word."

"Where are we going now?" Joe questioned.

"Don't know; oyster-beds most likely, from the way we 're heading."

It was an uneventful trip. A breeze sprang up out of the night behind them, and held steady for an hour or more. Then it dropped and became aimless and erratic, puffing gently first from one quarter and then another. French Pete remained at the tiller, while occasionally Joe or 'Frisco Kid took in or slacked off a sheet.

Joe sat and marveled that the Frenchman should know where he was going. To Joe it seemed that they were lost in the impenetrable darkness which shrouded them. A high fog had rolled in from the Pacific, and though they were beneath, it came between them and the stars, depriving them of the little light from that source.

But French Pete seemed to know instinctively the direction he should go, and once, in reply to a query from Joe, bragged of his ability to go by the "feel" of things.

"I feel ze tide, ze wind, ze speed," he explained. "Even do I feel ze land. Dat I tell you for sure. How? I do not know. Only do I know dat I feel ze land, just like my arm grow long, miles and miles long, and I put my hand upon ze land and feel it, and know dat it is there."

Joe looked incredulously at 'Frisco Kid.

"That 's right," he affirmed. "After you 've been on the water a good while you come to feel the land. And if your nose is any account, you can usually smell it."

An hour or so later, Joe surmised from the Frenchman's actions that they were approaching their destination. He seemed on the alert, and was constantly peering into the darkness ahead as though he expected to see something at any moment. Joe looked very hard, but saw only the darkness.

"Try ze stick, Kid," French Pete ordered. "I t'ink it is about ze time."

'Frisco Kid unlashed a long and slender pole from the top of the cabin, and, standing on the narrow deck amidships, plunged one end of it into the water and drove it straight down.

"About fifteen feet," he said.

"What ze bottom?"

"Mud," was the answer.

"Wait one while, den we try some more."

Five minutes afterward the pole was plunged overside again.

"Two fathoms," Joe answered—"shells."

French Pete rubbed his hands with satisfaction. "Vaire good, vaire well," he said. "I hit ze ground every time. You can't fool-a ze old man; I tell you dat for sure."

'Frisco Kid continued operating the pole and announcing the results, to the mystification of Joe, who could not comprehend their intimate knowledge of the bottom of the bay.

"Ten feet—shells," 'Frisco Kid went on in a monotonous voice. "'Leven feet—shells. Fourteen feet—soft. Sixteen feet—mud. No bottom."

"Ah, ze channel," said French Pete at this.

For a few minutes it was "No bottom"; and then, suddenly, came 'Frisco Kid's cry: "Eight feet—hard!"

"Dat 'll do," French Pete commanded. "Run for'ard, you Sho, an' let go ze jib. You, Kid, get all ready ze hook."

Joe found the jib-halyard and cast it off the pin, and, as the canvas fluttered down, came in hand over hand on the downhaul.

"Let 'er go!" came the command, and the anchor dropped into the water, carrying but little chain after it.

'Frisco Kid threw over plenty of slack and made fast. Then they furled the sails, made things tidy, and went below and to bed.

It was six o'clock when Joe awoke and went out into the cockpit to look about. Wind and sea had sprung up, and the Dazzler was rolling and tossing and now and again fetching up on her anchor-chain with a savage jerk. He was forced to hold on to the boom overhead to steady himself. It was a gray and leaden day, with no signs of the rising sun, while the sky was obscured by great masses of flying clouds.

Joe sought for the land. A mile and a half away it lay—a long, low stretch of sandy beach with a heavy surf thundering upon it. Behind appeared desolate marshlands, while far beyond towered the Contra Costa Hills.

Changing the direction of his gaze, Joe was startled by the sight of a small sloop rolling and plunging at her anchor not a hundred yards away. She was nearly to windward, and as she swung off slightly he read her name on the stern, the Flying Dutchman, one of the boats he had seen lying at the city wharf in Oakland. A little to the left of her he discovered the Ghost, and beyond were half a dozen other sloops at anchor.

"What I tell you?"

Joe looked quickly over his shoulder. French Pete had come out of the cabin and was triumphantly regarding the spectacle.

"What I tell you? Can't fool-a ze old man, dat 's what. I hit it in ze dark just so well as in ze sunshine. I know—I know."

"Is she goin' to howl?" 'Frisco Kid asked from the cabin, where he was starting the fire.

The Frenchman gravely studied sea and sky for a couple of minutes.

"Mebbe blow over—mebbe blow up," was his doubtful verdict. "Get breakfast queeck, and we try ze dredging."

Smoke was rising from the cabins of the different sloops, denoting that they were all bent on getting the first meal of the day. So far as the Dazzler was concerned, it was a simple matter, and soon they were putting a single reef in the mainsail and getting ready to weigh anchor.

Joe was curious. These were undoubtedly the oyster-beds; but how under the sun, in that wild sea, were they to get oysters? He was quickly to learn the way. Lifting a section of the cockpit flooring, French Pete brought

223

out two triangular frames of steel. At the apex of one of these triangles; in a ring for the purpose, he made fast a piece of stout rope. From this the sides (inch rods) diverged at almost right angles, and extended down for a distance of four feet or more, where they were connected by the third side of the triangle, which was the bottom of the dredge. This was a flat plate of steel over a yard in length, to which was bolted a row of long, sharp teeth, likewise of steel. Attached to the toothed plate, and to the sides of the frame was a net of very coarse fishing-twine, which Joe correctly surmised was there to catch the oysters raked loose by the teeth from the bottom of the bay.

A rope being made fast to each of the dredges, they were dropped overboard from either side of the Dazzler. When they had reached the bottom, and were dragging with the proper length of line out, they checked her speed quite noticeably. Joe touched one of the lines with his hands, and could feel plainly the shock and jar and grind as it tore over the bottom.

"All in!" French Pete shouted.

The boys laid hold of the line and hove in the dredge. The net was full of mud and slime and small oysters, with here and there a large one. This mess they dumped on the deck and picked over while the dredge was dragging again. The large oysters they threw into the cockpit, and shoveled the rubbish overboard. There was no rest, for by this time the other dredge required emptying. And when this was done and the oysters sorted, both dredges had to be hauled aboard, so that French Pete could put the Dazzler about on the other tack.

The rest of the fleet was under way and dredging back in similar fashion. Sometimes the different sloops came quite close to them, and they hailed them and exchanged snatches of conversation and rough jokes. But in the main it was hard work, and at the end of an hour Joe's back was aching from the unaccustomed strain, and his fingers were cut and bleeding from his clumsy handling of the sharp-edged oysters.

"Dat 's right," French Pete said approvingly. "You learn queeck. Vaire soon you know how."

Joe grinned ruefully and wished it was dinner-time. Now and then, when a light dredge was hauled, the boys managed to catch breath and say a couple of words.

"That 's Asparagus Island," 'Frisco Kid said, indicating the shore. "At least, that 's what the fishermen and scow-sailors call it. The people who live there call it Bay Farm Island." He pointed more to the right. "And over there is San Leandro. You can't see it, but it 's there."

"Ever been there?" Joe asked.

'Frisco Kid nodded his head and signed to him to help heave in the starboard dredge.

"These are what they call the deserted beds," he said again. "Nobody owns them, so the oyster pirates come down and make a bluff at working them."

"Why a bluff?"

"'Cause they 're pirates, that 's why, and because there 's more money in raiding the private beds."

He made a sweeping gesture toward the east and southeast. "The private beds are over yonder, and if it don't storm the whole fleet 'll be raidin' 'em to-night."

"And if it does storm?" Joe asked.

"Why, we won't raid them, and French Pete 'll be mad, that 's all. He always hates being put out by the weather. But it don't look like lettin' up, and this is the worst possible shore in a sou'wester. Pete may try to hang on, but it 's best to get out before she howls."

At first it did seem as though the weather were growing better. The stiff southwest wind dropped perceptibly, and by noon, when they went to anchor for dinner, the sun was breaking fitfully through the clouds.

"That 's all right," 'Frisco Kid said prophetically. "But I ain't been on the bay for nothing. She 's just gettin' ready to let us have it good an' hard."

"I t'ink you 're right, Kid," French Pete agreed; "but ze Dazzler hang on all ze same. Last-a time she run away, an' fine night come. Dis time she run not away. Eh? Vaire good."

CHAPTER XV. GOOD SAILORS IN A WILD ANCHORAGE

All afternoon the Dazzler pitched and rolled at her anchorage, and as evening drew on the wind deceitfully eased down. This, and the example set by French Pete, encouraged the rest of the oyster-boats to attempt to ride out the night; but they looked carefully to their moorings and put out spare anchors.

French Pete ordered the two boys into the skiff, and, at the imminent risk of swamping, they carried out a second anchor, at nearly right angles to the first one, and dropped it over. French Pete then ran out a great quantity of chain and rope, so that the Dazzler dropped back a hundred feet or more, where she rode more easily.

It was a wild stretch of water which Joe looked upon from the shelter of the cockpit. The oyster-beds were out in the open bay, utterly unprotected, and the wind, sweeping the water for a clean twelve miles, kicked up so tremendous a sea that at every moment it seemed as though the wallowing sloops would roll their masts overside. Just before twilight a patch of sail sprang up to windward, and grew and grew until it resolved itself into the huge mainsail of the Reindeer.

"Ze beeg fool!" French Pete cried, running out of the cabin to see. "Sometime—ah, sometime, I tell you—he crack on like dat, an' he go, pouf! just like dat, pouf!—an' no more Nelson, no more Reindeer, no more nothing."

Joe looked inquiringly at 'Frisco Kid.

"That 's right," he answered. "Nelson ought to have at least one reef in. Two 'd be better. But there he goes, every inch spread, as though some fiend was after 'im. He drives too hard; he 's too reckless, when there ain't the smallest need for it. I 've sailed with him, and I know his ways."

Like some huge bird of the air, the Reindeer lifted and soared down on them on the foaming crest of a wave.

"Don't mind," 'Frisco Kid warned. "He 's only tryin' to see how close he can come to us without hittin' us."

Joe nodded, and stared with wide eyes at the thrilling sight. The Reindeer leaped up in the air, pointing her nose to the sky till they could see her whole churning forefoot; then she plunged downward till her for'ard deck was flush with the foam, and with a dizzying rush she drove past them, her main-boom missing the Dazzler's rigging by scarcely a foot.

Nelson, at the wheel, waved his hand to them as he hurtled past, and laughed joyously in French Pete's face, who was angered by the dangerous trick.

When to leeward, the splendid craft rounded to the wind, rolling once till her brown bottom showed to the centerboard and they thought she was over, then righting and dashing ahead again like a thing possessed. She passed abreast of them on the starboard side. They saw the jib run down with a rush and an anchor go overboard as she shot into the wind; and as she fell off and back and off and back with a spilling mainsail, they saw a second anchor go overboard, wide apart from the first. Then the mainsail came down on the run, and was furled and fastened by the time she had tightened to her double hawsers.

"Ah, ah! Never was there such a man!"

The Frenchman's eyes were glistening with admiration for such perfect seamanship, and 'Frisco Kid's were likewise moist.

"Just like a yacht," he said as he went back into the cabin. "Just like a yacht, only better."

As night came on the wind began to rise again, and by eleven o'clock had reached the stage which 'Frisco Kid described as "howlin'." There was little sleep on the Dazzler. He alone closed his eyes. French Pete was up and down every few minutes. Twice, when he went on deck, he paid out more chain and rope. Joe lay in his blankets and listened, the while vainly courting sleep. He was not frightened, but he was untrained in the art of sleeping in the midst of such turmoil and uproar and violent commotion. Nor had he imagined a boat could play as wild antics as did the Dazzler and still survive. Often she wallowed over on her beam till he thought she would surely capsize. At other times she leaped and plunged in the air and fell upon the seas with thunderous crashes as though her bottom were shattered to fragments. Again, she would fetch up taut on her hawsers so suddenly and so fiercely as to reel from the shock and to groan and protest through every timber.

'Frisco Kid awoke once, and smiled at him, saying:

"This is what they call hangin' on. But just you wait till daylight comes, and watch us clawin' off. If some of the sloops don't go ashore, I 'm not me, that 's all."

And thereat he rolled over on his side and was off to sleep. Joe envied him. About three in the morning he heard French Pete crawl up for'ard and rummage around in the eyes of the boat. Joe looked on curiously, and by the dim light of the wildly swinging sea-lamp saw him drag out two spare coils of line. These he took up on deck, and Joe knew he was bending them on to the hawsers to make them still longer.

At half-past four French Pete had the fire going, and at five he called the boys for coffee. This over, they crept into the cockpit to gaze on the terrible scene. The dawn was breaking bleak and gray over a wild waste of tumbling water. They could faintly see the beach-line of Asparagus Island, but they could distinctly hear the thunder of the surf upon it; and as the day grew stronger they made out that they had dragged fully half a mile during the night.

The rest of the fleet had likewise dragged. The Reindeer was almost abreast of them; La Caprice lay a few hundred yards away; and to leeward, straggling between them and shore, were five more of the struggling oyster-boats.

"Two missing," 'Frisco Kid announced, putting the glasses to his eyes and searching the beach.

"And there 's one!" he cried. And after studying it carefully he added: "The Go Ask Her. She 'll be in pieces in no time. I hope they got ashore."

228

French Pete looked through the glasses, and then Joe. He could clearly see the unfortunate sloop lifting and pounding in the surf, and on the beach he spied the men who made up her crew.

"Where 's ze Ghost?" French Pete queried.

'Frisco Kid looked for her in vain along the beach; but when he turned the glass seaward he quickly discovered her riding safely in the growing light, half a mile or more to windward.

"I 'll bet she did n't drag a hundred feet all night," he said. "Must 've struck good holding-ground."

"Mud," was French Pete's verdict. "Just one vaire small patch of mud right there. If she get t'rough it she 's a sure-enough goner, I tell you dat. Her anchors vaire light, only good for mud. I tell ze boys get more heavy anchors, but dey laugh. Some day be sorry, for sure."

One of the sloops to leeward raised a patch of sail and began the terrible struggle out of the jaws of destruction and death. They watched her for a space, rolling and plunging fearfully, and making very little headway.

French Pete put a stop to their gazing. "Come on!" he shouted. "Put two reef in ze mainsail! We get out queeck!"

While occupied with this a shout aroused them. Looking up, they saw the Ghost dead ahead and right on top of them, and dragging down upon them at a furious rate.

French Pete scrambled forward like a cat, at the same time drawing his knife, with one stroke of which he severed the rope that held them to the spare anchor. This threw the whole weight of the Dazzler on the chain-anchor. In consequence she swung off to the left, and just in time; for the next instant, drifting stern foremost, the Ghost passed over the spot she had vacated.

"Why, she 's got four anchors out!" Joe exclaimed, at sight of four taut ropes entering the water almost horizontally from her bow.

"Two of 'em 's dredges," 'Frisco Kid grinned; "and there goes the stove."

As he spoke, two young fellows appeared on deck and dropped the cooking-stove overside with a line attached.

"Phew!" 'Frisco Kid cried. "Look at Nelson. He 's got one reef in, and you can just bet that 's a sign she 's howlin'!"

The Reindeer came foaming toward them, breasting the storm like some magnificent sea-animal. Red Nelson waved to them as he passed astern, and fifteen minutes later, when they were breaking out the one anchor that remained to them, he passed well to windward on the other tack.

French Pete followed her admiringly, though he said ominously: "Some day, pouf! he go just like dat, I tell you, sure."

A moment later the Dazzler's reefed jib was flung out, and she was straining and struggling in the thick of the fight. It was slow work, and hard and dangerous, clawing off that lee shore, and Joe found himself marveling often that so small a craft could possibly endure a minute in such elemental fury. But little by little she worked off the shore and out of the ground-swell into the deeper waters of the bay, where the main-sheet was slacked away a bit, and she ran for shelter behind the rock wall of the Alameda Mole a few miles away. Here they found the Reindeer calmly at anchor; and here, during the next several hours, straggled in the remainder of the fleet, with the exception of the Ghost, which had evidently gone ashore to keep the Go Ask Her company.

By afternoon the wind had dropped away with surprising suddenness, and the weather had turned almost summer-like.

"It does n't look right," 'Frisco Kid said in the evening, after French Pete had rowed over in the skiff to visit Nelson.

"What does n't look right?" Joe asked.

"Why, the weather. It went down too sudden. It did n't have a chance to blow itself out, and it ain't going to quit till does blow itself out. It 's likely to puff up and howl at any moment, if I know anything about it."

"Where will we go from here?" Joe asked. "Back to the oyster-beds?"

'Frisco Kid shook his head. "I can't say what French Pete 'll do. He 's been fooled on the iron, and fooled on the oysters, and he 's that disgusted he 's liable to do 'most anything desperate. I would n't be surprised to see him go off with Nelson towards Redwood City, where that big thing is that I was tellin' you about. It 's somewhere over there."

"Well, I won't have anything to do with it," Joe announced decisively.

"Of course not," 'Frisco Kid answered. "And with Nelson and his two men an' French Pete, I don't think there 'll be any need for you anyway."

CHAPTER XVI. 'FRISCO KID'S DITTY-BOX

After the conversation died away, the two lads lay upon the cabin for perhaps an hour. Then, without saying a word, 'Frisco Kid went below and struck a light. Joe could hear him fumbling about, and a little later heard his own name called softly. On going into the cabin, he saw 'Frisco Kid sitting on the edge of the bunk, a sailor's ditty-box on his knees, and in his hand a carefully folded page from a magazine.

"Does she look like this?" he asked, smoothing it out and turning it that the other might see.

It was a half-page illustration of two girls and a boy, grouped, evidently, in an old-fashioned roomy attic, and holding a council of some sort. The girl who was talking faced the onlooker, while the backs of the other two were turned.

"Who?" Joe queried, glancing in perplexity from the picture to 'Frisco Kid's face.

"Your—your sister—Bessie."

The word seemed reluctant in coming to his lips, and he expressed himself with a certain shy reverence, as though it were something unspeakably sacred.

Joe was nonplussed for the moment. He could see no bearing between the two in point, and, anyway, girls were rather silly creatures to waste one's time over. "He 's actually blushing," he thought, regarding the soft glow on the other's cheeks. He felt an irresistible desire to laugh, and tried to smother it down.

"No, no; don't!" 'Frisco Kid cried, snatching the paper away and putting it back in the ditty-box with shaking fingers. Then he added more slowly: "I thought—I—I kind o' thought you would understand, and—and—"

His lips trembled and his eyes glistened with unwonted moistness as he turned hastily away.

The next instant Joe was by his side on the bunk, his arm around him. Prompted by some instinctive monitor, he had done it before he thought. A week before he could not have imagined himself in such an absurd situation— his arm around a boy; but now it seemed the most natural thing in the world. He did not comprehend, but he knew, whatever it was, that it was of deep importance to his companion.

"Go ahead and tell us," he urged. "I 'll understand."

"No, you won't. You can't."

"Yes, sure. Go ahead."

'Frisco Kid choked and shook his head. "I don't think I could, anyway. It 's more the things I feel, and I don't know how to put them in words." Joe's hand patted his shoulder reassuringly, and he went on: "Well, it 's this way. You see, I don't know much about the land, and people, and things, and I never had any brothers or sisters or playmates. All the time I did n't know it, but I was lonely—sort of missed them down in here somewheres." He placed a hand over his breast. "Did you ever feel downright hungry? Well, that 's just the way I used to feel, only a different kind of hunger, and me not knowing what it was. But one day, oh, a long time back, I got a-hold of a magazine and saw a picture—that picture, with the two girls and the boy talking together. I thought it must be fine to be like them, and I got to thinking about the things they said and did, till it came to me all of a sudden like, and I knew it was just loneliness was the matter with me.

"But, more than anything else, I got to wondering about the girl who looks out of the picture right at you. I was thinking about her all the time, and by and by she became real to me. You see, it was making believe, and I knew it all the time, and then again I did n't. Whenever I 'd think of the men, and the work, and the hard life, I 'd know it was make-believe; but when I 'd think of her, it was n't. I don't know; I can't explain it."

Joe remembered all his own adventures which he had imagined on land and sea, and nodded. He at least understood that much.

"Of course it was all foolishness, but to have a girl like that for a comrade or friend seemed more like heaven to me than anything else I knew of. As I said, it was a long while back, and I was only a little kid—that was when Red Nelson gave me my name, and I 've never been anything but 'Frisco Kid ever since. But the girl in the picture: I was always getting that picture out to look at her, and before long, if I was n't square—why, I felt ashamed to look at her. Afterwards, when I was older, I came to look at it in another way. I thought, 'Suppose, Kid, some day you were to meet a girl like that, what would she think of you? Could she like you? Could she be even the least bit of a friend to you?' And then I 'd make up my mind to be better, to try and do something with myself so that she or any of her kind of people would not be ashamed to know me.

"That 's why I learned to read. That 's why I ran away. Nicky Perrata, a Greek boy, taught me my letters, and it was n't till after I learned to read that I found out there was anything really wrong in bay-pirating. I 'd been used to it ever since I could remember, and almost all the people I knew made their living that way. But when I did find out, I ran away, thinking to quit it for good. I 'll tell you about it sometime, and how I 'm back at it again.

"Of course she seemed a real girl when I was a youngster, and even now she sometimes seems that way, I 've thought so much about her. But while I 'm talking to you it all clears up and she comes to me in this light: she stands just for a plain idea, a better, cleaner life than this, and one I 'd like to live; and if I could live it, why, I 'd come to know that kind of girls, and their kind of people—your kind, that 's what I mean. So I was wondering about your sister and you, and that 's why—I don't know; I guess I was just wondering. But I suppose you know lots of girls like that, don't you?"

Joe nodded his head.

"Then tell me about them—something, anything," he added as he noted the fleeting expression of doubt in the other's eyes.

"Oh, that 's easy," Joe began valiantly. To a certain extent he did understand the lad's hunger, and it seemed a simple enough task to at least partially satisfy him. "To begin with, they 're like—hem!—why, they 're like—girls, just girls." He broke off with a miserable sense of failure.

'Frisco Kid waited patiently, his face a study in expectancy.

Joe struggled valiantly to marshal his forces. To his mind, in quick succession, came the girls with whom he had gone to school—the sisters of the boys he knew, and those who were his sister's friends: slim girls and plump girls, tall girls and short girls, blue-eyed and brown-eyed, curly-haired, black-haired, golden-haired; in short, a procession of girls of all sorts and descriptions. But, to save himself, he could say nothing about them. Anyway, he 'd never been a "sissy," and why should he be expected to know anything about them? "All girls are alike," he concluded desperately. "They 're just the same as the ones you know, Kid—sure they are."

"But I don't know any."

Joe whistled. "And never did?"

"Yes, one. Carlotta Gispardi. But she could n't speak English, and I could n't speak Dago; and she died. I don't care; though I never knew any, I seem to know as much about them as you do."

"And I guess I know more about adventures all over the world than you do," Joe retorted.

Both boys laughed. But a moment later, Joe fell into deep thought. It had come upon him quite swiftly that he had not been duly grateful for the good things of life he did possess. Already home, father, and mother had assumed a greater significance to him; but he now found himself placing a higher personal value upon his sister and his chums and friends. He had never appreciated them properly, he thought, but henceforth—well, there would be a different tale to tell.

The voice of French Pete hailing them put a finish to the conversation, for they both ran on deck.

CHAPTER XVII. 'FRISCO KID TELLS HIS STORY

"Get up ze mainsail and break out ze hook!" the Frenchman shouted. "And den tail on to ze Reindeer! No side-lights!"

"Come! Cast off those gaskets—lively!" 'Frisco Kid ordered. "Now lay on to the peak-halyards—there, that rope—cast it off the pin. And don't hoist ahead of me. There! Make fast! We 'll stretch it afterwards. Run aft and come in on the main-sheet! Shove the helm up!"

Under the sudden driving power of the mainsail, the Dazzler strained and tugged at her anchor like an impatient horse till the muddy iron left the bottom with a rush and she was free.

"Let go the sheet! Come for'ard again and lend a hand on the chain! Stand by to give her the jib!" 'Frisco Kid the boy who mooned over girls in pictorial magazines had vanished, and 'Frisco Kid the sailor, strong and dominant, was on deck. He ran aft and tacked about as the jib rattled aloft in the hands of Joe, who quickly joined him. Just then the Reindeer, like a monstrous bat, passed to leeward of them in the gloom.

"Ah, dose boys! Dey take all-a night!" they heard French Pete exclaim, and then the gruff voice of Red Nelson, who said: "Never you mind, Frenchy. I taught the Kid his sailorizing, and I ain't never been ashamed of him yet."

The Reindeer was the faster boat, but by spilling the wind from her sails they managed so that the boys could keep them in sight. The breeze came steadily in from the west, with a promise of early increase. The stars were being blotted out by masses of driving clouds, which indicated a greater velocity in the upper strata. 'Frisco Kid surveyed the sky.

"Going to have it good and stiff before morning," he said, "just as I told you."

Several hours later, both boats stood in for the San Mateo shore, and dropped anchor not more than a cable's-length away. A little wharf ran out, the bare end of which was perceptible to them, though they could discern a small yacht lying moored to a buoy a short distance away.

According to their custom, everything was put in readiness for hasty departure. The anchors could be tripped and the sails flung out on a moment's notice. Both skiffs came over noiselessly from the Reindeer. Red Nelson had given one of his two men to French Pete, so that each skiff was doubly manned. They were not a very prepossessing group of men,—at least, Joe did not think so,—for their faces bore a savage seriousness which almost made him shiver. The captain of the Dazzler buckled on his pistol-belt, and placed a rifle and a stout double-block tackle in the boat. Then he poured out wine all around, and, standing in the darkness of the little cabin, they pledged success to the expedition. Red Nelson was also armed, while his men wore at their hips the customary sailor's sheath-knife. They were very slow and careful to avoid noise in getting into the boats, French Pete pausing long enough to warn the boys to remain quietly aboard and not try any tricks.

"Now 'd be your chance, Joe, if they had n't taken the skiff," 'Frisco Kid whispered, when the boats had vanished into the loom of the land.

"What 's the matter with the Dazzler?" was the unexpected answer. "We could up sail and away before you could say Jack Robinson."

'Frisco Kid hesitated. The spirit of comradeship was strong in the lad, and deserting a companion in a pinch could not but be repulsive to him.

"I don't think it 'd be exactly square to leave them in the lurch ashore," he said. "Of course," he went on hurriedly, "I know the whole thing 's wrong; but you remember that first night, when you came running through the water for the skiff, and those fellows on the bank busy popping away? We did n't leave you in the lurch, did we?"

Joe assented reluctantly, and then a new thought flashed across his mind. "But they 're pirates—and thieves—and criminals. They 're breaking the law, and you and I are not willing to be lawbreakers. Besides, they 'll not be left. There 's the Reindeer. There 's nothing to prevent them from getting away on her, and they 'll never catch us in the dark."

"Come on, then." Though he had agreed, 'Frisco Kid did not quite like it, for it still seemed to savor of desertion.

They crawled forward and began to hoist the mainsail. The anchor they could slip, if necessary, and save the time of pulling it up. But at the first rattle of the halyards on the sheaves a warning "Hist!" came to them through the darkness, followed by a loudly whispered "Drop that!"

Glancing in the direction from which these sounds proceeded, they made out a white face peering at them from over the rail of the other sloop.

"Aw, it 's only the Reindeer's boy," 'Frisco Kid said. "Come on."

Again they were interrupted at the first rattling of the blocks.

"I say, you fellers, you 'd better let go them halyards pretty quick, I 'm a-tellin' you, or I 'll give you what for!"

This threat being dramatically capped by the click of a cocking pistol, 'Frisco Kid obeyed and went grumblingly back to the cockpit. "Oh, there 's plenty more chances to come," he whispered consolingly to Joe. "French Pete was cute, was n't he? He thought you might be trying to make a break, and put a guard on us."

Nothing came from the shore to indicate how the pirates were faring. Not a dog barked, not a light flared. Yet the air seemed quivering with an alarm about to burst forth. The night had taken on a strained feeling of intensity, as though it held in store all kinds of terrible things. The boys felt this keenly as they huddled against each other in the cockpit and waited.

"You were going to tell me about your running away," Joe ventured finally, "and why you came back again."

'Frisco Kid took up the tale at once, speaking in a muffled undertone close to the other's ear.

"You see, when I made up my mind to quit the life, there was n't a soul to lend me a hand; but I knew that the only thing for me to do was to get ashore and find some kind of work, so I could study. Then I figured there 'd be more chance in the country than in the city; so I gave Red Nelson the slip—I was on the Reindeer then. One night on the Alameda oyster-beds, I got ashore and headed back from the bay as fast as I could sprint. Nelson did n't catch me. But they were all Portuguese farmers thereabouts, and none of them had work for me. Besides, it was in the wrong time of the year—winter. That shows how much I knew about the land.

"I 'd saved up a couple of dollars, and I kept traveling back, deeper and deeper into the country, looking for work, and buying bread and cheese and such things from the storekeepers. I tell you, it was cold, nights, sleeping out without blankets, and I was always glad when morning came. But worse than that was the way everybody looked on me. They were all suspicious, and not a bit afraid to show it, and sometimes they 'd set their dogs on me and tell me to get along. Seemed as though there was n't any place for me on the land. Then my money gave out, and just about the time I was good and hungry I got captured."

"Captured! What for?"

"Nothing. Living, I suppose. I crawled into a haystack to sleep one night, because it was warmer, and along comes a village constable and arrests me for being a tramp. At first they thought I was a runaway, and telegraphed my description all over. I told them I did n't have any people, but they would n't believe me for a long while. And then, when nobody claimed me, the judge sent me to a boys' 'refuge' in San Francisco."

He stopped and peered intently in the direction of the shore. The darkness and the silence in which the men had been swallowed up was profound. Nothing was stirring save the rising wind.

"I thought I 'd die in that 'refuge.' It was just like being in jail. We were locked up and guarded like prisoners. Even then, if I could have liked the other boys it might have been all right. But they were mostly street-boys of the worst kind—lying, and sneaking, and cowardly, without one spark of manhood or one idea of square dealing and fair play. There was only one thing I did like, and that was the books. Oh, I did lots of reading, I tell you! But that could n't make up for the rest. I wanted the freedom and the sunlight and the salt water. And what had I done to be kept in prison and herded with such a gang? Instead of doing wrong, I had tried to do right, to make myself better, and that 's what I got for it. I was n't old enough, you see, to reason anything out.

"Sometimes I 'd see the sunshine dancing on the water and showing white on the sails, and the Reindeer cutting through it just as you please, and I 'd get that sick I would know hardly what I did. And then the boys would come against me with some of their meannesses, and I 'd start in to lick the whole kit of them. Then the men in charge would lock me up and punish me. Well, I could n't stand it any longer; I watched my chance and ran for it. Seemed as though there was n't any place on the land for me, so I picked up with French Pete and went back on the bay. That 's about all there is to it, though I 'm going to try it again when I get a little older—old enough to get a square deal for myself."

"You 're going to go back on the land with me," Joe said authoritatively, laying a hand on his shoulder. "That 's what you 're going to do. As for—"

Bang! a revolver-shot rang out from the shore. Bang! bang! More guns were speaking sharply and hurriedly. A man's voice rose wildly on the air and died away. Somebody began to cry for help. Both boys were on their feet on the instant, hoisting the mainsail and getting everything ready to run. The Reindeer boy was doing likewise. A man, roused from his sleep on the yacht, thrust an excited head through the skylight, but withdrew it hastily at sight of the two stranger sloops. The intensity of waiting was broken, the time for action come.

CHAPTER XVIII. A NEW RESPONSIBILITY FOR JOE

Heaving in on the anchor-chain till it was up and down, 'Frisco Kid and Joe ceased from their exertions. Everything was in readiness to give the Dazzler the jib, and go. They strained their eyes in the direction of the shore. The clamor had died away, but here and there lights were beginning to flash. The creaking of a block and tackle came to their ears, and they heard Red Nelson's voice singing out: "Lower away!" and "Cast off!"

"French Pete forgot to oil it," 'Frisco Kid commented, referring to the tackle.

"Takin' their time about it, ain't they?" the boy on the Reindeer called over to them, sitting down on the cabin and mopping his face after the exertion of hoisting the mainsail single-handed.

"Guess they 're all right," 'Frisco Kid rejoined. "All ready?"

"Yes—all right here."

"Say, you," the man on the yacht cried through the skylight, not venturing to show his head. "You 'd better go away."

"And you 'd better stay below and keep quiet," was the response. "We 'll take care of ourselves. You do the same."

"If I was only out of this, I 'd show you!" he threatened.

"Lucky for you-you're not," responded the boy on the Reindeer; and thereat the man kept quiet.

"Here they come!" said 'Frisco Kid suddenly to Joe.

The two skiffs shot out of the darkness and came alongside. Some kind of an altercation was going on, as French Pete's voice attested.

"No, no!" he cried. "Put it on ze Dazzler. Ze Reindeer she sail too fast-a, and run away, oh, so queeck, and never more I see it. Put it on ze Dazzler.

Eh? Wot you say?"

"All right then," Red Nelson agreed. "We 'll whack up afterwards. But, say, hurry up. Out with you, lads, and heave her up! My arm 's broke."

The men tumbled out, ropes were cast inboard, and all hands, with the exception of Joe, tailed on. The shouting of men, the sound of oars, and the rattling and slapping of blocks and sails, told that the men on shore were getting under way for the pursuit.

"Now!" Red Nelson commanded. "All together! Don't let her come back or you 'll smash the skiff. There she takes it! A long pull and a strong pull! Once again! And yet again! Get a turn there, somebody, and take a spell."

Though the task was but half accomplished, they were exhausted by the strenuous effort, and hailed the rest eagerly. Joe glanced over the side to discover what the heavy object might be, and saw the vague outlines of a small office-safe.

"Now all together!" Red Nelson began again. "Take her on the run and don't let her stop! Yo, ho! heave, ho! Once again! And another! Over with her!"

Straining and gasping, with tense muscles and heaving chests, they brought the cumbersome weight over the side, rolled it on top of the rail, and lowered it into the cockpit on the run. The cabin doors were thrown apart, and it was moved along, end for end, till it lay on the cabin floor, snug against the end of the centerboard-case. Red Nelson had followed it aboard to superintend. His left arm hung helpless at his side, and from the finger-tips blood dripped with monotonous regularity. He did not seem to mind it, however, nor even the mutterings of the human storm he had raised ashore, and which, to judge by the sounds, was even then threatening to break upon them.

"Lay your course for the Golden Gate," he said to French Pete, as he turned to go. "I 'll try to stand by you, but if you get lost in the dark I 'll meet you outside, off the Farralones, in the morning." He sprang into the skiff after the men, and, with a wave of his uninjured arm, cried heartily: "And then it 's for Mexico, my lads—Mexico and summer weather!"

Just as the Dazzler, freed from her anchor, paid off under the jib and filled away, a dark sail loomed under their stern, barely missing the skiff in tow. The cockpit of the stranger was crowded with men, who raised their voices angrily at sight of the pirates. Joe had half a mind to run forward and cut the halyards so that the Dazzler might be captured. As he had told French Pete the day before, he had done nothing to be ashamed of, and was not afraid to go before a court of justice. But the thought of 'Frisco Kid restrained him. He wanted to take him ashore with him, but in so doing he did not wish to take him to jail. So he, too, began to experience a keen interest in the escape of the Dazzler.

The pursuing sloop rounded up hurriedly to come about after them, and in the darkness fouled the yacht which lay at anchor. The man aboard of her, thinking that at last his time had come, gave one wild yell, ran on deck, and leaped overboard. In the confusion of the collision, and while they were endeavoring to save him, French Pete and the boys slipped away into the night.

The Reindeer had already disappeared, and by the time Joe and 'Frisco Kid had the running-gear coiled down and everything in shape, they were standing out in open water. The wind was freshening constantly, and the Dazzler heeled a lively clip through the comparatively smooth stretch. Before an hour had passed, the lights of Hunter's Point were well on her starboard beam. 'Frisco Kid went below to make coffee, but Joe remained on deck, watching the lights of South San Francisco grow, and speculating on their destination. Mexico! They were going to sea in such a frail craft! Impossible! At least, it seemed so to him, for his conceptions of ocean travel were limited to steamers and full-rigged ships. He was beginning to feel half sorry that he had not cut the halyards, and longed to ask French Pete a thousand questions; but just as the first was on his lips that worthy ordered him to go below and get some coffee and then to turn in. He was followed shortly afterward by 'Frisco Kid, French Pete remaining at his lonely task of beating down the bay and out to sea. Twice he heard the waves buffeted back from some flying forefoot, and once he saw a sail to leeward on the opposite tack, which luffed sharply and came about at sight of him. But the darkness favored, and he heard no more of it—perhaps because he worked into the wind closer by a point, and held on his way with a shaking after-leech.

Shortly after dawn, the two boys were called and came sleepily on deck. The day had broken cold and gray, while the wind had attained half a gale. Joe noted with astonishment the white tents of the quarantine station on Angel Island. San Francisco lay a smoky blur on the southern horizon, while the night, still lingering on the western edge of the world, slowly withdrew before their eyes. French Pete was just finishing a long reach into the Raccoon Straits, and at the same time studiously regarding a plunging sloop-yacht half a mile astern.

"Dey t'ink to catch ze Dazzler, eh? Bah!" And he brought the craft in question about, laying a course straight for the Golden Gate.

The pursuing yacht followed suit. Joe watched her a few moments. She held an apparently parallel course to them, and forged ahead much faster.

"Why, at this rate they 'll have us in no time!" he cried.

French Pete laughed. "You t'ink so? Bah! Dey outfoot; we outpoint. Dey are scared of ze wind; we wipe ze eye of ze wind. Ah! you wait, you see."

"They 're traveling ahead faster," 'Frisco Kid explained, "but we 're sailing closer to the wind. In the end we 'll beat them, even if they have the nerve to cross the bar—which I don't think they have. Look! See!"

Ahead could be seen the great ocean surges, flinging themselves skyward and bursting into roaring caps of smother. In the midst of it, now rolling her dripping bottom clear, now sousing her deck-load of lumber far above the guards, a coasting steam-schooner was lumbering drunkenly into port. It was magnificent—this battle between man and the elements. Whatever timidity he had entertained fled away, and Joe's nostrils began to dilate and his eyes to flash at the nearness of the impending struggle.

French Pete called for his oilskins and sou'wester, and Joe also was equipped with a spare suit. Then he and 'Frisco Kid were sent below to lash and cleat the safe in place. In the midst of this task Joe glanced at the firm-name, gilt-lettered on the face of it, and read: "Bronson & Tate." Why, that was his father and his father's partner. That was their safe, their money! 'Frisco Kid, nailing the last cleat on the floor of the cabin, looked up and followed his fascinated gaze.

"That 's rough, is n't it," he whispered. "Your father?"

Joe nodded. He could see it all now. They had run into San Andreas, where his father worked the big quarries, and most probably the safe contained the wages of the thousand men or more whom he employed. "Don't say anything," he cautioned.

'Frisco Kid agreed knowingly. "French Pete can't read, anyway," he muttered, "and the chances are that Red Nelson won't know what your name is. But, just the same, it 's pretty rough. They 'll break it open and divide up as soon as they can, so I don't see what you 're going to do about it."

"Wait and see." Joe had made up his mind that he would do his best to stand by his father's property. At the worst, it could only be lost; and that would surely be the case were he not along, while, being along, he at least had a fighting chance to save it, or to be in position to recover it. Responsibilities were showering upon him thick and fast. But a few days back he had had but himself to consider; then, in some subtle way, he had felt a certain accountability for 'Frisco Kid's future welfare; and after that, and still more subtly, he had become aware of duties which he owed to his position, to his sister, to his chums and friends; and now, by a most unexpected chain of circumstances, came the pressing need of service for his father's sake. It was a call upon his deepest strength, and he responded bravely. While the future might be doubtful, he had no doubt of himself; and this very state of mind, this self-confidence, by a generous alchemy, gave him added resolution. Nor did he fail to be vaguely aware of it, and to grasp dimly at the truth that confidence breeds confidence—strength, strength.

CHAPTER XIX. THE BOYS PLAN AN ESCAPE

"Now she takes it!" French Pete cried.

Both lads ran into the cockpit. They were on the edge of the breaking bar. A huge forty-footer reared a foam-crested head far above them, stealing their wind for the moment and threatening to crush the tiny craft like an egg-shell. Joe held his breath. It was the supreme moment. French Pete luffed straight into it, and the Dazzler mounted the steep slope with a rush, poised a moment on the giddy summit, and fell into the yawning valley beyond. Keeping off in the intervals to fill the mainsail, and luffing into the combers, they worked their way across the dangerous stretch. Once they caught the tail-end of a whitecap and were well-nigh smothered in the froth, but otherwise the sloop bobbed and ducked with the happy facility of a cork.

To Joe it seemed as though he had been lifted out of himself—out of the world. Ah, this was life! this was action! Surely it could not be the old, commonplace world he had lived in so long! The sailors, grouped on the streaming deck-load of the steamer, waved their sou'westers, and, on the bridge, even the captain was expressing his admiration for the plucky craft.

"Ah, you see! you see!" French Pete pointed astern.

The sloop-yacht had been afraid to venture it, and was skirting back and forth on the inner edge of the bar. The chase was over. A pilot-boat, running for shelter from the coming storm, flew by them like a frightened bird, passing the steamer as though the latter were standing still.

Half an hour later the Dazzler sped beyond the last smoking sea and was sliding up and down on the long Pacific swell. The wind had increased its velocity and necessitated a reefing down of jib and mainsail. Then they laid off again, full and free on the starboard tack, for the Farralones, thirty miles away. By the time breakfast was cooked and eaten they picked up the Reindeer, which was hove to and working offshore to the south and west. The wheel was lashed down, and there was not a soul on deck.

French Pete complained bitterly against such recklessness. "Dat is ze one fault of Red Nelson. He no care. He is afraid of not'ing. Some day he will die, oh, so vaire queeck! I know he will."

Three times they circled about the Reindeer, running under her weather quarter and shouting in chorus, before they brought anybody on deck. Sail was then made at once, and together the two cockle-shells plunged away into the vastness of the Pacific. This was necessary, as 'Frisco Kid informed Joe, in order to have an offing before the whole fury of the storm broke upon them. Otherwise they would be driven on the lee shore of the California coast. Grub and water, he said, could be obtained by running into the land when fine weather came. He congratulated Joe upon the fact that he was not seasick, which circumstance likewise brought praise from French Pete and put him in better humor with his mutinous young sailor.

"I 'll tell you what we 'll do," 'Frisco Kid whispered, while cooking dinner. "To-night we 'll drag French Pete down—"

"Drag French Pete down!"

"Yes, and tie him up good and snug, as soon as it gets dark; then put out the lights and make a run for land; get to port anyway, anywhere, just so long as we shake loose from Red Nelson."

"Yes," Joe deliberated; "that would be all right—if I could do it alone. But as for asking you to help me—why, that would be treason to French Pete."

"That 's what I 'm coming to. I 'll help you if you promise me a few things. French Pete took me aboard when I ran away from the 'refuge,' when I was starving and had no place to go, and I just can't repay him for that by sending him to jail. 'T would n't be square. Your father would n't have you break your word, would he?"

"No; of course not." Joe knew how sacredly his father held his word of honor.

"Then you must promise, and your father must see it carried out, not to press any charge against French Pete."

"All right. And now, what about yourself? You can't very well expect to go away with him again on the Dazzler!"

"Oh, don't bother about me. There 's nobody to miss me. I 'm strong enough, and know enough about it, to ship to sea as ordinary seaman. I 'll go away somewhere over on the other side of the world, and begin all over again."

"Then we 'll have to call it off, that 's all."

"Call what off?"

"Tying French Pete up and running for it."

"No, sir. That 's decided upon."

"Now listen here: I 'll not have a thing to do with it. I 'll go on to Mexico first, if you don't make me one promise."

"And what 's the promise?"

"Just this: you place yourself in my hands from the moment we get ashore, and trust to me. You don't know anything about the land, anyway—you said so. And I 'll fix it with my father—I know I can—so that you can get to know people of the right sort, and study and get an education, and be something else than a bay pirate or a sailor. That 's what you 'd like, is n't it?"

Though he said nothing, 'Frisco Kid showed how well he liked it by the expression of his face.

"And it 'll be no more than your due, either," Joe continued. "You will have stood by me, and you 'll have recovered my father's money. He 'll owe it to you."

"But I don't do things that way. I don't think much of a man who does a favor just to be paid for it."

"Now you keep quiet. How much do you think it would cost my father for detectives and all that to recover that safe? Give me your promise, that 's all, and when I 've got things arranged, if you don't like them you can back

248

out. Come on; that 's fair."

They shook hands on the bargain, and proceeded to map out their line of action for the night.

But the storm, yelling down out of the northwest, had something entirely different in store for the Dazzler and her crew. By the time dinner was over they were forced to put double reefs in mainsail and jib, and still the gale had not reached its height. The sea, also, had been kicked up till it was a continuous succession of water-mountains, frightful and withal grand to look upon from the low deck of the sloop. It was only when the sloops were tossed upon the crests of the waves at the same time that they caught sight of each other. Occasional fragments of seas swashed into the cockpit or dashed aft over the cabin, and Joe was stationed at the small pump to keep the well dry.

At three o'clock, watching his chance, French Pete motioned to the Reindeer that he was going to heave to and get out a sea-anchor. This latter was of the nature of a large shallow canvas bag, with the mouth held open by triangularly lashed spars. To this the towing-ropes were attached, on the kite principle, so that the greatest resisting surface was presented to the water. The sloop, drifting so much faster, would thus be held bow on to both wind and sea—the safest possible position in a storm. Red Nelson waved his hand in response that he understood and to go ahead.

French Pete went forward to launch the sea-anchor himself, leaving it to 'Frisco Kid to put the helm down at the proper moment and run into the wind. The Frenchman poised on the slippery fore-deck, waiting an opportunity. But at that moment the Dazzler lifted into an unusually large sea, and, as she cleared the summit, caught a heavy snort of the gale at the very instant she was righting herself to an even keel. Thus there was not the slightest yield to this sudden pressure on her sails and mast-gear.

There was a quick snap, followed by a crash. The steel weather-rigging carried away at the lanyards, and mast, jib, mainsail, blocks, stays, sea-anchor, French Pete—everything—went over the side. Almost by a miracle, the captain clutched at the bobstay and managed to get one hand up and over the bowsprit. The boys ran forward to drag him into safety, and Red Nelson, observing the disaster, put up his helm and ran down to the rescue.

249

CHAPTER XX. PERILOUS HOURS

French Pete was uninjured from the fall overboard with the Dazzler's mast; but the sea-anchor, which had gone with him, had not escaped so easily. The gaff of the mainsail had been driven through it, and it refused to work. The wreckage, thumping alongside, held the sloop in a quartering slant to the seas—not so dangerous a position as it might be, nor so safe, either. "Goodby, old-a Dazzler. Never no more you wipe ze eye of ze wind. Never no more you kick your heels at ze crack gentlemen-yachts."

So the captain lamented, standing in the cockpit and surveying the ruin with wet eyes. Even Joe, who bore him great dislike, felt sorry for him at this moment. A heavier blast of the wind caught the jagged crest of a wave and hurled it upon the helpless craft.

"Can't we save her?" Joe spluttered.

'Frisco Kid shook his head.

"Nor the safe?"

"Impossible," he answered. "Could n't lay another boat alongside for a United States mint. As it is, it 'll keep us guessing to save ourselves."

Another sea swept over them, and the skiff, which had long since been swamped, dashed itself to pieces against the stern. Then the Reindeer towered above them on a mountain of water. Joe caught himself half shrinking back, for it seemed she would fall down squarely on top of them; but the next instant she dropped into the gaping trough, and they were looking down upon her far below. It was a striking picture—one Joe was destined never to forget. The Reindeer was wallowing in the snow-white smother, her rails flush with the sea, the water scudding across her deck in foaming cataracts. The air was filled with flying spray, which made the scene appear hazy and unreal. One of the men was clinging to the perilous after-deck and striving to cast off the water-logged skiff. The boy, leaning far over the cockpit-rail and holding on for dear life, was passing him a knife. The second man stood at the wheel, putting it up with flying hands and forcing the sloop to pay off. Beside him, his injured arm in a sling, was Red Nelson, his sou'wester gone and his fair hair plastered in wet, wind-blown ringlets about his face. His whole attitude breathed indomitability, courage, strength. It seemed almost as though the divine were blazing forth from him. Joe looked upon him in sudden awe, and, realizing the enormous possibilities of the man, felt sorrow for the way in which they had been wasted. A thief and a robber! In that flashing moment Joe caught a glimpse of human truth, grasped at the mystery of success and failure. Life threw back its curtains that he might read it and understand. Of such stuff as Red Nelson were heroes made; but they possessed wherein he lacked—the power of choice, the careful poise of mind, the sober control of soul: in short, the very things his father had so often "preached" to him about.

These were the thoughts which came to Joe in the flight of a second. Then the Reindeer swept skyward and hurtled across their bow to leeward on the breast of a mighty billow.

"Ze wild man! ze wild man!" French Pete shrieked, watching her in amazement. "He t'inks he can jibe! He will die! We will all die! He must come about. Oh, ze fool, ze fool!"

But time was precious, and Red Nelson ventured the chance. At the right moment he jibed the mainsail over and hauled back on the wind.

"Here she comes! Make ready to jump for it," 'Frisco Kid cried to Joe.

The Reindeer dashed by their stern, heeling over till the cabin windows were buried, and so close that it appeared she must run them down. But a freak of the waters lurched the two crafts apart. Red Nelson, seeing that the manoeuver had miscarried, instantly instituted another. Throwing the helm hard up, the Reindeer whirled on her heel, thus swinging her overhanging main-boom closer to the Dazzler. French Pete was the nearest, and the opportunity could last no longer than a second. Like a cat he sprang, catching the foot-rope with both hands. Then the Reindeer forged ahead, dipping him into the sea at every plunge. But he clung on, working inboard every time he emerged, till he dropped into the cockpit as Red Nelson squared off to run down to leeward and repeat the manoeuver.

"Your turn next," 'Frisco Kid said.

"No; yours," Joe replied.

"But I know more about the water," 'Frisco Kid insisted.

"And I can swim as well as you," the other retorted.

It would have been hard to forecast the outcome of this dispute; but, as it was, the swift rush of events made any settlement needless. The Reindeer had jibed over and was plowing back at breakneck speed, careening at such an angle that it seemed she must surely capsize. It was a gallant sight. Just then the storm burst in all its fury, the shouting wind flattening the ragged crests till they boiled. The Reindeer dipped from view behind an immense wave. The wave rolled on, but the next moment, where the sloop had been, the boys noted with startled eyes only the angry waters! Doubting, they looked a second time. There was no Reindeer. They were alone on the torn crest of the ocean!

"God have mercy on their souls!" 'Frisco Kid said solemnly.

Joe was too horrified at the suddenness of the catastrophe to utter a sound.

"Sailed her clean under, and, with the ballast she carried, went straight to bottom," 'Frisco Kid gasped. Then, turning to their own pressing need, he said: "Now we 've got to look out for ourselves. The back of the storm broke in that puff, but the sea 'll kick up worse yet as the wind eases down. Lend a hand and hang on with the other. We 've got to get her head-on."

Together, knives in hand, they crawled forward to where the pounding wreckage hampered the boat sorely. 'Frisco Kid took the lead in the ticklish work, but Joe obeyed orders like a veteran. Every minute or two the bow was swept by the sea, and they were pounded and buffeted about like a pair of shuttlecocks. First the main portion of the wreckage was securely fastened to the forward bitts; then, breathless and gasping, more often under the water than out, they cut and hacked at the tangle of halyards, sheets, stays, and tackles. The cockpit was taking water rapidly, and it was a race between swamping and completing the task. At last, however, everything stood clear save the lee rigging. 'Frisco Kid slashed the lanyards. The storm did the rest. The Dazzler drifted swiftly to leeward of the wreckage till the strain on the line fast to the forward bitts jerked her bow into place and she ducked dead into the eye of the wind and sea.

Pausing only for a cheer at the success of their undertaking, the two lads raced aft, where the cockpit was half full and the dunnage of the cabin all afloat. With a couple of buckets procured from the stern lockers, they proceeded to fling the water overboard. It was heartbreaking work, for many a barrelful was flung back upon them again; but they persevered, and when night fell the Dazzler, bobbing merrily at her sea-anchor, could boast that her pumps sucked once more. As 'Frisco Kid had said, the backbone of the storm was broken, though the wind had veered to the west, where it still blew stiffly.

"If she holds," 'Frisco Kid said, referring to the breeze, "we 'll drift to the California coast sometime to-morrow. Nothing to do now but wait."

They said little, oppressed by the loss of their comrades and overcome with exhaustion, preferring to huddle against each other for the sake of warmth and companionship. It was a miserable night, and they shivered constantly from the cold. Nothing dry was to be obtained aboard, food, blankets, everything being soaked with the salt water. Sometimes they dozed; but these intervals were short and harassing, for it seemed each took turn in waking with such sudden starts as to rouse the other.

At last day broke, and they looked about. Wind and sea had dropped considerably, and there was no question as to the safety of the Dazzler. The coast was nearer than they had expected, its cliffs showing dark and forbidding in the gray of dawn. But with the rising of the sun they could see the yellow beaches, flanked by the white surf, and beyond—it seemed too good to be true—the clustering houses and smoking chimneys of a town.

"Santa Cruz!" 'Frisco Kid cried, "and no chance of being wrecked in the surf!"

"Then the safe is safe?" Joe queried.

"Safe! I should say so. It ain't much of a sheltered harbor for large vessels, but with this breeze we 'll run right up the mouth of the San Lorenzo River. Then there 's a little lake like, and a boat-house. Water smooth as glass and hardly over your head. You see, I was down here once before, with Red Nelson. Come on. We 'll be in in time for breakfast."

Bringing to light some spare coils of rope from the lockers, he put a clove-hitch on the standing part of the sea-anchor hawser, and carried the new running-line aft, making it fast to the stern bitts. Then he cast off from the forward bitts. The Dazzler swung off into the trough, completed the evolution, and pointed her nose toward shore. A couple of spare oars from below, and as many water-soaked blankets, sufficed to make a jury-mast and sail. When this was in place, Joe cast loose from the wreckage, which was now towing astern, while 'Frisco Kid took the tiller.

CHAPTER XXI. JOE AND HIS FATHER

"How 's that?" cried 'Frisco Kid, as he finished making the Dazzler fast fore and aft, and sat down on the stringpiece of the tiny wharf. "What 'll we do next, captain?"

Joe looked up in quick surprise. "Why—I—what 's the matter?"

"Well, ain't you captain now? Have n't we reached land? I 'm crew from now on, ain't I? What 's your orders?"

Joe caught the spirit of it. "Pipe all hands for breakfast—that is—wait a minute."

Diving below, he possessed himself of the money he had stowed away in his bundle when he came aboard. Then he locked the cabin door, and they went uptown in search of a restaurant. Over the breakfast Joe planned the next move, and, when they had done, communicated it to 'Frisco Kid.

In response to his inquiry, the cashier told him when the morning train started for San Francisco. He glanced at the clock.

"Just time to catch it," he said to 'Frisco Kid. "Keep the cabin doors locked, and don't let anybody come aboard. Here 's money. Eat at the restaurants. Dry your blankets and sleep in the cockpit. I 'll be back to-morrow. And don't let anybody into that cabin. Good-by."

With a hasty hand-grip, he sped down the street to the depot. The conductor looked at him with surprise when he punched his ticket. And well he might, for it was not the custom of his passengers to travel in sea-boots and sou'westers. But Joe did not mind. He did not even notice. He had bought a paper and was absorbed in its contents. Before long his eyes caught an interesting paragraph:

SUPPOSED TO HAVE BEEN LOST

The tug Sea Queen, chartered by Bronson & Tate, has returned from a fruitless cruise outside the Heads. No news of value could be obtained concerning the pirates who so daringly carried off their safe at San Andreas last Tuesday night. The lighthouse-keeper at the Farralones mentions having sighted the two sloops Wednesday morning, clawing offshore in the teeth of the gale. It is supposed by shipping men that they perished in the storm with, their ill-gotten treasure. Rumor has it that, in addition to the ten thousand dollars in gold, the safe contained papers of great importance.

When Joe had read this he felt a great relief. It was evident no one had been killed at San Andreas the night of the robbery, else there would have been some comment on it in the paper. Nor, if they had had any clue to his own whereabouts, would they have omitted such a striking bit of information.

At the depot in San Francisco the curious onlookers were surprised to see a boy clad conspicuously in sea-boots and sou'wester hail a cab and dash away. But Joe was in a hurry. He knew his father's hours, and was fearful lest he should not catch him before he went to lunch.

The office-boy scowled at him when he pushed open the door and asked to see Mr. Bronson; nor could the head clerk, when summoned by this disreputable intruder, recognize him.

"Don't you know me, Mr. Willis?"

Mr. Willis looked a second time. "Why, it 's Joe Bronson! Of all things under the sun, where did you drop from? Go right in. Your father 's in there."

Mr. Bronson stopped dictating to his stenographer and looked up. "Hello! Where have you been?" he said.

"To sea," Joe answered demurely, not sure of just what kind of a reception he was to get, and fingering his sou'wester nervously.

"Short trip, eh? How did you make out?"

"Oh, so-so." He had caught the twinkle in his father's eye and knew that it was all clear sailing. "Not so bad—er—that is, considering."

"Considering?"

"Well, not exactly that; rather, it might have been worse, while it could n't have been better."

"That 's interesting. Sit down." Then, turning to the stenographer: "You may go, Mr. Brown, and—hum!—I won't need you any more to-day."

It was all Joe could do to keep from crying, so kindly and naturally had his father received him, making him feel at once as if not the slightest thing uncommon had occurred. It seemed as if he had just returned from a vacation, or, man-grown, had come back from some business trip.

"Now go ahead, Joe. You were speaking to me a moment ago in conundrums, and you have aroused my curiosity to a most uncomfortable degree."

Whereupon Joe sat down and told what had happened—all that had happened—from Monday night to that very moment. Each little incident he related,—every detail,—not forgetting his conversations with 'Frisco Kid nor his plans concerning him. His face flushed and he was carried away with the excitement of the narrative, while Mr. Bronson was almost as eager, urging him on whenever he slackened his pace, but otherwise remaining silent.

"So you see," Joe concluded, "it could n't possibly have turned out any better."

"Ah, well," Mr. Bronson deliberated judiciously, "it may be so, and then again it may not."

"I don't see it." Joe felt sharp disappointment at his father's qualified approval. It seemed to him that the return of the safe merited something stronger.

That Mr. Bronson fully comprehended the way Joe felt about it was clearly in evidence, for he went on: "As to the matter of the safe, all hail to you, Joe! Credit, and plenty of it, is your due. Mr. Tate and myself have already spent five hundred dollars in attempting to recover it. So important was it that we have also offered five thousand dollars reward, and but this morning were considering the advisability of increasing the amount. But,

257

my son,"—Mr. Bronson stood up, resting a hand affectionately on his boy's shoulder,—"there are certain things in this world which are of still greater importance than gold, or papers which represent what gold may buy. How about yourself? That 's the point. Will you sell the best possibilities of your life right now for a million dollars?"

Joe shook his head.

"As I said, that 's the point. A human life the money of the world cannot buy; nor can it redeem one which is misspent; nor can it make full and complete and beautiful a life which is dwarfed and warped and ugly. How about yourself? What is to be the effect of all these strange adventures on your life—your life, Joe? Are you going to pick yourself up to-morrow and try it over again? or the next day? or the day after? Do you understand? Why, Joe, do you think for one moment that I would place against the best value of my son's life the paltry value of a safe? And can I say, until time has told me, whether this trip of yours could not possibly have been better? Such an experience is as potent for evil as for good. One dollar is exactly like another—there are many in the world: but no Joe is like my Joe, nor can there be any others in the world to take his place. Don't you see, Joe? Don't you understand?"

Mr. Bronson's voice broke slightly, and the next instant Joe was sobbing as though his heart would break. He had never understood this father of his before, and he knew now the pain he must have caused him, to say nothing of his mother and sister. But the four stirring days he had lived had given him a clearer view of the world and humanity, and he had always possessed the power of putting his thoughts into speech; so he spoke of these things and the lessons he had learned—the conclusions he had drawn from his conversations with 'Frisco Kid, from his intercourse with French Pete, from the graphic picture he retained of the Reindeer and Red Nelson as they wallowed in the trough beneath him. And Mr. Bronson listened and, in turn, understood.

"But what of 'Frisco Kid, father?" Joe asked when he had finished.

"Hum! there seems to be a great deal of promise in the boy, from what you say of him." Mr. Bronson hid the twinkle in his eye this time. "And, I must confess, he seems perfectly capable of shifting for himself."

"Sir?" Joe could not believe his ears.

"Let us see, then. He is at present entitled to the half of five thousand dollars, the other half of which belongs to you. It was you two who preserved the safe from the bottom of the Pacific, and if you only had waited a little longer, Mr. Tate and myself would have increased the reward."

"Oh!" Joe caught a glimmering of the light. "Part of that is easily arranged. I simply refuse to take my half. As to the other—that is n't exactly what 'Frisco Kid desires. He wants friends—and—and—though you did n't say so, they are far higher than money, nor can money buy them. He wants friends and a chance for an education, not twenty-five hundred dollars."

"Don't you think it would be better for him to choose for himself?"

"Ah, no. That 's all arranged."

"Arranged?"

"Yes, sir. He 's captain on sea, and I 'm captain on land. So he 's under my charge now."

"Then you have the power of attorney for him in the present negotiations? Good. I 'll make you a proposition. The twenty-five hundred dollars shall be held in trust by me, on his demand at any time. We 'll settle about yours afterward. Then he shall be put on probation for, say, a year—in our office. You can either coach him in his studies, for I am confident now that you will be up in yours hereafter, or he can attend night-school. And after that, if he comes through his period of probation with flying colors, I 'll give him the same opportunities for an education that you possess. It all depends on himself. And now, Mr. Attorney, what have you to say to my offer in the interests of your client?"

"That I close with it at once."

Father and son shook hands.

"And what are you going to do now, Joe?"

"Send a telegram to 'Frisco Kid first, and then hurry home."

"Then wait a minute till I call up San Andreas and tell Mr. Tate the good news, and then I 'll go with you."

"Mr. Willis," Mr. Bronson said as they left the outer office, "the San Andreas safe is recovered, and we 'll all take a holiday. Kindly tell the clerks that they are free for the rest of the day. And I say," he called back as they entered the elevator, "don't forget the office-boy."

About Author

Family

Jack London's mother, Flora Wellman, was the fifth and youngest child of Pennsylvania Canal builder Marshall Wellman and his first wife, Eleanor Garrett Jones. Marshall Wellman was descended from Thomas Wellman, an early Puritan settler in the Massachusetts Bay Colony. Flora left Ohio and moved to the Pacific coast when her father remarried after her mother died. In San Francisco, Flora worked as a music teacher and spiritualist, claiming to channel the spirit of a Sauk chief, Black Hawk.

Biographer Clarice Stasz and others believe London's father was astrologer William Chaney. Flora Wellman was living with Chaney in San Francisco when she became pregnant. Whether Wellman and Chaney were legally married is unknown. Most San Francisco civil records were destroyed by the extensive fires that followed the 1906 earthquake; nobody knows what name appeared on her son's birth certificate. Stasz notes that in his memoirs, Chaney refers to London's mother Flora Wellman as having been his "wife"; he also cites an advertisement in which Flora called herself "Florence Wellman Chaney".

According to Flora Wellman's account, as recorded in the San Francisco Chronicle of June 4, 1875, Chaney demanded that she have an abortion. When she refused, he disclaimed responsibility for the child. In desperation, she shot herself. She was not seriously wounded, but she was temporarily deranged. After giving birth, Flora turned the baby over for care to Virginia Prentiss, an African-American woman and former slave. She was a major maternal figure throughout London's life. Late in 1876, Flora Wellman married John London, a partially disabled Civil War veteran, and brought her baby John, later known as Jack, to live with the newly married couple. The family moved around the San Francisco Bay Area before settling in Oakland, where London completed public grade school.

In 1897, when he was 21 and a student at the University of California,

Berkeley, London searched for and read the newspaper accounts of his mother's suicide attempt and the name of his biological father. He wrote to William Chaney, then living in Chicago. Chaney responded that he could not be London's father because he was impotent; he casually asserted that London's mother had relations with other men and averred that she had slandered him when she said he insisted on an abortion. Chaney concluded by saying that he was more to be pitied than London. London was devastated by his father's letter; in the months following, he quit school at Berkeley and went to the Klondike during the gold rush boom.

Early life

London was born near Third and Brannan Streets in San Francisco. The house burned down in the fire after the 1906 San Francisco earthquake; the California Historical Society placed a plaque at the site in 1953. Although the family was working class, it was not as impoverished as London's later accounts claimed. London was largely self-educated.

In 1885, London found and read Ouida's long Victorian novel Signa. He credited this as the seed of his literary success. In 1886, he went to the Oakland Public Library and found a sympathetic librarian, Ina Coolbrith, who encouraged his learning. (She later became California's first poet laureate and an important figure in the San Francisco literary community).

In 1889, London began working 12 to 18 hours a day at Hickmott's Cannery. Seeking a way out, he borrowed money from his foster mother Virginia Prentiss, bought the sloop Razzle-Dazzle from an oyster pirate named French Frank, and became an oyster pirate himself. In his memoir, John Barleycorn, he claims also to have stolen French Frank's mistress Mamie. After a few months, his sloop became damaged beyond repair. London hired on as a member of the California Fish Patrol.

In 1893, he signed on to the sealing schooner Sophie Sutherland, bound for the coast of Japan. When he returned, the country was in the grip of the panic of '93 and Oakland was swept by labor unrest. After grueling jobs in a jute mill and a street-railway power plant, London joined Coxey's Army and began his career as a tramp. In 1894, he spent 30 days for vagrancy in the Erie County Penitentiary at Buffalo, New York. In The Road, he wrote:

Man-handling was merely one of the very minor unprintable horrors of the Erie County Pen. I say 'unprintable'; and in justice I must also say undescribable. They were unthinkable to me until I saw them, and I was no spring chicken in the ways of the world and the awful abysses of human degradation. It would take a deep plummet to reach bottom in the Erie County Pen, and I do but skim lightly and facetiously the surface of things as I there saw them.

After many experiences as a hobo and a sailor, he returned to Oakland and attended Oakland High School. He contributed a number of articles to the high school's magazine, The Aegis. His first published work was "Typhoon off the Coast of Japan", an account of his sailing experiences.

As a schoolboy, London often studied at Heinold's First and Last Chance Saloon, a port-side bar in Oakland. At 17, he confessed to the bar's owner, John Heinold, his desire to attend university and pursue a career as a writer. Heinold lent London tuition money to attend college.

London desperately wanted to attend the University of California, Berkeley. In 1896, after a summer of intense studying to pass certification exams, he was admitted. Financial circumstances forced him to leave in 1897 and he never graduated. No evidence suggests that London wrote for student publications while studying at Berkeley.

While at Berkeley, London continued to study and spend time at Heinold's saloon, where he was introduced to the sailors and adventurers who would influence his writing. In his autobiographical novel, John Barleycorn, London mentioned the pub's likeness seventeen times. Heinold's was the place where London met Alexander McLean, a captain known for his cruelty at sea. London based his protagonist Wolf Larsen, in the novel The Sea-Wolf, on McLean.

Heinold's First and Last Chance Saloon is now unofficially named Jack London's Rendezvous in his honor.

Gold rush and first success

On July 12, 1897, London (age 21) and his sister's husband Captain Shepard sailed to join the Klondike Gold Rush. This was the setting for some of his first successful stories. London's time in the harsh Klondike, however, was detrimental to his health. Like so many other men who were malnourished in the goldfields, London developed scurvy. His gums became swollen, leading to the loss of his four front teeth. A constant gnawing pain affected his hip and leg muscles, and his face was stricken with marks that always reminded him of the struggles he faced in the Klondike. Father William Judge, "The Saint of Dawson", had a facility in Dawson that provided shelter, food and any available medicine to London and others. His struggles there inspired London's short story, "To Build a Fire" (1902, revised in 1908), which many critics assess as his best.

His landlords in Dawson were mining engineers Marshall Latham Bond and Louis Whitford Bond, educated at Yale and Stanford, respectively. The brothers' father, Judge Hiram Bond, was a wealthy mining investor. The Bonds, especially Hiram, were active Republicans. Marshall Bond's diary mentions friendly sparring with London on political issues as a camp pastime.

London left Oakland with a social conscience and socialist leanings; he returned to become an activist for socialism. He concluded that his only hope of escaping the work "trap" was to get an education and "sell his brains". He saw his writing as a business, his ticket out of poverty, and, he hoped, a means of beating the wealthy at their own game. On returning to California in 1898, London began working to get published, a struggle described in his novel, Martin Eden (serialized in 1908, published in 1909). His first published story since high school was "To the Man On Trail", which has frequently been collected in anthologies. When The Overland Monthly offered him only five dollars for it—and was slow paying—London came close to abandoning his writing career. In his words, "literally and literarily I was saved" when The Black Cat accepted his story "A Thousand Deaths", and paid him $40—the "first money I ever received for a story".

London began his writing career just as new printing technologies enabled lower-cost production of magazines. This resulted in a boom in popular magazines aimed at a wide public audience and a strong market for short fiction. In 1900, he made $2,500 in writing, about $75,000 in today's currency. Among the works he sold to magazines was a short story known as either "Diable" (1902) or "Bâtard" (1904), two editions of the same basic story; London received $141.25 for this story on May 27, 1902. In the text, a cruel French Canadian brutalizes his dog, and the dog retaliates and kills the man. London told some of his critics that man's actions are the main cause of the behavior of their animals, and he would show this in another story, The Call of the Wild.

In early 1903, London sold The Call of the Wild to The Saturday Evening Post for $750, and the book rights to Macmillan for $2,000. Macmillan's promotional campaign propelled it to swift success.

While living at his rented villa on Lake Merritt in Oakland, California, London met poet George Sterling; in time they became best friends. In 1902, Sterling helped London find a home closer to his own in nearby Piedmont. In his letters London addressed Sterling as "Greek", owing to Sterling's aquiline nose and classical profile, and he signed them as "Wolf". London was later to depict Sterling as Russ Brissenden in his autobiographical novel Martin Eden (1910) and as Mark Hall in The Valley of the Moon (1913).

In later life London indulged his wide-ranging interests by accumulating a personal library of 15,000 volumes. He referred to his books as "the tools of my trade".

First marriage (1900–04)

London married Elizabeth "Bessie" Maddern on April 7, 1900, the same day The Son of the Wolf was published. Bess had been part of his circle of friends for a number of years. She was related to stage actresses Minnie Maddern Fiske and Emily Stevens. Stasz says, "Both acknowledged publicly that they were not marrying out of love, but from friendship and a belief that they would produce sturdy children." Kingman says, "they were comfortable together... Jack had made it clear to Bessie that he did not love her, but that he liked her enough to make a successful marriage."

London met Bessie through his friend at Oakland High School, Fred Jacobs; she was Fred's fiancee. Bessie, who tutored at Anderson's University Academy in Alameda California, tutored Jack in preparation for his entrance exams for the University of California at Berkeley in 1896. Jacobs was killed aboard the USAT Scandia in 1897, but Jack and Bessie continued their friendship, which included taking photos and developing the film together. This was the beginning of Jack's passion for photography.

During the marriage, London continued his friendship with Anna Strunsky, co-authoring The Kempton-Wace Letters, an epistolary novel contrasting two philosophies of love. Anna, writing "Dane Kempton's" letters, arguing for a romantic view of marriage, while London, writing "Herbert Wace's" letters, argued for a scientific view, based on Darwinism and eugenics. In the novel, his fictional character contrasted two women he had known.

London's pet name for Bess was "Mother-Girl" and Bess's for London was "Daddy-Boy". Their first child, Joan, was born on January 15, 1901, and their second, Bessie (later called Becky), on October 20, 1902. Both children were born in Piedmont, California. Here London wrote one of his most celebrated works, The Call of the Wild.

While London had pride in his children, the marriage was strained. Kingman says that by 1903 the couple were close to separation as they were "extremely incompatible". "Jack was still so kind and gentle with Bessie that when Cloudsley Johns was a house guest in February 1903 he didn't suspect a breakup of their marriage."

London reportedly complained to friends Joseph Noel and George Sterling:

[Bessie] is devoted to purity. When I tell her morality is only evidence of low blood pressure, she hates me. She'd sell me and the children out for her damned purity. It's terrible. Every time I come back after being away from home for a night she won't let me be in the same room with her if she can help it.

Stasz writes that these were "code words for [Bess's] fear that [Jack] was consorting with prostitutes and might bring home venereal disease."

On July 24, 1903, London told Bessie he was leaving and moved out. During 1904, London and Bess negotiated the terms of a divorce, and the decree was granted on November 11, 1904.

War correspondent (1904)

London accepted an assignment of the San Francisco Examiner to cover the Russo-Japanese War in early 1904, arriving in Yokohama on January 25, 1904. He was arrested by Japanese authorities in Shimonoseki, but released through the intervention of American ambassador Lloyd Griscom. After travelling to Korea, he was again arrested by Japanese authorities for straying too close to the border with Manchuria without official permission, and was sent back to Seoul. Released again, London was permitted to travel with the Imperial Japanese Army to the border, and to observe the Battle of the Yalu.

London asked William Randolph Hearst, the owner of the San Francisco Examiner, to be allowed to transfer to the Imperial Russian Army, where he felt that restrictions on his reporting and his movements would be less severe. However, before this could be arranged, he was arrested for a third time in four months, this time for assaulting his Japanese assistants, whom he accused of stealing the fodder for his horse. Released through the personal intervention of President Theodore Roosevelt, London departed the front in June 1904.

Bohemian Club

On August 18, 1904, London went with his close friend, the poet George Sterling, to "Summer High Jinks" at the Bohemian Grove. London was elected to honorary membership in the Bohemian Club and took part in many activities. Other noted members of the Bohemian Club during this time included Ambrose Bierce, Gelett Burgess, Allan Dunn, John Muir, Frank Norris, and Herman George Scheffauer.

Beginning in December 1914, London worked on The Acorn Planter, A California Forest Play, to be performed as one of the annual Grove Plays, but it was never selected. It was described as too difficult to set to music. London published The Acorn Planter in 1916.

Second marriage

After divorcing Maddern, London married Charmian Kittredge in 1905. London was introduced to Kittredge in 1900 by her aunt Netta Eames, who was an editor at Overland Monthly magazine in San Francisco. The two met prior to his first marriage but became lovers years later after Jack and Bessie London visited Wake Robin, Netta Eames' Sonoma County resort, in 1903. London was injured when he fell from a buggy, and Netta arranged for Charmian to care for him. The two developed a friendship, as Charmian, Netta, her husband Roscoe, and London were politically aligned with socialist causes. At some point the relationship became romantic, and Jack divorced his wife to marry Charmian, who was five years his senior.

Biographer Russ Kingman called Charmian "Jack's soul-mate, always at his side, and a perfect match." Their time together included numerous trips, including a 1907 cruise on the yacht Snark to Hawaii and Australia. Many of London's stories are based on his visits to Hawaii, the last one for 10 months beginning in December 1915.

The couple also visited Goldfield, Nevada, in 1907, where they were guests of the Bond brothers, London's Dawson City landlords. The Bond brothers were working in Nevada as mining engineers.

London had contrasted the concepts of the "Mother Girl" and the "Mate Woman" in The Kempton-Wace Letters. His pet name for Bess had been "Mother-Girl;" his pet name for Charmian was "Mate-Woman." Charmian's aunt and foster mother, a disciple of Victoria Woodhull, had raised her without prudishness. Every biographer alludes to Charmian's uninhibited sexuality.

Joseph Noel calls the events from 1903 to 1905 "a domestic drama that would have intrigued the pen of an Ibsen.... London's had comedy relief in it

270

and a sort of easy-going romance." In broad outline, London was restless in his first marriage, sought extramarital sexual affairs, and found, in Charmian Kittredge, not only a sexually active and adventurous partner, but his future life-companion. They attempted to have children; one child died at birth, and another pregnancy ended in a miscarriage.

In 1906, London published in Collier's magazine his eye-witness report of the San Francisco earthquake.

Beauty Ranch (1905–16)

In 1905, London purchased a 1,000 acres (4.0 km2) ranch in Glen Ellen, Sonoma County, California, on the eastern slope of Sonoma Mountain, for $26,450. He wrote: "Next to my wife, the ranch is the dearest thing in the world to me." He desperately wanted the ranch to become a successful business enterprise. Writing, always a commercial enterprise with London, now became even more a means to an end: "I write for no other purpose than to add to the beauty that now belongs to me. I write a book for no other reason than to add three or four hundred acres to my magnificent estate."

Stasz writes that London "had taken fully to heart the vision, expressed in his agrarian fiction, of the land as the closest earthly version of Eden ... he educated himself through the study of agricultural manuals and scientific tomes. He conceived of a system of ranching that today would be praised for its ecological wisdom." He was proud to own the first concrete silo in California, a circular piggery that he designed. He hoped to adapt the wisdom of Asian sustainable agriculture to the United States. He hired both Italian and Chinese stonemasons, whose distinctly different styles are obvious.

The ranch was an economic failure. Sympathetic observers such as Stasz treat his projects as potentially feasible, and ascribe their failure to bad luck or to being ahead of their time. Unsympathetic historians such as Kevin Starr suggest that he was a bad manager, distracted by other concerns and impaired by his alcoholism. Starr notes that London was absent from his ranch about six months a year between 1910 and 1916 and says, "He liked the show of managerial power, but not grinding attention to detail .... London's workers laughed at his efforts to play big-time rancher [and considered] the operation a rich man's hobby."

London spent $80,000 ($2,230,000 in current value) to build a 15,000-square-foot (1,400 m2) stone mansion called Wolf House on the property. Just as the mansion was nearing completion, two weeks before the Londons planned to move in, it was destroyed by fire.

London's last visit to Hawaii, beginning in December 1915, lasted eight months. He met with Duke Kahanamoku, Prince Jonah Kūhiō Kalaniana'ole, Queen Lili'uokalani and many others, before returning to his ranch in July 1916. He was suffering from kidney failure, but he continued to work.

The ranch (abutting stone remnants of Wolf House) is now a National Historic Landmark and is protected in Jack London State Historic Park.

Animal activism

London witnessed animal cruelty in the training of circus animals, and his subsequent novels Jerry of the Islands and Michael, Brother of Jerry included a foreword entreating the public to become more informed about this practice. In 1918, the Massachusetts Society for the Prevention of Cruelty to Animals and the American Humane Education Society teamed up to create the Jack London Club, which sought to inform the public about cruelty to circus animals and encourage them to protest this establishment. Support from Club members led to a temporary cessation of trained animal acts at Ringling-Barnum and Bailey in 1925.

Death

London died November 22, 1916, in a sleeping porch in a cottage on his ranch. London had been a robust man but had suffered several serious illnesses, including scurvy in the Klondike. Additionally, during travels on the Snark, he and Charmian picked up unspecified tropical infections, and diseases, including yaws. At the time of his death, he suffered from dysentery, late-stage alcoholism, and uremia; he was in extreme pain and taking morphine.

272

London's ashes were buried on his property not far from the Wolf House. London's funeral took place on November 26, 1916, attended only by close friends, relatives, and workers of the property. In accordance with his wishes, he was cremated and buried next to some pioneer children, under a rock that belonged to the Wolf House. After Charmian's death in 1955, she was also cremated and then buried with her husband in the same simple spot that her husband chose. The grave is marked by a mossy boulder. The buildings and property were later preserved as Jack London State Historic Park, in Glen Ellen, California.

Suicide debate

Because he was using morphine, many older sources describe London's death as a suicide, and some still do. This conjecture appears to be a rumor, or speculation based on incidents in his fiction writings. His death certificate gives the cause as uremia, following acute renal colic.

The biographer Stasz writes, "Following London's death, for a number of reasons, a biographical myth developed in which he has been portrayed as an alcoholic womanizer who committed suicide. Recent scholarship based upon firsthand documents challenges this caricature." Most biographers, including Russ Kingman, now agree he died of uremia aggravated by an accidental morphine overdose.

London's fiction featured several suicides. In his autobiographical memoir John Barleycorn, he claims, as a youth, to have drunkenly stumbled overboard into the San Francisco Bay, "some maundering fancy of going out with the tide suddenly obsessed me". He said he drifted and nearly succeeded in drowning before sobering up and being rescued by fishermen. In the dénouement of The Little Lady of the Big House, the heroine, confronted by the pain of a mortal gunshot wound, undergoes a physician-assisted suicide by morphine. Also, in Martin Eden, the principal protagonist, who shares certain characteristics with London, drowns himself.

Accusations of plagiarism

London was vulnerable to accusations of plagiarism, both because he was such a conspicuous, prolific, and successful writer and because of his methods of working. He wrote in a letter to Elwyn Hoffman, "expression, you see—with me—is far easier than invention." He purchased plots and novels from the young Sinclair Lewis and used incidents from newspaper clippings as writing material.

In July 1901, two pieces of fiction appeared within the same month: London's "Moon-Face", in the San Francisco Argonaut, and Frank Norris' "The Passing of Cock-eye Blacklock", in Century Magazine. Newspapers showed the similarities between the stories, which London said were "quite different in manner of treatment, [but] patently the same in foundation and motive." London explained both writers based their stories on the same newspaper account. A year later, it was discovered that Charles Forrest McLean had published a fictional story also based on the same incident.

Egerton Ryerson Young claimed The Call of the Wild (1903) was taken from Young's book My Dogs in the Northland (1902). London acknowledged using it as a source and claimed to have written a letter to Young thanking him.

In 1906, the New York World published "deadly parallel" columns showing eighteen passages from London's short story "Love of Life" side by side with similar passages from a nonfiction article by Augustus Biddle and J. K. Macdonald, titled "Lost in the Land of the Midnight Sun". London noted the World did not accuse him of "plagiarism", but only of "identity of time and situation", to which he defiantly "pled guilty".

The most serious charge of plagiarism was based on London's "The Bishop's Vision", Chapter 7 of his novel The Iron Heel (1908). The chapter is nearly identical to an ironic essay that Frank Harris published in 1901, titled "The Bishop of London and Public Morality". Harris was incensed and suggested he should receive 1/60th of the royalties from The Iron Heel, the disputed material constituting about that fraction of the whole novel. London insisted he had clipped a reprint of the article, which had appeared in an American newspaper, and believed it to be a genuine speech delivered by the Bishop of London.

Views

Atheism

London was an atheist. He is quoted as saying, "I believe that when I am dead, I am dead. I believe that with my death I am just as much obliterated as the last mosquito you and I squashed."

Socialism

London wrote from a socialist viewpoint, which is evident in his novel The Iron Heel. Neither a theorist nor an intellectual socialist, London's socialism grew out of his life experience. As London explained in his essay, "How I Became a Socialist", his views were influenced by his experience with people at the bottom of the social pit. His optimism and individualism faded, and he vowed never to do more hard physical work than necessary. He wrote that his individualism was hammered out of him, and he was politically reborn. He often closed his letters "Yours for the Revolution."

London joined the Socialist Labor Party in April 1896. In the same year, the San Francisco Chronicle published a story about the twenty-year-old London's giving nightly speeches in Oakland's City Hall Park, an activity he was arrested for a year later. In 1901, he left the Socialist Labor Party and joined the new Socialist Party of America. He ran unsuccessfully as the high-profile Socialist candidate for mayor of Oakland in 1901 (receiving 245 votes) and 1905 (improving to 981 votes), toured the country lecturing on socialism in 1906, and published two collections of essays about socialism: The War of the Classes (1905) and Revolution, and other Essays (1906).

Stasz notes that "London regarded the Wobblies as a welcome addition to the Socialist cause, although he never joined them in going so far as to recommend sabotage." Stasz mentions a personal meeting between London and Big Bill Haywood in 1912.

In his late (1913) book The Cruise of the Snark, London writes about appeals to him for membership of the Snark's crew from office workers and other "toilers" who longed for escape from the cities, and of being cheated by workmen.

In his Glen Ellen ranch years, London felt some ambivalence toward socialism and complained about the "inefficient Italian labourers" in his employ. In 1916, he resigned from the Glen Ellen chapter of the Socialist Party, but stated emphatically he did so "because of its lack of fire and fight, and its loss of emphasis on the class struggle." In an unflattering portrait of London's ranch days, California cultural historian Kevin Starr refers to this period as "post-socialist" and says "... by 1911 ... London was more bored by the class struggle than he cared to admit."

Racial views

London shared common concerns among European Americans in California about Asian immigration, described as "the yellow peril"; he used the latter term as the title of a 1904 essay. This theme was also the subject of a story he wrote in 1910 called "The Unparalleled Invasion". Presented as an historical essay set in the future, the story narrates events between 1976 and 1987, in which China, with an ever-increasing population, is taking over and colonizing its neighbors with the intention of taking over the entire Earth. The western nations respond with biological warfare and bombard China with dozens of the most infectious diseases. On his fears about China, he admits, "it must be taken into consideration that the above postulate is itself a product of Western race-egotism, urged by our belief in our own righteousness and fostered by a faith in ourselves which may be as erroneous as are most fond race fancies."

By contrast, many of London's short stories are notable for their empathetic portrayal of Mexican ("The Mexican"), Asian ("The Chinago"), and Hawaiian ("Koolau the Leper") characters. London's war correspondence from the Russo-Japanese War, as well as his unfinished novel Cherry, show he admired much about Japanese customs and capabilities. London's writings have been popular among the Japanese, who believe he portrayed them positively.

In "Koolau the Leper", London describes Koolau, who is a Hawaiian leper—and thus a very different sort of "superman" than Martin Eden—and who fights off an entire cavalry troop to elude capture, as "indomitable spiritually—a … magnificent rebel". This character is based on Hawaiian leper Kaluaikoolau, who in 1893 revolted and resisted capture from forces of the Provisional Government of Hawaii in the Kalalau Valley.

An amateur boxer and avid boxing fan, London reported on the 1910 Johnson–Jeffries fight, in which the black boxer Jack Johnson vanquished Jim Jeffries, known as the "Great White Hope". In 1908, London had reported on an earlier fight of Johnson's, contrasting the black boxer's coolness and intellectual style, with the apelike appearance and fighting style of his Canadian opponent, Tommy Burns,

'what . . . [won] on Saturday was bigness, coolness, quickness, cleverness, and vast physical superiority... Because a white man wishes a white man to win, this should not prevent him from giving absolute credit to the best man, even when that best man was black. All hail to Johnson.' London wrote that Johnson was 'superb. He was impregnable . . . as inaccessible as Mont Blanc.'

Those who defend London against charges of racism cite the letter he wrote to the Japanese-American Commercial Weekly in 1913:

In reply to yours of August 16, 1913. First of all, I should say by stopping the stupid newspaper from always fomenting race prejudice. This of course, being impossible, I would say, next, by educating the people of Japan so that they will be too intelligently tolerant to respond to any call to race prejudice. And, finally, by realizing, in industry and government, of socialism—which last word is merely a word that stands for the actual application of in the affairs of men of the theory of the Brotherhood of Man.

In the meantime the nations and races are only unruly boys who have not yet grown to the stature of men. So we must expect them to do unruly and boisterous things at times. And, just as boys grow up, so the races of mankind will grow up and laugh when they look back upon their childish quarrels.

In 1996, after the City of Whitehorse, Yukon, renamed a street in honor of London, protests over London's alleged racism forced the city to change the name of "Jack London Boulevard" back to "Two-mile Hill".

Works

Short stories

Western writer and historian Dale L. Walker writes:

London's true métier was the short story ... London's true genius lay in the short form, 7,500 words and under, where the flood of images in his teeming brain and the innate power of his narrative gift were at once constrained and freed. His stories that run longer than the magic 7,500 generally—but certainly not always—could have benefited from self-editing.

London's "strength of utterance" is at its height in his stories, and they are painstakingly well-constructed. "To Build a Fire" is the best known of all his stories. Set in the harsh Klondike, it recounts the haphazard trek of a new arrival who has ignored an old-timer's warning about the risks of traveling alone. Falling through the ice into a creek in seventy-five-below weather, the unnamed man is keenly aware that survival depends on his untested skills at quickly building a fire to dry his clothes and warm his extremities. After publishing a tame version of this story—with a sunny outcome—in The Youth's Companion in 1902, London offered a second, more severe take on the man's predicament in The Century Magazine in 1908. Reading both provides an illustration of London's growth and maturation as a writer. As Labor (1994) observes: "To compare the two versions is itself an instructive lesson in what distinguished a great work of literary art from a good children's story."

Other stories from the Klondike period include: "All Gold Canyon", about a battle between a gold prospector and a claim jumper; "The Law of Life", about an aging American Indian man abandoned by his tribe and left to die; "Love of Life", about a trek by a prospector across the Canadian tundra; "To the Man on Trail," which tells the story of a prospector fleeing the Mounted Police in a sled race, and raises the question of the contrast between written law and morality; and "An Odyssey of the North," which raises questions of conditional morality, and paints a sympathetic portrait of a man of mixed White and Aleut ancestry.

London was a boxing fan and an avid amateur boxer. "A Piece of Steak" is a tale about a match between older and younger boxers. It contrasts the differing experiences of youth and age but also raises the social question of the treatment of aging workers. "The Mexican" combines boxing with a social theme, as a young Mexican endures an unfair fight and ethnic prejudice in order to earn money with which to aid the revolution.

Several of London's stories would today be classified as science fiction. "The Unparalleled Invasion" describes germ warfare against China; "Goliath" is about an irresistible energy weapon; "The Shadow and the Flash" is a tale about two brothers who take different routes to achieving invisibility; "A Relic of the Pliocene" is a tall tale about an encounter of a modern-day man with a mammoth. "The Red One" is a late story from a period when London was intrigued by the theories of the psychiatrist and writer Jung. It tells of an island tribe held in thrall by an extraterrestrial object.

Some nineteen original collections of short stories were published during London's brief life or shortly after his death. There have been several posthumous anthologies drawn from this pool of stories. Many of these stories were located in the Klondike and the Pacific. A collection of Jack London's San Francisco Stories was published in October 2010 by Sydney Samizdat Press.

Novels

London's most famous novels are The Call of the Wild, White Fang, The Sea-Wolf, The Iron Heel, and Martin Eden.

In a letter dated Dec 27, 1901, London's Macmillan publisher George Platt Brett, Sr., said "he believed Jack's fiction represented 'the very best kind of work' done in America."

Critic Maxwell Geismar called The Call of the Wild "a beautiful prose poem"; editor Franklin Walker said that it "belongs on a shelf with Walden and Huckleberry Finn"; and novelist E.L. Doctorow called it "a mordant parable ... his masterpiece."

The historian Dale L. Walker commented:

Jack London was an uncomfortable novelist, that form too long for his natural impatience and the quickness of his mind. His novels, even the best of them, are hugely flawed.

Some critics have said that his novels are episodic and resemble linked short stories. Dale L. Walker writes:

The Star Rover, that magnificent experiment, is actually a series of short stories connected by a unifying device ... Smoke Bellew is a series of stories bound together in a novel-like form by their reappearing protagonist, Kit Bellew; and John Barleycorn ... is a synoptic series of short episodes.

Ambrose Bierce said of The Sea-Wolf that "the great thing—and it is among the greatest of things—is that tremendous creation, Wolf Larsen ... the hewing out and setting up of such a figure is enough for a man to do in one lifetime." However, he noted, "The love element, with its absurd suppressions, and impossible proprieties, is awful."

The Iron Heel is interesting as an example of a dystopian novel that anticipates and influenced George Orwell's Nineteen Eighty-Four. London's socialist politics are explicitly on display here. The Iron Heel meets the contemporary definition of soft science fiction. The Star Rover (1915) is also science fiction.

Apocrypha

Jack London Credo

London's literary executor, Irving Shepard, quoted a Jack London Credo in an introduction to a 1956 collection of London stories:

I would rather be ashes than dust!

I would rather that my spark should burn out in a brilliant blaze than it should be stifled by dry-rot.

I would rather be a superb meteor, every atom of me in magnificent glow, than a sleepy and permanent planet.

The function of man is to live, not to exist.

I shall not waste my days in trying to prolong them.

I shall use my time.

The biographer Stasz notes that the passage "has many marks of London's style" but the only line that could be safely attributed to London was the first. The words Shepard quoted were from a story in the San Francisco Bulletin, December 2, 1916, by journalist Ernest J. Hopkins, who visited the ranch just weeks before London's death. Stasz notes, "Even more so than today journalists' quotes were unreliable or even sheer inventions," and says no direct source in London's writings has been found. However, at least one line, according to Stasz, is authentic, being referenced by London and written in his own hand in the autograph book of Australian suffragette Vida Goldstein:

Dear Miss Goldstein:–

Seven years ago I wrote you that I'd rather be ashes than dust. I still subscribe to that sentiment.

Sincerely yours,

Jack London

Jan. 13, 1909

Furthermore, in his short story "By The Turtles of Tasman", a character, defending her ne'er-do-well grasshopperish father to her antlike uncle, says: "... my father has been a king. He has lived .... Have you lived merely to live? Are you afraid to die? I'd rather sing one wild song and burst my heart with it, than live a thousand years watching my digestion and being afraid of the wet. When you are dust, my father will be ashes."

"The Scab"

A short diatribe on "The Scab" is often quoted within the U.S. labor movement and frequently attributed to London. It opens:

After God had finished the rattlesnake, the toad, and the vampire, he had some awful substance left with which he made a scab. A scab is a two-legged animal with a corkscrew soul, a water brain, a combination backbone of jelly and glue. Where others have hearts, he carries a tumor of rotten principles. When a scab comes down the street, men turn their backs and Angels weep in Heaven, and the Devil shuts the gates of hell to keep him out....

In 1913 and 1914, a number of newspapers printed the first three sentences with varying terms used instead of "scab", such as "knocker", "stool pigeon" or "scandal monger".

This passage as given above was the subject of a 1974 Supreme Court case, Letter Carriers v. Austin, in which Justice Thurgood Marshall referred to it as "a well-known piece of trade union literature, generally attributed to author Jack London". A union newsletter had published a "list of scabs," which was granted to be factual and therefore not libelous, but then went on to quote the passage as the "definition of a scab". The case turned on the question of whether the "definition" was defamatory. The court ruled that "Jack London's... 'definition of a scab' is merely rhetorical hyperbole, a lusty and imaginative expression of the contempt felt by union members towards those who refuse to join", and as such was not libelous and was protected under the First Amendment.

Despite being frequently attributed to London, the passage does not appear at all in the extensive collection of his writings at Sonoma State University's website. However, in his book The War of the Classes he published a 1903 speech entitled "The Scab", which gave a much more balanced view of the topic:

The laborer who gives more time or strength or skill for the same wage than another, or equal time or strength or skill for a less wage, is a scab. The generousness on his part is hurtful to his fellow-laborers, for it compels them to an equal generousness which is not to their liking, and which gives them less of food and shelter. But a word may be said for the scab. Just as his act makes his rivals compulsorily generous, so do they, by fortune of birth and training, make compulsory his act of generousness.

[...]

Nobody desires to scab, to give most for least. The ambition of every individual is quite the opposite, to give least for most; and, as a result, living in a tooth-and-nail society, battle royal is waged by the ambitious individuals. But in its most salient aspect, that of the struggle over the division of the joint product, it is no longer a battle between individuals, but between groups of individuals. Capital and labor apply themselves to raw material, make something useful out of it, add to its value, and then proceed to quarrel over the division of the added value. Neither cares to give most for least. Each is intent on giving less than the other and on receiving more. (Source: Wikipedia)

Lightning Source UK Ltd.
Milton Keynes UK
UKHW011950050520
362772UK00001B/59